CAMAZOTZ CURSE

Book Three
Camazotz Trilogy

By Jennifer Foxcroft

Camazotz Curse
Jennifer Foxcroft
Copyright © 2019 by Jennifer Foxcroft

First Edition. June 2019.
Published in United States of America

Written and published by Jennifer Foxcroft
Cover design by Cate Pepper 2019

Print ISBN: 978-0-9909895-4-7

Acknowledgments

To my beta readers: Jen, Betsy, Stacey, Irene, and Dingbat. Thank you so much for the time you take to read my ramblings and give me awesome feedback. I appreciate it more than words can express. My brain is always too close to the story, but you all help make it better on every level. I love the questions you ask.

To my favourite line editor, Betsy. The thought of putting a book out into the world without you editing it first scares me beyond words. I trust your guidance and comma wisdom so much! Thank you for all the time and effort you put into catching all of my mistakes. I promise my next series won't have crazy names that make the spell checker go nuts!

To my proofreader, Ellie. Thank you. Thank you. Thank you. I love that your brains sees things [that] mine misses! LOL. I really appreciate the care you take literally reading every word. I'm so lucky to have you on my team.

To my very own Dingbat. Thank you for supporting me through every twist and turn on the journey that was book three. Thank you for turning off the TV and sending me off to write. Thank you for talking through ideas and giving me a fresh perspective. You are way more creative than you give yourself credit for, and one day, I hope to read your manuscript.

To my friends and family, and everyone who has purchased this book. Thank you for supporting an independent author chasing her dream into reality. My journey from Sanguine Moon to Camazotz Curse has been a difficult one, but you have stood by me through it all. Thank you forever.

Dear Readers,

Welcome to the final installment of the Camazotz Trilogy. Don't forget you can refer to the character guide if you are getting confused as to who is who in the Camazotz zoo.

Happy reading,
Jennifer.

"ROCKS can be human. Not a Camazotz, just an ordinary human," I say out loud, alone in my car, for the hundredth time. "An aeronaught, like me!"

The headlights of the oncoming car glow like the full moon, and I ease my old Honda over a little. The drive from Helen late at night surrounds me with the kind of darkness only found in the country. I need to concentrate on the road until I reach the safety of Atlanta's suburban streetlights, but my brain is reeling. "Human. Forever. Not a Camazotz. What the…"

The solitude of my drive gives me a chance to recover from the shock. I replay everything that has happened in the last twenty-four hours in my head. I'm honestly waiting for the day when my crazy life returns to normal. This past year has been intense to say the least.

Last night, my baby sister Mini was returned from being kidnapped and held by Enzo Ascari in his drug warehouse. My birth mother, Josie, was the one who gave the Feds the video footage Rocks filmed secretly as a bat to take down my murderous biological father. I'm assuming the Feds raided his warehouse and found the drugs, because they found Mini and returned her safely to my parents. Now, my time working as a money counter for Enzo is thankfully over.

Well, I hope it's over. The police didn't mention too many details to my folks, but I pray hard they arrested him. I swallow the lump forming in my throat.

After celebrating a family reunion with Mini over Easter brunch, Rocks and I headed to Sanguine Mountain market to see what was happening after the county-organized bat cull. On our way, we found poor little Moonshadow from the Duskwing colony wandering lost through the streets of Helen. I don't think I'll ever forget the look of fear and exhaustion on her face, or witnessing that fear morph into absolute relief when she recognized Rocks—a fellow Camazotz.

I thought the biggest shock of the night would be Moonshadow identifying Joey as the Camazotz Tronido, who is responsible for bat-napping the whole Duskwing colony. We finally know the real Camazotz identity of the bat that tried to murder Rocks by crushing his wing. But kidnapping a whole colony is taking his evil to a new level. Little Moonshadow was the only bat lucky enough to escape. Thankfully she found the Shadows market and told Strickland and the others what happened.

But, that wasn't the most shocking announcement of the night.

Rocks admitted he could be cured of his Camazotz bat side!

It's called the fix. He said he can be fixed in one state—either bat or human—forever.

"What the flip? I don't believe it," I mutter again, exiting the highway.

After Rocks made his 'I can be fixed,' jaw-dropping admission, our time together was cut short. Strickland needed him to deliver an important message to the roost on Blood Mountain about the Duskwing bat-napping, and since he's the fastest flyer, it was safer for him to take the message than any other Camazotz. I have so many questions about this mysterious fix it isn't funny. One day, I swear I'll have all the answers, but it doesn't feel like that day will be any time soon.

"Fixed." I say again to myself. "Holy crap!"

I start a mental list of questions to text him the second I'm not behind the wheel. I doubt he'll get any sleep tonight, as the colony will be on are-we-gonna-be-bat-napped-next maximum alert.

Strickland was in a chest-to-chest yelling match with Cypress when Rocks escorted me to my car. Previously, I've always been the cause for tension at the colony, but tonight was different. I've never felt stress levels like it. Then again, I've never seen two leaders at each other's throats the way Strickland and Cypress were. Bat-napping the entire Duskwing colony is beyond serious, but they need to keep their heads.

The tale little Moonshadow told astounded everyone. She identified Joey as the Camazotz Tronido from the news story I had brought about the bat cull. Obviously, the bat cull was just a cover for the Vuelo de la Muerte colony to kidnap the Duskwing colony, but it makes no sense. I get why the Sire and aeronaught-loathing Cypress were in a yelling match, but it won't change what's happened, or give us any answers.

The Vuelo de la Muerte have now become the Shadows' enemy number one, because with their newly acquired numbers, they could overthrow Strickland and take control of the Shadows too. I was stunned when Rocks explained that's why Strickland and Cypress were at it so aggressively—the fear that they might be next.

Who knew bat business could be this unscrupulous and complicated?

Pulling into my driveway at last, I'm not surprised the house is in complete darkness. I can't help looking over my shoulder as I run from my car to the porch. I have a Horror Movie Girl worthy scream ready if any bats materialize. I know for a fact they won't be Shadows' members as the whole colony is on lock down.

Since discovering the bat behind Rocks' wing break in December is the same bat responsible for bat-napping the Duskwing, my nerves are almost frayed to oblivion. Joey—or Tronido—worked for Enzo as a drug dealer, and before that for Enzo's competition, the Vipers gang. Tronido is a Vuelo de la Muerte colony member. How on earth did he get into doing business with Enzo?

My brain hurts from the endless, unanswered questions. I sneak up the stairs and beeline for Mini's room. Her little crib is empty. My heart momentarily stutters because that bed has been empty for too many weeks, and for a split second, I think she still isn't home. Taking a deep breath, I calm myself. I know exactly where I'll find her, and I shouldn't be surprised.

Down the hall, nestled safely between two sleeping forms is tiny Mini. Mom and Dad are clearly going to take a while before they let her out of their sight. I wonder if the news channel is broadcasting her return, or whether the cops are keeping it quiet until Enzo is charged with the slew of crimes for which they have evidence against him. Has Enzo even been arrested? I wonder again.

In the kitchen, I grab leftover cheesecake and a can of soda before settling in front of the TV. I have serious news watching to do, and if Kelly doesn't plan on letting me stay home from school tomorrow, then I'm calling out sick whether she likes it or not. I need to know if Enzo's goons could be lurking outside school to collect me. The instant relief I felt when Mini was returned is now being shadowed by the fact that I don't really know if I'm still on Enzo's radar. If he's been arrested, then I should be safe... I think. But I recall his opinion on the strength of blood—of family—and what he would do to protect his own.

Fudge!

I need to talk to the folks about what the cops said. But then again, the cops don't know my personal connection to Enzo, or that I was his little money counter, so of course they'll tell my parents I'm safe. Why wouldn't I be?

I rub my aching temples and shovel in more cheesecake.

I focus back on the news because I need to get as much information on the bat cull for Rocks as I can find. Any detail might give them a clue about what Tronido is really doing, but there doesn't seem to be any word of it on the news.

When I swap from watching the recorded news broadcasts to Google, all I get are old reports stating the bat cull will happen. Nothing about what actually happened—like the guy who was thrown out of the cave to his death. I wonder if that will ever get reported, and how Tronido will cover up his stupid, dangerous actions. That bat is playing with fire, and I can't work out why.

My next search is just as unsettling. There's not a word about Enzo Ascari. What the fudge? The cheesecake swirls in my gut. I'm safe. I'm safe. I'm safe, I chant over and over before closing my computer and heading upstairs.

Rocks hasn't replied to a single text, and I'm trying not to think the worst. He's fine. He's busy. I will not allow my imagination to run wild with horrible reasons why he can't text back. I send him one last message saying I'm coming to the market tomorrow before turning off my bed lamp.

"Connie, wake up! Get up young lady. It's a school day."

I shove my head under my pillow.

"Connie, get up this minute. You're going to be late."

"I'm not going." I grip my pillow tightly because any second she might snatch it up so she can give me the Kelly-means-business glare.

"Why ever not?" Her voice has risen to her 'what madness are you speaking, child' level. "It's a school day."

"Mo-om, Mini just got home. I should get the day off. I don't want to face the hallways again," I moan.

My bed groans as she takes a seat. She pulls at my pillow and I give in. Her eyes show too much emotion, and obviously concern, and I immediately feel guilty. I should've kept my mouth shut. "Honey, what do you mean?"

Kelly wasn't her usual self while Mini was kidnapped. She was doing the best she could, but she wasn't exactly aware of how Dad and I had to live. Being the freak at school with the missing baby sister was hell. But the threat to Mini coupled with working for Enzo didn't give me a lot of time to dwell on it. Today, I'll be the center of attention again, and I'm in no mood to face those questions and whispers.

"It wasn't fun having that kind of attention," I say. Hoping she'll understand. I don't really want to remind her of the Enzo threat since she's back to normal again. I hope that wanting to avoid the halls will be reason enough for her to agree.

It takes her a moment, but then what I'm talking about must dawn on her. "Oh, sweetheart, I hadn't even thought of that." She covers her mouth with her slender hand. She lets out a sigh. "I'm sorry. I really am, but this time it's a good thing. It's positive now. She's home safe and sound. The kids will be happy for you."

"It's all the gossip, Mom. Please. Please let me stay home."

"Whether you face them today, or tomorrow, or next week, you're still going to have to deal with it. Stay close to the girls between classes and let them help you. Now get up."

Here goes.

"What about Enzo's thugs? I watched the news late last night, and there's nothing about his arrest. What if they're waiting after school? We don't actually know the cops got him."

The color drains from her face. I have no clue if Johnson will be sitting outside the school again, and the thought does send a chill down my spine. What if Enzo knows I had something to do with the raid, which got Mini returned to us?

"I'm calling your father." She heads for the door and then turns on a dime. "Chad, I mean, I'm calling Chad." The look on her face is heartbreaking.

"Mom, I know who you mean when you say 'your father.'"

I've had months to come to terms with Enzo being my biological dad, but it's still new to Mom. She's only just found out that I know I'm adopted, and it's clearly difficult for her.

While she's out of the room, I log onto the laptop, and the news of the death during the bat cull is plastered over every site. What a difference twelve hours makes. Last night, there was nothing on the dead county worker, but today it's breaking news. I download everything because my phone's data plan won't cope with playing these over and over at the market.

When I have all the available news reports downloaded to the laptop, I head downstairs and snag the four newspapers Dad gets delivered each morning. That man's love of current affairs is proving incredibly useful. Mini starts to howl when I change the channel from the pig show she can't get enough of to the news. I hand over mom's iPad, and she loses interest in the remote control.

Not caring how mad Dad will be, I begin dissecting his newspapers. Mom returns to find the TV room littered with newspaper clippings, and the news playing on the TV, my phone and the laptop simultaneously.

I don't need to look at my mom to know her eyes are trying to bore a hole in my head. "What?" I pause the live news on the TV, and eventually meet her stare.

"What's this for?" She gestures to the floor, then her eyes narrow, and the look she gives me is hard to explain. "Why are you cutting out those bat reports?"

Crap. I can't tell her it's for Rocks. *Shit.*

"Did you know Parker Reed from school was collecting signatures to help this senseless slaughter take place?" I channel my inner animal lover. "He's a murderer, and I need all this to prove it to him." I look back at the TV because I really don't care to guess if she's buying my crabapple story or not. "And there's nothing on Enzo still," I add, pointing to all of my screens.

"Stay home until we know he's been arrested. But I'm calling to get your school work." She stares at the black and white pictures of the bats that appear to be dead on the bottom of the dark cave. I'm probably the only human on earth who knows they're unconscious and about to be loaded into special harnesses and taken against their will.

Mom wasn't pleased at the idea of me leaving her sight and driving to visit Rocks after I reminded her of the Enzo threat. I promised to be back inside the house before school lets out to be safe. I text Tiff and break the good news about Mini, and that I'm allowed the day off school. My phone blows up three minutes later with more messages than I have time to answer, but not one of them is from the boy I'm desperately waiting to hear is okay.

Spring is in the air today, and the sunshine helps my nerves settle. I can't shake the feeling I may still be under Enzo's surveillance, and the Vuelo de la Muerte have reason to keep tabs on me now too. Joey—or Tronido—has to know about Mini, and that I was working for Enzo. Who knows how much bat surveillance he and his gang were doing on Enzo's warehouse? My gut tells me they knew exactly what was going on there.

The gates at the market have a huge CLOSED sign hanging across them, and are chained shut. I park in the driveway, grab my backpack, and climb over the ornately carved, wooden barrier. At the fork in the path, I head left toward Rocks' shop, but stop when I hear voices drifting through the trees. Turning right, I head in the direction of the dairy.

Exiting the tree-lined path into the open space, I find a large gathering of Camazotz—maybe the whole colony. The members near the back of the crowd half jump out of their skins when I appear. So much for heightened security measures and sensitive Camazotz hearing. When they realize I'm no threat, they turn in unison back to whoever is having the yelling match in the center of the crowd. I push my way toward the noise, knowing I'll find Strickland.

"You're turning into a soft-hearted naught-lover like your son!"

The surrounding crowd reacts in equal parts of support and horror at those angry words. Cypress and Strickland are nose-to-nose again. Why is it always the leader of the Plant wing that's involved in issues at the colony?

"We need to attack them now before they come for us," Cypress yells, his gruesome tattoos on display on his bare arms. "But you would have us hide here as humans? Never have the Shadows been so weak!"

Cypress hates me more than anyone. He hates the fact I'm not a Camazotz, and I know way too many Camazotz secrets. I can't imagine how he'll react if I interrupt his rant.

"Stand down!" Strickland yells. "You have no right to even speak. I am the Sire! I decide what is best! Not a Fold member who was in bed with our very enemy and didn't even know it!"

Rocks is on the opposite side of the circle. I scan the crowd and see all the Fold members and their sons. Zada tugs on Rockland's arm and points in my direction. Rocks leans closer to Ash—who is standing next to him—and snarls something in his ear. I've never seen such anger on my boyfriend's face before. Rocks pushes through the sea of bodies and skirts around the two men still at each other's throats.

"I'm sorry I couldn't text. I thought it was going to get physical several times and couldn't leave Strickland's side. It's been excruciating." His long fingers slide into my back pocket, and he pulls my body closer to his, so we're touching side-to-side. "Did you bring any news?"

I nod, but can't take my eyes off Strickland and Cypress.

"As I previously decreed, no member of the Shadows is to leave the market," Strickland announces. "No member—under any circumstance—is to have any contact with the Vuelo de la Muerte! All members shall stay in human form until further notice. Do you understand?" he bellows.

Silence fills the space. Yet the looks of disgust clearly written on the faces of opposing members can't be missed. Colony politics has always been unstable, and it took me ages to wrap my head around how it works.

Every wing—no matter how small—gets to vote for a leader from their bloodline. This leader is called the Clip and is responsible for running their wing. The Clips have more power than they get credit for. They spend their nights making deals and promising support to other larger wings in return for protection and benefits.

The prime example of this is the Z wing and the Mythical Creatures wing. Zander was only blessed with female pups, so he doesn't have an heir to groom to replace him when it's time. As a result, he's done deals with Pegasus and promised to groom him to take over his position, so long as Pegasus allows the Z wing members to continue to enjoy the benefits of being part of a leader's wing.

All adult Camazotz get to vote on all the Clips until seven winners are chosen to form the Fold. One of those chosen Fold members is then voted into absolute power and becomes the Sire. The Sire rules and is supposed to be supported by each of his six remaining Fold members.

Although Cypress is a Fold member, he's never been a team player. All I have ever witnessed is him causing trouble and questioning Strickland's leadership. Macallister of the Mac wing, and Carnelian of the Gem wing always support Cypress. Strickland's allies are usually Judge and Zander. Judge is the kindest Fold member alive, and I'm still sad for him over the death of his eldest son, Decker.

The wing that sometimes sways a vote is the Hebrew wing. The oldest Fold member, Levi, most often sides with Strickland, but can fall prey to Cypress' aeronaught scaremongering. I stare at each of the powerful leaders watching their Sire in the center of the whole gathered colony.

"Kneel in acceptance!" Strickland roars. His face is redder with anger than I've ever seen before, and I've seen him absolutely flippin' furious.

The entire crowd drops to their knees as one—including Rocks. It's like when flocks of birds fly in formation, and all change direction in a beautiful, silent, choreographed dance. As the sole person standing, Strickland zeros in on me. One curt hand gesture from the Sire, and Rocks pushes me forward. Thankfully he follows close behind. The colony is still on their knees and I'm finding it really hard not to stare, particularly at Cypress bowed before his Sire. If hate could be seen as a physical thing, I imagine it would be oozing out of every pore on the man's body.

I fumble with the zipper on my backpack trying to free the laptop, but am painfully aware of the still-kneeling crowd. The newspaper clippings somehow scatter from the folder, and gasps of horror escape from those close enough to see the images of hundreds of unconscious bats on a cave floor.

"The news only broke this morning about the county worker that Tronido killed during this… abduction," I explain, opening the laptop and placing it in Rockland's waiting arms.

"What's this?" Strickland asks, glaring at my laptop. "Why aren't you using that telephone thing?"

"It's a computer, Sir. Bigger screen. I thought it would be easier."

Strickland doesn't look happy about new technology being introduced to the entire colony. I swap places with Rocks and point out the files to play. I want to make sure every Fold member can view the footage clearly. The news reports are played over and over. Rocks eventually hands the laptop to a very eager Jeremiah. Rocks' best friend doesn't say much on a good day, but I know he's super keen for any chance to get his hands on technology. Rocks and I take a seat away from the main crowd under the shade of a nearby tree.

His body slides as close as possible to mine, and I'm grateful for the contact. He looks up, then over his shoulder, but every Camazotz present is closing in on the laptop to watch a news broadcast for the first time in their lives.

"Don't mention Enzo, or the connection between… you know," Rocks says only loud enough for me to hear.

I lean a little away from him, so he can see my whole face and mouth the word Joey. He adds, "I think it's best if we keep that connection to ourselves for now."

"You don't want to give certain members any more ammunition to use against me?"

He nods. "I haven't slept a wink. There were meetings all night and still no one will agree on what to do."

"How come there aren't guards at the entrance? I just walked in here."

"It's chaos. No one can agree, so nothing is getting done. I'm hoping this news will scare them into listening to the Sire."

"I know you have a lot going on, but we need to talk about the fix. I have so many questions."

"I know. I'm sorry I dropped that on you. We will. Just let me get this sorted first."

Rocks reads all the newspaper clippings, while groups take turns watching the news. Finally, when the entire Clip—the leaders of all the smaller wings that never got enough votes to be Fold members—have seen the footage, Strickland comes over to us.

"Why do you think this was only reported today? They don't appear to know much. They aren't saying it was murder," he says, frowning and crossing his arms.

Rocks and I get to our feet. "No," I reply. "They seem to think it was an accident, but there'll be an investigation. When someone dies at work, there's always an investigation, so there'll be government people visiting their roost."

Hisses of horror echo through the crowd at the thought of more aeronaughts trespassing on a hidden, sacred Camazotz roost. "I don't know for sure," I add, looking at a multitude of worried faces. "I'm just guessing from what I know… of my world."

I hate talking in terms of 'us and them.' I hate how Rocks will hear those words, and if they'll make him feel as though he doesn't belong with me. But these bats don't understand how the modern world operates. They don't understand the legalities of what happened on that cliff face—Tronido doesn't understand. But nothing from the investigation should lead anyone to Sanguine Mountain market, and that's the only thing keeping me from panicking alongside the colony.

Macallister appears and stands next to Cypress behind Strickland. He whispers something for only Cypress to hear.

"I'll keep you updated on all the new reports I find," I promise.

Strickland nods. "Thank you."

"We don't need to stand around watching stories on machines. We need to take action. They will come for us next!" Cypress declares to the crowd.

Arguments erupt all over again as wings disagree, and smaller fights break out in the crowd surrounding us. I step forward, raising my hand, unsure of whether I'll be in more trouble for interfering in bat affairs.

"Quiet!" a voice yells next to me. The crowd and I turn to look at Rockland. He's so tall his voice booms across the crowd. It's impossible not to listen to him, and the Camazotz go quiet. His voice held so much authority I almost didn't recognize it. "Let Connie speak."

"I, ah, I was just wondering" —I swallow the nerves from having the entire colony focused on me— "I think you should be safe… at least for now."

Ash—Cypress' eldest son with the fang tattoos on his chin—surges though the huddle of Fold members. "What would you know, little—"

Rocks is across the space and grabbing Ash by the shirt. "Do not say it. She has a name, and it's about time you started using it."

Zander and Judge materialize so fast it's as though they just flipped, clearly to back up Rocks if things escalate. It feels like the slightest thing will cause violence to erupt. The colony is choking on its own fear.

Before Ash or Cypress say a word in answer, Strickland pushes Rockland back, forcing him to lose his grip on Ash. "Both of you cease! I want to hear what she has to say," Strickland says, turning to face me.

"The Muerte know you hate technology, so the only way you could possibly know about the cull is if you were reading the newspapers and watching TV. Which nobody here would ever do. So they're probably assuming you don't know what's happened to the Duskwing. They don't know Moonshadow escaped and alerted you. They don't know you know."

Silence fills the air as the Camazotz look to one another contemplating my idea. Rocks replies, "But Tronido knows I'm dating you. You're our connection to the modern world."

"But they also know the whole colony detest me and what I represent. Tronido is cocky. He thinks he's smarter than everyone else, so there's a chance he's overlooked that."

"She might be right," Strickland says.

"No, we must attack them," Cypress counters. "If they think we don't know, then we will have the element of surprise. They won't know what's hit them until it's over!" A few members cheer at this plan.

"No!" Rocks moves out from behind me. "The Sire is right. We cannot attack them. They have video surveillance. The surprise will be on us."

It takes a moment to explain what modern madness Rocks is talking about. I receive a few glares of dislike because I'm clearly the one who introduced Rocks to this evil magic. Never mind the fact the Muerte got video surveillance without my help.

"When we visited their compound to find out about the owl attacks, the gates opened by themselves. Remember?" Rocks looks around the group to the members who must have accompanied him on that mission. Several nod confirming he's speaking the truth. "That wasn't a coincidence. It was a hidden video camera. They knew we were at their front door. Sire, trust me on this. We will not have the element of surprise."

By the time they concede Rocks and I might be right, my stomach is growling. Strickland repeats his orders to not leave the market, to follow Judge's guard and patrol duty orders, and to stay human in case the Muerte do come for them. If they're human, they won't be easily overpowered by a loud noise like the unfortunate Duskwing were.

"Do you have enough supplies?" I wish I hadn't asked the second Strickland's eyes zero in on me.

"What do you mean?"

I swallow the lump in my throat. One day, I swear this man won't intimidate me, but that day is not today. "You know, food and stuff... since you'll all be human."

2
Ugly Boxes

STRICKLAND doesn't move a muscle. In fact, I'm not even sure he's breathing. He's either trying to control his temper, or he's deciding where to hide my body—again. Finally, his eyes shift to his son.

"Go with her and take care of this. Then transport half your goats to the roost. The confined will need a blood source."

Rocks, Jeremiah and I escape as soon as we are dismissed and head for Helen. Rocks explains that the very young, the pregnant, and the very old bats weren't able to make the flight from Blood Mountain. The Little wing volunteered to stay behind to protect them. Since Strickland has ordered them not to leave the roost under any circumstances, they'll need more goats to sustain them, than the ones currently residing deep inside Blood Mountain. These are the only members of the Shadows colony who are allowed to be in bat form.

"You hungry, Jez?" Rocks asks.

I've finally worked out the Camazotz only use nicknames when they aren't around colony leaders. Jez would never address Rockland as Rocks before the Sire or Fold. These bats are so old-fashioned it warms my heart.

"Always. Can we buy those Bavarian donuts you love?" Jez asks, leaning in to the space between Rocks and I from the backseat.

I snort trying to contain my laughter. Rocks looks at me and shrugs.

"Donuts are not going to be enough, but I vote we stop there for lunch, and then head to the superstore out of town for bulk supplies," I suggest.

The boys agree. It honestly doesn't take much for them to agree when it comes to food. The bakery in Helen is every bit as scrumptious as Rocks described. Picking one sweet treat from their glass cabinet is nearly impossible. Jez gets several stares from other waiting customers when he keeps taking long, slow, very audible drags of air into his lungs—like he's tasting everything through his nose.

To avoid a scene, I agree to stop again on the way back to the market, so they can stock up for later. Mr. Hollow Legs and his right hand bat are in food sampling heaven. Sitting outside in the sunshine is a nice break from the chaos and stress back at the market, and it's a rare treat for Rocks and I to eat together in public.

The supermarket is another first for both of the boys. Watching Jez and Rocks push their carts around the giant superstore is priceless. The backs of my ankles will never be the same again, and if we weren't purchasing so much bulk frozen food, I know for a fact the manager would have kicked us out. The two mysterious goth guys followed by the sunshine yellow girl do get some nasty stares from other shoppers. It makes me feel ashamed when other people judge the Camazotz on their looks alone.

The boys are simply being ordinary teenagers, having fun with shopping carts. In fact, I've seen the guys at school act much worse in public, yet because they look like 'All American' football players, nobody bats an eyelid. I'm starting to realize the adult world I live in has so many double standards it's unbelievable.

My cart has two microwaves, the biggest cutlery set we could find, and a leaning tower of paper plates. Enzo Ascari is bankrolling this purchase with a small roll of dirty bills, which were hidden in my trunk under the spare tire.

"Wow, who knew all this was inside, huh?" Rocks says to Jez, grinning.

"Wonder what's in all the others," Jez replies.

"What are you talking about?" I ask.

"These ugly boxes," Rocks replies, indicating to the roof and four walls of the store. "From the air, they're ugly boxes on the landscape, but inside is all this. I never knew."

I love getting a glimpse of their perspective on the world. Seeing how they view modern life transports me back in time to a simpler era.

"You shouldn't judge a book by its cover."

"Don't we know it," Rocks replies, looking at Jez and raising an eyebrow.

Yeah, he's noticed the ugly stares from the other shoppers too.

"Didn't you wonder why so many aeronaughts flock to these boxes?" I ask, not wanting to dwell on the negativity.

Jez shrugs. Rocks replies, "Some of your rituals and routines look really weird from above. Like the interstate for example." He stops his cart next to mine. "Hundreds of cars all wait to join thousands of other cars sitting still on one big road, when there are heaps of smaller roads all around with nobody driving on them. That's so weird."

"But the interstate is usually the fastest," I explain.

"Not from my view point it's not."

The boys want to buy one pack of every food available. I have to be the bad guy and limit their choices. Feeding a large group—half of whom are horrified at the idea of living on food—is not easy. Keeping things simple is best for now.

"This won't be the only shopping run. I'm guessing this will last a few days at best." I survey the contents of all the carts. "Wow, you're gonna need a lot of food to keep everyone fed if everyone eats the way you do." I poke Rocks in the stomach—his hard, muscled stomach. "Wait, I know what else we need, and it'll be much cheaper in the long run."

Rocks and Jeremiah couldn't be more relaxed on the way back to the market. Only two hours before, both boys looked tired and defeated, now they're wearing aprons—in my car—and playing with the long grill tongs. The small gas grill in my trunk will never be left alone for a second. I've made two bats' day, and surprisingly it had nothing to do with buying the bakery clean either.

Judge and Zander have unlocked the wooden gate, anticipating our return. The gentle giant, Pegasus, pulls it open, allowing me to park in their lot. The gate must weigh a ton, but muscle-bound Pegasus moves it with ease. As we get out, Bailey, Moonshiner, Baxter, Ireland, and new little Moonshadow lead a group of not-so-cooperative goats down the path to wait next to Zander. It's incredible how much Rocks' uncle looks like him.

"Thank you for your help, Connie, and for all the information you have given us. We owe you," Zander says, taking a small bow.

What the…

A Fold member—even one of the good guys—bowing to an aeronaught is totally unheard of. Rocks' handsome uncle smiles again. I'm pretty sure my face is showing my utter confusion at his gratitude.

"You're welcome. I'll do anything to help, because I owe Rockland for my baby sister's life."

Of course, none of the Camazotz present—except Jeremiah—know anything about what happened with Mini. Rocks gives a quick explanation, since they all remember the police showing up at the market wanting to question him. Next Rocks grabs Bailey and sends her off on a mission at top tiny Camazotz speed.

Judge gives Rocks a small head nod. "I'm very proud you could help Connie with her sister." The scar running down the Fold member's face doesn't look half as bad when he smiles so genuinely.

"I understand better than you might think what kidnapping feels like. Being powerless. Being controlled by evil people. I get why everyone's freaking out here," I say. He doesn't need to know I've experienced it firsthand.

"I'm glad your sister is safe, Connie." Judge lays a hand on my shoulder and gives it a gentle squeeze. His smile is sad, and my mind turns to his son, who never returned home safely. Decker is still an open wound that is painfully raw.

"I miss Decker too," I add, quietly.

Judge nods, turning away. It must be so hard being a leader and having to control his heartbreaking sorrow. I think of how Kelly and Chad reacted to having Mini gone, but still alive. Knowing for certain your kid was never coming home must be horrible to live with, and leading a wing of nervous, flighty Camazotz at the same must be near impossible.

Pegasus carries the two massive microwave boxes by himself. I stare at the enormous amount of frozen food, but before I worry about how we're getting it all down to Zola's industrial freezer at the dairy, an army of pups shows up to help. It's all the pups who got a Beanie baby, and in less than a minute, the Honda is empty.

Zander frowns at the supplies marching past him carried by the tiny worker bats. "How did we pay for all of this?"

"Connie," Rocks answers. "The Sire never thinks of those things, and I'm not happy about it."

The only reason Rocks and I didn't argue in the store was because I didn't want to cause a scene. Rocks swore he would pay me back when I handed over the dirty cash, but I don't want him to. It's Enzo's blood money. I don't like having it because it links me to very, very illegal dealings. I hate to think how much trace cocaine is all over it. So the sooner I spend it, the better. But my Victorian-era gentleman has an issue with me supporting his ungrateful colony members.

"Connie, we will repay you, but thank you again for providing for us," Zander says. "I do have one more favor to ask of you." He shoves his hands in his front pockets, exactly the same way his nephew does when he's nervous, or uncomfortable.

"Yes."

"The goats."

Rocks begins to laugh. It starts out small, but now he's laughing so hard, he bends over.

"Rockland!" Zander admonishes.

"You can't be serious?" Rocks replies, with the widest smile I think I've ever seen on his face, looking at his uncle.

"The van is full of hay."

"What's going on?" I interrupt, wanting in on the joke too.

"You tell her," Zander says, but his eyes avoid mine.

Rocks informs me the goats need to be transported to the Blood Mountain parking lot, and since they don't know how long they'll be in the cave, they have loaded their old, rusty van up to the ceiling with feed. The goats need a ride, and I'm the only other person with wheels.

"All of them, in there?" I point to my little Honda. "Can't you make two runs with the van?"

"It's going to take all afternoon to lug the hay, and herd these ones up the mountain. Strickland wants us all back here before nightfall. I'm sorry," Rocks explains.

I was hoping for some alone time with Rocks. But being alone with a car full of goats wasn't exactly what I was imagining.

"They better be potty trained! And Zander, please remind the Sire how unsuccessful today's plan would be without the help of a friendly aeronaught."

How many goats can you fit in an old, two-door Honda?

More than I care for is the answer. My poor little car will never be the same.

Actually it's six—three in the back seat, two in the trunk and a smaller one precariously perched on Rocks' lap.

"Sorry about this. I don't exactly agree with his plan, but Strickland is in no mood for arguments from me."

"What do you mean?" I ask.

"He's leaving the weakest members of the colony—and I don't mean that in a cruel way—at the roost, in case it has been compromised and the Muerte come. Strickland won't lose his young, strong Camazotz. And he hopes the Muerte won't know they don't have those strong members, until they take the bats to wherever they took the Duskwing."

"What? Are you serious?" Strickland is a piece of work. "But I thought they had some protection?"

"Yeah, the Little wing absolutely refused to leave vulnerable bats unguarded. I feel bad for them because they have a high female population, and that's why they lost power in the Fold. You remember how only males rule at the Shadows? Well, getting them a supply of goats is all I can do to help them."

"Strickland totally underestimates girl power, but don't feel bad. Doing this is literally a lifesaver for them, Rocks. They will appreciate what you're giving them."

The annoyance I felt at having goat passengers is lessening. Those brave Camazotz need all the help they can get, because their Sire is prepared to sacrifice the more vulnerable members of the colony.

"Thank you so much, Beans."

"Pfft, you're welcome, bat boy." We grin at each other like only couples do.

Usually my favorite smell on our little road trips together is the crisp, moonlit night smell that is all Rocks. When he's confined to my car, I get a heavenly full dose of him. Unfortunately, my nose is overloaded with goat and goat pee. His little dinner snacks are definitely not toilet trained, but since I'm helping out some brave females, I can't be mad. "Tell me about this fix. We have time," I say to distract myself from the stench.

Rocks sighs. "It's... It's what we suspect Celand did. She tried to get fixed as a human, so she could live with her boyfriend. I don't know for sure, but it's the only logical explanation."

"Shit, Rocks! Celand died. There is no way you're risking your life for that."

"But I'm sick of how half the colony look at me. I want to belong."

"You do belong. They listen to you. I've witnessed it."

Rocks shrugs his shoulders, and our conversation ends when two of his snack packs in the backseat think my golden hair is delicious hay. For the rest of the trip, Rocks has to safeguard my locks from nibbling goat lips—not exactly the lips I want on my neck and shoulder—but his long fingers do caress my neck. I'll take what contact I can get.

I'M HOME WELL before Mom needs to worry. Again, I set up in front of the TV with my laptop, phone, the remote control, and two newspapers I picked up at the store. I've set off an air freshener bomb in the Honda to hopefully make tomorrow's trip back to Rocks bearable.

Tiffany, Brandy, and Mary Lou all arrive with gifts for Mini once school gets out. That kid is happier than a Camazotz at the blood bank. Mom has made her famous death by chocolate cake and is clearly touched by the girls' non-stop cooing over Mini.

Mini grabs fistfuls of cake and shoves it in her mouth. Mom doesn't mention her unused fork, letting her thoroughly enjoy her chocolate feast.

"More," Mini says, with at least three-quarters of her first piece still on her plate.

"I agree, Mini. I want more too," jokes Tiff. She's got a soft spot for Kelly's cakes. "My parents cried when I told them the good news, Mrs. Phillips."

"I must call them," Mom replies. "When things settle down, we'll have them over for dinner. Tell Louise, will you?"

"Lola, where's Lola?" a tiny voice chirps. All eyes are on Mini.

"No, Louise. That's my Mom's name, Mini. Louise."

"No, Lola. Where Lola? Lola here?" Mini leans as far out of her chair as she can, looking around Tiff toward the entrance hall.

Memories of the thin, young girl in the red underwear flood my brain. I suck air into my lungs. Lola was the girl who told me she was looking after my sister in that concrete jail cell. I pray Lola wasn't there the day they got raided. I guess I'll never know what happened to her, but I'm so grateful she took care of my sister when none of us could.

When I look at Kelly, she's staring at me, her hand covering her mouth. The color is draining from her face. The specter of shattered Kelly is too fresh in my mind, and I don't want to upset her unnecessarily so soon. It's only been a few days since Mini was returned, and Mom is understandably fragile.

"Let's go into the TV room. I've got bat research to do to shove in Parker's face when I go back."

I take my usual seat with my newspapers and devices resting all over the arms of the chair. The girls hit the three-seater.

"Show us your nail perfection," Brandy says.

"What?"

"Your nails. You had a day off from school, which means you would've let your inner nail art queen reign supreme."

I make fists to cover my uneven, unloved nails. That's the last thing on my mind right now. "Didn't get a chance."

I don't miss the looks they exchange.

Tiff asks if the scissors and folder are really mine, because she thought I was joking about Parker. My TV set up is a little over the top from their point of view, I guess. But it's not if you're related to Enzo Ascari. Or if your boyfriend is the same kind of bat that got culled this week.

There still hasn't been any news on Enzo's arrest, and I wonder what exactly went down when the Feds raided his warehouse to rescue Mini. If they didn't catch him there, I have no clue how they'll find him. I'm sure he's got a serious network of hiding places to choose from.

Maybe even the next site he was planning to use for the warehouse relocation.

Later that night, Chad watches me as I check the backdoor is locked and all the windows too. Since the girls left, I haven't been able to settle. The darkness is giving me claustrophobia. I toss and turn all night trying to sleep. Focusing on the bat cull helps to put Enzo from my mind, but Mini mentioning Lola this afternoon has me feeling spooked.

Every time a neighbor's dog barks, I'm convinced there are dark figures skulking across the lawn. It's completely illogical, but there's unfinished business with my biological father. I count the hours until sunrise, and the creeping shadows retreat. I'll be glad to get back to Rocks tomorrow. Even with how stressed the colony is, I feel calmer there—off grid—surrounded by them all.

STEPPING OUT OF my car, the aroma of meat grilling masks the usual pine needle freshness. A new day has dawned for the Shadows, which involves food, but I bet they won't like to admit it. I head for the dairy and find a long, snaking line of Camazotz slowly drifting toward the tiny grill. Rocks and Jez are the grill masters in charge. Zada and Zander are handing out plates and buns for the sizzling dogs to rest on. Next shopping trip, I must buy mustard and onions.

Rocks waves his tongs in the air for me to join him, but I'm intercepted by Strickland, who looks as grumpy as ever. He continually screws up his nose as though the aroma from the meat is a noxious gas.

"You tried one yet?" I ask, pulling out the newspaper clippings I gathered this morning.

He glares, takes the folder and stalks off. As I watch him go, I notice Judge with a large group of fledgers huddled around him. He's on microwave duty, and I must admit I'm impressed. I try not to laugh as the whole group of teenage bats jump when the microwave beeps its completion.

"Try the sweet potato ones," he encourages, holding out a fresh plate. The group of teens look hesitant, their noses working overtime analyzing all the scents.

Little Moonshadow from the Duskwing takes a handful and proudly announces to the group, "Potatoes are my favorite food. You can eat them so many different ways, and wait until you can dip them in ketchup."

Judge is lucky to escape with his hand intact as the plate is emptied. Little Moonshadow smiles up at the old, scarred Fold member, and they nod to each other.

Two fingers slide into my back pocket, making me lean back into a warm body. He smells of the grill, and it's so at odds with his usual scent. "She's got a kind of godlike status amongst the young ones." We both watch Moonshadow drift from the microwave over to the grill— her entourage trailing behind. "There's a rumor floating around she used magic to escape."

That makes me face him. "Seriously?" He nods. I scan his face for signs as to whether he believes it too. All I notice are the dark circles under his eyes. It's so hard for me to think of magic as real. Yet witnessing Rocks flip turns me into a hard-core believer. But when everyone's in human form, acting like any other human, my skepticism returns. "You?"

"Nah, she was just in the right form at the right time. Come on, there's another meeting, and it's time we tell them about Tronido."

The meeting is held in the large workroom behind the candle shop. It smells heavenly, with notes of vanilla, different fruits, and essential oils lingering in the air. The Fold and their sons, the Clip and their sons, and what looks to be all the mates of these influential members are present. All the females gather in a group at one end, and I feel odd standing close to Rocks near the center of business amongst the males.

"It's clear the Vuelo de la Muerte released the owls that have plagued us," the oldest Fold member, Levi, says to the group. "Now they have taken the Duskwing. We need to work out their plan. Why the owls? When we visited with their Fold, they too had owl injuries."

"But did they really?" Zander asks. "Or was the young male, Tronido, controlling his Sire?"

People hiss at the suggestion. I'm guessing that's close to treason.

"Well, let's confront them and find out," Cypress suggests. It doesn't escape my notice that the gruesome tattoos of humans gushing blood—

which cover his arms from neck to wrist—are still bare. Surely I'm not the only one to have worked out he's not eating aeronaught food. Rocks always felt the cold more when he survived only on Mom's hospitality, so I scan the group and take note of those wearing less revealing clothes. It's harder to tell since spring is in full swing, but many of the females aren't showing off their usual amount of flesh.

"Without the answers for why they released the owls and why they took the Duskwing, it's too dangerous," Rocks says, moving forward. "Unfortunately, I have proof the Vuelo de la Muerte are in a dangerous business in the aeronaught world. It gives them power, and more money than you can imagine."

Everyone present starts speaking at once. It's chaos with questions and accusations flying. Of course, the Plant and Mac wings immediately implicate me, after Rocks explains the basics of illegal drug dealing. I don't blame them. It is because of me and my bio-daddy we know the Muerte are in the business. But it would be much worse if we didn't know this crucial fact.

"But isn't it better we know about this?" I defend. "This says a lot about what they're capable of. Otherwise we would be blind."

"We?" Ash hisses. "When did you become one of us?"

"When I paid for the food that's keeping you all healthy and alive." I shouldn't snap when all eyes are on me, but that bat is getting on my nerves. The fangs tattooed on his chin make me want to grab a sharpie and draw a giant curly moustache on his top lip. "Do *you* have the kind of cash it takes to support *your* colony?"

Strickland immediately orders for me to be reimbursed from the colony treasury. Snowcap is a small, wiry, elderly gentleman—I've never seen before— and he limps away at his Sire's command. He's from another wing I've never heard of, and I wonder at the honor of being in charge of the colony's funds.

"Rockland is correct," Judge says. "There's no point in visiting the Vuelo de la Muerte's Fold. They lied to our faces once, and now there's more at stake. It's too risky."

A debate breaks out as to whether members believe the Muerte would interact so much with aeronaughts to actually sell drugs. I don't mention how hypocritical that is since the Shadows run a shopping market, and they aren't exactly selling stuff to themselves. When tempers flare, Rocks pulls me though the frustrated crowd and out into the sunshine.

"I can't take those meetings any longer," he says, grabbing two fistfuls of his hair. "Let's go to my wagon. I need to hold you."

My frustration from the meeting dissolves into a tingling that starts in my stomach. It's been forever since Rocks and I have gotten to be carefree, in-love teenagers. "Yes, please," I answer, taking his hand.

The second we're alone in the wagon, Rocks is all over me, and I love every second. He kisses me hard and pulls me close. A moan escapes me, and I'm a little embarrassed. We haven't made out in so long, I'm almost shy about it.

"God, I miss you," he whispers in my ear. "I miss kissing you so much."

His lips find my neck and I stand up on my tippy-toes to be closer to him. My flesh is on fire.

"Oh, gross!"

Rocks is two-feet from me in half a heartbeat. We turn to see three shocked little faces standing in the open doorway of his wagon.

"It's not gross, Moonshiner. It's called love," little Bailey states, pushing past her half-brother and coming to say hello to me. "Thanks for those hot dogs, Miss Connie. Can you please bring more donuts next time? The hot dogs are good, but those donuts are my dragon's favorite. He needs more of them, please."

Bailey is going to be a female to be reckoned with when she comes of age. Strickland had better watch out. Moonshadow has taken a seat on the bench running along one side of the wagon. Poor Moonshiner is still on the doorstep, looking like he's gonna puke. Boys are so funny when they're still in the 'girl germs' phase, but boy, do they get over that quickly once their hormones kick into gear.

"What are you doing here?" Rocks asks. I'm guessing he's wishing he locked the door, or at least closed it.

"Some of the fledgers are saying Moonshiner helped the Muerte kidnap Moonshadow's family," Bailey explains. "I said you would know because you know everything." She's looking up at her big brother with her one good eye, like he's got the secrets of the universe tucked in his back pocket.

"But I didn't know those harnesses I engraved were going to be used for that," Moonshiner replies, looking like he's a nanosecond away from bursting into tears. "I swear, Moonshadow, I didn't."

Rocks kneels down to his height and opens his arms. The normally silent little boy accepts a hug, as Rocks explains to Moonshadow the Shadows do lots of business with both colonies and never before has it had this type of consequence. When Moonshiner regains his composure, he asks Rocks to clarify something.

"She said her mom is a Fold member, but I know that's wrong because females can't be Fold members, right?"

I recall meeting Moonshadow's mother on my visit to the Duskwing colony. The slender female Fold member, with the peaceful face and stars tattooed on her palms comes to mind. Her brilliant blue eyes were passed down to her daughter.

"Moonshadow's right. Her mother—Starjewel—is indeed a Fold member, and a very good one. You need to understand not all colonies put females below the worth of males. One day, I hope the Shadows recognizes their value, so always be nice to the girls."

"I swear I'm gonna look after you, Moonshadow, while you live here. We're family. To prove it, I'm gonna get planets tattooed all down my arm." Moonshiner gestures from shoulder to wrist, and it makes me remember the solar system tattooed on Moondust's arm. Moondust is the Sire at the Duskwing colony and father to both little Moonshiner and Moonshadow.

"I can take care of myself, thank you. I'm older than you, remember." Moonshadow retorts, her sapphire blue eyes showing how serious she is. "Let me draw our father's tattoo for you."

"Hold on," Rocks interrupts. "We'll discuss you getting tattooed another day. Now, Bailey, go tell those fledgers to talk to me if they have a problem with Moonshiner and the harnesses. Got it?"

If Bailey knew how to salute her Captain, I know she would be doing so right now. Her idol has given her an important task. Heaven help the older fledgers when she's done with them. Her dragon will undoubtedly burn them alive if they don't listen to what her big brother has decreed.

"Isn't he too young to get tattooed?" I ask, slightly horrified at the idea when we're alone again. "Surely, he has to wait until he's eighteen? I mean he's still growing."

"Why would he wait until then?"

"Because it's big decision getting ink. I mean, it's forever. He's too young. Won't the ink stretch?"

"My ink stretches from human-sized to bat-sized all the time. Does it look bad?" he says, holding out his immaculately tattooed arms.

"Nope. But—"

Rocks informs me many Camazotz start getting tattooed around twelve. Moonshiner is a bit young, but since he's so artistic with his carving and engraving, it's hardly a surprise. Before Rocks can reach for me again, Ezra shows up and tells him it's his turn to patrol the perimeter.

I decide to head home to get started on the schoolwork the girls dropped off yesterday. I've been so distracted this term I hate to think what my grades will be like, and I can't risk getting further behind.

Traffic is flowing nicely all the way back to Atlanta. I feel free and easy, and the worry from last night over Enzo is a distant memory. Rocks centers my world like nobody else. I know I'll sleep well tonight. I smile at the memory of the pups catching us making out, but my smile fades the second I turn into the drive.

There are cop cars everywhere.

Again.

3
Suspicions

ALL conversation ceases the second I walk through the door. I scan the room.

Mini is safe.

Mom and Dad are safe.

I breathe again.

A bunch of cops and detectives are in the living room with Mom and Dad. Mini makes a beeline for me the second she spies me. The way she throws her arms around my legs and stands behind me tells me she's not happy about our guests. I try to breathe normally, but my blood pressure is slowly creeping up.

"Connie, the police were informing us that Jasmine's abductor has been arrested. News reports will probably break tomorrow, so..." Dad says. His eyes are giving me the 'you know who I'm talking about' look. My brain is processing this information, and then I notice all eyes are on me.

"You got whoever did this?" My voice sounds super weird—even to me. "Thank God." Bending over, I pick up my baby sister. She clings to me, and I bury my face in her little neck, so the cops can't scrutinize my face. I have no clue what my emotions will tell them, but I can't risk them getting suspicious about a single—damn—thing. "I'm hungry," I lie. Thinking of the easiest thing to escape their stares.

I head to the TV room instead and collapse in the single armchair. Mini wants down and grabs the remote, but she has no clue which button turns it on yet. I close my eyes and say a silent prayer of thanks.

Enzo Ascari has been arrested.

It seems to take an eternity for the cops to leave. Mom and Dad find me seconds after I hear the door close. There are tears and hugs, and more tears. My emotional elevator doesn't know which way is up. We order Chinese, and all three of us take up residence in the TV room, scanning the news channels.

According to the folks, the police couldn't share the details of how he was arrested, but they did tell them it was the Ascari Organization behind her kidnapping, but they have no clue as to why Jasmine was taken. This information makes Dad feel confident I'm in the clear, but Mom and I aren't so sure. If those detectives actually earn their paychecks, they'll figure out my family connection. Depends how deeply they dig, I guess.

The late news talks of nothing but Enzo's arrest. There's one photo of him in handcuffs, being pulled from the back of a car. A couple of strands of blond hair have come loose from his pony-tail, but that's the only telling sign Enzo Ascari is—for once—not in total control. Seeing that picture on the screen is surreal. Less than a week ago, I was working for him against my will. Now, his operation is leaderless. I wonder about Sophia and what will happen to her.

The last I read in the newspaper weeks ago, she was still in WITSEC after giving evidence on the Vipers' gang members. Sophia swore she witnessed the Vipers kill two cops. I shudder when I remember the video Rocks got of Enzo going at Brick with a tire iron. Brick used to pick me up each day from school for Enzo, and he wasn't so bad as far as drug thugs go. I hope the footage of Brick being questioned by Enzo about how he knew Sophia had lied can somehow be used to put her away too. My stomach rolls and I feel a headache coming on. Not how I thought I'd react to knowing Enzo is off the streets.

"It will be months and months before this goes to trial, and we get a conviction," Mom says, almost reading my thoughts.

"It's okay, sweetheart. He won't get bail. The police said the prosecuting attorney is petitioning for no bail. Connie is safe now."

I can tell Mom wants to believe Dad as badly as I do. "But what if he says something in the trial? What if he mentions her?" Mom asks, looking panicked. Mini must pick up on her feelings and starts to whine. Then again, it is way past her bedtime.

I take a long, deep, calming breath. If one thing matters to Enzo Ascari, it's blood. I know this deep in my bones, in my gut, in my heart.

"He won't. I'm his kin, and nothing will make that man crack." As little as I know about my biological father, I know that much. He won't turn me in. The Ascari's have a weird sense of honor. If he ever gets out of prison and connects me to his arrest, then my life will be over, but otherwise, he won't touch me. And I'm guessing he'll make sure his networks and enemies know not to touch me either.

A cold shiver runs up my spine at the thought of what he would do to Chad, Kelly, Mini, and I if he did ever find out I was the reason he's been arrested. I was the mole in his crime syndicate.

Shit.

"I'm going to bed."

The next morning, the smell of sizzling bacon and fresh pancakes lure me downstairs, but the kitchen is deserted. Dad is mirroring me with all of his newspapers spread out, while he watches the news. Kelly is a living statue, sitting with her hands clasped over her mouth, looking no less worried than last night.

"Breaking news in the Ascari case," the serious-looking news caster reports "Sophia Ascari, the daughter of crime boss, Enzo Ascari, has been arrested. New evidence has come to light that Ms. Ascari gave false evidence as a witness in the murder trial of Mitchell 'The Finger' Jones and Raymond Ramirez. This follows on the heels of her father's arrest. Our sources report an anonymous tip resulted in the biggest drug bust in Georgia history."

"They got her too," Mom says, holding out a hand to me. I take a seat next to her. "You hungry?" She asks, offering up her completely untouched plate.

I shake my head. I was hungry two minutes ago, but the media has new footage of Enzo and Sophia, and my stomach is churning. I text Rocks. I wonder if Mom sees me when she looks at the girl that's so similar to me on the TV screen it's spooky.

The guilt I lived with while Mini was kidnapped is creeping back into me. I can't explain it. Why do I feel guilty for that evil man being arrested? Human brains are way too complicated. Somewhere in my subconscious, I must feel something... for Enzo. It disgusts me, while simultaneously making me angry.

Crap! I need to stop thinking and feeling.

Enzo is a criminal.

Enzo deserves to go to jail.

The end.

TIFF AGREES TO meet me in the parking lot. The news hadn't mentioned anything to do with Mini—yet—but I'm in no mood to face the halls alone this morning.

"I thought there would be a news report on Mini's return," she says innocently, holding the door open for me.

I'm trying to focus on her and not the stares of the other kids, and the gossip I'm sure is a text-second away from hitting the school network.

"Does everyone know?"

"Oh yeah, Principle Skenner made an announcement yesterday, and thanked us all for our thoughts and prayers." We walk toward the main building entry.

"What the…" I can't contain my eye roll.

"Don't worry about it. There's a football game on Friday night, so you'll be forgotten in no—"

A kid I've never even seen before engulfs me in a bear hug. "Such good news about your sister," she gushes. I pull away trying to control my face. I don't want to be broadcasting a look of abject horror at being hugged by some freaky stranger. Tiff's face mirrors mine, but it's okay for her. Nobody will say she's ungrateful, or a bitch for not wanting hugs from randoms.

"Thanks," I say, stepping away.

"Yo, Cons. She's back," one of the football team hollers at me, while giving me a high five. "Nice one!"

In the hall, three other boys follow in his wake with more high fives. I hope I packed my hand sanitizer. No one on earth is happier than I am my sister is home safely. But the breaking news about Enzo has me in no mood for this weird shit. The business with Enzo doesn't feel over, and that scares me. People getting in my personal space today is making me jumpy.

This absurd, totally ridiculous behavior continues for most of the day. Kids, I have no clue if they even go here—that's how well I know them—are acting like I'm a long, lost cousin. I force Tiffany to make a blood oath—well, not quite, but it feels as serious—to body block Parker Reed from hugging, or touching me, in any way, shape, or form during English.

The last bell is usually my favorite sound of the day, but today it makes my stomach churn. I stay close to the girls heading out to the parking lot. As casually as I can manage, I scan the street for a waiting car. My chauffeurs are nowhere to be seen. My eyes spend more time in my rearview mirror driving home, than on the road ahead of me. I'm not followed. I have to believe I'm in the clear and perfectly safe.

Ignoring my homework, I sit with Mom watching yet more news updates. Nothing has changed, except they show pictures of inside the warehouse, and the bags of product they seized. When Dad gets home he hands me a folder with a disclaimer saying he doesn't want to upset me, but he thought I'd want the latest articles from his work newspapers.

More black and white pictures of 'dead' bats.

'Tragic accident' are the two words I read, before closing the folder.

"Surely not all those bats had rabies?" he asks.

"Of course, they didn't."

"It's sad. I hope they never find our cave."

I hug him hard. He goes on to talk about how special that day was, even though he still believes the bats were watching him. He tells Mom how not one single creature came near him or I the whole time we were in their home. Then it hits me—why he's giving me the articles. One of his own met his death doing what my father loves to do whenever he gets half a chance. Rappelling. The rappelling community is in shock and mourning too.

"They're saying it was a faulty harness, but I find that hard to believe."

When I look at Mom, she's staring at me—almost studying me. I excuse myself to do homework to get away from her weird scrutiny. Something is on her mind, and my gut is telling me I don't want to know what it is.

The second I'm in my room, I read the articles. As dad said, the county has officially ruled it a tragic accident blaming an equipment failure. The next clipping takes my breath away. Tronido is front and center outside some government building shaking hands with the Mayor. What the fudge! That weasel is an evil, drug-dealing, bat-napping liar, and he's on a first name basis with the Mayor! Where is the justice in this world?

Looking up, Kelly is standing silently in my doorway. I hope she blames the angry look in my eyes on the injustice of innocent animals being slaughtered. She takes a seat on the bed next to me. Her eyes scan the article I'm clutching. I close the folder, placing it behind me.

Next her eyes land on my bat necklace from Rocks. I swallow. She *cannot* know. It's impossible.

"This cull has really upset you, hasn't it?"

I nod.

"There's been a lot going on lately. It's been emotional," she adds. The coward in me simply nods again. "The arrest. It got me thinking of the footage. Odd how it was upside down, don't you think? Something about how Rocks filmed it just…"

I shrug. Where is she going with this? I wonder, trying to keep my cool.

"I wonder if the bat that broke its arm survived. What do you think?"

"Don't you mean wing? The bat broke his *wing*."

"Hmm… I guess." She smiles and her eyes return to my necklace. I have the urge to cover it, but remain still. "Rocks is a good, young man. I hope he knows we never really believed him capable of hurting Mini. It just doesn't fit his nature."

The vein in my neck is pumping blood at an alarming rate. Conversations about bats, followed by Rocks are not what I want to be discussing with anyone.

"Lots of strange things have happened lately, haven't they, sweetheart? Rocks breaks his arm. That bat you rescued had a broken wing. You were attacked by bats. Parker was attacked by bats at the dance behind the gym. I don't suppose you know what Parker was doing behind the gym, do you?"

I look away. I know she knows I was there. She has this look in her eye, but I'll admit to nothing. This line of thinking is dangerous. It's bad enough I know the Camazotz secret, but Kelly absolutely *cannot* know.

"Then we had the little bat roost on our porch. Remember? Odd, huh? The footage Rocks filmed... well, I'd swear he was hanging upside down in the warehouse if I didn't know better. Wouldn't you?"

Fuck! Fuck! Fuck!

If I learned one thing from my time with Enzo, it's that hiding from your problems solves nothing. And Enzo tackles his problems head on, holding nothing back. Without telling Rocks and Josie about the trouble I was in, we never would have rescued Mini. I take a deep breath.

"What are you trying to say, Mom?" There's no way in hell she'll voice the absurdity she's implying. By tackling her idea head on, I pray she'll back down.

"Nothing, darling, I'm just thinking out loud. Odd coincidences lately." She leans over and places a delicate kiss on the tiny scar across my eyebrow. "I'll let you do your homework."

My thumbs move at the speed of light texting Rocks of Kelly's suspicions. He calls me immediately and assures me there's no way she knows. He goes on to tell me how worried he is about the colony members confined at the roost. His goats have an appetite, and he needs to know when they will require more hay, but Strickland won't let him fly to find out.

I update him on Tronido's appearance with the Mayor and agree to bring him the clippings for Strickland.

SATURDAY MORNING, Rocks and his crew of pups are waiting in the parking lot. I've brought more frozen supplies for the whole colony.

"Can we go somewhere private?" I ask.

Rocks' eyes widen momentarily before he grins. Boys! My ears burn. I wasn't thinking along *those* lines. I open the zipper on my stuffed backpack and let him peak inside.

"Wow. Yeah, let's go to my wagon."

"I'm coming too," announces Bailey.

"No, you aren't, but go tell Jeremiah, Judge, and Zander to meet me at my wagon." He takes my hand and we head in the opposite direction of the little helpers unloading my trunk.

Spread out across Rocks' dark green bedspread are seven brand-new burner phones. You should have seen the look the guy at the store gave me, and then to make myself seem even more suspicious, I paid with dirty Enzo cash. I don't know if it's just me, but I swear that money smells of cocaine. I need to google if hand sanitizer gets rid of cocaine residue.

"From what you told me last night about the chaos of the patrols and not knowing who is where, I thought it was time each wing had one."

Rocks turns toward the doorway. "Just come in," he says. The entrance is empty. He squints and tilts his head listening again. "Except you, Bailey. Go play."

Oh, to have his batty hearing.

A moment later, Judge, Jez, and Zander enter looking worried. "Look at the gift Connie has given us."

My cheeks start to heat. I don't know why, so I take a deep breath to shrug it off. I'm helping the colony, and I'm proud to say it feels good. For a second, I feel as mature as Rocks always appears to be.

"One is for each wing, and one for the roost, so they won't be stuck out there all alone and can give you goat reports. Rocks already has the Land wing covered with his phone," I explain.

"You mean I get a phone?" Jez asks, looking like Mini when she's given the go ahead to raid the presents under the Christmas tree.

"No, your wing gets one," Zander corrects. "You'll get some use of it, if you volunteer for patrols."

"I volunteer! Every patrol. I'll do it!" He edges around Rocks to be closer to the plastic wrapped techno goodies.

Judge smiles. "Thank you, Connie. I'm guessing our Sire is not aware of this gift?"

Rocks replies, "I wanted to get your opinions first. If you approve, then I'll go to battle with Strickland. But if we get them all set up and the three of you trained, we can give him a demonstration of how fast the whole market and roost can have the same information."

"For the safety of all," I add.

Jez happily unwraps all the phones, while I explain texting and calling to Judge and Zander. Rocks and I demonstrate to their pure amazement. Judge keeps trying to look at the back of the phone, as though he'll somehow catch a glimpse of the magical text leaving my screen on it's way to Rocks'. I bite my lip so I won't laugh.

"I'll meet you at the dairy," Jez says, clutching a canvas bag tight to his chest loaded with the phones and cables. "I'll do my best to not let anyone see how many I'm filling with electricity."

"Charging," I correct.

"I'll be charging," he says, proudly, heading for the exit. I remember the days when Jez hardly said a word, but with Decker around back then, he barely got a chance.

"Get Ezra to help you," Zander suggests, pushing up his sleeves. It reveals swirls of ink covering both arms that look so much like Rockland's design. "And Bailey will make the perfect lookout if certain wing members get too close."

"We need to convince Strickland, Carnelian, and Levi, without Cypress and Macallister getting wind of it," Judge says, taking a seat on the edge of Rocks' bed. Exhaustion seems to seep from his bones. "If five of us vote yes, they can't protest."

We all head to the dairy with our plan for convincing Strickland first. He'll be the toughest to crack. Rocks goes in search of him, while I arm Jez, Ezra, Judge, and Zander with a phone each. I enlist the help of Jez and Ezra to load the numbers of each cell into the address book. Our demonstration needs to be as efficient and as effective as possible, because we might only get one shot at it before Strickland explodes.

When Strickland enters the dairy kitchen, Rocks quietly closes the door behind him.

"You have an update for me?" he barks.

"Yes, and a weapon to give you an equal advantage against the Muerte," I say, feeling braver than I ever have in the Sire's presence.

"What weapon?" Strickland notices the large number of Camazotz crammed into the kitchen, but his eyes eventually land on me.

"Phones!" I say, pointing to the group. Each member slowly reveals his new device.

"What? All of you are working behind my back with *her?*" Strickland sneers.

"No, Sire," Judge replies. "Never. Connie surprised us with these, so we summoned you immediately. But let her give you a demonstration of their power before you decide."

Strickland growls. The body language of all the Camazotz present explains why it feels like there isn't enough oxygen. We can't afford to have Strickland leave without seeing how useful the phones will be to the whole colony—especially those risking their necks out on patrol. Even though Rocks has had a phone at the colony since last Christmas, he tries not to let Strickland see or hear him using it.

"That is not power!" He folds his arms over his chest as though the matter is closed.

Rocks is counting on me, so I step forward. "There's an old saying... knowledge is power. It's true. If you know where your patrols are, and what they're seeing a second after they do, then you have the instant power to act," I say calmly.

Strickland narrows his eyes at me. It's starting to be my favorite look.

"Plus, my father always says 'know thy enemy.'"

"Know thy enemy," he repeats. He's silent for a long moment before turning on me. "How would you know anything about my enemies?"

And I've gotcha, oh Grand Daddy of the Stink Eye!

"I know more than you think." I open the folder and take out the photo of Tronido shaking the Mayor's hand. "See?"

Strickland takes the clipping and scrutinizes the photo. "What?"

"There. In his hand." I point to his left hand and what he's holding. "Your enemy uses a cell phone, so that all his lieutenants know exactly what's going on every second of the day. See? Know thy enemy. Fight fire with fire. You're at war with the Vuelo de la Muerte, so learn the rules they play by if you want a chance at beating them."

Rocks is beaming at me from across the kitchen. He flicks his long hair out of his eyes and stands tall next to Zander. "Sire, let us show you."

The men give a demonstration of how fast a message can pass from one patrol member to each and every wing in a matter of seconds. We prove almost instantly the alert can be raised and the wing members can plan evasive action.

Strickland's face is turning scarlet. He hasn't uttered a single word. I'm a little concerned he's having a silent heart attack—except I'm not sure the man has a heart.

"Sire?" Zander breaks the silence.

Strickland stares at Judge and then Zander and back again. "Are you still with me?"

Zander and Judge both look as though Strickland slapped them across the face. Zander drops to one knee and bows his head. "Sire, if you reject this technology, I will stand with you. I will always stand with you. You are my Sire until death." He raises his eyes and looks up at Strickland. "But I will also fight to the death for my colony, and I believe Connie is arming us with what we need to keep us safe from our enemies."

Strickland looks to Judge. The older Fold member bows his head. "On my wing's honor, my Sire."

Strickland turns on his heel. "Bring them!"

Without the ability to use their bat telepathy, it takes a lot longer to assemble a meeting. This helps promote how useful my gift really will be for the colony. Luck is on our side when the first Fold member we find is Levi. Seeing his two sons—Jez and Ezra—wielding the technology without fear definitely helps our cause. After briefly examining the phone—including giving it a long sniff—Levi nods his head, announcing he's onboard.

As we approach our next Fold member, Judge has somehow fat-fingered his way into the settings screen. While the group show Carnelian the phones, I take a moment to give Judge a one-on-one lesson behind the others.

"Decker would've loved this," Judge says.

I smile. "Yes, he would have. Did you know he was saving up for one?" It's Judge's turn to smile, even though his eyes are sad. "Rocks misses him, and so do I."

Judge sighs and nods his head. He lowers his voice. "I worry about him," —he indicates toward Rocks with a jerk of his head— "about the responsibility that is coming to him—as the next Sire. I always knew that, with my son standing by his side as a Fold member, he would find the strength to lead. Rockland would never let his brother down, and therefore, the colony would be in very safe hands. Now I worry for him, and where the balance of power will fall—for or against Rocklands' aeronaught-friendly ways."

4
Politics 101

Bat POV

ROCKLAND searches through the settings on his phone to stop the vibrations. Jeremiah is turning out to be a budding techno-bat and is texting his friend non-stop. Not one message has been patrol related, but it makes Rockland smile. He tosses up whether or not to teach Jez about emojis, or if that will only make him worse. Then again, he remembers his early days of phone ownership, and how he used to stare at the screen willing Connie to text him, even when he knew she was fast asleep.

In the time it took him to turn off the vibration, there are thirty-four unread messages. But one of them isn't from Jeremiah.

> Can we talk

Rockland gets off his bed and finds his boots as easily in the darkness, as if he had electric lighting. Before he replies another text arrives.

> That was a question
> Not a command
> At the Trade Wing platform

He must show Judge where to find the punctuation marks when texting, he muses striding through the dark forest. Having the whole colony in their human form, under the command from their Sire, has been entertaining to Rockland. Watching the members that were only human when they had to be, and how they're learning about their human side amuses the young male. Thankfully, it's not winter, or he's sure there would be a blood mutiny.

Rockland was almost the only member who owned long-sleeved shirts, but since their blood supply has been cut off, the colony seamstresses have been besieged with a sudden demand for less revealing clothing options. Many of the Camazotz are discovering for the first time in their lives that their blood diet keeps them warm.

His hair blows across his face in the cool night breeze as he takes a deep breath of forest fresh air. It's a nice night for a stroll, he thinks to himself. Flying is always easier, but he loves having the excuse to walk through the forest on foot. And presently, nobody can give him grief for his human preference. After nineteen years of persecution, he's finally free to enjoy himself without justification.

The forest leading to the open wing-shaped space is thick and dark. He ducks and weaves around trees and low hanging branches. The night is quiet, and he can't sense any other nocturnal creatures nearby. No raccoons scrounging for worms. No deer sniffing out juicy greens. But more importantly, no owls waiting for unsuspecting bats. He hopes the lack of Camazotz in bat form has allowed those foul, evil birds to move on in search of better feeding grounds.

Feeding grounds.

He scrunches his eyes closed and takes a slow, deep inhale. He tries to block the last, violent moments of his brother's life from his imagination. It usually works, but not tonight. *Decker.* Decker didn't deserve such an end. He was a Camazotz of worth—worth more than many of the colony's hateful members. Why did he have to be taken from them he wonders for the millionth time?

The Vuelo de la Muerte will pay in blood for Decker's death.

"Brother?" he says, looking up at the twinkling stars peeping down between the tree branches. "That's my oath to you. I will avenge you entering the next world too soon—far too soon. I will make Tronido pay."

A moment later, the tallest member of the Camazotz reaches the clearing used for the blood ceremony. The shape of the bat's wing is only visible from an aerial viewpoint. The young male scans the open space. The area holds seven raised wooden platforms, each belonging to one of the Fold wings currently in power. When large gatherings occur for the entire colony, the members of those influential wings get to sit above the lower wings on their private dais.

Looking across the clearing, the Land wing platform is empty, but to the right, Rockland sees the group expecting him. He strides across the open grass field and steps up and over the boardwalk running down the middle. He remembers how nervous his gorgeous sunshine girl was the night she came to donate her blood for the protection ceremony. She was so strong and brave, even back then, but she didn't know that about herself. He loves how much stronger she has become since he's known her. Watching her stand up to his father with the phones made him so proud.

"Thank you for joining us," Judge says quietly.

Rockland nods at each member present. He's a little surprised, but then again colony politics is rather predictable. The chess game has commenced.

"You checked our privacy?" he asks just as quietly, while looking up at the trees lining this section of their meeting place. No Camazotz should be in bat form, but then again, he's lost count of how many times he's disobeyed his Sire over the years.

"As best we can," Mazal replies. Mazal is Levi's heir and full brother of Ezra, while being half brother to Jeremiah. Rockland wonders at Levi's absence. Fold members usually attend alliance meetings. Is it because Levi doesn't want to be seen aligning himself, or because he's not aware of the new empire his heir is building?

Mazal's buzz cut is new, revealing once more the gruesome gothic bat covering the back of his skull. The wings wrap around his head and come to a point across his temples where the ends of the wings touch his eyes—giving the appearance of thick eyeliner. It's not a look that would go unnoticed amongst the aeronaught population. Standing close to him is his mate, Foxpaw, and beside her is her younger brother, Foxfire.

Rockland acknowledges his third cousin. "New ink?" he asks.

Foxfire's hand moves to the open collar of his black button up shirt. He pulls it open further to reveal the painfully new looking fox head tattooed on the side of his neck. "Yeah. Like it?"

Rockland grins. "Nice."

He shoves his hands in his front pockets and waits to see who'll speak next. He's guessing Foxpaw has hatched this plan and put it into her mate's head. If Mazal pledges his support to the Trade wing, Judge will endorse Mazal's brother-in-law for a Fold position. The Fox wing will then have a solid chance of regaining power with one daughter mated with a future Fold member of the Hebrew wing, and now a son being groomed for a chance at the Fold via the Trade wing.

Rockland eyes his cousin again. The young male with shaggy hair has always been ambitious. When they were pups, they used to fly together often, but after Celand disappeared, Foxfire kept his distance. Rockland knew it was at Foxfire's father's request. The Fox wing has been vocal about their dislike of being in human form. They aren't exactly disrespectful aeronaught haters—like the Plant wing—they simply have a preference for their animal side.

Rockland tries to put the sadness of Decker's death from his mind for the second time this evening. He knew the take-over politics would commence soon, but he had hoped not to be this involved. However, Judge has always treated Rockland like a son, so it's not surprising the Fold member would ask for his opinion on a matter of this magnitude, which will directly affect Rocks for decades to come.

The Land and Trade wing have been strong allies for decades. When one wing makes a new alliance with a smaller wing, it's always common courtesy to run it by their current political partners. After the owl attacks killed so many members, many stable alliances were fractured, so new deals and pacts are being negotiated across the Shadows. This kind of political posturing is why Strickland has been ashamed of Rockland's preference for his human form all his life. It's made his Sire's negotiating over the years more complicated, and armed his enemies with a strong argument not to support the Land wing.

"As we all know my next son, Baxter, won't be considered as my heir due to his young age, so I must select a replace—" —Judge falters, clearing his throat— "a replacement to groom to supersede me in the Fold one day. It is my duty to the colony."

Rockland stares down at the wooden platform. He wants to hug Judge and offer him comfort, but doesn't want to embarrass him in front of other wings. Rockland knows no matter whom the wise Fold member selects, that candidate will never replace Decker.

"Decker was well respected, and liked by all. A valuable member of the Camazotz," Foxfire adds. "It truly is a great honor to my bloodline that you're even considering me as a candidate, Sir."

"To be open and honest with you, the Red wing has approached with a candidate also," Judge says. In the pitch darkness, the scar running down his face is less formidable.

"Who's their candidate?" Mazal asks.

Judge looks to Rockland. The young male shrugs his shoulders, unsure if it should be confidential or not. He knows the gossips will soon spread it anyway.

"It's RedWish," Judge tells the others. "But I don't want there to be political games now you know his identity."

"What?" Rockland grumbles. "Like every other day at the Shadows?" Rockland has felt the direct sting of political blowback from his actions with Connie, and all the years without her too. The Shadows wouldn't know how not to play games if they tried. "Don't take that personally, Foxfire. I'm simply reminding Judge that this will get ugly— very ugly—before it's done."

"It doesn't need to be. In memory of Decker, I ask everyone to act as he would," Judge says.

"That I can do with ease," Rockland promises. He watches Mazal, Foxfire, and Foxpaw. The three of them nod their heads and make the promise to Judge to act with dignity.

Judge talks to Mazal and Foxfire of alliances and what both of them wish to see as the colony's future. Rockland pulls his phone from his back pocket and requests the patrol's location from Jeremiah. He doesn't want this meeting to be witnessed by the Plant or Mac wings.

"We should go," he reports to the others. "The patrol's headed this way."

Judge and Rockland head back toward the market, while the other three disappear into the forest moving south.

"I know you don't want to think about all this, but as the future Sire, you must."

"I'm not so sure I ever will be Sire. You know it's a long shot now."

Judge lays a hand on Rockland's shoulder. "Do not doubt yourself. Do not let the Sire's anger at the world feel like it's aimed at you."

"It is aimed at me! You know it. I don't believe my father wants me to succeed him, Judge. In my heart, I honestly don't know anymore, and without Decker, I don't know that I can do it," Rockland admits. "I will have to fight for every single thing."

"You have the strength to fight because you have been fighting for every single thing since the day you were born. Yes, it will be a struggle, but if I choose carefully, the struggle will be a little less for you. Zander is grooming Pegasus. That Camazotz is on your side. Malachite will side with whoever he believes will help the Gem wing stay in power—"

"I disagree. Malachite will not vote with me. Ash has been in his ear too much with anti-aeronaught hate. Don't forget Malachite tried to attack Connie to scare her away from me."

Judge frowns. "Hmmm... maybe Ash does have his ear, but his father is loyal to Strickland. Carnelian is a swing voter and usually sides with Strickland to gain favor."

"True, but I still don't trust Malachite. He can be manipulated."

"Well, if Mazal pledges himself to you, if I select Foxfire, then it will give you the advantage over Ash and Mackie. You know Levi has always been a swing voter, going with whoever could do the most for him? This will mean the Hebrew wing is your ally, as well as the Fox wing. You will have the numbers."

"Barely. Four to three is not the kind of vote that I would want to be Sire. That's still too many wings to undermine me behind my back."

"It's almost impossible to get everyone to agree. You know this, but I want to give you the best chance I can of leading us into a great future."

Rocks nods even though he's unsure of Judge's plan. "I'm going this way."

"I'll walk with you. It's a lovely night, and thankfully, not unusual for us to be seen together," Judge adds.

"SEEN ROCKLAND?" a cold voice whispers.

"No, not since this morning at the grilling machine," Lavender replies to her cousin. "Why?"

"It's time you do your duty," Ash replies.

"What duty?"

"The blood bond with Rockland. It's time. Call it in."

"But he said no to AuburnSky when she asked him, and I don't think Rockland is ready now either. His aeronaught is here all the time."

"Forget her! Put the colony first, and remind him that he should do the same. As a female, you can't fight, but you can breed. Breed now to sustain us. We will need new fighters if darker times descend on us, so do your duty. Go to him and demand he gives you what he owes for the blood you sustained him with. Understood?"

The female with the sprigs of lavender tattooed down each forearm nods her head at her cousin's command.

"Do you know where I can find any of the other females he owes a bond? It's so annoying being in this form."

"Phoenix is usually by the dairy helping the Z wing, since her brother will be their heir," she reports.

"He won't be their heir if she doesn't do what I order," Ash snarls, before turning on his heel and slinking into the darkness behind the shops.

THE REST OF the night was calm. The cell phones have made a huge impact, allowing members not on patrol to get sufficient rest. The patrol can keep in constant contact with each wing via texts, rather than the members not on patrol needing to run back and forth on foot with messages. Messages get confusing by the end of one shift—let alone three rotating shifts.

Rockland has had eight glorious hours of uninterrupted sleep. With his eyes still closed, he wakes slowly, stretching his arms and legs under the soft bed covers. He rolls over on his side and suddenly his senses light up. He's not alone in his wagon.

His eyes flash open to find three little bodies are sitting cross-legged on the floor by his bed staring at him.

"What are you doing here?"

"Would you like me to get you some breakfast?" Bailey asks, standing up and straightening out the creases in her dark grey dress. Her dragon is sitting on Rockland's bedside table. "Today is waffles, and dragon highly recommends you try them before we run out." Bailey turns on her heels and leaves, not waiting for an answer.

"What are you doing here?" Rockland repeats, sitting up and revealing his naked torso.

"See?" Moonshiner points. "I told you he didn't have the Land wing tattoo anywhere."

Moonshadow is leaning from side to side trying to get a better look at his naked chest and back. Rockland grabs the sheets, pulling them up to his neck. "Moonshiner, what's this about?" He frowns at the pup, scanning the space for his nearest shirt.

"My tattoo. Moonshadow has drawn what my father at the Duskwing has, and we're trying to design my Moon wing tattoo. Since I'm the only member here, I get to design it. I told Moonshadow you didn't have the Land wing emblem, but she didn't believe me. She wants to see what it looks like. I asked Graceland, but she yelled at me and told me to go away."

At the mention of his younger sister, Rockland wonders how she's coping with having to be human. The only time any Camazotz is allowed to be in bat form is for the brief forced flip every thirty-six hours because it can't be controlled, or avoided. "Where is she?"

"With Malachite."

Rockland has yet to forgive the young male who tried to scare Connie in the park. He knows he will need to for the sake of his sister, but not yet. Connie has done nothing but try to help his colony and bullying her will never be acceptable.

"We tried to spy on the Sire taking off his clothes, but Zada shooed us away," the young pup admits.

Rockland visualizes the massive tattoo of his wing's emblem covering Strickland's entire back. It's a magnificent tattoo, but he can just imagine how well received pups trying to get a glimpse of it would be to his already cranky Sire. Zada probably saved their lives.

"Give me a pen, and pass me that shirt."

When Bailey returns with two waffles covered in honey on a plate, Rockland's stomach growls. He continues his sketch of the intricate tattoo, despite how excited his nose is about a new breakfast experience. The Land wing's design is an octagon, mostly black image, but the north, south, east and west edges are shorter than the four edges between them. It changes the shape, so it doesn't seem like a regular octagon.

The edges have Aztec style triangles and circles in white relief along the border. In the middle, is a white triangle with a black crescent moon inside it. Around the three points of the triangle is a white circle, and inside each circle are black bats silhouettes. On each side of the top triangle point is a white tree with no leaves. The busy design needs large real estate for it to look it's best, which is why their Sire devoted his entire back to this one tattoo.

Each wing has a tattoo to represent their bloodline. It's customary for the first tattoo a fledger gets to be the mark of his or her wing. Rockland made a stand years ago by not getting the Land wing ink, but the Shadows colony emblem instead. Both arms bare the ink of the intricate bat design. He argued he wanted to show he belonged to the whole colony rather than one bloodline. Zada had to go to battle with Strickland over it. She was proud her son wanted to represent the entire community, instead of just a portion of it.

"Wow," Moonshadow says quietly, when the sketchpad is swapped for the waffles. "I don't know how we can incorporate this. Look at all those details."

"What do you mean?" Rockland asks, swallowing his first mouthful of sweet goodness.

"He wants to represent both colonies."

Rockland frowns. Tattoos represent a lot to the Camazotz, and the last thing Moonshiner needs to do is alienate himself from the Shadows, because they think he's aligning himself with the Duskwing. The fact little Moonshiner sees himself as a Camazotz from both colonies is a good thing, but many at the Shadows will view it as a betrayal.

"Nope, design it for yourself. Represent you," Rocks suggests.

"But I want my father to know I respect him. That I didn't help with those harnesses used to carry him away on purpose."

"Moonshiner," Rockland interrupts. "Listen to me. Your father will not blame you for doing your job. You were ordered by the tanner to do the work. You did your job. Your father will respect that. None of us knew what those harnesses were to be used for."

"But what if... what if..." Little Moonshiner's eyes dart to his half-sister sitting next to him.

She sighs. "You can say it. It's okay."

"What if he's never rescued? What if I never get to meet him?"

"Your father is one tough Camazotz. He's alive. I'm sure of it. But he would want you to have a tattoo for you—not to represent him."

"But I want it to represent both parts of me—the Shadows and the Duskwing."

Rockland smiles. He couldn't be more proud of his little half-brother if he tried. The innocence of children is ruined by adulthood. Politics and power, hate and segregation, alliances and control is what's ahead of these young pups. Rockland wonders if the world wouldn't be a better place if the innocent ruled it.

"Moonshiner, I want what's best for you. So you need to trust me. You don't want to blur the lines between which colony you belong to. Or where your allegiance lies. Okay?"

The boy nods.

"If you want to get some planet tattoos when you're older to represent your father, then that's fine. But this tattoo needs to be about your wing. When people see it, they will instantly know the person with it is a member of the Moon wing at the Shadows colony."

"Your colony really is stuck in the dark ages," Moonshadow says. "My mother says that all the time. You won't let females rule, you hate aeronaughts, and now tattoos are political? Wow."

Rockland tries not to laugh at the truth uttered from this young Duskwing pup—an eleven-year-old more open-minded and inclusive than half of his supposed wise leaders. Bailey and Moonshiner are talking non-stop giving examples of all the ways they don't hate aeronaughts.

"Hey." The noise coming from the young ones drowns him out completely. "HEY!" he yells. Three sets of surprised eyes land on him. "Thank you for breakfast, Bailey. Now all of you get out of here, so I can put on some pants."

M Y homework is interrupted for the best reason. Rocks' text saves me from mathematics that I didn't have the answers for anyway.

Leaving market. I need a visit.

Suddenly I'm aware that my room looks like a dump truck unloaded in it, but I've got time to straighten it out before Rocks will witness the carnage. His wagon is so pristine, even on a bad day, that I can't let him see this chaos.

Come in the front door. Mom made ribs and beans.
To die for.

His reply makes my heart happy. He's the sweetest boyfriend a girl could have.

Beans' beans? Your favorite?

I don't know why giving me a nickname and using it makes me feel like I can fly too. Giving up on my math answers, I start shoveling the clothes that have erupted from my closet back into it.

Kelly acts completely normal with Rocks. I was curious to watch her after our little bat chat the other day. If she truly suspects something supernatural about Rocks, then she sure is good at not showing it. She heats him leftovers and commands him to leave enough room for pie before going to bathe Mini.

We both bring a slice of pie loaded with vanilla ice cream up to my room. Rocks takes up his usual position in my armchair, while I sit facing him cross-legged on my bed.

"You okay?" I ask. I know there is no way he got permission to leave, but I'm glad he did.

"Yeah, sick of the meetings, sick of the Fold talking around everything, sick of the politics. It's so ruthless."

He tells me about the secret meetings he and Judge have been forced to endure to find a replacement trainee for Decker. I'm shocked. Decker's only been gone for five weeks, and I can't imagine how raw that must feel to Judge.

"Are you really okay?"

He flicks his hair out of his eyes and shrugs his shoulders. "You'd think with all the losses at the colony last year, I'd be better prepared for it."

"He was your brother and best friend. Nothing could prepare you for that."

We sit silence and savor the perfection of Kelly's homemade apple and blueberry pie.

"Losing Celand was one thing, but Decker. Fuck, it hurts. With Celand, I felt so guilty about her—until I met you."

I can't stop my eyebrows rising. After I swallow a massive mouthful of pie, I ask, "But don't I remind you of what you lost?"

"It's hard to explain. You entering my world helped me get out of my head because I suddenly had a purpose again. I was learning about my other side. It distracted me from obsessing over every conversation I had with her in the weeks before she left."

I nod. I know what that's like. I would analyze every word Enzo said for days after, trying to find hidden meaning to make sense of it all.

He continues, "I don't feel guilty that I think about her less because what happened to her was about following her heart. I would have gone with her if she asked me. But, Decker, man, that's a hurt I don't think will ever heal, and I don't deserve it to. I can't forgive myself." He shakes his head when I go to argue. "He was my little brother—only by two years, but I'll never forget seeing him for the first time."

Rocks explains he was five-years-old when Decker finally flipped into human form. The day a pup first flips is sort of a right of passage for the Camazotz. He had been waiting what felt like an age to a small child to finally meet the voice that was in his head when they talked. "I should've been there with him that night." He wipes the corner of his eye before shrugging his shoulders.

I feel incompetent at this. Rocks has lost two siblings. It's hard to comprehend how I would feel in his shoes. When Mini was abducted, kids at school would walk up to me, but once they stopped in front of the girl with the missing sister, their voices would vanish. They would stare and move from one foot to the other. I mean, what words are right in that fudged up situation? I wonder.

I understood their discomfort, but I remember wanting to hurt Parker the day he made it sound like Mini was dead. I got lucky. I got my sister back—alive and unharmed. And the pain in my heart when I think of Decker is minuscule in comparison to what Rocks is feeling. I want to find the right words to comfort him.

"I'm so sorry, Rocks. Decker loved you. If he could have predicted the outcome of that flight, he would never have wanted you on his wing. He would never put you in danger. You know the boys fly with you to protect their future Sire."

Rocks lowers his head into his hands, his elbows resting on his knees. His voice is quiet. "No member of the colony should be thought of as more important than another. If anything, those of us with responsibility should give ourselves for the protection of others. My father is wrong leaving the weaker bats unprotected at Blood Mountain right now. It's wrong."

I wonder quietly if Ash or Mackie would sacrifice themselves for young pups from a small wing the way Decker did.

I take his hand and place a gentle kiss on his long, strong fingers. Hopefully reminding him I'm here for him, even if my words are inadequate.

He pulls me up off the bed and onto his lap. We're a tangle of arms and limbs until I get settled across his legs.

"I need you closer," he explains, and I don't argue. "I've been thinking about why Celand wanted to get fixed. She wasn't like me—born human and always in this form—but she made the decision to do it. I think I know why now." His dark blue eyes stare into mine. The intensity almost takes my breath away.

"Why?" I whisper.

"Because she found her soul mate. Like I've found you."

I place a hand on his cheek and study his gorgeous face. Rocks talks about how, while we were broken up, he started to examine relationships at the colony. He wonders if his father's constant state of anger and frustration is because he witnesses Zada partner up with so many influential males. Sharing mates can't be healthy in the long run. The jealousy and uncertainty it can cause must be hell to live with. Bats might happily mate with the strongest partner, but humans are way more complicated.

"I know you think I have a harem of females, but I never 'flew' with them much." I shift on his lap, but he holds me there. Thinking of him doing that with the girls at the colony always makes me uncomfortable and jealous. "Hear me out, please."

I nod. "Okay. I asked you to share yourself in every way, so I'll listen."

"I love you, Connie Phillips. I've never felt this way for any Camazotz. Never. I think it's because you make me feel secure in who I am. You love *me*. You *only* want to love me. It makes me feel like I can conquer the world, the universe, and whatever is beyond."

I lean in and brush my lips gently against his. I don't want to interrupt, but I need to kiss him.

He continues, "I used to be drawn to Rebekkah. I won't lie. But I knew she would want other males too. She's ambitious. She craves power, and I always felt like I was just a stepping-stone for her. We weren't true mates. What I never realized until now is that it was my human longing coming out in me, my need as a man to be faithful to one woman. It's *so* not how the colony operates, and I never realized what it was before."

Rocks stares at me again. His eyes roam my face. He reaches up and pulls the elastic from my hair, freeing my ponytail. I shake my head to help my hair fall around my face. His smile is breathtaking. I'm not sure I'll ever get used to the sight of him smiling. He runs his fingers down the length of my hair.

"I want to get fixed for you, Connie, for us," he whispers.

"What?" I half yell. "Are you serious? Rocks, Celand died doing this!" This time I do get off his lap. I walk to my window and back again. I can't believe Rocks wants to get fixed into his human form and give up all that being a Camazotz allows him. "What if you regret it? What if it works and then you hate not being able to fly, or smell things in the next county, or see in the dark, or hear what the neighbors are saying? Huh?" I stand in front of him with my hands on my hips. I can't believe he's thinking of giving up all those animal abilities—for me.

"Firstly, I can't smell things in the next county."

"You know what I mean."

"You might think I said no to the blood bond mating with AuburnSky for you—and I did—but I also did it for me. I drank from the girls to survive—to come back to you. I never did it to enter into those bonds, but Strickland set it up that way. He trapped me on purpose because he knows I try to do the right thing by Camazotz law. But being faithful to the one girl I love is the right thing for me. I finally understand this part of myself. So I know getting fixed is what I'm meant to do."

His admission breaks my heart. He wants me and only me forever. But this is dangerous. Celand didn't survive. But I can't stop him doing what he needs to in order to belong.

"You need to think long and hard about this. I want you to take note of every time you use your bat senses and think of what it will be like living without those. Promise me?"

He nods.

THE NEXT FOUR days, I think of nothing but Rocks getting fixed. Rocks wants to be human—and only human. I'm nervous to say the least. My gut is screaming at me that this is the worst idea ever, but I don't know how to tell him. My gut hasn't exactly been reliable over the years. Rocks has always been way more in touch with his intuition, and if he feels this is the right thing to do, then who am I to question him. I don't want him to think he won't belong here in my world either.

I question how much I love Rocks for Rocks, and how much I love the fact he's a shape-shifting Camazotz. All I know is that I can't answer that question. I love *him*—every bit of him. And he is a Camazotz. Both parts create the guy I fell for, but I will admit I was totally in awe of his abilities when we first met—after I got over the freaking shock of it. I mean, he can freakin' fly. Will I feel differently about him if he suddenly can't?

I can't make any comparisons that feel the same. What if Rocks was a racecar driver when I fell in love with him, and then he changed careers and was something really ordinary and normal, would that make a difference? The longer I think about it, the more I'm sure I wouldn't really care what he did for a living, so long as it made him happy. But this is way more than a job change. It's magic that's going to change him. He's always been a Camazotz, so it's not like it's magic that's going to turn him back to what he was before the spell. He's never known anything other than this.

My shift at the Bun Lovin' Barn is dragging so slowly it feels like time has stopped completely. Tiff has restocked everything fifteen times, but no one's in the mood for hot dogs. The slowness allows my mind to wander back to the topic of Rocks and this magical fix.

Mini was watching *Beauty and the Beast* when I left home. That's given my brain something of a comparison, but still no answers. Belle falls for the beast, and then ends up with the man.

"Why do you think they never made a *Beauty and the Beast 2?*" I ask Tiff. She's zoned out watching the line of ravers waiting to get into the club across the street.

"What?"

"*Beauty and the Beast*. It was a massive hit. They seem to always make sequels to cash in on popular franchises, so why do you think they never made a second one?"

"Huh! Never thought of that."

"Do you think it's because the beast regrets becoming a plain, old prince again? He lost his ability to leap across the castle rooftop without fear of hurting himself," I ask.

"Or now he can't save Belle from wolves if they get lost in the forest," Tiff adds, immediately following my line of thought as only best friends can.

"Do you think they live happily ever after? Would they ride off into the sunset never thinking about the time he was an animal ever again?"

I look at her and she's frowning, deep in thought.

"Hmmm, I don't know. It would be different, wouldn't it? Maybe that's why they never made a second one because it's just a story about two people in love. Nothing special really."

"But maybe that's the best kind of love?" I ask. "Ordinary, rock solid love."

Questions! I really, really, REALLY dislike questions. I seem to be a magnet for them like a dog is to fleas. When will I get some damn answers for a change? And these questions are even harder, because I'm trying to guess how Rocks is going to feel. I can't predict how I'm going to feel in five minutes time let alone how he'll feel after he's changed. What if the magic somehow changes his personality?

Tiff sighs. "I wish I had any kind of love in my life. You're so lucky having Rocks. I really thought in my senior year I'd have a boyfriend."

"I didn't! I never ever thought I'd be this lucky."

"Yeah, you hit the jackpot. You seen Jeremiah lately? Has he come down for a visit with Rocks?" She starts wiping down the already gleaming stainless steel counter top.

"No, I told you they've been busy up at their market."

"Can I come see the market one day? We could make a road trip of it. How much fun would that be?" She beams.

Oh crap!

The last thing I need to do is bring Tiff to the market. Strickland would flip.

"Well, ah, they're sort of renovating, so it's closed to the public?" My voice has risen so high it sounded like a question. I make an effort to lower it and it sounds even weirder. "When they reopen. Sure." I add, sounding like a guy.

The next morning, Mom has baked up a storm. Four containers sit stacked high on the bench with a lone raspberry muffin perched on a plate on top. It's still warm. I shove a third of it in my mouth.

"Wafs ssis faw?" I ask, covering my mouth.

She smiles. The only time I get away with eating like an animal is when Mom knows I'm in home-baked heaven unable to resist her creations.

"Mmm, delicious," I add, after I swallow. "It's still warm."

"These are for Rockland and his family. If they're busy renovating, a mid-morning snack will be appreciated."

My cover story for Rockland's sudden absence is his family is renovating the market. Tiff didn't seem to question that lie, so I thought I'd stick with it.

"You didn't have to do this, but these will vanish in a nanosecond. Thanks, Mom."

Each time I take aeronaught supplies, the Camazotz seem to be more adventurous and eager to try new foods. Kelly's baked goods will knock their Goth socks off.

Weather in May in Atlanta still has days when the humidity doesn't completely blow. Today is one of those gorgeous, pleasant days. My royal blue sundress is the perfect choice. I'm kinda over wearing black to blend in, because my hair is a beacon of difference, so I might as well embrace it. Today I'm wearing blue for Rockland. He loves seeing me in colors, so I plan on ignoring any stares from the haters. They glare at me whether I wear black, blue, or pink and green polka dots.

I cringe spying my unpainted toenails when I step out of the car in the market parking lot, but before I give them a second glance, two strong arms circle my waist and pull me against his lean muscled body.

"God, you look amazing," he breathes against the bare flesh of my slightly exposed shoulder. He places three soft kisses there and sends my nerve endings into overdrive. I wrap my arms around his shoulders, standing up on my toes to reach him. His fingertips find the edge of my knee-length skirt and slowly run up the outside of my thighs.

"Oh, God," I sigh, melting against him. I thread my fingers into the short hair on the back of his head and pull him to my lips. We kiss like it's been a millennium since we saw each other. Before I'm even close to done, Rocks pulls away and shoves his hands in his front pockets. He must see the 'what the' look on my face.

"We have company." He nods his head over his left shoulder.

Sure enough Bailey, Moonshiner, Moonshadow, Pegasus, and Jeremiah walk down the path.

"They're here to help unload the supplies," he explains, as a touch of pink colors his cheeks. I bite my lip grinning back, willing my heartbeat to return to normal in case these sneaky bats can hear it running wild from our way-too-brief encounter.

"You look pretty in blue, Miss Connie," Bailey gushes. "Maybe I can get a blue dress too." She looks up at her big brother.

"I don't know. Ask Zada," Rocks replies. "Are you ready to help?"

She holds out her little arms waiting for a parcel to carry. When I pull the canvas bag holding Mom's baking from the front seat, six noses twitch. Almost in unison, they take a long, slow intake of air.

"Your Mom baked?" Jez asks, looking hopeful.

"That smells incredible," the gentle giant Pegasus comments.

"What's in there, Miss Connie?"

"Cupcakes, muffins, and cookies." I pull out the top container and remove the lid.

Mom would be reveling in this moment if she were here. The wide-eyed looks of wonder as four of the six Camazotz stare at the glistening, sprinkle-covered cupcakes. Mom has decorated them as though she's entering the county fair. The group is in awe of the perfectly piped, pink icing with silver balls, and tiny, green sugar stars sprinkled with frightening precision across each vanilla cake.

Jeremiah and Rocks share a knowing glance. They understand just how good these are going to taste.

"Helpers get a cupcake each," I announce, as though it's a written rule.

Watching them each devour their cake, licking the icing from their fingers and lips, and moaning and smiling at each other makes me feel way better about my manners earlier. Kelly's cooking has the power to transform anyone with working taste buds into a pig. I pass around the napkins Mom thoughtfully packed. Grabbing one, I place a cupcake in the center and gently fold the sides around it.

"Take this to your mom." I hold the cake out to Bailey. Her one little eye widens in delight as she takes the cake and runs at top speed back up the path. Rocks leans over and kisses my forehead.

"Do you have any news for Strickland?"

"Nope. No news."

"Okay, I'll meet you at my shop. I'll help them take this stuff to the dairy, and I'll let him know. He's been extra... ah, extra..."

"Shitty?" finishes Jez with a cheeky grin. "Just admit it. He's been *extra* shitty."

I try not to laugh. "Thanks for the warning. I'll stay out of sight then."

I watch the group leave before heading back to the front seat. I stashed some cookies and a muffin in a separate container for Rocks. Knowing he'll give up his share because Mom didn't bake enough for the whole colony to try, I've put some aside for him.

Turning around, I almost scream. "Jeez, personal space issues much?"

I'm face-to-face with the bat *biatches*. And I mean face-to-face. The girls are practically on top of me, so I step back.

"'Naught," Rebekkah sneers. Her elf-like features make her so pretty, but the hate that's always in her eyes cancels it out.

Rolling my eyes is the only response she's gonna get. I really don't care if they call me nothing now, because I know I'm not nothing to the one person here that matters to me.

We stand in silence eyeballing each other. I glance around the group and notice a few faces I don't recognize. Of course, my least favorite Camazotz—Zabreena, with the large scar running from her lip under her chin—is standing close to Rebekkah. I recognize the girl with the bob hairstyle and swirling tatts on the back of both hands. I'll never forget her because she came looking for Rocks in his shop the night we broke up. I'm pretty sure her name is AuburnSky, or something close, and Rocks owes her a blood bond.

The next girl surprises me, because she's short and... dumpy. It's weird how I'd never noticed the absence of larger girls at the colony. I guess their blood diet and speedy metabolism keeps them all slender—well, all except this chick. She gives me the evil eye, and I notice the large Mac wing symbol tattooed on both her bare shoulders. Miss Mac-Meany is clearly not a fan of mine.

On the other side of her is that annoying little Violet. The scars down her arms and face have healed considerably since the last time I saw her, but they're still angry red and puckered. I can't imagine healing from those wounds without any painkillers.

"Take a long, hard look at us, naught," Rebekkah boasts. "We're ALL his now."

"Liar!" I shot back at her. "Zabreena's his cousin." I will not let them play me again.

"All of us, except her," she corrects. "Let me introduce the ones you might not know, but *he's* going to know intimately soon enough."

Dumpy is introduced as Macantia, and next to her is AuburnSky. What does surprise me is the Plant wing has two representatives. The girl standing next to Violet is called Lavender, which explains the sprigs of lavender tattooed up and down her forearms. I wonder if Strickland was trying to placate Cypress by promising two pups from Rockland to the Plant wing.

"That's Madison," Rebekkah says, pointing to the girl with a severe undercut pixie hairdo. Her bangs are so long they almost cover half her face down to her chin, but I see the reason for keeping it so short at the back. Her neck, from collarbone to chin, is tattooed with a fine lace pattern, and it continues down her back into her corset. The ink is absolutely stunning, and I remind myself I'm supposed to hate her instead of complimenting her.

The last girl is drop-dead gorgeous. I clench my fingers into fists and take a deep breath.

"And last, but definitely not least is the beautiful RedFaith."

RedFaith smiles. It's cold and evil, but she's still unbelievably attractive. I'm normally not a lover of any kind of facial studs, but RedFaith makes the matching butterfly kiss piercings under her eyes look sexy. That's when I notice the tall, slender beauty has one blue and one brown eye. "What ever does he see in her?" she asks the group, as though I can't hear her.

"Nice to meet you too," I reply, turning my sarcasm up a notch.

"Beats me," Rebekkah replies to the Camazotz supermodel. "But he won't be interested in blonde hair and boobs after he's done his duty with us. Oh, and the Sire had twelve of us bond with him in total, so we're not *all* the females he owes."

I will not be tricked into believing these biatches.

I.

Will.

Not.

I trust Rocks, and I'm gonna trust my gut for once.

"I know you think I'm worried about sharing Rocks," I say, inspecting the chipped clear varnish on my fingernails. "Well, I used to be, and you used to be able to get under my skin. That was before. Now I know *I'm* what makes Rockland happy. And for the record, he doesn't like to share either." I watch them each realize their innuendos are no longer going to trick me into being upset with him. They've played me two times too many, and it's stopping here and now.

"But he's—" Macantia starts, but I cut her off.

"No, he's decided to give the aeronaught style of dating a go, and I believe him because if there's one thing you can say about Rocks, it's that he's honest and dependable, right?" I grin and scan the faces standing around me. Rebekkah's eyes are getting narrower and narrower. If she's not careful, they'll disappear altogether. "Yeah, don't bother answering because we all knows it's true. When he says he only wants to be with me, I believe him. So run along and try intimidating someone else, you bunch of *biatches*."

The knowledge that none of them know what a *biatch* is gives me a thrill like riding the world's biggest roller coaster without holding on, and adds to the smile I feel stretching across my face. I predict more aeronaught style insults will be headed their way if they try to get inside my head again.

I'm well aware the blood bonds with all of them are still officially hanging around Rocks' neck. But he turned down AuburnSky and is unofficially planning on evading the rest of them too.

The girls are still standing there. I've completely and utterly shocked them. "If you'll excuse me," I say, pushing past them. "I've got a date with your colony heir."

I practically skip all the way to Rock's jewelry shop. He's not here, so I take the opportunity to walk around his workshop, looking at his silversmithing tools and equipment. On his workbench is an unfinished filigree heart. Its intricate design is breathtaking, and must have taken hours and hours of painstaking work.

When Rocks arrives, I can hardly stand still. The arch of one eyebrow tells me he's curious about the happiness oozing from me. So much can be learned from body language, and I was so oblivious to it until I met him.

"I hope that smile's because you've missed me," he comments with a cheeky grin.

I walk around the workbench separating us and into his open arms.

"Actually, I told your old harem, you're mine, and their mind games no longer work on me."

His eyes widen. "You did?

I nod. "Yep."

His arms and body wrap around me. "I'm so proud of you. At long last, there will just be the two of us in this relationship." He takes in a slow, deep breath, and I wonder what I smell like to him. I can't be half as enchanting as a moonlit night in the forest. His fresh, clean smell still sends tingles all the way to my toes.

A buzzing starts against my leg. Rocks pulls away and reaches into his pocket for his phone.

"Oh shit," he says, looking at the screen and turning off his reminder. "I almost forgot. Follow me."

He leads the way out of his shop and around to his wagon. Instead of heading inside, we go behind to where the last of his goats are still living. He stands by the gate and uses all of his senses. He closes his eyes to concentrate, and I can't help looking up, down, and behind us to make sure we really are alone. I want to ask what's going on but remain silent.

He takes one last look down behind the row of shops opposite and then opens the gate to the goat enclosure. "We need to give them fresh water," he says a little too loudly.

"Oh, cool." I'm watching his face for clues because who cares if we are giving them water. He's acting odd.

He goes through the motions of connecting an ancient looking rubber hose to an even older faucet. It squeaks and squeals as he twists it on, his bicep bulging to open the water flow. The water eventually bubbles out of the hose end, and he places it in the long metal tub, flushing out the stagnant water.

Several goats come to him and lean against his legs. His spare hand finds the sweet spot between their horns and scratches them for as long as they stand there. He glances around once more before leaving the hose and leading the largest goat he was giving a head scratch to back under the shade of several very close young pine trees. I follow.

"All set," he says, under his breath, while looking up at the back corner of his wagon where the roof pushes against the trees. He leans over and starts talking in a soothing voice to the goat. It kneels down against the trunk of a tree, and he bends down with it, still rubbing between its horns.

Rocks is a goat whisperer, and I never knew it. The goat—called Sunflower—seems to almost be in a trance, or hypnotized by his soft words and constant touch.

A scratching sound above my head makes me nearly jump into his lap. But Rocks ignores it and continues giving his attention to sleepy Sunflower. Looking up, a bat crawls out from a tiny space just under his wagon's roof. The bat jumps into the nearest pine tree, but it's clumsy and hits its nose on the closest branch. It then half falls, half jumps from branch to branch on an awkward descent toward the resting goat. I realize I have my hands out ready to catch it, and then what's happening here finally registers.

Rocks is feeding a Camazotz—in bat form—against all of Strickland's commands.

I spin around to make sure nobody has come up behind us. He would be in big trouble for this. The bat—whose fur is tinged with grey—works its way down the tree, but with none of the grace and agility Rockland displays when he's a bat. It's almost like each branch surprises the little bat.

When it starts to feed, he signals for me to crouch down with him. He leans over and softly whispers directly in my ear. "This is my only living grandparent, Cappella. She's Zada's mother. She can't see very well, so prefers to stay like this cause her senses are slightly better. Only Zada knows I'm doing this."

Wow. Rockland's grandmother.

I watch as she finishes feeding and fumbles around trying to get back to the tree trunk. Rocks gently grabs her and reaches up to place her at the entrance to the almost hidden nook under his roof. She bumps her nose on the edge of the wagon, before finally disappearing into the tiny, dark hole.

"Her eyesight is really bad now. She can hardly see anything in front of her nose."

We walk back to the water trough, and it's overflowing with fresh, clean water. Nobody is around and I see his shoulders relax.

"I've never seen any older Camazotz."

He nods. "That's because there aren't many. Cappella is among the few, and her eyesight makes it almost impossible for her to fly freely to feed."

"How old is she?"

"Fifty-seven and without Zada she wouldn't make it to fifty-eight."

"Jeez, Rocks. That's crazy. I mean, she's old, but she's not like *old* old! She couldn't even retire if she worked in the aeronaught world."

"I know, but without access to medicine and care, we have no hope of living an aeronaught life span."

6
Chess Moves

Bat POV

ASH and Cedar are waiting by the stream. The soft trickle of water and the gentle rustle of the wind moving through the new foliage are the only sounds disturbing the quiet night. The moon has shifted behind a cloud, adding an extra layer of darkness to the forest.

"Send him a text," Cedar says.

Ash—despite his avid hate for Connie and all that aeronaughts represent—slides the shiny, new cell phone from his pocket. He's usually the only member of his wing to have possession of the miracle device. It's communication capabilities are faster than even Rockland can fly, and Ash has adjusted his opinion of the device, since it makes holding secret meetings far, far easier.

Where are you?

His screen lights up with an immediate reply from Malachite.

Near the old oak.

Ash swears as his thumbs punch out his response.

I said the holly tree. The angry, young male replies.

"He's going to be a couple of minutes," Ash tells his half-brother.

"I don't know if this plan is genius or insanity," Cedar replies. "The Gem wing have voted with Strickland recently. Why do you think Malachite will go against his father and give you his allegiance?"

"Because he's weak and not very smart."

"But do you think he's got what it takes?" Cedar asks.

Ash smiles, making the fangs tattooed on his chin look even more sinister. "We're going to find out, aren't we? Depends how much he wants the power of being a Fold member, and a Fold member who also gets what he wants. When I'm the new Sire, I can make his life easy or hell."

"Do you think Graceland will be a problem? He cares for her deeply, and it's no secret."

"She knows her place, and she can't stand her brother's love of 'naughts. She won't interfere."

"But what if he doesn't succeed?"

"Malachite will. He must."

"Be careful, brother. We may need him regardless, especially now the traitor Levi has shown his true colors. How could he possibly think Cypress wouldn't hear about him supporting Foxfire to replace Decker?"

"That's not what bothers me the most. It's that a lowly female influenced a Fold member. His son's mate is the one behind this power play. How could he be so weak as to listen to her? I never really liked Levi, but I despise him now." Ash spits on the forest floor.

"That means Mazal will never vote with you if his mate has his ear. We need Malachite more than he actually needs us."

"Shhh… let's hope he's too stupid to work that out."

They end their conversation and wait in silence, listening to the signs the forest gives them.

A bat bursts out of the branches and a second later, Malachite materializes in front of them.

"What the hell are you thinking?" sneers Ash. "If you were sensed by another Camazotz, we will all pay for breaking the Sire's command. You idiot!"

"I'm sorry. I got lost. I know this forest like the back of my wing, but walking through it on foot all the trees look the same from the ground. I didn't want to keep you waiting." He wipes the sweat from his forehead.

Cedar folds his arms and shakes his head in silence.

"I said I was sorry. We don't have long."

Ash agrees and launches into his well-prepared speech of honor and power, and allies and blood—blood that ties and unites all things.

"Carnelian was lucky to win his place on the Fold. You know it. The whole colony knows it. As a result, he usually sides with the Sire to keep in favor, but that's weak. That shows no backbone. The Gem wing needs to start showing strength instead. My father stands his ground and stands up for what's right, even if it means fighting the Sire. I will ensure your wing doesn't lose power if you do what I ask. Are you ready?"

"I swear I'll do whatever it takes if you help me join the Fold."

"I will, but first you need to get Rockland out of our way—forever."

Malachite's eyes' widen. He looks from one brother to the other and back again. "What?"

"I don't repeat myself."

Malachite nods and swallows. "But... how? What are you suggesting exactly?"

"Think! To be a Fold member you need to have what it takes up here," Ash says, pointing to his temple. "You have several choices open to you. The most obvious being to force Strickland's hand. Rockland believes in Camazotz law, and the threat of a blood sentence might show us where his allegiance really lies."

Malachite doesn't say a word. He watches the two males for signs they might be toying with him, setting him up for some joke. Neither of them moves a muscle. He realizes the brothers are actually asking him to force Strickland to give Rockland a blood sentence for breaking Camazotz law.

"But without Rockland... you would then be next in line to be Sire? Are you serious?"

"Do I look like I'm joking?"

Malachite swallows and shakes his head.

"Now prove to the Plant wing you have what it takes to hold a position on the Shadow's Fold. Prove your loyalty to me."

ROCKLAND STANDS IN the early morning sunshine waiting until Zander has finished giving the Sire his report. After his uncle is dismissed, Rockland steps forward.

"Sire, we need to move more goats to the roost. LittleSong sent... word." Rockland chooses his words carefully around his father. Even though the cell phones at the colony have more than proven their efficiency for communicating, he knows Strickland still isn't comfortable about them.

"Why?"

"One of my goats died this morning. They're being fed from too frequently. I think the restrictions should be reduced. Strong bats should be allowed out to feed, but if you won't sanction that, then I must take them more goats."

Rockland waits in silence, allowing his father time to digest his suggestions. All of which will be unwelcome to his overly cautious and increasingly paranoid leader.

"Father, there have been no sightings of any bats and no contact from the Muerte. I'm not suggesting we let our guard down, but I sense they're busy with their own affairs."

"I need more than a *sense* from you to risk my colony."

Rockland bites his tongue. He hasn't forgotten that his father only weeks ago was prepared to leave the weaker and older members of the Shadows at the roost totally unguarded and vulnerable to attack. Now he doesn't want to risk them. Rockland takes a deep breath.

"Or I could take them food supplies." He waits.

"As in blood?"

"No, food as in food. I need to take Judge to the store today, because we're critically low again, so I can pick up some supplies for the roost while I'm there."

"Take them the goats," he almost growls. "Go to town with Judge first, then deliver the goats."

MALACHITE TAKES GRACELAND'S hand and places a soft kiss on her fingers. "Thank you," he says. "This is nice and private."

Deep in the woods to the north of the market, the couple arrives at the meeting place. Three shapes are waiting under the shade of the dense branches—Rebekkah, Madison, and RedFaith.

"Thank you for meeting. When are you all requesting Rockland honor his blood bond?" Malachite asks, eyeing each female. "It's time."

The tall, stunning female answers, "He's not ready. He's so infatuated with that girl."

"And soon he'll be infatuated with you, if you try hard enough."

RedFaith rolls her eyes, crossing her arms. She looks Rockland's sister up and down. The young female is pretty. She has the same fine, high cheekbones inherited from the Z Wing. Her skin is clear, but the gorgeous female can't see what else is so special about Graceland. "Why are you so keen for your brother to mate?"

Graceland blinks at the direct question. "Because... because—"

"Because she knows what her brother's duty is to this colony," interrupts Malachite. "Now do *your* duty and be quiet about it." He glares at the other two.

"I'm ready," states Rebekkah. "And I will succeed too."

"Good. When?" Malachite demands.

RedFaith has always gotten away with a little more attitude than the other females in her wing. She knows it's her looks that allow the males to cut her more slack. "Why's the timing so important to you, Malachite? We have our bond—our debt—and can call it when we're ready. Why are you so interested in when we do it?"

Malachite sucks in air through his teeth. He turns on her and steps closer, forcing her to move away from him. "You would do well to remember this with that loose tongue of yours. When I'm a Fold member, I can make life easy, or hard for your wing. And if your brother—RedWish—is to have any hope of getting Judge to take him on as his heir, then you better stop asking questions and simply do what females were made for! If you don't, RedWish and your wing will only have you to blame!"

PHOENIX CARRIES THE tub of plates down to the stream, which runs along the far end of the market. The dairy has always used it as a water source for their milking cows, but now it's in much higher demand. The horde of hungry Camazotz were going through paper plates at an alarming rate. Judge and Rockland went to a local camping store and stocked up on enamel plate ware. It means the Camazotz eat in sessions now, but it's more cost effective and better for their beautiful forest. The Camazotz have always been sensitive to aeronaught trash and annoying plastic bags too easily get caught on wings during windy night flights.

She lifts her skirts clear of the muddy edge and begins her duties. Lost in the repetitive task, her mind wanders, and she fails to hear the large male approach from behind.

"Leave those and come with me," Malachite orders, walking past her toward the edge of the trees. "Now!"

The slim female, with the delicate stars tattooed around her eyes, drops the plate and follows. She looks above and behind her, breaking into a slow jog to keep up.

Once under the cover of the nearest tree, she asks, "What's wrong? Is there danger?" She looks out at the open sky.

"You have a duty, and you haven't fulfilled it yet."

"But I was! I'm not done yet. The plates will be ready before the next meal," she says, exasperated at this annoying male's suggestion. She can only go so fast.

"Not the dishes. Rockland! You haven't called on your blood bond yet. Why?"

Phoenix gasps and covers her mouth with both hands. "That's my business!" She says around her fingers. Her tone is harsher than she would normally speak to a male, but she's disgusted by the young Camazotz, who isn't her father, or in power, asking her such private questions.

"Watch it, little bat. I'm only looking out for you."

Phoenix frowns. Malachite is mean. He's always been mean, even before he tried to attack Connie in the park. "How so?"

"Your brother needs you. Don't you see?"

"Go on." Pegasus is the kindest older brother a girl could ever wish for. He looks after her and makes sure she has plenty to eat, even though supplies are short most days. He's respectful and caring and asks for her opinion whenever he has a big decision to make. She would do anything to help him succeed. The Mythical creatures wing has been forgotten for too long. Now that Pegasus is aligned with the Z wing, life has gotten much better.

"If you have a pup with Rockland, the Land Wing and the Z Wing will give you their allegiance. That will practically guarantee Pegasus will get a seat on the Fold in the years to come."

"But Pegasus already has an alliance with the Z wing," she says, confused.

Malachite huffs out a breath and grits out between his teeth, "Does he have one with the Land wing?"

"Not exactly, but—"

"Quiet. Do you want him in favor with Strickland or not?" he growls.

His logic suggests he's trying to help her, but she knows better. His eyes are hard and his hands keep fidgeting. From what Pegasus has shared with her about the colony politics, this doesn't make sense. Malachite isn't their ally, so what's his game?

Phoenix knows all too well what a pup from Rockland would mean to her wing. And more importantly, what it would mean to her to be with a male she loves... but Rockland isn't ready. Rockland probably won't ever be ready because he's found his girl. Focusing on her feelings for her brother, and the respect she has for their future Sire, she takes in a deep breath. She needs courage. She summons the vague memories of her mother. She was a strong female. She would know what to do if a male was treating her in this manner.

"How does my brother getting voted in benefit you?" She places her hands behind her back, so the dominant male won't see them shake. She stands tall.

"Females shouldn't ask those kinds of questions—"

"And unrelated males shouldn't ask the kind of questions you just asked me." The adrenaline pumps down her veins, and it feels good to defend what's right and stand up when it matters. She thinks of Rockland and knows he would be proud of her too.

"Let me be clear then. If you don't call on Rockland, I'll make sure Pegasus never takes a position on the Fold. It will be my mission to weaken your wing and push you back down to where you belong. Now, demand Rockland fulfills his duty with you!" he snaps, only inches from her face.

Letting out a breath, she pictures her mother, then her brother, and the only male she never ever wants to hurt, or see disappointment in his eyes.

"No, I will not. My brother would be ashamed of me if he knew I was forcing our future heir into a union he didn't want. He wouldn't be able to look at me, because Pegasus *is* a male of worth. Pegasus respects females and would never threaten, or manipulate one to win power. Pegasus—unlike you—earned the respect he has from the other members, and you will never be able to take that away. Now if you'll excuse me, I have real work to do, and no time for dangerous games that will only weaken our colony in the long run."

PHOENIX WASHES THE pile of dishes faster than ever before. Her fingers are still shaking, but she can't hide the smile of satisfaction she got from speaking the truth. She needs to find her brother, or Rockland, and tell them what Malachite is doing. She senses she isn't the only female from the dozen Strickland forced into a blood bond, but she doesn't have proof of that. Just her instinct telling her Rockland is in trouble.

She lugs the heavy tub of clean plates, back to the grilling machine. Rockland is nowhere to be seen. He's always so keen to help with the cooking, but Jet and Mackie are draping the aprons over their necks.

"Where's Rockland?" she asks, scanning the line of hungry Camazotz starting to form.

"Don't know," Jet replies. Mackie ignores her.

She plays the conversation with Malachite over in her mind. She knows she's missing something, but can't figure out what. Why would my pup with Rockland help Malachite? she wonders.

She asks everyone she sees on her way to the dairy if they know where Pegasus or Rockland are. Nobody knows. One of the hardest parts of staying in human form is locating people. As bats, they send mental messages to each other, until someone knows their whereabouts, but as humans, it takes much longer.

She jogs along the path, dodging the people walking toward her. If only she could flip, and fly to his shop. Their bat sonic radar means even in a crowd of bats, none of them fly into each other. But in human form, they're clumsy—except Rockland. He's graceful in either form. She bumps into two females who glare at her.

Backing away, she looks around for anyone else. "Have you seen Pegasus?" she asks two passing pups. They shake their heads in a negative response.

The urge to flip surges through her, but she knows Strickland would punish her. It would embarrass Pegasus and then she would be disappointed in herself. Rules are there for a reason—for the protection of all. She continues on foot to the dairy.

Zola is working in the kitchen when she enters. Her cheese production is supplementing their diet and Phoenix was pleasantly surprised how delicious the gooey yellow substance is when melted over hamburgers on the grill. She never knew it could be eaten that way.

"Hi, Zola, have you seen Pegasus recently?" she asks. "I've been on dish duty and can't find him."

Zada's cousin looks up from the giant wheel of cheese she's about to start slicing. "Hello, Phoenix, yes, Pegasus left with Rockland and Judge to deliver more goats to the roost. He won't be back yet."

"Oh."

"Would you like a slice?" Zola says, holding up a thin yellow piece.

"No, thank you. I love it melted now."

Zola nods her head in understanding and returns her focus back to the task at hand. Phoenix leaves the kitchen and stands outside, watching the moving traffic of Camazotz heading for lunch at the grilling machine. Since she can't talk to her brother, or Rockland, about what Malachite is up to, she wonders if Rebekkah will know.

Rebekkah used to be her friend. They used to hang out and fly together regularly, but Phoenix saw an ugly side to her friend once Connie arrived. Phoenix never knew Rebekkah hated aeronaughts as much as she does. Rebekkah would deny it, but Phoenix is pretty sure she just hates Connie for taking Rockland away from them all.

She starts the long hike through the trees to find the girls. When they're in human form, they spend time near the herb garden Sylvana— the Shadows resident shaman—tends to for her medicinal needs. The sage and lavender and rosemary make the fresh forest air smell even more intoxicating. The spot is isolated which is why the girls feel safe gossiping there.

Phoenix can hear their voices long before she sees them. From the sounds of it, Rebekkah, Zabreena, Macantia, and Lavender are all here. It surprises Phoenix that chubby Macantia is here. Rebekkah usually only surrounds herself with the 'right' kind of friends, and Macantia is larger than superficial Rebekkah normally allows.

"Hi," Phoenix announces when she steps out into the clearing the girls are occupying. There's a small break in the tall pine trees that allows the sun to hit the forest floor. Tiny wildflowers sprout up from their bed of pine needles, and the girls usually lounge in the sunshine picking the delicate blooms to twist into their braids.

"Long time since you've decided to join us," Zabreena sneers. "What do you want?"

"I've been working on dish duty each day! Pegasus volunteered me to help every shift." It's not exactly the truth. Phoenix is more than happy to help the colony when needed, but she needs the girls to think she's been busy, rather than purposely choosing to avoid them.

"Yes, I've seen you dragging those dishes around," Rebekkah replies. "Thank the bats above I don't have to do it."

If Phoenix thought Macantia's presence here was surprising, then it's nothing compared to the shock she tries to hide from her features, when she spies Madison sitting at the edge of their clearing. The Son wing is a medium-sized wing that has never risen to any substantial power. Again Rebekkah has either lowered her standards on whom she's seen with, or there's something more going on in the group.

"Hi, Madison," Phoenix says. "What brings you here?" She's nervous Zabreena will be all over her for asking questions, when she hasn't spent much time with her friends, but Phoenix needs to try. None of the girls are members of the Gem wing, so she's not sure how forward she wants to be about Malachite's conversation with her.

"Madison has been sitting with us because she's one of Rockland's chosen too," Lavender replies. "We thought we should all stick together since we have him in common now."

Phoenix doesn't miss the flash of anger in Rebekkah's eyes as Lavender speaks. Rebekkah used to lord it over all of them that Rockland only had eyes for her. Now he has a blood bond with all the girls present, it must be eating away at Rebekkah's ego. Her social status isn't quite as elite as it was before Rocks broke his wing.

"Have you decided when you're calling in your bond?" Lavender continues, totally oblivious to the death stare shooting her way.

Phoenix swallows, "Um, no. Have you?" She's relieved she didn't have to mention it. Maybe she can collect more information on what's behind Malachite's plan.

"Tonight," Lavender replies, casually looking around the circle of females.

"So soon?" Phoenix replies. "Don't you want to wait until the threat is over, and the colony returns to normal?"

"No. And I'm not the only one that will be visiting Rockland later," she boasts.

"What?" Phoenix gasps, looking to Rebekkah. She wants to ask if Malachite has anything to do with their decisions, but Rebekkah has always made her feel inadequate and stupid. She wonders again how Malachite would benefit from all of them having pups now with Rockland. If anything, that will only gain Rockland more votes to become future Sire because he will have more ties to each wing.

Rebekkah stretches her arms out to give them maximum sun exposure. "Maybe tonight, maybe not, but I'll be the one deciding when," Rebekkah states.

I'll be deciding when.

Phoenix is sure that means Malachite has spoken to her.

"You told him you were ready?" Lavender screeches. "You can't change your mind."

Rebekkah looks down her nose at the younger Lavender. "I am ready, but I never told him when. That's for me and Rockland to know, isn't it?"

Never told him when.

Phoenix decides the *him* must mean Malachite.

Zabreena announces she has work to do at the candle shop and convinces the group to move their conversation to the picnic tables outside the store.

"I can't. I'm scheduled to eat in an hour," Madison replies, running her fingers through her undercut pixie hairstyle.

"Me too," Phoenix adds, staring at Madison's intricate lace collar tattoo. The art completely covers her neck. Phoenix dreams of getting a tattoo that large. "We can walk together."

Zabreena, Rebekkah, Macantia, and Lavender all head west into the forest, while Madison and Phoenix move south to make their way back to the grilling machine. Asking about Malachite will be easier with just the two of them.

"I know you think it's weird that I'm sitting with them now, but they approached me after Graceland asked me to meet them in the forest two nights ago," Madison explains. "I was so shocked I couldn't say no."

Phoenix understands all too well the draw to those with influence, when you belong to a smaller wing. But what's Rockland's sister got to do with all of this. "Graceland asked you to meet her in the forest?"

"Well, she was just helping Malachite."

7
Betrayal

Bat POV

"**H**ELPING Malachite?" Phoenix asks.

"Yeah, to arrange a meeting with us. He thinks it's important we call in the mating bonds."

Phoenix stops in her tracks to face Madison. The girls are standing under the low branches of a massive, gnarled tree about half way back to the market. She knows nobody will overhear them talking here, but she doesn't want to get any closer to the market. "Madison, that makes no sense. Why would he care when we all have pups with Rockland? It's not like he cares about everyone—like Rockland does. Malachite only cares about himself, so it seems odd to me that he wants us to mate."

"I know, but he got really angry with RedFaith when she asked him those exact questions. You know what she's like."

"RedFaith was there too?" Phoenix confirms.

Madison nods her head. Phoenix takes a seat on the soft ground and leans against the trunk. The wind has picked up slightly, but the trunk offers them protection. She pats the forest floor for Madison to join her. Sitting in the quiet shade, the girls each ponder silently what Malachite would get out of their bonds since they're both from less influential wings.

Here!

The girls both jump from the unexpected gruff male voice echoing inside their heads. Phoenix clasps a hand over her mouth in shock and stares wide-eyed at Madison. Madison flicks her chin length hair away from her eyes and stares in silence back at her friend. There is a Camazotz in bat form, so it can't be a Shadows member.

Phoenix uncovers her mouth with her hand and takes hold of Madison's. They grip each other tightly, as the fear the Muerte are here freezes them in place, unable to move. Madison places one slender finger over her lips, and Phoenix agrees to stay absolutely silent.

Boots crunch on the forest floor on the other side of the large tree they are taking shelter under. The branches grow low to the floor and have made a nice hidey-hole for the girls to sit in out of the wind. Phoenix relaxes a fraction when she realizes they are sitting down wind of the two males. She knows they are male because she can smell them now. She bites her lip and prays to the bats above for protection.

"Is it done?" The same gruff voice growls.

"Yes, it will be," the other male replies. "All of them are ready."

Madison's fingers squeeze hard, forcing Phoenix to look at her. Both girls continue their wide-eyed stare. Those voices belong to Shadows' members. Shadows' members who were just in bat form breaking Strickland's command.

"All?"

"Well, maybe not all, but enough."

Phoenix is positive the young male voice belongs to Ash, and he's talking with his father, Cypress.

"Are you sure?" Cypress growls.

"Yes."

"Can anyone trace it back to you?" The tone of his voice is laced with anger.

"I was discreet. Mackie and I got Malachite to ask most of them, so our wings are clean," Ash replies.

The girls blink at each other. Malachite was asking members to do something on behalf of Ash—in secret. This can't be a coincidence.

"If you fail me, there will be consequences."

"Father, I swear to you on the blood in my veins that Rockland will be dead, or bleeding out at least, by sunrise."

Phoenix musters all her courage not to make a single sound. Those words make her want to cry out at just the thought of harm coming to Rockland, but she presses her lips together hard to remain undetected by the males. When she looks at Madison, she sees she has closed her eyes and is holding her breath.

"Is this your ego talking?"

"No. One is going at dusk, and Lavender and Violet have sworn to ask tonight too. They won't let their own wing down, so Strickland will be forced to give him a blood sentence, or our Sire will be breaking a sacred law. The Fold won't be able to save his heir this time, because breaking more than three blood bonds will seal his fate."

"Excellent. The reign of the Land wing is almost over," Cypress spits. "I'll be by the grilling machine when it's time to summon me. Clear?"

"Yes, father." The males both flip and the girls try to press their bodies as close as possible to the ancient tree. If they're spotted after what they just overheard, who knows what Cypress would do. They wait several minutes before daring to make a sound.

"Did you hear that?" Phoenix whispers. Madison nods her head, tears forming in her striking brown eyes. Their knuckles are turning white from the pressure of clasping each other's fingers. "What do we do?"

Madison shrugs, still too scared to speak.

"We have to warn Rockland," Phoenix whispers. "I'm flipping. I know it's illegal, but it's the only way to cover enough ground to find him. He might be back by now."

The girls argue about what will happen if they're caught in bat form, versus what will happen if they can't find Rockland to warn him. They decide the risk is worth it and both transform.

ROCKLAND IS STANDING in the middle of the doorway to his jeweler's shop. He stinks of goat after the long hike up Blood Mountain carrying one of them around his shoulders. Standing before him is RedFaith, wearing not much of anything. Her corset is tied so tightly her chest looks four sizes bigger, and the skirt is so short she might as well not have bothered to put it on. What Rockland never knew was that RedFaith has butterflies tattooed on her upper thighs. Her long skirts normally cover the ink that matches the design covering both her arms.

"I officially ask you to do your duty by me and give me the life you owe."

"What?"

"What do you mean what? I'm calling in my blood bond, Rockland."

"When?"

"Now."

"Now?"

"Is there something wrong with your hearing? Yes, now. Right now."

Rockland fully enters the shop and turns to close the glass fronted door. He needs to have a serious conversation with RedFaith about how he feels about his duty to the colony, and his duty to his girlfriend. Looking down the row of shops to see who might be around to witness this, he spies Ash and his gang of supporters. Rebekkah, Zabreena, Lavender, Ash, Mackie, Macantia, and Malachite are all sitting on one of the picnic tables near the candle shop. It still saddens him that Rebekkah is so supportive of the Plant wing's heir now.

"RedFaith, I'm really sorry—"

"Don't you dare deny me," she says, cutting him off. "You owe me."

Rocks frowns, wondering why her voice is so tense, and she's so aggressive in her request. Something feels off about her approach. "Are you okay?" he asks.

She flinches at his kind words. "Yes, now will you honor the bond?"

"No." Rocks braces himself for the fight he knows will now follow.

"Swear on *my* blood in *your* veins that you are officially denying me my right of a blood bond," she snaps. "Swear it!"

He doesn't miss her attempt at guilting him into compliance with the mention of blood.

"I will be forever grateful to you for saving my life, but I need to stand for what I believe in now. You and I both know my father trapped me into these bonds. My family would have sustained me if given the opportunity. But I will swear on *your* blood that I'm not fulfilling my duty to you. Now or ever."

Without another word, the sultry female storms from his shop. Rocks pulls his phone from his back pocket. He needs to send a quick text to Jez to inform him about what just happened, and one to Connie to let her know he's back safely. Before Rocks finishes his first text, Lavender strolls in and stops with her hands on her hips opposite him.

"I officially ask you to do your duty by me and give me the life you owe."

Rocks closes his eyes and takes a deep breath. He thinks about his father, his mother, all of his younger siblings. He thinks about Judge and Zander, and what they will say. But most of all, he pictures his beautiful, golden girl, Connie.

Connie.

Opening his eyes, he clears his throat and looks Lavender in the eye. "The answer is no, and I will swear on all the blood in this universe and the next if you want me to."

Without a word, she also leaves.

The trap has been set. Rockland looks at the empty rafters above him. Bats above, why didn't he see this coming? He wants to kick himself for assuming nobody would play this dirty to win control of the colony.

He rests his chin on his chest and takes another deep breath. He doesn't need to look out the window to know another female from Ash's posse will soon be marching in and making another blood bond demand. He doesn't know what happened at the market in the hours he was gone, but he knows he's been set up—and set up to fail with potentially deadly consequences.

The Sire's hand will be forced now. Rockland slumps onto the wooden bench that runs the length of his shop window. He waits while the deepest sadness he's ever known fills his soul. Of all the requests his Sire could have made of him, a blood bond was the only one that he wouldn't fulfill. But his father knew that when he made the decree.

Seconds later, Rebekkah enters. He doesn't even raise his head to look at her. Betrayal from someone he considered a close friend once stings even harder.

"Look at me," she snaps.

"Just get on with your betrayal, Rebekkah," he says, still staring at his scuffed boots.

"My betrayal?" she scoffs. "You are the one betraying us."

Rockland finally looks at her. "No, I'm not. I've devoted my entire life to making this colony a better, safer place for us, and future generations. I work from dusk until dawn doing all that I can to help, while you slink around in the shadows playing games that will only weaken us."

"That's not true."

"Whatever. Just get on with what you were *sent* here to do."

"Why do you think I was sent?" she asks.

"Because I've been playing these political chess games my entire life, and the three of you coming in here all at once reeks of manipulation. What I don't understand is why smart females let disrespectful males bully and control them. If you stand up to those bastards, you'll take away their power."

"It's not that simple."

"No, I know it's not. But if you don't make a stand when there are males of worth that will support you, then nothing will ever change. Did you go to Jeremiah, or Levi, and report whoever told you to do this?" He waits for her to answer.

Rebekkah looks at the dusty, wooden floorboards.

"No, you didn't, because deep down you get a sick rush from playing these games. But if you stand back and look at the big picture, you'll see you're being used. When those males don't have a need for you, you'll be nothing to them again. So get on with your betrayal because I've got shit to do."

THE SIRE AND the Fold have been summoned to the jewelry store. Rockland waits, sitting on the edge of the cracked, wooden veranda. He didn't want the confrontation he knows is coming to take place inside his shop. His workspace has been a place of salvation for him since he learned his trade. It was always a space he felt at ease being in his human form. The more jewelry he produced, the less his critics could complain, because bats can't silversmith.

He sees the small army marching up the path past the candle shop toward him. The surprise is that Cypress is leading the mob and not his father. He shakes his head at himself for not guessing who would be behind this maneuver.

The Plant and Land wings have historically never seen eye-to-eye, but they have always stood together for the sake of the whole colony—until now.

Rockland stands up and steadies himself for the punishment he is owed because he denied the three females their blood bonds. He doesn't want to remind anyone that it's actually four bonds he hasn't honored, but if they have forgotten about the bond he rejected with AuburnSky, then he's not going to remind them. But then again, can the look of disappointment he knows his father will give him get any worse?

Hardly.

When the group finally assembles, Cypress and Strickland are front and center. The Fold stands in a semi-circle panning out from the two center figures. Rockland stands opposite with his head held high. He doesn't regret his decision because he knows in his heart it's the right one for him. What he won't relish is looking at Zada, Judge, and Zander and witnessing their shame and dismay because of him.

Cypress begins, "I have called forth witnesses to be present for the hearing of a blood sentence against Rockland, son of Strickland."

He continues to report that three worthy females—who sustained the colony member when he needed blood the most, and thereby saving his life—have been shunned by this male when asked to return the life they gave him.

Zada has pushed her way to the front of the crowd and is standing directly behind Strickland. Pain lances straight through Rockland's heart when he meets his mother's desolate gaze. He mouths the words 'I'm sorry' to her.

"I call forth the first denied female, RedFaith," Cypress announces. He asks her to state for those present an account of events. Some members of the crowd hiss in shock when she says Rockland swore on her blood that he would not repay his debt. "Do you confess to this?" Cypress asks Rockland.

"I do," he says, loudly with a steady voice. He couldn't live with himself if he did anything other than deny her.

The hearing continues with Cypress calling the other two females and Rockland admitting to his refusal of them both.

"As all present have witnessed, Rockland has broken one of the Camazotz most scared vows—not only once, but three times. He is, therefore, guilty of a blood sentence and shall pay with his life. The life he stole ungratefully from these willing, innocent females—"

"Stop with the theatrics, Cypress," Judge intervenes. "We all know those females were doing what their Sire ordered. It's not like Rockland coerced and tricked them into saving his life. In fact, we all witnessed him not wanting to bond with any of them."

"That is irrelevant. He did!" Cypress retorts.

Judge continues, "Sire, let us hear from Rockland. Let all present hear what he has to say regarding his denials. He surely has good reason—"

Macallister steps up. "Just because you helped raise the boy, Judge, doesn't mean you can bend colony laws to protect him. It doesn't matter why he said no to the females. He knows our law. In fact, maybe your influence is to blame for his lack of Camazotz commitment."

The crowd gasp at the insult.

"Leave Judge out of this," Rocks says. "His loyalty to the Shadows is not to be questioned because of my decisions."

There's a moment of silence. Cypress stands staring at his Sire, while Strickland looks across at his first-born son. The usually angry Sire is almost emotionless. It's as though the young man standing before him is already dead to him.

"Get on with it," Cypress hisses.

"Wait," Judges speaks. "Is there anyone present who can speak in his defense?"

More silence. Nobody steps forward.

Strickland clears his throat. "I hereby issue, using the power bestowed to me by each and every Camazotz, issue a—"

"Wait, Sire," Zander speaks. "Surely we can vote on this? Surely?"

The desperation in his uncle's voice is another blade to the young man's heart. He tries to keep his face devoid of emotions. To help himself stay strong, Rockland focuses not on his caring, loving uncle, but on the coldness seeping from his father.

"Not according to law. It's too late for that now," Cypress states. "He's broken three blood bonds."

"Zander, you are the youngest of the Fold," Levi says calmly. "You're not as familiar with our ancient laws of old, but Cypress is correct. When three blood bonds are denied, it's an automatic blood sentence. Taking blood and not repaying the life owed means one forfeits their own life. Like it was lost had they not received the life saving blood."

Zander tries again, "But, Sire—"

"Enough! It's the law," Strickland bellows. "And not only do I have to deal with this, but two females were caught earlier in bat form. They've been caged, and I need to deal with them when they regain consciousness. So let's proceed. I hereby issue a blood sentence upon Rockland, son of Strickland. Your life will be forfeit from this day onwards."

Rockland hangs his head and closes his eyes. He won't look at his mother or uncle. His heart pounds faster and faster inside his chest.

"And according to laws of old, the Camazotz sentenced gets to choose instant death, a death flight, or to be banished forever. Let the boy choose," Judge announces to the crowd.

"No!" Cypress cries. "With his intermixing with the 'naughts, he will survive. That's *not* what the elders of old had in mind when they gave banishment as an option. Back then, the banished would surely die, and slowly at that. He will run to her! That's not allowed!"

A murmur passes through the onlookers.

Judge steps out in front of the circle and faces the crowd. "Well, until we all vote to change the laws of old, they currently still stand for *this* sentencing, so where he may seek shelter for his banishment is of no concern of ours. Rockland will lose his family, his home, and his legacy, isn't that punishment enough?" Judge says, making eye contact with each Fold member. "But maybe I'm sensing a suspicious keenness for the young man to die, Cypress? This better not be personal, or you would be breaking another law of old yourself."

"Don't insult me. I merely want justice for the females he has turned his back on," Cypress defends.

"Quiet!" Strickland roars. "We are not going to debate this for half the night. I'm more concerned with the safety of every member here from the threat of the Muerte, than what my son is doing—or not doing—with any females! I'm astounded, Cypress, that you're so focused on his love life, rather than our security," Strickland glares at Cypress for several seconds before continuing, "But as you have stated, he has broken the law and will be punished according to that law. Rockland, son" —Strickland swallows— "son of Strickland, I hereby find you guilty of breaking a Camazotz law laid down by our blood from generations past. A law designed to protect our numbers and keep our members prosperous. You are sentenced in blood. What do you choose as your fate?"

"Banishment," Rockland declares.

Cypress and Ash hiss at his answer. Judge eyes Zander and the two of them step closer to Rockland. Creating a physical barrier between the young Camazotz and Cypress.

"You have until sunset, three days henceforth to leave," Strickland declares. "And I ask the Shadows' members to stay away from him during those three days. It's simply to get his affairs in order. The less contact, the better."

Zada drops to the ground, covering her face. Her shoulders heave in silent sobs. She has lost another of her dearly loved pups—first Celand, then Decker, and now Rockland.

8
Evicted

TIFF leaves straight after dinner. She came over for a study session after school, but we ended up painting Mini's nails. That kid is the ultimate distraction and at the moment, nobody wants to tell her no.

I sit at my desk, staring at my handwriting scrawled across the page. Finals are next week, and then I'm done.

Done with high school forever.

Where did it go? At times, I never thought I'd get here. But now it's almost over, I'm sick to my stomach about what I'll do next. My year was so turbulent compared to how I thought it would go this time last year. So much has happened. Maybe that's why I feel like this year has slipped away from me.

Learning I was adopted, discovering the Camazotz, witnessing the magic of shape-shifting, falling head over heels for the most amazing guy ever, finding my real parents, wishing I never found my real parents, getting kidnapped, Rocks getting hurt by Joey, Mini getting kidnapped, working for Enzo, getting evidence to put away the biggest drug lord on this side of the continent, the Camazotz getting batnapped, all those lies upon lies upon more lies. No wonder I'm freaked out the school year is about to end. That's a lot for a girl to have time to do in less than a year.

Open your window.

My phone pulls me back to the here and now.

Opening my window, Rocks is sitting on the roof that stretches over the wide porch below.

"What are you doing? Why didn't you text me earlier?"

He shrugs.

"Are you okay?" It's weird that ninety-nine percent of the time when someone asks that particular question, people already know the answer, and it's not good.

"I needed to get away fast. Sorry. I should have let you know. I can go, but…"

"Pffft, don't be silly, bat boy. Get in here," I say, stepping back from the window.

"Connie?" he says quietly.

Poking my head back out the window, I look into his eyes. A deep sadness is reflected back at me. "Rocks?"

"I don't want to come in. I can't be confined right now. Can we go somewhere? The park maybe?"

"Can I tell Mom and Dad you're here? Or would you rather stay unannounced?"

"Unannounced. Sorry."

Shit. I really don't want to sneak out. I feel like for the first time this year, I'm back in the good books with Mom and Dad. Sticking to the truth as much as I can makes me feel good, and I'd rather not sneak out on them either.

"Um, ahhh…"

"How about you come out here, and we sit and talk up here? I'll be able to hear if they come upstairs."

My answering smile tells Rocks all he needs to know. "You hungry?" He nods, biting his bottom lip. "Gimme a sec."

Returning from the kitchen, I shove the sealed, heated dishes into my backpack along with the snacks and sodas, and the crocheted throw off my bed. I grab my coat and a beanie just in case it's cooler out there than I expect. Rocks helps pull me out the window. He's so steady it calms the adrenaline that's starting to pump through my system at the idea of a roof picnic.

Before helping me up to the top of our roof, he gives me a quick hug, but there's a longing to his hold. Getting me up onto the roof above my bedroom isn't exactly graceful. There's lots of pushing and shoving, and giggling. I'm convinced I've made enough noise to wake not only Mini, but also half the neighborhood.

We're headed to the other side of the roof, where the guest room juts out from the house. No nosy neighbors should be able to see us here. It's not until we sit in the L shaped corner facing each other, that I take a look at the horizon.

"Wow, it's so beautiful." I'm stunned. There isn't much of a view from our windows, but from the roof it's a different story. Being higher than the neighboring houses, I can see the city in the distance. The soft twinkle of the lit high-rises is spell binding.

"You don't mind the height?"

"I don't actually want to look down, but I'm not scared of heights—usually." I put the fact that my feet are only inches from the edge of our guttering out of my mind.

"I won't let you fall. Trust me."

In all those action movies, when you see someone fall off a bridge, or building, and they dangle waiting for their friend to pull them back up to safety, I can't help but think how ridiculous that is. It would be almost impossible to pull someone back up in most cases, but I know in my heart, Rockland has the upper body strength most ordinary aeronaughts don't possess. He'd be able to pull me back to safety and probably quite easily.

"I do trust you." I smile and start unpacking his feast, and my second dessert for the night.

It's not until he's eaten his meal followed by the chocolate silk pie that he takes my hand and places a soft kiss on my knuckles.

"I wanted you to know I'm now debt free."

It takes a moment to register exactly what he's talking about. The blood bonds—all those girls he owes a bond.

How could I forget? There are so many questions filling my head, but I don't know where to start. Questions I'm not sure I really want the answers to, but questions I know will eat away at me unless I ask. I've learned that being brave enough to ask a difficult question is way better in the long run. If only I'd asked Kelly and Chad about my adoption…

"You're gonna need to start explaining that before I panic." I swallow down the fear bubbling up from the bottom of the pit inside me.

"Oh my God, Connie, it's not like that," he says, eyes wide.

A second later, his hair drops over his eyes while he studies our entwined fingers. He takes a deep breath, and I know he's ready to finally talk when he flicks his hair back off his face again. "I refused to honor my blood bonds. I've walked away. That's why I'm debt free."

"But I didn't think you had a choice."

"I always had a choice. It was only the consequences that were the problem. In the end, I decided honoring those bonds would hurt the only girl I love, so I said no—to all of them."

The sadness in his eyes earlier, and the sag of his strong, muscled shoulders doesn't add up with the awesome good news he's sharing.

"Rocks, is there something you aren't telling me?"

He looks out over the neighboring houses. "I'm on my own now."

"What do you mean?"

He looks at me again, and I see disappointment mixed in his dark blue eyes. He sighs. "I've been exiled from the colony. They're letting me stay there—for the moment—but I have to make plans to leave in the next three days."

"What? No!" I half yell.

"Shhh, your neighbors will hear us," he whispers, taking hold of my cheeks and leaning closer. "It's okay. This is the only way."

"Rocks, you can't let them kick you out. I won't let that happen," I angry whisper back at him.

"Connie, the alternative is not an option for you—or me. I want you, and I'll lose you if I honor those bonds. I won't let that happen. You're too precious to me. And I don't want those females in that way at all. Ever."

I'm wishing I had snuck off to the park, so I wouldn't have to try to control my voice so much, or the desire to pace around. "But you'll lose your family. You won't see Bailey, or Moonshiner, or any of the pups again!"

Rocks stares back out over the horizon, and I wait for him to speak. "I was never a good influence on them anyway."

"Bullshit! You are amazing. Go back there and honor those bonds. I won't let you give up everything for me." I pull my hand out of his and shuffle myself further up the roof. "It's too much!"

Rocks flips and before I know it he's reappeared behind me. His long legs and arms circle my whole body as he takes a seat behind my back. His warmth and touch is exactly what I need. I cover my face with my hands because I don't want him to see my tears. He's about to lose his whole family and life because of his father's hate for aeronaughts.

I can't hide the shake of my shoulders as the tears begin to fall. He pulls me back against his body. "Shhh, Connie, don't cry. It's okay."

"It's not okay," I sob, imagining him never seeing Bailey, or Zada, or Jez, or any of his other young siblings again. "It's so not okay, and Strickland should be ashamed of himself. The Fold should be too."

He wraps me up in the best Rocks hug ever, and we sit in silence watching the three quarter moon moving in and out of the drifting clouds.

Rocks is about to lose everything for me. The thought of letting him go—of breaking up with him again—sends an indescribable ache tearing though by chest. I can't do it. I'm too selfish. But Rocks has done so much for me. He's risked so much—including his life—that it wouldn't be fair of me to not give him back his family since he gave me mine.

"Rocks, this breaks my heart to even think it, let alone say it, but I can't be your girlfr—"

"No, Connie," he interrupts. "No. We are not breaking up. I'm not giving you up again. Last time, I let you go, it left me feeling incomplete. Some part of me was missing, and it was you. Being apart is not an option."

"But…"

"But nothing. I love you with my heart and soul. You're the only person who has ever accepted me and not worried about the consequences. Decker accepted me, but in our early years, it cost him greatly. He would get teased and picked on because of me. You, however, love me for me."

My tears erupt at his gorgeous words. All I can do is nod and cry more, while he gently rocks us both back and forth.

"I love you so much, Rocks. I'm so sorry Strickland has done this to you," I sob. "Is there any chance he won't make you leave?"

"No, none. It's called a blood sentence. When certain Camazotz laws are broken, the Camazotz must face a blood sentence."

"That sounds bad."

"It is. There are choices… an instant, painless death, but most choose a death fight."

Rocks explains a death flight is when a Camazotz is to fight for his life—but not just once—three times. The fights take place as bats. If a bat has broken the law and is faced with a blood sentence, the bat will fight three opponents back-to-back. It's common for bats to fight and survive, but when a bat has to fight two fresh combatants straight away, it usually ends badly for the convicted. Torn wing membranes and blood loss are the biggest causes of death.

"That's horrible. Who did you fight? Are you hurt?" I try to turn around to make sure Rocks is in one piece and doesn't need another trip to Dr. Gandy's veterinarian surgery.

"God, no, I fled."

Rocks tells me that the convicted bat has a choice to take his life and leave the colony—forever banished—rather than face the three fights. Since most Camazotz don't have much interaction with the aeronaught world and have been brainwashed into fearing it mostly, leaving the safety of their home colony is as good as suicide. Most never integrate and die alone in an unfamiliar forest somewhere. The other colonies are also forbidden from taking in those convicted of a blood sentence. It's shameful and no other colony would want a spineless law-breaker joining them.

"So now I'm a coward too."

His words make my blood boil. As difficult as it is on the roof to turn around, I manage it. I take Rocks' face in my hands and force him to look at me.

"Listen here. That's bullshit. You are the bravest man, Camazotz, and bat I know, so I never want to hear you say that ever again. This blood sentence thing is archaic and barbaric. You have rescued me every time I needed you, and you didn't even hesitate about the danger!

I know for a fact, you would have done exactly what Decker did to save those pups. This blood sentence isn't justice, it's murder!"

"Thank you. I would hate it if you thought I was a coward."

"Never say that word again! And what the hell are Zander and Judge thinking? Surely they didn't vote against you?" The more I think about this, the more I want to slap some sense into those stupid bats.

"No, they were the only two who attempted to save me, but this crime made it impossible."

"It wasn't a crime!"

"It was Cypress. Phoenix reported that Malachite was going to each of the females and demanding they call in their blood bond now. He threatened her and Pegasus, but she stood up to him and refused. Jez and Zander pieced this all together. Phoenix risked a lot to help me, but it was too late. She was unconscious in bat form when I was sentenced. Cypress then made sure nobody would listen to her.

"They think Ash put Malachite up to it to get me kicked out for good. That opens up the way for Ash to become the future Sire. To ensure the colony can't turn on the Plant wing, Ash made sure he wasn't the one directly responsible for my exile. That's where Malachite comes in. I bet Ash promised Malachite a Fold position, since there's so much uncertainty with Decker gone. Judge was holding all the power, but now Cypress has stolen it all back," Rocks explains.

"Those sneaky fuckers!"

"Shhh!" Rocks smiles at my insult, and it reaches his eyes. He looks around to see if any new lights in the neighboring houses have turned on if they heard my outrange. "They are sneaky fuckers," he says, starting to laugh, but trying to muffle his laughter in his elbow. Seeing him suddenly look happier, makes my anger evaporate, and I cover my mouth with my hands to try to contain my laughter too. "I love it when you defend me," he says when we both settle down.

"It's my job."

"Do you think your parents might let me stay for a while?"

Shit. Rocks is going to be homeless after the weekend. I know Mom is still feeling extremely guilty for sending the police to his family's market, and I think that's our ticket to success. It doesn't thrill me to play on her guilt, but Rocks being homeless is way worse.

"Let me handle it. I'll talk to them tomorrow, and then we can plan to move you in here on Saturday and Sunday." Saying this out loud is making it real. Rocks is going to be leaving the colony and joining my world. "Wow, this is crazy. I can't believe it."

"Me neither. God, I hope they say yes."

"Does this mean the Shadows aren't on high alert anymore from the Muerte attacking?"

"Cypress had a speech all planned out for Strickland afterward. I didn't get to hear it, only the Fold did. But apparently he had collected texts about each patrol proving no owls or other Camazotz have been seen in the area, so therefore the colony can do without a blood traitor like me, since it's safe to be bats again."

The technology Cypress was so dead against he used to help his case against Rockland.

"I *hate* him so much. I know I shouldn't say that, but I do. And why is Strickland so hell bent on you becoming a dad so young? It's not like you committed a real crime. All you're guilty of is not getting a bunch of girls pregnant!" The football team members would all be given awards by the Principal if they were able to keep it in their pants, and poor Rocks is about to lose everything.

"Strickland was the only child my grandfather, Richland, sired. It was tough for Strickland to survive and then gain power and become the next Sire as well. As a result, he made sure he had plenty of pups to carry on his legacy, and he wants me to do the same. Since the average Camazotz life span isn't great, it does make sense." He shrugs.

I sense he's taking his refusal to fulfill the blood bonds to heart way more than he's allowing me to know. Rocks takes colony law very seriously, so I know deep inside he really does feel like he shouldn't be allowed to live there. I remember seeing his half-blind grandmother feeding from his goat. Without medicine and simple things like glasses, old age is rough at the colony.

"No, it doesn't make sense. If Strickland's truly worried about the survival of his colony, then he would allow modern technology and access to medical treatment. And he would want the best leader to take over from him, regardless of whether he's sired a dozen pups or not."

Rocks cocks his head to the side. I listen too. "Your folks are locking the back door."

"Shit, they're getting ready for bed. I've got to get back in there."

FRIDAY AT SCHOOL, I tell Tiff, Brandy, and Mary Lou about Rocks getting kicked out of his family. If Mom and Dad agree to let him stay, then the girls are going to find out anyway, so I might as well use their brains for the best way to broach the subject with the folks.

It takes me a while to back track and explain how they sent the cops looking for Mini at his family market. Not being able to mention anything about bats and blood bonds makes it hard, but it's kind of like a practice run. If I can get the girls on side with my story, then I might be able to convince Mom.

"Oh. My. God. Your boyfriend is going to be living down the hall from you," Brandy chides.

"Stop that! Be serious. He's going to be living on the streets if I can't convince them," I reply, praying my ears are not burning red hot. I should have worn my hair down today. Note to self, I absolutely must wear it down when I talk to the folks.

"Your mom owes him. If he's being kicked out because of what they did, they can't say no. I'll cover for you tonight at work," Tiff offers. "You'll need time to talk this over with them, 'cause Brandy's right, there's gonna be way more rules at your house now if he moves in." She grins.

The girls all snicker, and I feel my cheeks burn too. I give up trying not to be embarrassed. If this plan works, Rocks is going to be sharing my bathroom. I'm gonna have to get up at the crack of dawn so he doesn't see my bird's nest, morning hair.

"Holy crap, it's kinda just sinking in what I'm proposing to them!" I add, biting my bottom lip. My stomach rolls. Rocks is depending on me. If I can't convince them, he's really screwed.

"And don't wait for dinner," Mary Lou suggests. "Make sure you ask your mom before your dad gets home. United they conquer, but divided they fall. That's what my parents always say, so now my brother and I ask them serious stuff separately."

The girls leave me armed with every defense of Rocks and the situation they can think of. I'm ready. I find Mom in the upstairs bathroom bathing Mini when I get home.

"Nee." Mini beams at me standing behind Mom.

"Hello, gorgeous girl. Hi, Mom."

"Hello, sweetheart, how was school?" Mom's sitting on a child-sized chair next to the tub. I take a seat on the tiles in front of her and wink at Mini watching me.

I do honestly hate lying to them now, but Rocks has secrets that must be protected, and he needs my help. These lies have a higher purpose.

"I have bad news."

I launch into my prepared speech about Rocks' parents not being able to forget the sight of the police showing up on their doorstep accusing him of kidnapping a baby. I explain they're suffering hard times due to their market being closed for renovations, and they simply can't afford to feed and clothe him any longer, so they asked him to leave. Now he won't set a bad example to his many younger siblings. It's not exactly the truth, but it's not that far from it.

Mom is devastated.

She offers to call his parents and beg for their forgiveness, but I tell her it's too late for apologies. Her and Dad doubted Rocks' moral integrity, and his parents won't forget that in a hurry. Having Mini playing in the water beside us is the perfect reminder of exactly what Rocks has done for this family. I lean over and squeeze the rubber duck floating on the warm water. She giggles and starts squeezing all the toys that make noise.

"He saved her for us, Mom. I know it's a lot to ask, but we owe him. Letting him stay until he can sort out something more permanent is only fair."

"Oh my God, I feel so responsible."

"Can he stay for a bit? Please." I bite my bottom lip. I watch the emotions flit across her face. It's a big ask, but so was getting involved with Mini's abduction. "What would we have done without him?"

It's a low blow, but it's also the truth. Mini hands the duck to Mom and smiles her little heartbreaking smile.

"Of course, he can stay." I watch her features. She nods her head and looks at me. "Yes. He can stay. He can stay as long as he needs."

It's almost as though she's convincing herself each time she says it, but I don't care. The answer is yes. I scramble off the floor to hug her. "Thank you so much. He's been so worried. I'll text him now. Do you think Dad will be okay?"

"I'll worry about him, but I'm sure he's going to have a thing or two to say about having a young man in the house."

My guilt meter kicks into high gear. Maybe it's time I came clean about us dating, since it's going to be way obvious in a matter of days.

"Um, well, about that. You see, um, well—" I stutter because I totally didn't prepare this admission.

"You two are dating?" she asks, with a look of such hope in her eyes, it makes me laugh.

"Yes," I say, smiling.

"Oh, sweetheart, you have a boyfriend. And such a lovely, young man. I've been hoping you two would get together."

"Mo-om, stop." I can feel the heat return to my cheeks.

"Sorry, I don't want to embarrass you, but I couldn't be happier, but let's not mention this part to your father just yet."

9
New Beginnings

WHEN I arrive at the market the next morning, I'm as nervous as I originally used to be coming here. I'm not sure what to expect, whether the Camazotz will be back to being their hostile, hating selves, or if the colony will be in mourning at the loss of a great member. Or maybe they'll be back to blaming me for everything, and I guess I am partly to blame for Rockland's decision.

But, the place is a ghost town.

Not one single person is between the parking lot and Rocks' jewelry shop. I listen like Rocks always does, and the silence is eerie after the hive of activity the market has been for the last few weeks. I send a text to find out where Rocks is.

A few minutes later, a bat flies in the door of Rocks' shop, and Jez appears.

"Rocks is busy, but he sent me to get you. He said you're early."

When I first met Jeremiah, I couldn't help but focus on his half-missing ear. Now I hardly notice it. Maybe it's because he talks way more than he used to.

"Yeah, I couldn't sleep. I got up and started driving. Is everything okay?"

He shrugs. "This all sucks. I don't know if any of us are really okay about it, but the Sire has spoken. Follow me."

"Hey, you were just a bat. Is that allowed?"

"Yep, Strickland rescinded the command to stay human."

That explains why the market is back to its usual almost empty feeling.

We walk out the back around past Rocks' wagon. Beside the goat pen is a half-hidden track that leads through the trees. I've never noticed the path before, and since it's lined closely with young fir trees, it's well concealed.

"Where are we going?"

"You'll see. And I don't even care if you're 'allowed' or not. You're giving him a home, so I'm giving you permission." I watch his square shoulders disappear around a bend in the path.

What the heck can he be talking about? I wonder. I trot to keep up with him, unsure of what the hurry is. The air is so clean and fresh. Taking in deep breaths of it, helps my nerves from earlier to unwind. Like he said, I'm taking their heir into my home, so they can all go flip themselves if they have a problem with me today. I follow in silence, and we must hike along this secret path for a good twenty minutes before arriving.

Yet again, the Camazotz continually amaze and surprise me. Nestled amongst a thicket of fir and spruce trees is what can only be described as a giant lean-to structure. The building has a slanted roof and two sidewalls offering support, but the main support comes from two old pine trees. Their trunks are about thirty-feet apart and the structure is large enough to accommodate the dozen or so people crammed inside.

"What's this?" I whisper, not wanting to interrupt the scene before me. Something is on the ground in the center with several people kneeling around it. Rocks is in the thick of it, sitting on the floor, leaning over doing something with both hands. "What are they doing?" I stand up on my tip-toes, but it doesn't help.

My words bring a halt to activities. An older man is next to Rocks with his back mostly to me. He twists around to stare, and then goes back to whatever he's doing.

"Moonshiner's getting his first tattoo," Jez replies quietly. "Come have a look. I know he loves you, so he'll be proud for you to witness this too."

What the?

Moonshiner's just a little kid. I can't believe they're letting him get inked. As I approach, I can't see him, and the area everyone is centered around is too small. He must be in bat form.

The members of the inner circle are all kneeling near little Moonshiner's bat body, while the second tier is standing watching from behind. Zada, young Moonshadow, Bailey, Baxter, Zander, and Ezra are all present. There's another guy about Rocks' age kneeling opposite the old man.

"Moonshiner wanted Rocks to help with his tattooing. That's why he's getting it done now. It's a big honor to be chosen to hold the skin while the tattooing takes place," Jez explains. "None of us are technically allowed to mingle with 'the banished,' but I just don't give a shit anymore."

I should've known their tattoos had a ceremonial meaning. A thin swirl of light grey smoke rises from the back corner. Sniffing the air, I guess it is sage to cleanse the process. Several small objects hang from the main beam holding the roof up between the two pines. Amulets or wards I'd bet. They sway in the breeze, and some of them look like small bones.

Rocks acts so normal—in an aeronaught way—it's easy for me to forget his colony is so wrapped up in ancient traditions and superstitions. Since so many of the members have tattoos representing their bloodlines, the serious atmosphere doesn't surprise me.

Rocks leans over and speaks quietly. A moment later, he signals for me to come in under the shelter. The little bat is lying on his stomach while Rockland, and the two unknown males work on inking the black rubbery membrane of his wings.

"Hi, Moonshiner," I say quietly.

Hi, Miss Connie.

It's been so long since I've had voices in my head. Zada smiles at me from across the group, but it doesn't reach her eyes. When I look at Bailey, she's sitting with her arms folded and the biggest pout possible on her little face. Clearly, she's here against her will.

"Connie, this is Jackson of the Son wing and our resident tattoo master," Rocks explains.

The old man—most probably in his sixties—gives me a curt nod and returns his focus to Moonshiner's skin.

"And that's Jackson's grandson, Jenson, his newest apprentice."

Jenson doesn't appear to have an inch of un-inked skin—well, of the skin that's visible. His ink is a mad swirl of patterns and color on his right side, and I make a mental note to ask Rocks what his design shows when he's a bat. On his left side, the designs were done while human. He might have been practicing on himself because some of the work is rough, but thankfully not nasty, like all the ink Cypress sports.

Moonshiner has made the choice to show his tattoo design only when he's in bat form.

I place a hand on Rocks' shoulder and watch the men work. There's no buzzing of an electric tattoo machine. Rocks is using both hands to stretch flat the wing membrane, while Jackson welds the rustic instruments. The long stick in his right hand has a needle attached at a ninety-degree angle. He places it with careful precision before hitting it with the thicker, carved stick in his left hand. Jenson is holding a bowl of black ink and one of red in his palm. He hands his mentor a different tool with lots of small points attached to it.

"We use traditional methods," Rocks adds. "The needles in the different tools are made from organic materials. Carved bones, cactus needles, fish bones. That sort of thing."

I wonder what design Moonshiner came up with and look forward to seeing it when it's complete. I imagine Rocks, laying here as a bat, while Jackson worked on the intricate design of the Shadows' bat on each wing. Using these old-fashioned methods must have taken a very long time and seems like it would be more painful. And no quick shots of alcohol to calm any nerves before they start either.

BACK IN ROCKS' wagon, Moonshiner is resting amongst the piles of belongings on Rocks' bed. The little bat isn't allowed to flip into his human form until his tattoos have completely healed. According to Jackson, flipping stretches out the skin and can wreak havoc with the design until it has properly set.

Rocks' wagon isn't the same. Two ancient, leather trunks are by the door. All his remaining worldly possession—which aren't many—are in neat piles on his bed.

"Can I take a load back today?" I ask. "And then come and get you and the rest tomorrow. Is that cool?"

Rocks nods. I walk over and wrap my arms around him. He returns my hug, and we simply stand, holding each other.

"I have an idea that might cheer you up," I say.

"What is it?"

"I found an optometrist only fifteen minutes away. We could take Cappella and get her eyes tested. I'll buy her some contact lenses from Enzo's cash. She should be able to see again as a bat, or a human. You won't have to worry about who will take care of her."

Rocks gives me his shy, little smile—the one that's my absolute favorite. "I'll get her. She's still up in my roof," he says, pointing to the starry, wooden ceiling above us.

Rocks returns with a small bat lying over his shoulder with one wing clinging to his front and one to his back.

Strickland hates modern ways.

Her croaky, old lady voice reverberates in my head.

"He's coming around," Rocks replies. "Each wing has a cell phone now." He holds his phone so close to her face it almost touches her little batty nose.

"Plus with your eyesight back, you'll be able to help Zada make candles again," I add.

I'm beginning to understand how these bats think. They hate being a burden on the colony. I'm guessing Cappella has felt useless since she hasn't been able to see. Why else would she be hiding away in Rock's roof when there's always work to be done at the colony?

Really?
I could see that well?

"I'm pretty sure, but we won't know until a doctor has a look at your eyes."

Our trip to the optometrist is very uneventful. The old female flipped before taking up the front seat. Cappella enjoys the car ride and leaves the window all the way down, so the wind blows her long, greying hair. It's the same thing Rocks used to do when he first started riding with me.

Her clothing is thankfully more modest than the younger generations, but she's in black from head-to-toe. Her neck shows faded tattoos of stars and bats. The tats on her arms are too blurry to distinguish. My curiosity gets the better of me, and I ask her about them. She's proud to tell me that she's fifty-seven years old, and she's had some of her ink since she was twelve. She looks older than that—way older—but without face creams and the easy life of an aeronaught, I guess I shouldn't be surprised.

The optometrist is stunned Cappella has never had glasses before. He confirms she probably hasn't been able to read anything for several years. Again, I can't imagine such craziness. Reading glasses aren't even modern anymore. Since there aren't any other customers, I pay the extra fee, and the optometrist makes her glasses on the spot.

The look on her face when she slides the glasses up her nose and can read again is absolutely priceless. She walks around the store reading every advertisement in sight out loud before coming over and taking Rockland's face between her hands. She studies his features as though she's seeing him for the first time in a long time. Next she walks over and wraps me in a hug.

"It's a modern miracle."

I bite my tongue and pay for the glasses and several boxes of disposable contact lenses. We're gonna need Zada's help in caring for the delicate contacts, but I know she won't mind. If her mother will be able to fly safely wearing them, I'm pretty sure she might even keep it from Strickland.

Back at the market, we don't have much time left after explaining Cappella's good-as-new eyesight to Zada and Zander. Putting Enzo's drug money to good use makes me feel right about having it. The glasses have changed not only Cappella's quality of life but Zada's too.

Zada sadly admitted to preferring her mother spend her days in a dark, isolated roof void, rather than risking her life each time she took to the air—almost totally blind.

Rocks and Jez carry the large trunks to my Honda. "I wish we had more time together," I say.

"Soon we'll have all the time. Actually, soon you'll get sick of me."

"I will not."

"Will too." He grins.

"Is Bailey okay? She looked rather grumpy at the tattooing."

"You noticed?"

I raise one eyebrow. "Of course, I noticed her pouty face, and the fact she ignored me. Bailey never ignores me."

"She's mad at you."

"What?" I half yell. "What did I do?"

"She figured if I had no place to live, Strickland would change his mind. Since you're taking me in, she's blaming you for me leaving. I've tried to explain it isn't that simple, but at times like this, she acts her age."

"Yeah, it's easy to forget she's only five."

"Acts like she's forty-five half the time," he says, smiling. But it fades too quickly. "I'm gonna miss that little mother hen."

Before I can reply, two Camazotz enter the parking lot carrying large boxes. Rocks immediately goes to their sides and takes one of the boxes from the older of the two females.

"This is Zada's cousin—Zola—who runs the dairy," Rocks introduces.

"Nice to finally meet you, Connie. I was wondering if you wanted some cheese? Since the market has been closed for business some of this will go bad if it isn't eaten soon, and Strickland hasn't announced when the market will reopen. I was able to use the plain cheddar varieties while everyone was human. But my specialty produce is going to waste without aeronaught customers."

I don't know what to say. This is so kind it catches me off-guard. "Sure. Thank you. My parents love cheese."

My reply makes her and her helper smile wide. "No need for thanks. You're doing me a favor. There's nothing worse than seeing your own labor of love rot in a refrigerator." She opens the box Rocks is holding and starts pointing out the different cheeses. Some of them look like the kinds Mom brings home from the market deli she loves. The pungent, artisan cheese probably turned the noses of most of the aeronaught-weary food eaters.

"Wow, these are gourmet cheeses, Zola. You could sell them to restaurants on the internet."

She smiles and hands them over, but I know she doesn't really understand what I suggested. Strickland is sitting on a gold mine with the artisan talents housed at the Shadows, and the worst part is he doesn't even know it.

MOM AND DAD help me lift the trunks from the car and take them to Rocks' new room. He's going to be sleeping here from tomorrow night—indefinitely. A concept I can't quite get my head around.

Mom has done what she does best and turned his room upside down to clean every inch. It smells of lemon and fresh linens.

"I want to apologize to his parents in person," she announces, straightening the already straight cushions on the bed. "To try and explain."

"No, Mom. No, that won't help."

Shit. Shit. Shit.

If Kelly gets in the car and drives to the market, I don't even know what will happen. I swallow the lump in my throat. "I truly get why you want to, but think about Rocks."

"I am, sweetheart. I feel responsible."

"Mom, how did you cope when you thought Mini wasn't coming back?" I hate to remind her of this dark hour, but she cannot go barging into the colony to apologize. I sit on the bed and motion for her to join me.

"Oh dear." She covers her mouth with her hand. Her eyes reveal her shame at the dreadful memory. "I fell apart completely."

"And would you let Dad or I help you?"

Her eyes begin to water. She shakes her head to tell me the answer I already know.

"No, you didn't, and we're your family. Imagine how you would've felt if Rocks' mom barged in here and started telling you what you should be doing? We were lucky and got Mini back, but his parents are still mourning the death of Decker. They lost a son and aren't coping well."

It's not the reason Rocks is banished, but it's a reason she can relate to and will hopefully keep her away.

Her tears spill over, and I'd bet she's thinking about if Mini never came back. She takes a moment before saying, "How did you get to be so mature, my beautiful girl? How? It certainly wasn't from my example when Mini was gone. I'm still so ashamed of how I behaved. Leaving you and your poor father to cope alone."

"Don't worry about it, Mom. We all did the best we could. But promise me you won't go visiting the market in Helen to help. Just the offer of a bedroom is all the help Rocks needs. He's so relieved to have a place to call home."

"I promise. Tell him, he can stay as long as he needs. There's no rush to rent an apartment. His parents will most probably realize what they've done and come around. I'm going to the store to stock up the pantry with his favorites, and to buy more crackers for that delicious cheese."

My mom is the best mom ever.

The next day, I make one final trip to the market to get the rest of Rocks' stuff. I was surprised when he decided to fly down to my place after sun down. He said he wanted to spend as much time as possible with the pups and say goodbye alone. Being Rocks, he apologized profusely in case he'd offended me. He said the flight would clear his head and get him in a better frame of mind to face Chad and Kelly.

I don't blame him one little bit.

I wait on the porch swing for him to materialize near the trees. Mom calls me in for dinner when he hasn't arrived by eight p.m. I'm trying not to worry, but I can't help myself. What if he's done something stupid? Then, I calm down because this is Rocks I'm talking about, and he never does anything stupid when he's upset. Emotional stupidity is more my style.

At nine, the doorbell rings, and the tension in my shoulders subsides the moment I lay eyes on him. He's unharmed and is here in one piece.

Rocks hands Kelly a beautiful bunch of flowers, which smell of a forest glen. There's no cellophane wrapping, just a simple black satin ribbon, which explains his late arrival. "Sorry I'm late."

"Oh, Rocks, these are magnificent, but you didn't have to," Mom purrs.

As soon as I can, I pull Rocks upstairs to my room. It feels like forever since we've had proper time to talk.

"I'm not going to ask you if you're okay because you wouldn't be normal if you said yes. You don't need to talk about it either, unless you want to."

Rocks takes my hand and kisses my knuckles. It's a gesture that always makes me smile. "I think I'm in shock. When I left, Strickland told me I was doing what's best for the survival of the colony."

"Bullshit! I can't believe Strickland won't evolve with the world he's living in. How can the colony prosper if members aren't allowed to celebrate their strengths and be who they are? You have so much to give and being in human form doesn't lessen it one little bit. If they can't see your value, Rocks, then don't worry because I know one family who can. You won't ever be alone in this world."

Rocks pulls me off my bed and onto his lap in his corner chair. He wraps me in the kind of hug I have missed lately. "That is why I have really and truly decided to get fixed.

"But..."

"I've thought hard about it, Connie. Believe me. But it's who I want to be."

Rocks has always supported me—no matter what. Finding Enzo and Josie changed my life forever, and not in the way I was imagining. This is going to change Rocks' life forever too.

"So will you help me find the fix?"

I stare at him for a while. My eyes wander up and down the ink patterns swirling across his muscled arms. "Can I ask you something first?"

He rolls his eyes. "Anything, Beans."

"Won't your bat tattoos haunt you? In fact, why did you get bat tattoos if you always wanted to be human?"

Rocks smiles. "Took you long enough to ask." I raise an eyebrow at him. "I was trying to embrace the Camazotz in me, and show others that... well, that I'm proud of who, or what, I am."

"Proud? But, are you?" Wanting this fix suggests otherwise.

"Sort of. It's something I'm working on because so far I'm not allowed to be me—the man who's also a bat, as opposed to the bat who's also a man. So I'm picking you and your family, Connie. For now, that's all I can do."

As much as my gut is screaming at me this is wrong, I respected Rocks for never questioning me on my search to find where I belonged in the world. I suspect he knew way before me that my place was with Chad and Kelly, but he helped me on my road to discovery all the same.

"Then I'll help you find this fix if it's what you want."

If Rocks is serious about wanting to only be human, I need to respect his choice.

"I have a confession," I admit.

"Do tell."

"When you first told me about the fix, I googled shape-shifting spells. *Half a million* results came back, and people were saying it's real."

His eyes go wide. "Why didn't you tell me?"

"I didn't want to give you false hope if they're all full of shit. And I didn't want you to think I didn't like you just the way you are. You know I don't want you to change, unless that's what you really want."

"It is. I want to do this. I can't stop thinking about Celand. I understand her so much more now. It's sad I can't tell her."

It reminds me of what I learned about myself from my brief time with Enzo and Josie. I know where I get certain looks and traits. Maybe Rocks is also learning about who he is and why. I know nothing on this earth would have persuaded me from going on my journey of self-discovery, so it would be completely hypocritical of me to try to change his mind.

I can't deny I'm worried about what killed Celand in the process, but I should have been worried about my murderous father and surviving him instead. But I did survive Enzo, and I have to believe that with the help of the Internet—which Celand most probably didn't have—Rockland will survive too.

10
Peaches

THE next day, it feels like my alarm goes off before the birds even sing, but I think I'll need every extra minute. I shower and spend a ridiculous amount of time staring at my wardrobe options. I want to look casual, not too casual, but I want to impress him. I text Tiff, and she takes my 'my boyfriend lives with me' wardrobe dilemma extremely seriously.

My hair is pulled up into a high ponytail; I straighten my top in the mirror and smudge my lip gloss a little more. Mom better not say a word about me looking so nice *before* breakfast.

Taking a deep breath, I exit my bedroom and barrel straight into Rocks' chest.

His BARE chest.

His hard, muscled chest.

And did I mention it's completely bare?

And gorgeous.

And warm from being fresh out of the shower.

I step back and watch his eyes land on my obviously flaming red ears. He looks down and smirks, his wet hair falling over his eyes.

"Good morning," he croons.

I swallow. I try to stop looking at the shape of his chest. I try to keep looking up into his eyes. I try. Honest.

Stop ogling.

I get so mad when boys stare at my chest—and it's never bare. But this is different surely. Right?

Crap. It's no different at all.

"You're beautiful." I mutter

Oh, double crap.

"I'm sorry," I add, trying to re-engage my brain cells. I turn away from his nakedness so fast and end up with my nose against the wall. I rest my palms on the wall beside my head and squeeze my eyes closed, but all I can see is Rocks in his freshly showered, bare-chested glory. It's seared into the back of my eyelids.

"Don't be sorry. I forgot my clothes."

I crab walk along the wall to pass him without facing him again. He chuckles behind me, and I bite my lip. "I hate my ears," I announce because I have clearly not regained control of the words spilling from my mouth.

"I love them. They show your emotions and give me clues as to what you're feeling."

God, if only he knew what my body was feeling! I cover both my ears and continue my weird side step around him. When the stairs come into sight, I know I will survive this delicious torture. "I'll see you downstairs with your clothes on, Mister."

Before I enter the kitchen, I pull the elastic from my hair and check my cheeks in the entryway mirror. Entering the kitchen, Mom has gone into her old Rocks-needs-feeding mode and has baked a continental breakfast to out do any five-star hotel I've ever seen.

"You so didn't need to do this."

"It's his first morning. Speaking of which, what's he planning to do all day?"

This is the first of a long string of questions that continue even after Rocks joins us. I keep my distance from him and circle the kitchen island as he tries to come near me. He gives up eventually and winks at me across the divide. My eyes flash to Mom, but she's fussing with the dishes at the sink and thankfully missed his cheekiness. She's still asking question after question.

Rocks answers with his usual grace. He's planning to spend his day at the library. Kelly assumes this is for his job search, but I know the truth.

She begins fishing for information about the time gap between the police showing up and his parents evicting him. It's only natural because it is a flaw in our story, but Rocks is way ahead. He changes the subject and completely distracts her.

"Mrs. Phillips, can you teach me how to cook? I never had a need to learn before now."

I say goodbye to Mom, but I'm fairly sure she doesn't compute my words. She's babbling about the lessons and what to teach him first. At my car, I'm almost inside, when two arms wrap around my middle.

"You can't leave for school without a goodbye kiss," he whispers. I turn in his embrace and his lips sear my soul. I'm sure they leave burn marks on my skin because I want him so badly.

Rockland—the housemate—is going to be the very slow death of me.

WHEN THE FINAL bell rings, I'm in the Honda and speeding home a nanosecond later. The girls are excited for tomorrow's lunchtime episode of 'Living with Rocks.' He texted me during last class to say he was back from the library and getting ready for his first cooking lesson.

I don't want to miss a second of this show.

I enter the kitchen right as Rocks shovels a huge mouthful of fluffy whiteness into his mouth. The look on his face is priceless. It's almost as funny as the time he showed me his bat nipple piercing, and I couldn't stop laughing then either. His features screw up and he tries not to gag. I'm at his side peering into the mixing bowl, giving it a quick sniff.

Egg whites.

Whipped egg whites to be exact.

When I look at Kelly, she's gaping at him. "What on earth did you eat that for?" she asks horrified.

He downs two glasses of water from the faucet and is still scrunching up his nose in disgust. "It looked interesting, but I'm sorry to say it doesn't taste very nice."

I have to sit on a stool because my legs can't hold up my shaking upper body. I laugh and laugh and laugh.

"Connie," Mom admonishes—ten minutes later—when I'm still

snickering every time I look his way. I will never forget the look on his face.

"Why are you teaching him to make meringue? It's not like he's going to be having a fancy dinner party."

"You never know, and it's good to learn the basics."

Basics?

Boiling an egg is basic for a Camazotz. "I think when he asked he meant more like how to make your baked beans. The sort of food that will keep a guy satisfied."

The word satisfied does strange things to my insides.

Thankfully, Kelly ignores me and returns the bowl to the mixer to slowly add spoonful's of sugar. Rocks doesn't look impressed, and I hang around to see how Kelly's going to coax him into tasting it once it turns into thick, sticky goo for piping.

"Didn't your mother teach you any of this?" she asks.

Rocks shakes his head. "She's not much of a cook." I love how he manages to avoid lies with versions of the truth. Zada isn't much of a cook. That's certainly no lie.

MORNING TWO AND I find myself leaning up against my closed bedroom door, staring at the glowing number on my alarm clock. It's the exact time of yesterday's bare chest fest. I want to leave my room in case I catch another glimpse of his half-naked glory, but at the same time, I don't want to be that ogling girl. I breathe in and out as slowly as I can. I hope to god his batty hearing can't hear my labored breaths.

In the end, I open the door. I'll let fate decide if I get a show or not before breakfast. Before I step out, I glance at the bathroom door, and watch it open slowly. Rocks steps out with his blue t-shirt slung over one shoulder. I stand transfixed in my bedroom doorway as he saunters past me down the hall, not saying a word, but the grin on his face tells me he's discovered my new Achilles heel.

Thank goodness Dad leaves for work early.

And so begins my new morning routine. The only days his chest is covered is if Mini, or Mom, happen to still be upstairs. Life is so beautiful at times it isn't funny.

In fact, my last two weeks of high school are awesome. I head off to school each day, while he spends most of his time scouring different county libraries for any evidence that shape-shifting magic exists. After school, Kelly's cooking classes fill up his afternoon.

After dinner, we work on the spreadsheet I created to track his findings. The libraries haven't given us anything, so he's been working his way through an extensive list of shape-shifter websites. Rocks emails asking if these people claiming to be shape-shifters, can show him how it's done. None of the fakers are ever willing to share their secrets. Part of me wants him to meet one of them and flip in front of them to see if they run screaming for the hills. That way we'll know for sure if they have any true magic abilities or connections.

The problem is both Rocks and I know shape-shifting is possible. He does it at will. Bat-to-human. Human-to-bat. What we don't know is if any of the ancient magic survived the purges and cleanses of history.

"Are you absolutely sure a shaman cursed your ancestors' village? I mean is it possible that your ancestors were simply born as shape-shifters, and there's nothing to un-do?" I ask

I'm on the laptop going cross-eyed from too much data entry. Rocks is in his chair listing the email responses he has received in the last twenty-four hours.

He puts his phone down and looks across the room, staring into space. I wait. He frowns before looking at me. "Holy shit. You know I never even thought of that. The Shadows don't actually have any proof of our history that I can think of."

"I don't mean to doubt. It's just a thought."

"I know." We both return to our tasks and eliminate another dozen websites.

"So can you ask anyone at the colony about the fix?"

"Banished remember."

"Sorry."

"It's cool. Even if I wasn't, it's not something anyone talks about openly at the Shadows. My colony love being bats, so most would never want it. I think they don't talk about it 'cause the thought of being trapped in human form scares them more than a parliament of hungry Great Horned Owls."

Entering the kitchen Friday afternoon, Mini is helping with the cooking lessons. She's been following Rocks around like an annoying little fly. It's super cute, but a pain when we want to spend some time alone. I'm not game to talk about shape-shifting in case the little mimic says something in front of my folks. Kelly hasn't said anything about Rocks and bats since our odd conversation, but I don't want to open that can of worms a second time.

Today's lesson is orange and poppy seed muffins. Rocks has his hands full measuring the flour with Mom by his side. Mini leans over from her chair and knocks the poppy seed jar over. Before anyone can react, half the jar of poppy seeds litter the floor.

"Oh Mini!" Mom scolds. "Connie, be a dear and get the vacuum for me. I want to get these in the oven ASAP."

I drag the vac into the kitchen, plug it in, and suck the mess of poppy seeds into oblivion. What I fail to miss is Rocks on a technology high. As I begin to retract the power cord, I look up and witness—as though in slow motion—Rocks picking up the remaining poppy seeds and upending them all over the kitchen tiles.

"What—"

"Rocks?" Mom asks, just as astonished. We both stare at him, while he's staring at the magical vacuum device still in my hands.

"I wanted a turn," he says, pointing at the unit. Suddenly, he blinks and looks at the floor, then the empty bottle of poppy seeds and finally at Kelly. The color that floods his cheeks is like nothing I have ever seen before. He's super cute when his totally embarrassed. I have to bite the inside of my cheek to stop the urge to laugh. "I'm so, so sorry, Mrs. Phillips," he says, looking wide-eyed. "I'll buy you some more. I've never used one of those before is all," he says, pointing to the vacuum cleaner.

Mom's frown of annoyance fades, and she takes the machine from me and hands it to Rocks. "Well, when you're done here, you can vacuum the whole house. No need to ask. No need to scatter poppy seeds. Vacuum whenever you want. Mini leaves food in places you wouldn't believe."

Rocks looks like he's just won the lottery. "Really? I can vacuum whenever I want?"

SATURDAY MORNING I need a break from the lies that fill each email Rocks' receives. More excuses about why nobody is willing to give a display of their shape-shifting abilities. We discuss again if he should meet with them and flip, but it's a secret the three colonies have managed to keep under wraps for five hundred years, and that's too great a risk.

"Grab a jacket. We're getting out of here. I know something you're gonna love!" I say, contemplating internally if I should change my outfit or not.

"Where are we going?"

"To the movies."

In the theatre, the giant screen mesmerizes Rocks. His hand is constantly going from popcorn to candy to chips in a continuous loop. I stifle the urge to giggle because I don't want to distract, or embarrass him. His Camazotz metabolism sure is super charged. I let him enjoy the snacks and the movie because I want this to be the most amazing experience he's ever had. I settle in next to him and focus back on the screen.

The movie continues, but it doesn't hold my attention. I'm fidgeting. Normally, I love the movies, but this is the first time I've been with a boyfriend—and not just any boyfriend—one who completely owns my heart.

Watching Rocks exit my bathroom each morning is taking its toll on me. My mind and other parts of my body want more. I fold my arms to stop myself from touching him. I can't imagine how intense seeing a movie on the big screen must be for him. I've grown up with it. It's normal. My overexcited hormones should not ruin this first for him.

But there's a restlessness inside I have a feeling only Rocks will be able to still. As always, he senses my mood and looks over. The smile I receive—illuminated by the glow from the screen—almost stops my heart. He leans over and kisses me sending my pulse through the roof.

"This is the best. Thank you, Beans."

An explosion on screen draws his eyes. Glancing at my watch, I calculate another plan before folding my arms again and relaxing back into my seat.

When the movie ends, we sit watching the credits roll to the very end. Rocks is reading every word, still entranced by the magic and wonder of the big screen. So often he sends me back in time with a real understanding of history. I picture the first moviegoers and how amazed they would've been, and films back then were boring black and white with no sound.

Rocks shakes his head smiling. He has no words. And I couldn't be happier.

"Want to go again?"

His eyes widen. "Can we?" His happiness dims as a frown creases his brow. "Only if you want to. I know this isn't new for you."

"Don't."

"What?"

"Feel bad about what you've never had the chance to experience in my world. Watching you is a first for me that I'm loving. Believe me!"

That earns me the shy smile. "Can we see the same movie again?"

"I was hoping you'd say that because I want to show you what teenagers do in the back row." His eyebrows lift in question. "Don't ask because I'm not telling, but I will show you. I promise." Just the thought sends a tingle through my whole system. I'm going to be making out with the hottest guy in the world in less than an hour. The best part is my parents and little sister will not be able to interrupt us.

We head for a bathroom break, and I notice Rocks has demolished every morsel from the candy bar, but he declines my offer of more aeronaught treats. I tell him after the movie we'll go for ice cream at Cold Stone. He'll be in mix-in heaven.

The butterflies begin at the box office buying tickets to a movie we just saw, and they intensify as I climb the stairs in the theater headed for the darkest corner of the back row. With Rocks' eyesight, I know it's probably as bright as day back here. I fumble along the row and feel his hands move to my waist to steady me. In the far corner, I pull down the seats.

"Hey, is there anything on this seat I shouldn't sit on?" I might as well make use of his super Camazotz senses while I can.

"Nope, all clear."

Ten minutes in, I raise the armrest between us and snuggle in against his warm side.

"Remember that driving lesson in my backseat?" I whisper.

"God, yes."

"Well the back row of a movie theater is just as much fun."

LATER THAT NIGHT at the Bun Lovin' Barn, I share my first trip to a movie with my boyfriend. Tiff sighs and squeals, hanging on every word, as I pause my storytelling between paying customers.

"God, you're so lucky. I wish I had a boyfriend to jump in the back of the movies."

"I didn't jump him." I say, starting to flush.

"Yeah, but it's only a matter of time. He loves you. You love him. It's the next step."

I can't speak. I wipe down the counter and tidy up the condiments.

"Are you telling me you haven't thought about sleeping with him?" Tiff asks. She couldn't be more serious.

"Um," I bite my lip. I know my ears are flaming red and I don't care. It's good to be able to talk about this stuff with an old friend who really knows me. "Lately, I've been thinking about it more and more. You should see his body, Tiff. He drives me *crazy*. What am I going to do? It's such a big step."

"Yes and no. You'll know when the time is right. And Rocks is so not the type of guy to pressure you. He's got the most old-fashioned manners of any guy I've ever met. Plus, it's not like he's going to dump you after getting what he wants. He lives with you now." She grins. "Don't stress, Con. Just do what feels right."

Thirty minutes before closing, Rocks hasn't replied to any of my texts. Mom and Dad were hosting a dinner party with some of Dad's work friends, and Rocks had promised me he would come and walk me home.

Tiff and I close up, and Rocks isn't anywhere to be seen. I send another text. My gut radar starts to beep that something's not right, but I can't even imagine what or why. When Tiff offers me a ride home instead, I take it. She's kind enough to drive the same route Rocks would walk if he was coming to get me. I also scan the skies in case he flew because he was running late. Rocks makes sure to flip every night before bed. Neither of us want to risk him losing track of time and accidentally flipping, like he did the night I met him in the forest.

I jump out of Tiff's car on the street and run up the drive still full of extra cars. The folk's dinner party is in full swing, and from the distant laughter I can hear, I'm guessing they're all drinking on the back deck.

I hit send to call Rocks' phone and nearly jump out of my skin when I hear it ringing to my right. I dart between the cars and head for the front lawn. There in the middle of the grass is a body splayed out on the lawn.

"Rocks!" I rush to his side. "Are you okay? What's going on? Why didn't you come meet me? Are you hurt?" My hands have moved over his long limbs to check for breaks or damage.

"Connie?" he says, lifting his head and staring at me like I just flipped. He tries to sit up, but half way loses his balance and falls back across the grass, arms spread wide, and begins to giggle.

And giggle. And giggle.

Frowning, I grab my phone and turn on the flashlight app. Shining it in Rocks' face, I see he's perspiring. His hair is sticking to his forehead, and he rolls away from the brightness, shielding his eyes.

"Hey, bright. That super hurts," he mutters, and then lets out a deep sigh.

I lean over him and take a long, deep inhale.

Peaches.

I smell peaches and alcohol.

I sniff again, getting closer to his mouth. "Oh my God, have you been drinking?" I roll him back over onto his back.

"Yep!" He giggles again. "Yous mom's peaches. Look at the mooooooon, Con. Looks sooo pretty."

He raises both arms and is pointing with all ten fingers at the enormous white ball rising slowly overhead. I sit next to him and rest my face in my hands. My parents have a patio full of guests and my shape-shifting boyfriend is drunk on the front lawn. *Awesome.*

"We need to get you inside."

"Okay." Rocks sits up, and I grab him before he falls back over again. But the next minute, he's vanished.

The little bat squeaks and nose dives, head first into the lawn.

Ouch. That's gonna hurt tomorrow.

"Shit. Flip back." I scan the street to make sure nobody saw his change.

Flip.

Rocks is back. Now he's lying face down on the lawn. "Whoops. Don't know how that happened." He spits a blade of grass out of his mouth.

Rocks flips three more times in as many seconds.

"How much did you drink?" I ask, helping him to roll over again.

"What was left in the bottle. It's delicious. Like de-li-cioussss. New favorite."

Flip.

He's little batty Rockland again.

"Okay, stay as a bat," I order, as I start to dump the contents of my backpack on the lawn. "I'm gonna put you in my back pack and then I'll take you up upstairs and lock you in your bedroom. Nobody will see you flip in there. Got it?"

Eeeekkkkk.

I ignore the guilt as I carefully pick up Rocks. I hate putting him in carry cages—or backpacks—like a common animal. His wings are folded neatly around his body and ever so gently I place him in my backpack.

"Stay still and do not speak to me telepathically, okay?" I pull the zipper slowly closed and hoist it onto my back.

I take three steps and then…

Wham!

I'm face down on the lawn with human Rocks sprawled all over me.

"What the hell?"

"Ouch!" he groans.

"Ouch? You're saying ouch? Get off me," I whisper yell. God, the neighbors are in for a show tonight. Rusty, the dog next door, starts to bark. "Shit!" I crawl out from under Rocks. He's a mess of arms and legs. My poor backpack is in pieces surrounding us. "You owe me a new backpack, Mister. That one was my favorite."

"Where's your backpack?" he says, looking around. I roll my eyes and help him sit up again. I need him to concentrate on staying human. This is late for my parents to still be entertaining, and if he flips in front of their guests too, we're doomed.

Kneeling in front of him, I take his face in my hands and force him to look at me. "Focus, Rocks. You are a guy. Say it with me... I'm a guy." I grab his shoulders and try to get him to focus.

"Yous is girl," he says and does a weird hand gesture to his chest.

"Not me! You. Focus. If you flip in front of my parents, they'll flip, and you'll never be able to see me again. Got it? Think guy thoughts." His eyes go straight to my boobs. I'd smack him if he wasn't looking so cute about it, but at least I know he's focusing on being human.

He's got some serious explaining to do tomorrow.

ROCKS IS NOWHERE to be seen at breakfast. It's so not like him to miss a meal. I text him at ten to make sure he's okay.

My head hurts.

And I feel awful.

His replies do not surprise me. I text back.

You need to drink a gallon of water.

What you're feeling is called a hangover.

I head to the kitchen and grab some water for him. When I'm outside his door, my phone beeps again.

Hangovers are not my favorite.

"You can come in," he says, before I have a chance to knock. It's kinda cool that he can hear exactly where I am in the whole house.

The room is in darkness, and he moans at the light from the doorway.

"What on earth were you thinking?" I hand him a glass of water and hold the jug ready to fill his glass again.

"It smelled so good. So sweet and fruity. I just wanted to try it."

"But you're underage. You could have gotten us both in big trouble."

Rocks sits up. "What?"

I sigh. "Don't tell me you didn't know you have to be twenty-one to drink legally?" The silence that follows is deafening. I take a seat on the bed beside him and fill his water glass. "You're so lucky nobody saw you flipping out."

"I'm sorry. I didn't know that would happen. When I used to go to the dance club, I always wanted to try alcohol, but it's not cheap. Last night, your parents made these cocktails—"

"Wait? Did they make one for you?" They've never offered me a cocktail.

"No, but they smelled like heaven. I couldn't help myself. I'm really sorry."

Rocks pulls himself out of bed and takes a shower. He comes into my room when he's feeling better. He sits in his chair, as I close up my mathematics book.

"I don't know if... well, I..." he starts. I wait for him to try again. He's staring out my window. "I feel like I don't belong in your world either."

"What are you talking about?"

"Connie, face it. I don't know much about the aeronaught world. I could have gotten you into trouble because my nose couldn't resist the smell of a stupid drink. I've never been to the movies. I don't know the rules. I'm as useful as Mini in this world."

"That's not true. And don't be so hard on yourself. How are you supposed to know all this stuff? You weren't raised with it. It's like me at the colony. I see all your traditions and rituals, and I'm clueless about it all. But how can I be expected to know what's going on? It's not my world."

"Exactly! Your world isn't mine. Maybe I have no right wanting to join it. I don't belong in my world either, but at least I understand it."

"Are you having doubts about getting fixed?"

"I don't know."

I need to tread carefully. I remember having all sorts of doubts when I was looking for Enzo and Josie, but that didn't mean I didn't want to continue my search in the end.

"What are you saying?"

He's silent for a long while.

"Maybe your doubt is because you're suffering from a killer hangover and weren't expecting that to happen."

He grins, and the tiniest hint of color touches his cheeks. "Maybe," he admits. "My head really hurts."

I bite my lip to stop myself from laughing. There is so much for him to learn about the aeronaught world. The last thing I want is for Rocks to feel like he doesn't belong anywhere.

"Well, researching your options won't hurt. Just because we find out the information doesn't mean you have to go through with it, right?"

The frown creasing his forehead eases. "Right. It's just information. Thank you. I can't tell you what your support means. Besides without the colony to ask, I don't even know what we'll be able to find out. The Camazotz love their secrets, but this time I really want to get to the bottom of it."

EXAMS are done.

My high school career ended two hours ago.

I'm secretly a little freaked out about the fact I will never walk those halls again, but I'm so glad to be free.

The girls and I are at the mall. It's been our tradition since we started high school, and it's only fitting we spend our last afternoon shopping together. Who knows where everyone will end up at college in the fall. I know it's a decision I've been delaying as much as possible.

We're each in fitting rooms trying on new clothes to wear tomorrow night. I have no idea what style I want to go with. I want to impress Rocks and look sexy, but I'm nervous about what he considers as sexy. The Camazotz girls have taken raunchy to new heights, and I don't think I can compete with them. I also don't want to look absurd trying to dress up like a goth whore.

"So is Jeremiah coming to my graduation party?" Tiff asks for the millionth time from the fitting room next to mine.

"Depends if he can get away."

"Is he bringing any friends?" Brandy asks from the other side.

"No clue."

I'm so nervous about taking Rocks to our first party together. I don't know why I feel this way. I know he won't embarrass me, but since he's been living with me, all I can think about is taking things to the next level. At Tiff's house, we might have a chance to really be alone.

Last year, Brandy and Mary Lou both did it for the first time, and they weren't as serious with their guys as Rocks and me. I have a feeling the Camazotz are haunting me. What if I'm not good at it? All the talk of blood bonds and pups. I take a deep breath. I do not want a kid at this age. I wonder if he knows about condoms. I don't need to look in the mirror to know my ears are turning red. God, I hope he knows what they are because that will be one crazy conversation.

For some reason, I can talk to Rocks about anything—except sex and guy stuff.

I pull up the zipper and am blown away by my reflection. I've found the winner.

Stepping out of my change room, I feel beautiful. The soft fabric of the skirt brushes against my legs.

"Wow. You're buying that," Tiff comments, coming to stand next to me. "Hey, girls, check out Con in this."

My dress is blood red and strapless. The sweetheart neckline and tight waist is super flattering. I spin and look at myself from all angles.

This is way more skin than I've ever revealed to Rocks before, and I think he's gonna love it. I hope he's gonna love it.

"Sold," says Brandy, poking her head out from behind her curtain. "You look killer in that."

"You might be needing some alone time with you-know-who wearing that," Tiff whispers to me, grinning from ear-to-ear.

I bite my bottom lip and smile back at her. "You really think so?"

"Hells yeah!"

OUR HIGH SCHOOL graduation ceremony was held at the local community hall. Dad took the morning off work, so we could attend as a family. I painted my nails and Mom's with the school colors. The folks were so supportive about Rocks attending as part of our family that Dad even loaned him a jacket. I asked Rocks if he bought the dark grey, pinstriped suit with him that he wore to dinner when he first met Chad and Kelly. Turns out it belongs to Zander. But he looked amazing in his dark jeans and dark red button up, matched with Dad's black suit jacket and shiny, gunmetal grey tie.

It sent a shiver though my system every time I looked at him because nobody else knew about the sexy ink covering his arms, hidden underneath the suit. He really looked the part, and got too many extra long glances from the female population in attendance—both student and adult.

Mini got a super cute, new, blue dress and was the superstar of the day, since all the parents wanted to see for themselves that she really was back safe and sound. Mini ate up every ounce of attention from the safety of Rocks' arms. He's still her absolute favorite and was content to be held by him for the whole event. I secretly think she enjoys the vantage point he offers with his six-foot-four height.

It felt surreal to wear my cap and gown and walk across the stage to collect my diploma. High school is officially done. But the whole time, my gut was churning with nervous anticipation about attending tonight's party with Rocks—as my official boyfriend.

Tiff's house—unlike mine—has a basement. The party is down here to contain the noise from the music. I recognize Mom's contributions on the food table. Half the kids, mostly the girls, can't take their eyes off Rocks. He sticks close to me and doesn't seem to mind the stares and whispers.

It occurs to me he can probably hear what they're saying. "Are they talking about us?" I ask, sipping my icy soda.

"Mostly about me. But they're curious how we met, and where I'm from. A few of them don't trust me."

"Do you mind?"

"It's nothing I haven't heard before. I know I look different." His hands slide around my waist. "Although those girls in the far corner think my tatts are super sexy. I might go chat to them." He winks. I will admit I had requested he wear short sleeves tonight, so his tats could be seen. I think Rocks is the most gorgeous creature alive and couldn't wait to show him off properly.

I grab a fistful of his dark cotton tee. "You will do no such thing, Mister," I say, eyeing my competition in the corner. I stand up on tiptoes and kiss him. When I pull away, Rocks is grinning down at me.

"I like my Beans jealous."

"You're all mine."

"And proud of it. Let's dance. It's been so long since I've had the chance."

I recall the only other time Rocks and I have hit the dance floor at the club across from the Bun Lovin' Barn. It suddenly feels way too hot in here. That dance was all kinds of close, and we weren't even dating back then. I swallow and follow him to the adjoining room that's the makeshift dance party.

The lights are off, but Tiff hung two strands of soft, white, twinkling stars across the ceiling. It's awesome mood lighting. Rocks guides me through the moving crowd to the back corner. When we face each other, the song changes to a slow beat. He wraps his arms around me and pulls me close.

We stand and sway together in time to the slow groove. "I didn't tell you earlier because I couldn't find the right words, and even now, I know I won't get this right, but you look stunning tonight. This dress was made for you." He runs his long fingers down the side of my neck and across the bare expanse of my shoulder. "Your skin is so soft and perfect. You're so beautiful; you take my breath away."

My heart skips a beat. I'm suddenly not close enough to him, despite the fact that we're flush against each other still moving to the gentle beat. His hard muscles flex as he turns us around, and my mind flashes to him walking bare-chested down my hallway. Those same muscles move under my hands as I run them down his chest. Knowing exactly what's under his tight tee is all the more intoxicating.

"Sorry, 1 need to be alone with you. Let's go," I barely whisper, knowing he heard every word.

Rocks doesn't argue and follows me up the stairs, out the front door and back to my old Honda. He pushes me up against the door before I have a chance to open it and kisses the life out of me. When his lips move to the exposed flesh of my neck and shoulder, I know we need some privacy.

"Let's get in." I sound like I'm half starved of oxygen.

We're a tangle of arms and legs, and for the first time ever, Rocks slides his hand up under my skirt. The feeling of his fingers running up my thigh sends jolts of electricity firing between us.

"Is this okay?"

"Yes," I moan, kissing him hard.

His fingers find me, and I'm lost to the sensations. I never knew being with a guy could feel this intense. I pull up his shirt and kiss his chest the way I've wanted to every morning. He moans and I know I'm ready. I reach for the front of his jeans.

"Oh shit," I say, stopping.

"What?" Rocks cups my cheek, and I make out a worried frown in the glow from Tiff's porch light. "What is it?"

"Did you bring any, ah, you know?"

"Any what?"

Crap.

I knew I should have talked to him about this earlier. My stupid inability to discuss sex is going to be a major cock blocker.

"You know? Protection?"

"Protection? I'll always protect you, Beans."

I roll my eyes and push him away. I'm gonna need space to put a stop to this.

"What's wrong?" he asks, trying to pull me back close to him. "Did I do something wrong?"

"Oh, God no, we just can't because we don't have a condom," I mumble. But while I'm feeling brave, I continue, "They stop me getting pregnant because you put it on. There. So we're done. Here. Now. With this." I take a deep breath to calm my racing heart. "I want you so badly. I don't want you to think otherwise. What you did just now felt amazing."

I don't care that I'm probably blushing wildly. I want him to know how he made me feel. For a guy that's never fooled around much as a human, he sure knows what buttons to push.

"No sweat," he replies, leaning back against the window. "You know I want you too."

We sit in silence watching each other from opposite sides of the car. My legs are draped up over his knees, as he's stretched his long legs across to my side. He takes hold of my hand and entwines our fingers making me smile.

"I'm sorry if I gave you the worst case of blue balls," I blurt.

Me and my crazy mouth!

Rocks sits up straight, and I can just make out another deep frown.

"They are not!" he says, indignantly. He eyes me like I'm a freak and lets go of my hand. "They are dark brown, and it's not fair that you get to check me out when I'm a bat. I can't help not wearing pants," he huffs. "And I'll have you know size and proportion from species-to-species isn't exact. Okay? So no judging."

Oh.

My.

God.

I want to die.

"OMG, you did not just describe your bat junk."

Of all the embarrassing conversations we have ever had, this is the winner.

"You started it. You said they were blue."

"I did not—"

"You just said I had blue balls," he protests, folding his arms over his chest.

"Keep your voice down. We don't want the whole party knowing." I stare out into the darkness aware that we most likely aren't the only ones wanting to be alone. "And I didn't mean it like that."

He glares at me from his side of the car.

"God, I wish you were from this century." I sigh.

"Explain."

"No."

"I'll ask your mom when we get home."

I sit up like I've been electrocuted and glare at him. "It's when guys and girls don't... you know... and guys say... their... you know... balls... will turn blue and drop off... if girls don't." I continue to glare, praying he understands my absurd explanation.

"How on earth did you pass biology with explanations like that, Beans?"

I close my eyes and fight the smile starting to form. "Please tell me you get it."

"I do," he says, leaning closer to me. I can feel the warmth of his breath on my cheek.

When I open my eyes, he's mere inches from my face, and the way he's looking at me makes my stomach flip.

"Just glad you weren't judging my junk." He smirks.

I hate boys.

"For the record, I've never checked out your bat bits," I say, but he's giving me that 'yeah whatever' look, and suddenly I feel brave. "Although if they were that remarkable, then I'm sure it would've been hard for me *not* to notice them flapping in the breeze."

HA!

I've hardly had time to give myself a mental high five when he pounces, tickling my ribs so hard I can't bear it.

"They do not flap!"

I try to muffle my squeals, so Tiff's neighbors don't call the cops. He stops tickling me, and somehow in his attack, I've ended up mostly underneath him. That feeling from earlier is back as I become aware of where his body touches mine. The look in his eyes is so intense.

"So where do I buy these condoms you said I need?"

THAT NIGHT, I get no sleep. I can't settle because I'm hyper aware of the guy sleeping just down the hall. He's so close, but so far away at the same time. I mentally start to build a plan for us to be alone, and alone long enough to take our relationship to the next level. It feels right.

Saturday night, I tell Tiff I won't be working at the hotdog stand anymore. It's not like I need the money, and I want to enjoy the freedom of my whole summer. She also tells me that if Rocks and I are going to do this properly, I need to book a hotel room.

In the days that follow, her words make more and more sense. It feels like Mom is onto us because my weekdays are plagued with her, or Dad, or Mini giving us zero time for privacy. Rocks doesn't complain when we can't catch a moment alone, but the looks he gives me across the room send my system into overdrive. I sense he's super aware of me, just as I am of him.

My first week of summer is spent researching with Rocks full-time. I asked him again if he was still having second thoughts about wanting the fix. He said he just wants answers. How does it work? Is it painful? Who is powerful enough to perform the ritual? What went wrong for Celand to die?

He wants lots and lots of answers and our research is getting us nowhere near close to answering.

With two of us working on finding clues, we eliminate so much more. The Rocks I fell in love with is so even and dependable. His colony upbringing gave him a maturity I always found appealing. Seeing Rocks disheartened and losing faith with the search is hard to witness. Reply after reply, which says they can shape-shift, but aren't willing to help us, is past the point of annoying.

Are the Camazotz the only ones left? I wonder yet again. There's always an excuse why nobody will demonstrate in person their magical powers—the moon's in the wrong phase, they need to make a blood sacrifice first; it drains their energy, blah, blah, blah.

The replies I hate the most say they will show him only after he joins their 'cult'—that's my description of these groups, not Rocklands'. They ask him to pay stupid amounts of money, along with agreeing to insane conditions. The money isn't the issue. I don't want him mixed up with a bunch of fakers, who don't have the abilities Rockland was born with.

We try to come up with our own list of demands as if it was Rocks who was willing to show people his abilities. What would I require from them before I let them see him flip. I guess I would want them to join my crazy cult too. Maybe some of them really can do it, and this is for their protection. The confusion of not knowing who to believe, combined with the fact that I can't be alone with my boyfriend, is fraying my nerves.

We're sitting on the back patio, watching Mini ride her unicorn on wheels around the paving. Mom brings out iced tea and closes the door behind her when she leaves us.

"I'm sorry I'm in a shi—" —his eyes dart to Mini— "sugarplums mood," he says, trying not to smile.

"I'm sorry too. This is making me crazy! I just want to know if it's possible."

"Tell me about it. You know, I never thought I'd be here doing this. My whole life, deep down I sort of sensed the Shadows wasn't going to be my home forever, but I never really thought about doing *this* seriously. I thought it was a myth, and maybe it is."

He sips his tea watching me over the rim of the glass.

"I thought I might end up joining the Duskwing, but now they're gone. Sometimes I think we spend so much time in our heads thinking about the future, yet the future is so uncertain we should simply enjoy the present," he says.

I smile and think about all the worries and fears I had starting my final year of high school—all of them totally irrelevant now. Rocks is so right.

"I wish I could talk to Celand. I keep playing over every detail of her last few weeks in my mind. Now that I'm searching for what I know she was searching for, I'm trying to see her words and actions in a different light. Hoping I'll remember some clue to help me, but nothing comes to mind."

"Don't you think she'd tell you not to do it?" The fact his sister died trying to be human weighs heavily on me. I try to block it from my thoughts because I want to support him the way he always supports me, but some days it plagues me.

"Yeah, but I feel we have an advantage. We now know this is dangerous—like deadly dangerous—so I'm not going to take any chances. I don't know how much support her boyfriend gave her, but I know you've got my back."

"Promise me that if you feel it's too dangerous to continue, then you'll stop?"

Mini comes racing between our chairs —a blur of pink and glitter. He reaches for her as part of their game, and she zooms off giggling.

"Yeah, I promise. Jez texted me last night and was asking when I'm coming up that way for a visit. He said it's been too hard for him and Ezra to get away to come down here. Now that school's over, do you mind taking a trip to Helen?"

"Helen! Helen! Helen!" Mini echoes, zooming between our chairs again.

"Quiet, you little brat. That sounds perfect cause I was thinking about when" —I lower my voice so that only Rocks and the dog next door will hear me— "we can spend some more time alone."

He leans forward and takes my hand. "I've been thinking about that too. Just pick the day."

"Let's aim for Wednesday after the long weekend and traffic has totally cleared."

"I'll let Jez know. God, Connie, I can't wait." He grins and I grin back. Rocks is about to take a major step to be with me permanently in my world, so it feels right that we do this together first. It kinda feels like my way of making a physical commitment to him since he's going to be changed physically forever soon for us.

RINGING.

Buzzing.

There is an annoying buzzing near my face. I swipe my hand past my ear.

The contact wakes me; I open my eyes and realize my phone is going nuts. It's vibrating so much it's moving along my bedside table. I squint at the window, but it's still dark.

What the?

I frown when I see the picture of Rocks on my screen. I snatch it up to answer. "Rocks?"

"Can I come in?" he replies. I turn toward the door because I swear I can hear him speaking outside my room.

"Yeah." Before I get the word out, he storms in sniffing the air.

I sit up, clicking on my bedside lamp. The light is so bright my eyes automatically close. I can still hear him sniffing like a bloodhound on a scent. I take a deep breath through my nose, but my senses come up with nothing.

"I smell fresh blood. Are you hurt?"

"What?" I lift my covers and check my body. "No. Blood? Are you sure?"

He gives me a 'really?' kind of look, taking in another deep drag of air. His head snaps towards the window. He slowly moves my curtain and swears softly.

"What is it?"

"You don't want to see this."

I'm out of bed and by his side in a heartbeat. Looking out the window, I wish I had listened.

I want to be sick. I turn away, scrunching my eyes closed. "Wh-Who?" I stutter, swallowing the bile. "Who is that?"

Rocks pulls open the window, and now I can smell the pungent carnage on my roof. Fresh blood. My throat heaves, and my shoulders jerk on reflex.

"Go," he says. "You don't need to be here."

I swallow hard. "No, it's okay. I'll help. What do you need?"

The image of the dead bat on my porch roof is seared into my eyelids. But it's not just a dead bat. It's a dead bat missing both its wings. Severed. Hacked off by the looks of it. Two little bloody stumps are all that's remaining.

"Fuck," Rocks whispers. "I don't know who this is."

"Who would do this?"

"I don't know." He grabs two fistfuls of his hair. "Fuck! Fuck!"

"What's wrong? I mean apart from…" I indicate to the bloody mess. I'm trying to stay calm, but when Rocks panics, then it means things are super effed up, and my blood pressure immediately starts to rise.

"I'm banished. Banishment means I can't contact the Shadows—ever. My texts to Jez are highly illegal and could get him in really serious trouble. I have to tell them, but I'm not allowed to. Fuck!"

"Is this some kind of sick test?"

"I don't know. Maybe. Cypress was really pissed off I chose banishment because he knew I would come to you and survive. Fuck! Surely, this is beyond even his hate?"

"Is there a way to know who this is?"

Rocks shakes his head. "Only if someone notices a member missing. Without the wings, we have lost any tattoo identification. That's why so many of us get ink on our wings as bats."

"Wait, we're going to Helen in two days. Maybe Jez will tell you if someone is missing?"

"Connie, this Camazotz has been brutally murdered. You're asking me to do nothing for two whole days?"

"If it means you're safe and pass whatever sick test this is, then yes."

Rocks pinches the bridge of his nose. He takes a long, steady breath. I watch his chest expand and slowly contract again. He opens his eyes. "You're right. I can't say anything. Any mistake could be deadly—for me or Jez. And now they've involved you too. I don't know what this threat means, but we're going to be smart about it. If I look like I'm about to text Jez, take my phone off me. We can't be sure he's the only one that will see it."

"Deal. If it helps, I think this is a very smart plan." I try to copy Rocks and fill my lungs with air too. It helps, but won't erase the vicious image of the poor creature outside my window.

Rocks asks for a box for the remains, cold water, and something to scrub the stain off the roof tiles.

By the time he's done, the sun has peaked over the horizon. Neither of us knows what to say. What this means. My gut has commenced a slow churn, and I pray Jez will have some kind of answer for us.

Rocks takes the shoe box and heads outside to place it in my trunk. This unidentified Camazotz will need a resting place.

THE LAST TWO days, time has felt like it's stood still. Rocks decided not to contact Jez at all—in case the dead bat is a warning sign to Rocks because he was banished. We also decided not to speak of it because unknown Camazotz were on my roof. One of them dropped off the body and there is no telling how long they were out there. With their hearing, we don't want the murderer to know anything about Jez, or our search for the fix.

Jeremiah texts, asking if we're still headed to Helen tonight. Rocks hugs me hard and replies yes.

"Oh, thank God he's okay," I sigh.

"I know!" Rocks agrees. "And I'm pretty sure he would have texted me by now if someone was missing. The relief I feel is huge. Now we can actually enjoy ourselves again." He winks.

Knowing Jez is alive and well, allows me to get more excited about our plans for some quality alone time in a hotel room. The dark cloud of the dead bat is lifting a little.

I'm overly paranoid Mom and Dad know what we're planning, so I read between the lines of everything they say. Mom has asked me three times if I'm feeling okay, and I know she knows something's up because I'm acting like a freak.

"So you'll both be back tomorrow?" Mom asks over breakfast.

"Mm-hmm." I swallow my mouthful of cereal. "Just stopping in to visit his family. Back tomorrow." I can't look in Rocks' direction. The tension between us has reignited and is rocketing off the charts. I'm so far past even knowing how to act normal.

Mom's eyes go from me to Rocks and back to me. "Okay, I'll drop Mini at daycare then. Be sure to drive safely."

"Always do." I stand, rinse my bowl and tell Rocks I'll meet him at the car.

Exiting the driveway, we both grin at each other. We roll down the windows, Rocks selects songs from my phone, and we travel in silence mostly, sharing the occasional quick glance.

I don't know if it's my nerves firing up, but we seem to arrive in Helen only moments after we left Atlanta. I drive down the backstreets of the quaint little town to ensure we aren't seen, and we pick a hotel advertising a nightly special. The hotel backs onto the small river that runs through town.

None of the Shadows' members should be anywhere near this part of town.

When we get into the room, it's generic and worn-looking, but clean and private.

Rocks takes a long inhale and screws up his nose.

"What? What can you smell?" My heart races remembering the last time he smelled something.

His eyes widen momentarily. "Oh, sorry, no, nothing like last time. Relax."

"Phew!" I start sniffing, walking from the door through the long, thin room. "I can't smell anything."

He sniffs the air again. "It's stale and I don't know how to describe it, but our first time isn't going to be here. You deserve better, and it annoys me that I don't have more money to treat you to better."

"What?"

Rocks is at the window looking out toward the river. He opens it and starts fiddling with the screen.

"Rocks, what are you talking about and what are you doing?" I'm by his side and on autopilot start helping him with the screen.

"I know just the place. I'll be back in two hours. Do you mind?"

"Two hours?"

"Please. Not here. I don't want it to be here."

"Okay. But I'm super curious now."

He removes the screen and leans it inside against the wall. Next he stands still and closes his eyes, cocking his head slightly left and then right. He's listening, and I begin to focus on every little sound too.

"The coast is clear," he reports. Rocks pulls me into his arms and kisses me deeply. It immediately ignites the fire that's been a slow burn for the past couple of weeks. He steps me back against the wall, and I can feel him everywhere. I think I'm going to explode.

When he steps back, we're both breathing hard. "Wanted to give you something to think about while I'm gone." He grins.

"Ugh! You're so mean." I playfully swat his shoulder. "You've got ninety minutes, Mister. Now get moving."

Faster than my eyes can register, there's a bat flapping his wing inches from me. It's so magical to witness I can't really describe it. Seeing his transformation again really does make me wonder about all those people we've contacted. Rocks pumps his wings and is out the window a second later. He heads for the large, tall trees, which line the river, and soon I can't see him amongst the branches.

It's time for a lazy, long soak in a hot bath.

12
Cathedral

"DO you trust me?" he asks.

"Pffft, of course I do, silly."

We're standing in the forest next to a tiny hole at ankle height, just large enough for an adult to crawl through. It doesn't look like much, and most people wouldn't even notice it's there. Blades of long grass hang over the edge, partly obscuring it from view. Rocks returned on time and gave me instructions to drive about twenty minutes from town. We left my car on the side of the road and hiked a little ways down a steep-ish slope through the trees.

"Good. 'Cause it's going to be really dark for you."

I watch as he crouches down, pushes the blanket he borrowed from the hotel in, and disappears into the hole, which seems way too small for him, but somehow it works. When it's my turn, the hole is deceptively large, but super freaky. I don't even get any dirt on my navy-blue sundress as I crawl in.

Inside the cave it isn't dark—it's pitch-freaking-black! The astonishing part is I can almost stand up straight as soon as I'm only a few feet in the hole. The light at my feet tapers out faster than I'm okay with. My eyes are constantly drawn to the strong glow from the outside world, highlighting my feet and ankles. Each time I blink and look anywhere but at the stupid hole near my feet, I see hole-shaped white patches on my eyelids. I need to stop focusing on the light.

"Rocks?" I blink, trying to make out where he is. "I can't see a damn thing!" My hands move to my back pocket to reach for my phone. The flashlight app will guide me.

"No, I'm here. You don't need your phone." His hands find mine with no fumbling whatsoever. "Trust me. Just walk normally. I'll lead you safely."

I feel him turn away from me. He's holding my hands behind his back and sets off at a slow pace. It takes all my courage to step into the darkness after him, but considering what we're about to do, I like that this is proving my trust in him. The urge to look back toward the light hits me hard, but I know I need to move forward with him.

"Can you really see in here?"

"Yep, as clearly as I could outside."

"Wow. I'm like, totally blind. I can't see you at all." The path takes a sharp turn, and I can't stop myself. I look behind and now there is no sign of the little bit of light that was keeping my blood pressure under control. He gently tugs me forward again.

"Just wait. Give your eyes time to adjust." I bump against the cold stone wall to my left. "Sorry. This part is narrow. We're walking down a thin fissure in the mountainside. Reach out. You'll feel the cave on either side of you."

We stop and I slowly spread my arms. He's right. There's stone surrounding us on both sides. It's smooth and cool under my fingers. The air in here is fresh and cool—much nicer than the fake floral scent of the hotel room.

I close my eyes and let Rocks lead me further under the earth. He describes what he can see as we make our way along the winding path. The air moves my hair slightly, as he explains another path has joined ours, and the area we are in could be considered a small cave.

Listening, our footsteps reverberate a little, and his voice sounds like there is more room around us.

"I hear water."

"Very good. There's a stream running down the left side of the cave we're about to enter. Open your eyes. We're almost there. What can you see?"

Blinking them open, I'm disappointed to discover I can't see anything. "Nothing! Absolutely nothing."

"Really? Not even my silhouette?"

I laugh. "Is there any light source you can see in here?" I ask, knowing the answer.

"No."

"Well, then I can't see shit. Jack shit to be exact," I joke.

"Not even a little bit?" I jump because Rocks has leaned in close, and I couldn't tell until I felt his breath on my face.

"Nothing. I don't think you really understand how dramatically your senses are going to change when you get fixed. I'm totally blind and depending on you."

"How many fingers am I holding up?"

"Oh my God, I don't know!" I laugh, waving my arms through the air impersonating a blind zombie, and trying to find his hands, so I can feel how many fingers he's holding up. "Rocks?"

He's not in front of me. I take a step forward and reach out as far as I can.

Nothing.

"Rocks, where the hell are you?"

"Here," he says behind me.

"Fudge me!" I jump.

"Wow, you really can't see for shit."

"Ugh, you're so annoying."

A little deeper into the mountainside, he announces we're here. Handing me the blanket, I hear him messing with something on the ground.

A small spark appears as he strikes a match. The glow from the one single flame feels so bright after the total darkness. Rocks lights a thin taper candle and stands holding it between us.

"You had candles this whole time and didn't use them?"

"I wanted to guide you."

I roll my eyes.

"Hold it exactly like this for a second." He pulls my arm up and places the tiny candle between my thumb and index finger.

He flips catching me off-guard, as his moving bat shadows dance on the far wall. Rocks, the bat, swoops in and takes the long, thin candle in his mouth. He flies up into the lofty darkness, his crazy shadow now dancing as he ascends. Hovering close to the stone sides, he lights a small white candle. After a couple of minutes, he's flown up and down the wall around the cavern and lit a dozen different colored candles.

The glow from the colored, still flames is breathtaking on the giant rock cave. Pink. Blue. Green. White. Purple.

"How did you do that?"

A second later, he's a man by my side. I stare up at the enchanting lights. The cave is large with a very high ceiling. The walls are dark stone and have jagged lines running horizontally in places. Most of these lines are small ridges that he's placed the tiny candles on, where the rock has moved under pressure.

"This is amazing."

"Do you really like it?"

"I love it, but, Rocks... um,"

"What?" His body moves up close to mine and he wraps his arms around me. Even though the temperature down here is pleasant, the warmth from his body thrills me.

"There's no, um, well, bed." There I said it. "There's no bed."

"We need to get you up there." Rocks points to the wall behind me. Now that my eyes have adjusted to the low light, I can tell there is an edge about ten feet up. "Ready?"

He moves me over to stand before the sheer rock face, and then he bends down. I place my hands on the stone for balance as he wraps his arms around my knees. Slowly, he stands up and I can see the ledge getting closer. I reach up and get a grip on the edge and try to help him hoist me up. It's definitely not ladylike, but I manage to scramble up onto it.

Rocks has covered the area with a bed of soft, green grass. I catch the faint scent of pine and spy the odd pine needle amongst the sea of lush green. Before I know it, Rocks is beside me with the blanket. He spreads it out and it couldn't be more perfect.

"Wow, this is way better than the room."

"I'm glad you think so. We'll remember this forever."

We lay down, and I snuggle in close to his warm body. We both stare up at the glowing, colorful lights on the cavern walls. It reminds me of a cathedral somehow. Rocks' fingers trace patterns on my back.

I'm so relaxed, but his touch ignites the wanting that's been plaguing me since the bare-chested bathroom incident.

I lean up on my elbow and look down at his gorgeous face. My breath catches yet again when I realize he's mine and about to give himself to me in a way he's never done with any other girl. I'm the luckiest girl alive.

Ever so slowly I lean down, hovering just above his lips. He smiles. I hope the anticipation is killing him as much as it's killing me. He bites his lips and I'm pretty sure that confirms it.

"I want you," I whisper, and then kiss him hard.

We kiss, and kiss some more. Then I make the first move as I sense he's waiting for my lead. I grab the bottom of his shirt, and he helps me remove it.

My god he's even more gorgeous!

His chest is so defined from all the flying. It's weird to think muscles he uses as an animal can tone up his human form. His arms are magnificent—not bulging, body builder muscles—just beautifully defined biceps and triceps. He's god-like and so unaware of how sexy he is.

"You're so beautiful, Rocks," I say, running my hand over his shoulder and down his arm. His ink is glorious. I want to feel every inch of his naked skin. His moonlit night smell seems to be more intense. I'm surrounded by him and I still can't get enough. I plant gentle kisses across his chest causing him to moan.

"I want to see you too."

My breath catches. This is it. But it's Rocks. He makes me feel so beautiful with my clothes on, I know he'll think the same when he sees me without them. I unbutton the front of my sundress and let it gape open. His eyes drop to my chest. I fight the embarrassment I have always felt being larger chested than all my friends. But he starts to worship me, and I suddenly feel like a goddess.

"I'm a lucky, lucky man. You are the most beautiful creature on this planet." He kisses me everywhere he can access. And when he gets frustrated, my dress is the next thing to go.

We take our time exploring each other's bodies, until we can't stand the feelings of wanting a second longer. Soon we become a tangle of bare flesh, and he's so gentle, I fall in love with him even more. The cave walls seem to echo the sounds of our passion. His mouth. His hands. Every part of his flesh touching mine I'm hyper aware of. It's too much, yet not enough.

It's intense.

It's sublime.

It's way better than I imagined.

My body comes alive when it's with his.

But it's over faster than we both expected.

Rocks pulls the blanket around us, and we return to looking at the colored glow on the walls while our breathing returns to normal.

"I love you," he says, placing a kiss against my temple.

"I love you too."

"I've never felt anything so intense in all my life," he says. "I'm glad I waited to find you and be in love before doing that."

"Me too."

WHEN WE RETURN to Helen, we're both ravenous. We grab burgers and fries to go and sit under the tree behind the hotel by the river. It's peaceful with the sound of the running water, and perfect for how I'm feeling. Rocks and I share grins over mouthfuls of food. Neither of us need to speak, yet we sit so our legs touch—easing a new desire to have contact with the other.

I catch subtle hints of Rocks listening to the sounds of dusk. Evening is approaching, and we both know the kinds of creatures that come out after dark in these parts. We're so close to home—but it's not his home any longer. He's not welcome, and I can't even begin to imagine how he feels. I was worried about sitting outside and being safe, but Rocks is convinced the kind of brutality it takes to mutilate a bat isn't present in any Shadows' member.

"When's Jeremiah coming?"

"As soon as it gets dark," he replies. "I can't wait to see him."

My heart aches for this beautiful boy whose father has banished him over antiquated laws.

"It must be hard being so close, but not…"

He nods. "It is. But now this town will represent us, not what I lost, so I'm glad we came here to share this. Come here." He scrunches up his trash, moving it to the side and indicates that he wants me to sit between his legs. Once I'm settled, he leans back against the trunk of the tree and wraps his arms around me. This is the happiest I think I've ever felt in my life.

The sun slowly sinks, and we wait for Jez to appear.

"Thank you, Connie." He kisses my temple.

"For what?"

"Being my girl. Sharing your body with me. Loving me despite what I am. The list is endless."

"Rocks, you are not some freak." I turn around to face him. "You are amazing and have a special magical ability that you never asked for." Before I have time to continue, Jez appears.

Rocks jumps to his feet and embraces his friend.

"You look exactly the same," Jez comments, stepping back. "Thought you'd be fatter with twenty-four-seven access to her mom's refrigerator." His nose twitches once. "Didn't you leave any for me?" he asks, indicating to the scrunched up paper bags.

"Let's go get you something," I suggest.

"Let's talk first," Rocks says. "Do you think you were followed?"

Both boys scan the sky. It's too dark for my eyes to be of any use. There's no moon tonight, so I watch them instead.

"I don't think so. Nobody knew you were going to be here."

"How is everyone?" Rocks asks. I wait holding my breath and would bet Rocks is doing the same thing.

However, Jez gives a rundown of each family member Rockland is missing terribly. He then goes on to discuss how effed up everything is politically. With Rocks gone, there are two empty spots to be filled, and the infighting to win those places has gone crazy. Wings are fighting with wings they once were allies with, nobody trusts anyone, and everyone is spying on each other.

Rocks glances at me quickly from where he's standing, and I know he's secretly relieved too. The murdered bat doesn't belong to the Shadows. That's at least one answer to our many questions.

I focus my attention back on Jez.

"I think Cypress is after Strickland. Like he wants him gone, and he's building up his allies and trying to move them into power. It's turning nasty, man."

"But now I'm gone why would Cypress care? His beef was always with me, and what I might introduce should I be the next leader."

"Trust me, Zander and Judge are just as surprised by it. He's up to something, but nobody knows what."

Rocks shakes his head as he paces in a tight circle. He covers his eyes and lets out a sigh. "I can't help him. For once, I'm not there to have his back. This is shit, but Strickland has brought it on himself. Fuck, this is hard." He walks a little way over to the river's edge, but a moment later, he paces back to us. "Well, that's Strickland's problem now. I can't help him. Anyhow, I might need your help. Connie and I have hit a brick wall with the fix."

"The what?" Jez half yells, staring wide-eyed at Rockland, and then at me and finally back at Rocks. "You're not!"

Rocks nods.

"No, fucking way. Are you crazy? After what happened to Celand? Elm and Oak too probably? Tell me you don't support this nonsense?" Jez finishes, looking at me.

I don't know what to say. For some reason, I assumed Rocks would have told Jeremiah. "Ahh, well…"

"Leave Connie out of it. This is my decision." Rocks stands tall. It's an old habit of pulling rank silently with the bats. I wonder if he's even aware he's doing it.

Jez doesn't seem to be bothered. He walks right up to Rockland and points a finger in his face an inch from his nose. "You are crazy if you follow that myth. You have the perfect life now, and you'll screw it up. Don't be an idiot!"

"You don't understand—"

"I don't understand?" Jez echoes, his face a mirror of disbelief. "I understand what it's like to lose more people than I care to count for nothing, and now you're telling me you're going to risk your life for nothing too?"

"It's not for nothing. It's so I'll belong," Rocks yells back.

"You already belong! Connie's family has practically adopted you. You've got an awesome girlfriend, and you have a set of abilities most aeronaughts would kill for, and the best part is you don't even have to use them if you don't want to. Just live your aeronaught life and flip once a day. Big deal. Don't risk your neck chasing ghosts. The shamans of old are all dead, and you know it."

The boys stare at each other in silence. Jeremiah has a good point—many actually.

"Should we go get you something to eat?" I ask, unsure of the tension between them. I've never seen these two fight before.

"I've lost my appetite," Jez replies. "You wait until I tell Zada."

"Don't."

"Why not? Huh?" Jez throws his arms up when Rocks doesn't answer. "Because you already know how risky it is. You know, brother, you *already* know!"

"I just want to find out how, and then I'll decide," Rocks says quietly.

I'm glad he's still thinking that way. When he was suffering his first hangover, we decided to learn if it was possible, and then he would figure out what to do. It eases my worries a little knowing this is still his plan. Information surely can't be all that dangerous.

"If you aren't actually serious about doing it, then why go to all that bother?"

"Because it might be something I want to do. If I think it's safe and can work out what went wrong with Celand, then why not do it?"

"How are you going to work on what went wrong with Celand's attempt when she's not here to ask? Huh? Have you lost your senses? You will be going in as blindly as she did."

I don't like the fact Jeremiah is this upset about the idea of Rocks getting fixed. I bite my lip.

"Why have we never seen a Camazotz that suddenly doesn't have to flip anymore?" Jez asks. "If it were possible, one of them would have come back to a colony and said 'hey, look at ordinary, old me.'"

"Maybe they did, but they were disposed of to prevent a mass exodus."

"Mass exodus? You, Celand, Elm and Oak? I would hardly describe that as a mass exodus."

Jez is the most eloquent I have ever heard him, and his logic is hard to argue against. But the answering look Rocks gives him makes it difficult for me to contain myself, despite the seriousness of the matter.

"You know what I mean," Rocks adds.

"Yeah, I do, but you need to re-think this plan of yours. The Fold might be desperate at times, but they aren't that desperate to hide evidence if it were really true."

The boys take a seat on the grass by the river in silence, and I sense they want to be alone. I tell Rocks I'm going to shower to give them a chance to catch up. I trust Rocks will share any important information with me later.

I lie down on the bed and wait for Rocks. I remember having to leave Mini's side each shift at the warehouse—not trusting when I would see her again. Rocks must be suffering a somewhat similar feeling with Jez, since he's banned from entering his old home. How long will it be before he sees his brother again?

Before I fall asleep, he climbs in the window. He crawls across the bed and pulls me into his arms. "He's going to help me," he whispers.

I pull back wanting to see his eyes. "What? How?"

"I need to talk to Sylvana about—"

"You can't trust that hag!" I interrupt. "She detests your human-ness. She hates me. And she hates you for liking me."

"Loving," he corrects with a smile.

"Yes, loving me." I smile back and feel my nerve endings twitch. "However, she can't be trusted."

"I don't trust her, but she knows more about this than either of us have discovered. I need to know what she knows." His hand slides down my back ever so slowly before resting on my thigh. "Enough talking." His eyes seem to sparkle, and his grin confirms he's up to something. "Let's see how it feels in an aeronaught bed," he adds.

I laugh out loud before kissing him.

Round two is just as mind-blowing as the first time, although maybe better. I will never tire of seeing his naked body, and the way his muscles move. We lay entwined staring at the boring ceiling. It can't be compared to the almost magical, colored flames from earlier illuminating our cave.

"So do you still want the fix now?" I'm curious since he's experienced sex as a human whether that will alter his decision.

He looks at me for a moment. "You think doing this as a bat is better?"

I don't reply. I know I'm being self-conscious.

"Let me tell you, those bats are missing out. You are amazing."

I let out the breath I didn't know I was holding. "I'm glad."

"I never knew it could be like this, Beans. It's the difference of being in love. So no, I won't be upset to lose the bat in me. Besides it really might be my only option of belonging."

"No, it's not. Look how far you've come just in the time you've been living with me. You know so much more about our world. Jez might be right."

He pulls a face. "It's nice of you to say so, but people still sense me as a predator. Your party confirmed it. I'm hoping once blood isn't part of my diet any longer, that will change."

We lay wrapped up in each other in silence again. I wonder if the crazy levels of hate and judgment he feels won't actually change at all. Humans hate other humans based on looks alone. It's got nada to do with being a predator. Rocks views himself as different, so isn't surprised by their stares, but he isn't aware of how many laws exist to stamp out discrimination. How do I explain that level of ugliness? Or the constant, never-ending fight for equality?

"I don't know," I finally reply. "You know how you get treated by the Shadows for preferring to be human?"

He rolls his eyes instead of answering, and I try not to laugh.

"Well, aeronaughts are just as cruel to aeronaughts they think are different, but who aren't really. Like, for their preferences, or race, or what they believe."

His eyes get serious, and I'm sorry I've ruined our bliss with such a somber conversation. "You think I'll always be treated like this no matter where I live?" he asks.

"I don't know, Rocks. I'm just saying that the low opinion Strickland has about aeronaughts isn't entirely unjustified."

13
Truth

Bat POV

TWO nights after Rockland's trip to Helen with Connie, Jeremiah texts him the whereabouts of Sylvana. Rockland replies and tells his friend to delete the messages in case anyone scrolls through the phone. Jez assures him he's the only one to have possession of the miracle device.

The large bat takes to the sky several blocks from Connie's house. To be extra vigilant, he walked a few streets over. Still unsure of who is behind the murder of the dead Camazotz, he can't be too careful.

The flight from Atlanta will be good exercise. Besides he has no other choice. He hasn't gotten his driver's license yet. Connie was clever enough to get him the papers he will need to apply, but his life has been too upside-down to study the driving manual again.

Letting his beautiful golden girl drive him into the heart of colony territory was far too dangerous—for them both. If he's caught, he doesn't know what they'll do to him. Would they really end him? He scans the evening sky for scents of predators and listens. He needs to focus on his surroundings and at least make it there in one piece.

The journey is uneventful—pleasant even. He hasn't flown this far in weeks, and it feels good to use his muscles once more. He's been trying not to fly to see how it would affect his headspace. As much as he resents the animal inside of him, he does love flying. The freedom it gives him is like nothing else.

He knows driving a car is fun and gives him a slight adrenaline burst, but it fades too quickly. It doesn't compare to diving nose first toward the earth and folding his wings in tight. Plummeting faster and faster.

The wind whooshing past his face, and the uncertainty of not really knowing if he will pull out of his death dive in time.

He flies on trying to think about something else. He will miss flying. But if that's the price he has to pay for belonging, then he'll pay it.

Jez had texted him where Sylvana was last seen. That female is sly. She's often not where she's supposed to be. Her hut is deep in the woods. She prefers her solitude and says it's better for her magic to live alone. Her magic must flow freely so she can perform her secret rituals to keep the colony protected. Strickland has never questioned her methods the whole time she's been with the Shadows.

Rockland wonders about her history. Nobody seems to know it, and Strickland punishes anyone who questions her. It was part of the deal she made when she joined the Shadows years ago.

Rockland lowers his altitude. He's entered colony territory, and if the patrols are doing their jobs properly, they could be this far south. He winds between the tree trunks faster than most other bats could do safely, so it doesn't really slow him down. There are several streams, which flow down Blood Mountain, and Sylvana uses their water for different purposes. Jez saw her headed for a small rock pool she frequents at dusk.

Most Camazotz keep their distance from the mystical female. They never want to risk her wrath, in case it involves a spell, or curse.

Rockland slows his pace. He's deep in the Shadows homelands now and must use caution. He tries to quiet his mind. He listens telepathically for patrol calls. The patrols never communicate when on high alert—like after the Duskwing were abducted—but often, on quiet nights when they feel safe, they send out brief messages.

His keen nose picks up the sent of white sage and rosemary. Sylvana is definitely nearby. He leaves the safety of the treetops and heads for ground level. Before flipping, he lands on a low branch and steadies his racing heart. He can't deny his adrenaline is pumping being this close to home illegally. Tonight he won't need to do death dives for the same effect.

The forest is quiet. He can't sense any approaching creatures—Camazotz or otherwise.

Flip.

The carpet of pine needles silences his heavy boots. He takes a deep breath of the pine-scented air. He misses the clean scents of the forest. Cars may be fun, but they smell horrible. He nimbly sidesteps the dry twigs trying to stay undetected.

Sylvana is bending over the dark pool of water. The stream bubbles over small stones, but there's a large, peaceful pool before the water bends to the left and goes on its way downstream. The last hint of twilight has faded, and the new moon has yet to rise. He uses his Camazotz eyesight in the fading light. He's still astounded by how blind Connie was in the cave. Maybe he'll miss his perfect night vision when it's gone.

But that's a thought for another time.

Focus.

Knowing the surrounding area is quiet, he leaves the safety of the trees and waits.

"I knew you would come," she says, still hunched over the water. "You took longer than I predicted. Occasionally, the bones are wrong."

"So you'll help me?"

"It depends on what you can do for me."

Rockland closes his eyes and lets out a deep breath. He was sure she would say no and turn him over to Cypress the second he showed himself. This is actually progress if she's willing to bargain.

"Name it."

Sylvana finally stands and turns around slowly. Rocks takes a step back because she has streaks of mud running down her face as though she was finger painting herself. The dark mud drips down her neck, adding to her weirdness. "A thousand dollars, and three strands of golden hair."

"What?" he asks, totally confused.

"You heard."

"Is this what you required from Celand? There's no way she had a thousand dollars. Or access to blonde hair!"

"The transaction between your sister and myself is none of your concern."

"Tell me what you told her." Rocks knows the Sire and the Fold questioned Sylvana when Celand disappeared, but as usual it was done in secret.

"Your sister didn't succeed, so why would I tell you what I told her?"

Rocks pinches the bridge of his nose. He's aware he needs to keep his cool, because one distress call from Sylvana, and he'll be in deadly trouble, but she's being her usual infuriating self.

"Maybe you don't really know about the fix at all," he replies.

Sylvana cackles loudly. The next instant she rushes over to him and is stalking around him like she's performing a ritual.

"I know more than you. Had any luck locating a shaman to perform the reversal spell? Hmmm?"

Rockland glares at her, knowing he doesn't really need to answer. She already knows. "No."

"Well, it appears you do need me because I know a living shaman. A powerful, mighty conjurer that may help you, but only if what you bring forth is worthy."

The tall male wants to growl at her for always speaking in riddles. *If what he brings forth is worthy.*

"Do we have a deal?" she snaps.

"Yes. Now tell me what you know. I don't have the money with me, but I'll bring it to Helen."

Sylvana stops in front of him and stares up into his eyes. Rockland tries hard not to break her stare, but the mud dripping off her is distracting.

"Deal," she replies. "Use Jeremiah to arrange the time when you're ready."

Her assumption he's still in regular contact with Jeremiah still concerns him. He hopes it doesn't mean Jeremiah is under surveillance—particularly if the political games are as out-of-hand as Jez suggested. That could be very, very dangerous.

She rummages in her deep pockets hidden by the yards of loose fabric that make up her skirts. Pulling out a smudge stick, she lights the end of it and blows the pale gray smoke toward the tall male. She cups her free hand around the burning ember and whispers an ancient chant.

Rockland prays that if the patrol gets a whiff of her fresh herbs, they'll keep their distance. The superstitious beliefs that many of the Camazotz hold could be a blessing right now.

She swirls and twirls around him coating him from head-to-toe in smoke. Cleansing.

When she's done, she walks to the pool's edge and extinguishes the end of the smudge stick in the water. She dips two fingers in the soft, dark mud and draws another pattern on her already filthy forehead before turning to face him.

"What I know is this. You need to collect the items for the spell. Then take them to the sacred place on the right moon."

"What sort of items? What place? Did you tell Celand this?"

She scowls at him and snorts. "Yes! But we will not speak of her again. Although, she was far more cooperative than you!"

"Sorry." Rocks pulls his beloved cell phone from his back pocket. When the screen illuminates, the medicine woman hisses. He opens the voice recorder and asks, "What items?"

She produces a tiny vial from those deep pockets again. "Colloidal silver." She holds it up to the sky. "You will also need three gemstones to represent you. Something close to your heart. You must carve a dagger from red cedar wood. Cedar wood represents the sun, since you wish to walk in it and turn from the night. But you must soak it in either clary sage or rosemary oil to represent the moon; opposites for balance. You need the bones of a dead ancestor and finally—"

"I will never get a bone from an ancestor," he interrupts. "The only way I can access the burial cavern is through the heart of the roost—by air. That's impossible. And you know it."

She smiles and it makes the hairs on the back of his neck rise a little. Her cunning runs deep, and the young Camazotz tries to gauge her next move.

"That's why I requested the money. I will get you your ancestor's bones, but I deserve payment for disturbing the dead from their rest. The older the ancestor, the better the connection is to the original spell, so leave that to me. Your final task is to seek the place where the sanguinaria grows in the shape of the crescent moon."

"Bloodroot?"

"Yes, bloodroot! Don't underestimate the power of herbs. Bloodroot—or sanguinaria—is a powerful magical herb. It protects and brings luck. You will need all the protection you can get to survive the power of this spell, and a little bit of luck won't go astray."

"Where does it grow like that?"

"That's for you to discover!" she snaps. "Your journey is part of the ritual you seek. You seek a body-mind journey to change your essence. It is all connected in the elements." She waves her hands at the stars as though tracing their invisible path. "I do know there is only one place like it. Once you have all of this, bring my payment, and I will tell you the last piece."

"Tell me now."

Before his eyes, Sylvana flips and flies off into the night. The second she's gone, he realizes his mistake. His heart races as he spins around on the spot, trying to decide whether to flip and outfly the male Camazotz he only *now* senses standing in the dark tree line. He let his guard down listening to her list of tasks and in doing so has been discovered.

Strickland steps into the clearing. Rockland scans for more Camazotz. Did Sylvana betray him somehow? He hopes this doesn't mean Jeremiah is in trouble for assisting a banished bat.

"I'm alone," Strickland announces. "Luckily for you. I wanted to speak with Sylvana, and who do I discover instead?"

"I'm sorry."

"Save it. But answer me one last question. Why are you so determined to betray us?" His look of disgust says a lot more than the words he uttered.

"I'm not betraying anyone. I'm not part of this '*us*' you speak of. I'm on my own, remember?"

"You're still a Camazotz, but for how long, huh? I heard what she told you. You *are* betraying us!"

"You see this as betrayal?"

One curt head nod is all he gives his son.

Rockland studies the hard man before him. His arms crossed over his solid chest. The deep furrowed lines between his eyebrows form the near permanent scowl he wears as regularly as his cracked leather vest.

Rockland tries to recall the last time he saw his father smile, or bat's above, dare to laugh.

"You owe me why," Strickland adds.

"Because you've left me no choice! The Camazotz rejected me, so I'm rejecting the Camazotz inside of me. I want to live somewhere free of judgment, and that's not at the Shadows! If I can't live with my own kind and not be persecuted for being myself, then I must fully embrace my human side in order to integrate and survive. I'm getting fixed, so I'll finally belong somewhere."

"You could belong here if you tried harder and stopped indulging yourself."

"Indulging myself? Why do you keep using that word? You think that's what I'm doing?" Rocks rolls his eye and shakes his head, trying to contain the less than flattering words he wants to spit at his Sire. "My interest in the aeronaught world is about trying to improve *our* chances of survival. It's about ensuring our future in a world we share with them. But you've heard this all before. You don't care."

Strickland narrows his eyes at his heir but remains silent.

"Okay, I admit it's also about what feels comfortable to me—being in this form." Rocks says, gesturing to his human body. "But is being comfortable an indulgence?" He waits, but his Sire still doesn't speak. "There are Camazotz who stay at the roost and are hardly ever human. You don't persecute them! They don't even contribute to the market to help us earn the bare minimum in order to survive."

"They contribute in ways you don't understand. You talk about our survival like you're an expert. They breed!" The Sire snarls.

"That's not all there is to our survival, Father, and you know it. How many times do you issue the command to flip because it's more convenient to be in human form? At Fold meetings? Clip meetings? And let's not forget your order to be human—and only human—after the Muerte attack on the Duskwing. Why? Huh? I don't recall you worrying about the dangers of being in this form too long then! I don't understand why not being in my bat form is such a crime? I'm *still* a Camazotz!"

"But for how long?" Strickland spits on the ground between them. "Never return here, or you will never leave."

Flip.

The bat hovers at Rockland's head height for a brief moment before disappearing into the trees.

"Goodbye, Father," Rockland says softly, knowing full well his Sire heard him.

Rockland searches the ground for something to pierce his skin. He usually flies with a tiny pin in his wallet, but he started carrying only what aeronaughts need after he moved to Connie's place.

He picks up a jagged stone and inspects the edges to see if they will break his skin. He throws it back in the pool. He walks to the trees. If he hits the old, rough trunk hard enough, it should cut him. He lines up his knuckles with a particularly gnarly section of the trunk.

"Wait, dear boy," a quiet voice says from behind.

Bats above! His senses must be dull after spending so much time in the aeronaught world trying to blend in. The fact his grandmother has crept up on him is almost shameful. He must be extra vigilant flying back to Connie's if he's not aware enough to hear her coming—she bumps and crashes around in the forest like a pig rooting for mushrooms.

"Cappella, how did you find me?"

"Oh, by accident, Rockland. I was sniffing out Sylvana for a rub for my aching joints, and suddenly I hear the Sire shouting, and here you are. Also, I drink from this pool because I'm sure the water has healing properties. Why else would she spend so much time here? She practically rolls around in that mud."

Rockland shrugs and carefully takes in his grandmother's appearance. Her hair is tied back in her usual soft bun, with a few grey strands lining her face. Around her neck is a thin, faded piece of red leather with a carved, wooden pendant.

"You found it?" he says, pointing to the three worn stars at her neck.

"I did! These things I wear in my eyes, your girl got me, are incredible. I can see again. I've found lots of things I thought I'd lost forever."

She takes both his hands in hers and looks at him—really looks at the young male standing tall before her.

"You have grown into a man now. I'm sorry they banished you. It's an absurd law." She shakes her head. She reaches up and touches his face. "It's so good to see you clearly."

"I can't stay long, Cappella. I shouldn't be here."

"I know, but it's hard to let you go. This may be the last time I ever see you, and that breaks my heart." Tears well in her eyes. She closes them and blinks. "I'm not allowed to rub my eyes with these things in. Zada has been very specific." She laughs. "She doesn't want to lose her newest and hardest worker if I break them."

Rocks smiles, but it hurts deep inside his chest. He wishes he were still at the colony to witness Cappella making candles again. She always had a special talent for the art, making the most beautiful multi-colored candles. As though she could control where she wanted the wax to flow by only thinking about it.

"Please thank Connie for me."

The tall male can't hold back his smile. Connie makes him so proud, particularly when members of his colony see her worth.

"Oh, I have missed seeing you smile, my boy," Cappella adds, smiling back him. "But I worry about what you're trying to do."

Rockland raises an eyebrow at her.

"My hearing is just fine—it was only ever my eyesight—and the Sire wasn't being subtle. You're trying to get fixed."

"Yes, but I'm doing it because it will make me smile more when I finally belong."

She shakes her head. "You do belong. Both sides of you belong because you were born into this world just the way you are. Now that you are free of those judgmental eyes, embrace your human side. Love it, but keep the bat too. Please."

Rockland sighs and leans back against the pine tree he was about to strike. "I need to do this. Or at least find out. It might give me more answers about what happened to Celand. I hope you understand."

"I understand you wanting answers about your sister. That's different. Just promise me you will think this over long and hard. Because once they take your wings away, you will never get them back. And I know in your heart how much you love flying."

Rockland wishes for the millionth time females were allowed to hold positions of power—like become Clip or Fold members—at the Shadows. He wonders what a different place it would be to live if the wisdom of females was used to make decisions. "I promise. I will find out what I need to do, and then I'll think about it."

She hugs him around the waist, tucking her head under his chin. "Good. Now do you need to borrow my hairpin? It looked like you were about to punish this innocent tree for nothing."

He holds out his hand and watches as she slides the pin from her bun. Her streaked grey hair falls past her shoulders as she gives him the silver pin.

"Is this?" He holds it up closer to his face, as the moon still hasn't risen. "It is!"

"Of course. I found that too." She laughs. "It's the first thing you ever gave me after you finished your apprenticeship. You always had a way with silver. At least you have a skill to take with you out into the world."

Rockland pricks the end of his finger and waits for a small dot of blood to gather. He takes the vial of colloidal silver from his pocket and smears a little on the tiny jar before tucking it back in his pocket.

Cappella takes the pin and pricks her own finger. The magic spell was smart enough to know the item must travel with the owner of the most recent blood to touch it. If she didn't, the pin would disappear with Rockland when he flies home.

"Did you ever hear of a place where sanguinaria grows in the shape of a crescent moon?" Asking one of the oldest members of the colony has to be a good start.

"Hmmm, nowhere in these parts. Not in our territory at least. I would head west if I were you."

Rockland places a kiss on her forehead. "Thank you, Cappella. I love you, and I promise today won't be the last time you see me."

14
Clues

WHEN I enter the kitchen on Saturday morning, Kelly is giving Rocks a lesson in baking her death-by-chocolate cake. I overslept and am keen to know what he discovered last night on his illegal visit. I waited up as long as I could, but sleep claimed me against my will. The sneaky little bat didn't wake me like I asked him to when he returned.

I head to the fridge in search of juice, but Mom's words freeze me to the spot.

"Do you know much about bats, Rocks?" Kelly says, working on the first layer of frosting.

I turn to watch the horror show. To my surprise, Rocks' face is a calm sea. I'm pretty sure mine resembles a raging ocean storm. "As a matter of fact, I do, Mrs. Phillips. Why do you ask?"

"No reason." Kelly sees me across the kitchen, and her eyes zoom in on the filigree bat necklace hanging at my throat. It almost singes my skin, but I fight my urge to cover it. She looks back at Rocks. "How did you learn about them?"

"Well, there are lots of bats that roost at my parent's market. They love sleeping up in any open roof space. So if there's a hole in your roof, they'll find it. I guess they prefer rural areas, because I've hardly seen any since I moved here."

I can't handle this. I turn away and shove my head in the fridge, so Kelly won't see my emotions advertised across my face.

There's a lot of bats that roost at my parent's market.
No lie.

"What's the significance of Connie's necklace—if you don't mind me asking?"

Holy shitballs.

I know I can't stay hiding in the fridge for much longer, but I can't face her. I put the juice bottle to my lips and drink straight from it. Mom *hates* it when I do this, so it might throw her off the bat trail.

"They fascinate me. Did you know they're the only mammal on earth who can fly?" he replies, still calm as cucumber. "I guess it's my spirit animal."

I spray juice all over the floor from my mouth and nose.

Spirit animal?

"Connie! How many times have I told you not to drink from the bottle? Clean that up!"

Coughing up the OJ in my lungs prevents Mom from seeing my face properly. I wave at her that I'm fine, because I don't want her any closer.

"Your spirit animal," Mom repeats. "Here, you put the frosting on this layer." She hands over the equivalent of her magic wand but hovers close at his side.

"Plus, bats are a cool shape. Cool shapes make great jewelry patterns. I tried making a chinchilla necklace for her, but everyone agreed it looked like an overweight mouse."

Mom laughs. "Yes, I guess it would, but they're so cute. Do you think a chinchilla is Connie's spirit animal?"

"Pfft, as if," I reply, dumping the used paper towels in the trash. "Have you seen how Feathers runs for half the night on her wheel? My inner animal isn't half as fit as she is."

Before Mom can return to Rocks and bats, I get us out of here. "Mom, Rocks doesn't need to learn how to pipe fancy frosting on cakes. Can I borrow him for a bit?"

Mom agrees since she's soooooo OCD about frosting this cake it isn't funny. She's probably secretly relieved at my suggestion. We head to my room because Mr. Spirit Animal has some talking to do, and I don't want to worry about her eavesdropping.

"Shit! Are you trying to kill me?" I ask when we get out of earshot. "Spirit animals and mouthfuls of juice don't mix! Some warning would be good next time."

Rocks grins and actually looks slightly embarrassed. He shrugs his shoulders. "I had to say something. It was the first thing I thought of. Besides, it's not a lie. I have quite an intense bat spirit, wouldn't you say?"

I roll my eyes. Only Rockland could get out of those questions without lying.

"Seriously though, she's suspicious. I don't know how, but she is. That's like the third time she's asked me questions about bats and you!" My chest starts to wheeze. Rocks rubs his long, fine-boned fingers up and down my back as we sit on my bed.

"Relax, Connie. I'm never ever going to flip in front of her, and soon that won't even be a worry. Very soon I'm going to be a man only—the animal in me banished forever. There'll be nothing for her to find out."

"I thought you were finding out how to get fixed and then deciding."

He shrugs. "The more I think about it, the more I feel I want to do it. I only won't go through with it if it turns out to be way too dangerous. I'm comfortable with what I will be giving up."

I swallow the fear his words cause. I need to trust his instincts on this. If he feels it's okay, then I have to support him. Besides, we're a long way from having all the answers we need.

"So tell me what happened last night. I need every detail."

Rocks recounts his whole evening. I feel sick when he mentions Strickland showing up, but because he's here on my bed in one piece, I know it didn't end badly. He plays the recording of Sylvana giving him the list of items he needs. Not at all what I was expecting, but then again I have no clue how to perform a magical shape-shifting spell.

"Wow, some are easy and some are hard."

"Yeah, I know."

"And who is the powerful conjurer?" I ask.

"I have no idea. I half wondered if it's someone from one of those websites we contacted. I guess we have to trust her on that."

"*Awesome*. But what the hell does that crazy bitch want three strands of my hair for?" The thought makes me shiver.

"She didn't say *your* hair. She said three strands of golden hair. I have it recorded. I'll be paying your neighbor's dog a visit. Golden Retriever's have 'golden hair,' don't they?"

"Oh. My. God. That's genius," I snicker, imagining the look on her face when she finds out. "But you better hope Sylvana never learns any shape-shifting spells, or we'll be toads!"

"So long as she turns us both into toads, I don't care."

"Well, I do!"

He winks, making me smile. "I'm gonna start searching for where the sanguinaria grows in a crescent moon tonight."

"As in." I make a wing flapping hand gesture.

He nods. "Google hasn't helped with this one, but you're much better at searches than me. Maybe you can do research here and text me anything you find?"

"Whatever you need."

"Wait here. I need to get something." He goes to his room and is back a moment later. I wonder what he's got when I spy his closed fist.

He sits on my bed opposite me, pulling up one knee, so he can face me.

"You are so amazing. I can't believe I got so lucky. The fix is… well, it is dangerous, but you're staying so calm. You're supporting me in a way I've never had in my entire life—unconditionally. I can't really explain in words what it means to me. I know you're worried, because to be honest, so am I. I don't want to do anything to risk being separated from you." He looks into my eyes, and I'm lost in the emotions swirling behind them.

I think about how much my parents have always supported me, and what it would really feel like to never have that kind of love. I take his free hand.

"To be honest, I'm not that suppo—"

"Wait, you don't have to say anything. I know you struggle with the idea of the fix. Deep inside I know that, because if the situations were reversed I wouldn't want you doing it. But I appreciate you letting me find out more, and following this as far as I can take it safely. Thank you, baby." He opens his palm revealing a dark red, velvet bag. "This is the last thing I made at my shop. I want you to have it, because technically it's already yours."

I try not to the let the sadness overwhelm me because it's the last piece of jewelry he made at the market—his home. I hope when we're done with the fix, we can find him a job using those incredible skills.

I take the bag and hold it in my hands, leaning over to kiss him. He reaches up and gently slides his hand around my neck, holding me in place as he lengthens our kiss. I love it when he gives me subtle hints he wants me as much as I constantly want him.

I open the bag and let the necklace fall into my palm. My eyes fly to his. "Your heart is mine?" I can't stop the smile.

He nods mirroring my grin. "It always will be, and now you can wear it."

The intricate work is breathtakingly beautiful, and I remember seeing this piece on his workbench. The filigree heart is absolutely perfect. Tiny twisted wires spiral and swirl through the middle of the heart. I can't imagine how long it took him to create.

"Thank you. It's absolutely beautiful."

He takes it as I gather up my hair, and we replace the bat that's hung at my throat for what feels like forever.

"It might distract your mom too," he adds, grinning.

My fingers rub over the new shape, learning the feel of it. He places the bat in my hand, and I can't stop the frown.

"It's okay, baby," he says, and I wonder again if he can actually read my mind.

"What is?" I ask.

"I know you're sad giving up my bat." I look up at him wide-eyed. Is he talking about the necklace? As that's not the only bat I'm going to miss.

He smiles. "I love your face and your expressions. I know you love this," he says, wrapping both his hands around the fist holding the little silver bat. "But I know you love the animal in me too."

I let out the breath I was holding. "I do," I admit. "I am sad at the thought of you giving him up."

"Part of me is too. But like I said, I appreciate your support while I find out all I can. So thank you."

I grab him and hold him tight. The relief that he knows I love the bat inside him, and that I'm trying so hard not to freak out, somehow settles the panic that's been simmering below my skin. He's not being reckless, he's simply trying to find the answers he needs, and I do understand that driving desire.

BY DAY FOUR, Rocks is exhausted. He's out most of the night flying low over miles and miles of terrain in circles radiating out from the roost. Each night, he widens his search, but so far it's been a waste of energy. With no good reason to tell my parents why Rocks is out all night, he's not getting a lot of sleep. Thankfully, Mom takes Mini with her to a luncheon with two college friends in town for a few days.

Rocks sleeps while I continue our internet search. I discover bloodroot blooms in spring, so the crescent moon shaped patch of white flowers he's been looking for won't exist now. Summer is in full swing in Georgia, and that means finding this place at night is going to be even harder. I want to say it's like finding a needle in a haystack, but don't want to add to his ever-increasing disappointment.

Rocks has chosen his three gemstones, but I figure it's best if he selects the actual stones. I could go buy them to save him the trip to the store, but since this is for a spell—which will banish the animal inside of him—I don't want to take any chances. What if the stones need to call to him in some way? I wonder. What if that's part of the whole process? I scan the list to see if there's anything else I can do.

He stumbles into my room, rubbing his eyes, and lies down on my bed. It's almost four p.m. and he's got the sexiest case of bed head going on. I want to run my fingers through his hair, but I leave him to doze. He's not quite awake.

Ten minutes later, he sighs. "Hi."

Sitting on the edge of the bed, I kiss him gently and receive my most favorite grin in return. It amazes me he still has the power and magic to totally stop my heart and restart it again with a simple look.

"Did you find anything?" he asks.

"Nothing good. Don't look for the white flowers because they've probably already bloomed and dropped their petals. Now you're looking for a crescent moon shaped patch of green in a forest. Sorry. But I did find an awesome gem shop in town, and it sells all the stones you need."

"Thank you, Beans. I'll head out after sundown, but I won't stay out long tonight. Tomorrow we can go to the gem shop."

I'm relieved he won't be out alone all night again. Having him doing so much flying makes me nervous without his boys on his wing keeping him safe. Both of us have calmed down a little—and I mean only a teeny weeny bit—from the murdered bat incident. If it was a warning, then it wasn't very clear. Maybe the fact he never reported it to the Shadows was the test, and he passed it.

"I was also thinking about..." He stares up at the ceiling not finishing.

"About?"

"Celand."

"Oh."

"I'm wondering if she found the sanguinaria. I can't imagine she would have left the colony without knowing where it was first. And if she did locate it, she might have told Alex Greene where it was."

"Her boyfriend?"

"Yep, I think it's time for a visit."

"Why on earth haven't we gone to see him sooner? Maybe he knows other stuff that can help."

"Strickland forbid anyone from going to Alex after we initially questioned him. I was following my Sire's command, but it dawned on me that since I'm not a member of the Shadows anymore, I guess I'm not bound to uphold his rulings. Except the one banishing me, of course."

Poor Rocks. But he's right. He's on his own now and can make his own rules.

Rocks uses the aerial view of Google maps to get me a physical address for Alex Greene. He's not sure if the guy still lives there, but it's worth the drive across town.

We assume he's got a day job, and figure a visit before dinner might be perfect timing. I park on the street outside his apartment block, and we wait. Rocks says it's been a while, but he'll never forget the face of the first aeronaught who gave him hope for integration one day.

Our large coffees are long gone when Rocks comes alert. A guy is walking down the sidewalk with a laptop bag tucked under one arm.

"That's him. Let's go."

Rocks is out of the car and striding towards him, before I've even slipped my flip-flops back on my feet. As I jog to catch up to Rocks, Alex looks our way. He's paused at the secure gated entrance that leads into the apartment complex. Then his eyes widen, and he starts scrambling to get his keys from his pockets.

"Shit, hurry." Rocks runs towards the panicking young man, but Alex has opened the gate and firmly closed it by the time Rocks gets there.

"Leave me alone!" he yells, before running down the garden path and disappearing into the courtyard of his complex. The building appears to be built in a U-shape with dense trees growing in the center.

The silver metal bars of the fence rattle from the force of Rocks shaking it. Locked.

"What'll we do?"

"I have to get in there before he gets to his apartment and locks the door." Rocks scans up and down the street twice. Apart from three cars driving along, it's pretty quiet. "Shit. I need to flip. Cover me."

"What?"

Rocks walks to the nearest parked car and ducks behind it. Trying to stay calm, I follow close on his heels and use my body to cover him in case anyone in the apartment building is watching. The summer sun is still setting, so we don't have the luxury of the cover of darkness to hide his transformation. My gut rolls when I think about how bad this can go on so many levels.

A second later, Rocks flaps his wings and zips over the gate and disappears into the thick foliage of the courtyard. I pray nobody witnessed his change, and that Alex doesn't live on the first floor. If he has to take some stairs, then my money is on Rocks beating him to the door.

My feet won't keep still as I move from the gate to the car where Rocks flipped and back again. My hands go from my pockets to my hair to my side and start the circuit all over again.

Shit.

I try to take a deep breath to calm my racing heart. Public flipping is an adrenaline rush I wasn't expecting, and don't ever want to experience again.

Bzzzzzzz...

The gate buzzes and I'm hot on Rocks' heels. I follow where I saw Alex head and hope that once I'm around the corner, Rocks will guide me. Sure enough, he's standing on the third floor leaning out of an apartment. He must have flown to the door faster than Alex could run up the stairs, get his key in the lock and slam the door shut again. Thank goodness. The less of a disturbance we cause the better.

When I enter the apartment, Alex is sitting on the floor, crammed in the corner beside his couch and half behind the small table holding a lamp. Actually sitting isn't the right word—he's cowering, covering his face and begging. I have no clue how he managed to wedge himself in the tiny space so quickly.

"Please don't hurt me. Please. Please."

I look at Rocks. He shrugs and his face shows he's as bewildered by Alex's behavior as I am. Rocks does add that he had to shove his way in, but apart from that he hasn't touched the guy.

"Nobody's going to hurt you," I say.

Alex looks up and stops his pleading. His eyes roam from head-to-toe and stop again on my golden locks.

"You... you..." His eyes flick to Rocks and fill with fear instantly. "You aren't one of them?"

I take a step closer and kneel on the faded carpet, but Alex tries to push himself through the wall to maintain as much distance from us as possible, still covering his face with both arms.

"No, I'm not a Camazotz. We're not going to hurt you."

He lets out a rough laugh—the kind that shows utter disbelief. "They said they'd kill me if they had to come back."

Rocks stands at my side. "Who did?" His voice has the commanding tone of when he's at the market giving orders.

Alex wipes his nose on the back of his arm. "Your kind! You hate me. For the millionth time, I don't know what happened to her."

Rocks swears on the blood in his very veins that he will not harm Alex. The guy takes a long time to calm down, but eventually we make progress. When he lowers his arms from protecting his face, I can see he's taken a real beating in recent weeks. My guess is a broken nose, he's missing a front tooth, and he's got a scar on his cheekbone, and one on his upper lip.

"Did the Camazotz do this to you?" I ask, indicating to the damage.

"Who else! But, like I told them, I don't know anything about owls, or missing kids, or your effing sister! Do you hear me!" he yells.

Rocks asks for a description of his attackers. There's no mistaking the distinctive and hideous ink that covers Cypress. Rocks is livid, but it doesn't surprise me. Cypress is cruel and calculating. Yet the fact the Fold member came here in person to give a beating to an aeronaught is risky. If Strickland didn't sanction this visit—as Rockland claims—then Cypress could end up excommunicated the same as Rockland.

"Banished? Cypress could be banished for this?" I point at Alex. Rocks nods. "We need to tell Strickland. Maybe they'll let you go back if you report this."

Rocks shakes his head. "It won't save me. I broke the law." He focuses back on Alex. "Alex, I swear on my blood and all the bloodlines of old, I won't harm you. Please tell me everything Celand told you once she decided to leave. I'm after the place where bloodroot grows in a crescent moon."

Alex looks as though Rocks is speaking Swahili. He frowns and blinks, still pushed up against the wall.

I creep closer on my knees. "I got this scar from a Camazotz too." I point to the one above my eyebrow. "I understand how scared you feel, but we aren't here to hurt you. I promise. Please tell us what happened."

It takes a few minutes, but eventually Alex speaks.

"They paid me a visit asking questions about kidnapping y'all. I mean, what the fuck would I want to kidnap a bunch of bats for? I curse the day I found out your crazy shit even exists." He stares up at Rocks. "Just leave me the fuck alone, man. And if I were you," —he looks at me— "I'd run very fast and very far away from these...

these…" He points at Rocks without finishing his sentence. "You don't need their shit in your life when we've got our own human problems."

"He is human," I reply, crossing my arms over my chest. I take a deep breath because hating this prick won't help Rocks. "Don't let Cypress make you hate all Camazotz. You loved one once, remember?"

My guess pays off. Alex's face scrunches up as though he's trying not to cry. He nods his head before burying his eyes in the crook of his elbow. "I did. Once," he sobs softly. "I lost the only woman who ever truly understood me. It breaks my heart I didn't go with her, but she was so insistent she needed to do this alone." He slowly raises his head.

"Go on."

"I know she had a list of things to do, but she said it was Camazotz business, and she couldn't ask for help. She wanted to test herself. If she couldn't do these things in human form, then she figured she had no right asking to be fixed in human form."

Rocks slumps onto the edge of the faded couch and covers his eyes with both hands. "God, that's so Celand," he sighs.

"Hmmm, and sooooo someone else I know," I add, giving Rocks my evil eye. After what Alex just said, when the time comes, Rocks will not be chasing this fix alone. I'm going with him whether he wants me to or not.

A hint of a smile crosses Alex's face. He nods. "She was so independent, but I was worried sick. I left her in a parking lot off I-575 at her instruction. She said she was headed east, but that's all I know, and I never saw her again."

"Does that mean anything to you?" Rocks asks. I nod.

When we leave, Alex is almost calm and has told us all he knows, but he's still wedged in his corner by the couch. The sorrow that seems to ooze from him over Celand chills my blood. The thought of losing Rocks to this magical spell causes a stabbing pain to linger between my lungs. I rub the delicate heart hanging at my throat. The more we discover, the less I want Rocks to go through with his plan. I cling to his promise of him not wanting to leave me either.

We're silent in the car heading home. Seeing Alex has sent a chill to my bones. I swallow, glancing over at Rocks.

"I know you need my support, and I'm ready to give it. But that doesn't mean I don't get to have an opinion on all this," I say.

Rocks looks at me and agrees.

"The more we find out, the more I don't want you to do this, Rocks," I say, pulling up at a red light. "It's too dangerous."

He runs his hand along my thigh. "This might help me find answers about Celand. If I can find the sanguinaria, I might find out what really happened to her. And I agree it feels... off... or, I don't know exactly. But it feels almost wrong."

"Yes, it does."

I know I would want answers about Mini, so I can't be a hypocrite. Those hours she was gone before Enzo let me know he had her, I will never ever forget. The panic. The loss. The helplessness of not knowing. I get why he needs answers more than anyone else does. And Alex has just given us a fresh clue. I doubt he would've told the others an aeronaught Interstate number. Silence fills the Honda the rest of the way home.

Before I've closed the front door, Dad is standing behind us in the entryway. He walks up and places a kiss on my forehead. "Come with me."

We follow him through the kitchen—where Rocks snags a slice of cold pizza—and into the TV room. The TV is paused with the words Enzo Ascari Trial along the bottom.

"Already?" I ask, collapsing on the couch.

Dad beams. "At long last more like it."

The newsreader reports the successful selection of a jury to commence the Enzo Ascari trial. I sag against the soft fabric.

"Isn't that the best news you've ever heard?" Dad asks, still smiling. "That bastard is going down, and I couldn't be happier."

"Don't get too excited. They've only picked a jury. Josie said this trial could go on for months—maybe even years."

He flicks the channel hoping to find another news report on Enzo. If I thought Dad was obsessed with the news before, I know he's gonna be a down right psycho about it now, following every scrap of new info on the trial he can find. But it makes me feel safe. My *real* Dad has my back and will keep me informed of anything I need to know. He'll make sure I'm protected no matter what. I grin and kiss Dad as the aroma of pepperoni pizza lures me back to the kitchen.

Rocks pours two sodas and settles himself in front of the pizza boxes on the counter. Tracking down old boyfriends and interrogating them is hungry work. But the doorbell chiming prevents me from joining him. Opening the door, I find Tiff waiting patiently.

"Quick. Get in here. Rocks is alone with a whole pizza, and if you want some, we better hurry."

"Pepperoni?" she asks.

"Is there any other kind worth ordering?" I grin.

Rocks can't speak when Tiff enters, but he stands and pretends to raise his imaginary hat to her as he chews madly. All the extra flying he's been doing is burning up calories.

"Awww, Rocks, you're so sweet. Sit. Please sit." She motions for him to be seated again. "I do love how you get up from the table when a lady enters."

"A lady?" I ask, raising one eyebrow.

"Oh, shut it, you! Yes, I'm a lady now. High school is done. We're adults! Can you believe that shit?" She covers her mouth and scans the area for Mini. "Can you believe it, though?"

I shake my head no since my mouth is jammed with delicious cheesy goodness too.

"I know right!" she replies. "It's totally crazy."

Rocks takes a sip of soda before asking, "To what do we owe the pleasure of your surprise visit, Tiff?"

"I'm glad you asked. Has Con told *you* which college she plans on attending in the fall? Cause I'd sure as hell like to know."

15
Price

ROCKS stares from me to Tiff and back again. His mouth opens and closes again. He places his half-eaten slice on his plate.

"Connie?" he asks.

I feel like complete and utter crabapples. My college acceptance letters have sat unopened hidden under my bed for weeks—actually closer to months now. Each week at school, Tiff would ask if I'd decided where I was going, and I'd tell her I didn't want to think about it yet. I had too much going on with Mini. Then all that's happened since her return at the colony—including Rocks living with us—college was the last thing I had time to decide.

"Yes?"

"College?"

"What?" Tiff interrupts. "You haven't told him?"

I close my eyes. "I haven't decided *yet*," I spit out through gritted teeth.

"Haven't decided?" she half screeches. "Connie, you've no doubt missed all the deadlines. What are you doing? This is serious."

"Deadlines?" Rocks mimics again, still clearly shocked that I kept such a big decision a secret from him.

I wince. "I know. I know. It'll be fine. I've still got time." I wonder when the acceptance deadlines were, and if my offers are still open—that's if I was accepted at all to begin with. The pizza churns in my gut. Fudge. I hope I've still got time to sort out my future.

"Rocks, I promise to tell you all about this later. Tiff, if you want to stay for pizza, swear on your favorite book boyfriend's life, you won't mention college in front of my folks, and I'll give you an extra large piece of Mom's death-by-chocolate cake. Deal?"

"Deal. But you don't play fair, and it's only because I love you I'm asking."

"I love you too."

Dad reluctantly hands over the remote and stops his obsessive and futile news scanning. There is absolutely no update on the trial at this hour. Rocks is restless all through the movie, and the tension in my gut only worsens as the night wears on. I should have talked to him about college, but it was so hard with everything going on, and I hate to admit this, but I don't know if I want to go now if it means being away from him.

Rocks and I just shared the most amazing thing ever. Sleeping with him was way better than I ever thought my first time would be. But it's not only that. He stood by me though the craziest shit. The thought of leaving him—especially if he gets fixed—is totally out of the question. He gives up his entire life and part of his existence to be with me in my world, and I flit off to live in another state to study? Yeah, that's not gonna happen.

But at the same time, I know I need to go to university and get an education. I want to get a degree, but I want to be there for him while he adjusts to his life without super bat senses.

Fudge.

Being an adult fucking sucks.

"I better get going," Tiff says, stretching as she stands. "Call me tomorrow, or I'll be back and I'll bring re-enforcements."

Rocks and I head upstairs without a word. I think of all the times I was mad at him for not sharing his bat business. I slink into my room as he follows, understanding all too well how he's feeling.

He sits in his corner chair but says nothing.

"Look, I know I should have talked to you. I know that. I'm really sorry. It's such a big decision, and I always thought to myself 'tomorrow I'll decide. Tomorrow will be quieter. Tomorrow I'll have time.' Or at least, less stuff going on, but if it's not one thing with us, it's another."

He doesn't say a word.

"I'm really, really sorry."

"Does this have anything to do with my fix?" His voice is too quiet. He sounds hurt, and that absolutely kills me.

"Sort of, yeah. I can't leave you and study out-of-state if you get fixed. God, I hate using that word. Can we call it something else?"

"Call it whatever you want, but, Connie, I don't want you missing out on going to college because of me. That's not right. I don't want to hold you back."

"It's more complicated than that. I've been through so much this year. You're possibly about to go through even more. I'm not sure the time is right, but I don't know... It's hard. What I do know is that you are where I want to be. I love that you want me to get a good education. But not going this fall doesn't mean I'll never go. Come here." I open my arms and beckon for him to join me on my single bed.

He lies down with me, and we wrap our arms and legs around each other—totally entwined. We lay together breathing in unison for what feels like ages. He kisses my forehead.

"I want us to face everything together, Beans. If that's college for you? Or me and this crazy spell? Or whatever? I want us to be a team."

"Me too." I rest my head on his shoulder, so relieved he finally knows. And the best part is now we can decide together. I'm such a slow learner when it comes to asking for help. Rocks has never once refused to help me. He's always been there for me, so I don't really know why I didn't tell him.

"You gonna show me these letters, or what?" His voice has returned to normal. I'm forgiven.

I jump up and scramble half under my bed. There are five large envelopes still unopened.

"You open them and tell me if I got accepted or not." I cross my fingers.

He frowns. "You can't possibly be scared about getting in."

"I am. Please open them. You'll bring me luck."

That earns me an eye roll. God, I love it when he does that.

"I applied to six schools and got letters back from five of them, so clearly I'm not as smart as you think."

"Pfft, whatever." He focuses on ripping into the first envelope, but remains quiet as he reads, then he picks up the next one.

"Well?"

Silence. He pulls the second letter free and starts to read.

"Come on, Rocks. What did the first one say?"

Still silence, but now with a tiny smirk. Cheeky bat. He opens the third envelope and reads that letter too—to himself. When he goes to take the fourth envelope, I snatch the open letters from his lap and scan for the one word I'm looking for... congratulations.

"Oh, thank goodness," I sigh, clutching one letter to my chest.

"Congratulations. They're all acceptance letters. Tell me about each school and why you applied."

Rocks and I get comfy on the bed again, and I tell him everything he wants to know. The University of Georgia is little more than an hour's drive away in the town of Athens. If all goes well with Rocks, then that might be where I end up this fall. We could both live there. But we agree to wait a little longer before deciding to see how everything goes with the fix first.

The next day, we head to the gem store to purchase the stones Rocks needs for the magic spell. I suggest he buys the biggest ones possible. The shop has a great selection, and even sells huge amethyst geodes. They're similar to thunder eggs, but hollow inside. The large eggs are cracked open, and the hollow inside is lined with deep purple, jagged crystals of vibrant amethyst. I walk along the line of geodes for sale and want to touch them all.

"You definitely need to get one of these!"

"Have you seen how much they are?" he whispers.

"It's on Enzo, silly. If this is going to protect you during the you-know-what, then it's cheap at the price."

We both try not to say any words to raise suspicion amongst eavesdropping aeronaughts. From some of the emails I got from the 'shape-shifting' community, this is exactly the type of shop they would frequent.

Rocks is drawn to a magnificent geode. It stands a foot high, and the amethyst crystals start a pretty, light shade of purple at the top and graduate down into a rich aubergine purple at the base. It's spectacular.

The sales assistant starts to hover nearby, and if she gets paid on commission, I'm sure she'll close up early.

Rocks chose amethyst because it is said to protect the wearer and strengthen intuition. It's believed it will even out emotions and heals both spiritually and physically. Rocks thought this suited his situation perfectly.

The second gemstone he chose is charoite. This stone is violet in color with swirls of purple and black and is believed to have healing properties and to remind the wearer to live in the here and now, to enjoy the present, and to let go of the past. Rocks wants to let go of the magical spell from his past, and his old colony, and belong in the present, modern world.

His final choice seemed obvious to both of us—moonstone. It's always been linked to the moon, just as Rocks feels his bat side is too. Moonstone is believed to help one on a spiritual journey to discover what's inside or is missing. Since Rocks is on a journey to discover his human side, he couldn't go past the pale, white, iridescent glow of a beautiful, round moonstone.

We exit the store and head to the car. Rocks places his purchases in the trunk so carefully you'd swear he was handling a newborn.

A thought hits me about Rocks' rocks.

"Hey, do you know when the next full moon is?" He usually does since he loves flying those nights, even though he's more likely to be spotted by owls.

"Not for a week and half. Why?" He slides into the passenger seat already wearing his sunglasses.

God, he's hot.

Focus!

"Um," I swallow. "You're so hot in those sunglasses. I just had to tell you."

He beams at me, before leaning over and nibbling my bottom lip. In an instant, we're a hot mess making out like it's the last five minutes the planet will exist. He smells so intoxicatingly good. I pull away when I hear a car door close next to us. He reaches up and slides his fingers through my long ponytail.

"Wow." He grins.

I bite my bottom lip, grinning back at him. I never thought I'd ever be this lucky.

"What were you saying about the moon?"

"Oh, yeah. I heard you're supposed to cleanse crystals under a full moon. We must put them in the moonlight next time it's full."

He frowns. "I hope to be using them before then."

"But we still haven't found the sanguinaria."

As though Sylvana has the ability to listen to us miles away, Rocks' phone buzzes with an incoming text.

"It's Jez," Rocks reads. "He said Sylvana came looking for him and asked him to contact me with a message."

"What's the message?"

"She said 'I have what he needs. Tell him to meet me by the river in Helen in two days. Don't forget what we agreed. Bring it all.'"

"Do you think she means she got those bones?"

He nods. "I hope disturbing an ancestor at peace is worth it." He rubs his eyes under his sunglasses. He replies to Jez instructing him to tell her to meet at noon. Knowing Sylvana she'll pick some odd hour, and that'll be difficult to explain to my folks.

Mom and Dad have been more than gracious about Rocks living with us, but I know they're keeping a close eye on us. Not that it's done any good, but I don't want to push our luck.

Rocks is back out flying for most of the night trying to find the crescent moon bloodroot. I showed him where I-575 is located, and he's confused when it's not near Blood Mountain. He said he isn't familiar with the territory surrounding it at all, which makes me worry about deadly owl populations.

When I wake the next morning, my nose twitches. A strong, foresty smell fills the air. Blinking from the light streaming in my open window, there's a sizeable hunk of wood resting on the roof outside my window and partially hanging inside. It's hard to say if it's a branch, or part of a trunk.

What the?

When Rocks goes out at night, he still uses my window. I can't comprehend how he managed to fly with that thing. From the smell and small leaves on one side, I know it's the red cedar he needs to carve his dagger.

Carved wooden dagger.

What's that witch on?

Is she for real? I wonder. Or is this a crazy stunt? More questions. Always questions. Never enough answers.

"Connie," Mom calls up the stairs.

I drag myself out of bed, closing my bedroom door and head in search of her. I'd rather not have to explain the chunk of red cedar hanging in my window.

Mini is running around the kitchen island as Mom pours creamer in her coffee. I snag the whole cup from her hands. The soft tendrils of steam rising from the caramel liquid make my mouth water. I know this is going to be coffee perfection—like everything Kelly creates in the kitchen. I take a small sip and moan.

She smiles at me, pouring herself another cup from the fresh pot.

"Mmmm, you always put exactly the right amount of cream and sugar. I don't know how you do it," I murmur, savoring the perfect flavor.

"I need you to watch Mini today. I'm about to head out, and I'll be back around three."

"No sweat, but tomorrow I can't, 'cause Rocks and I are going for a drive."

"Where to?"

"A picnic maybe." I swallow the lie, and my coffee doesn't taste as sweet as it did a moment ago. I can't tell her we're going to Helen to meet a witch—although she'd probably give up on asking bat questions if I did. Witch questions I can handle without having to lie. I don't believe Sylvana is capable of any magic—at all—ever! She's a total faker, but nobody in the colony seems to see it.

"How lovely. Do you want me to bake you something?" she asks.

I don't want Mom going to any trouble when I'm not being wholly honest with her. Although if she does bake something, I'll insist Rocks and I stop to eat it somewhere scenic, so then I won't be a little liar. We will be having a picnic, and I'll just be omitting the witch parts.

"You don't have to do that."

"I want to."

"Thanks, Mom, but don't go to too much trouble. Something portable and easy."

She grabs my hands and inspects my pinstriped nails. It's a simple, yet effective design, and one I know she loves. "Later in the week, I'll paint your nails. I promise. Think about what colors you want." I say.

Leaving my coffee on the counter, I start gathering my supplies. "Mini, I'll be right back."

With the laptop, my phone and the last of my coffee, I settle on the sofa in the TV room. Mini enters and heads straight for her toy boxes. In no time at all, the entire carpet is littered with Lego, farm animals, and happy meal toys. I watch her sifting through the chaos she's created in search of some particular prize. She's content, and I'm relieved she doesn't show any signs of trauma or stress from her time at Enzo's warehouse.

I know Mom and Dad have kept a close eye on her, but she seems totally fine. The relief, which fills my chest every time I watch her and know she's okay, still astounds me. Even though it's been two months since that harrowing ordeal ended, I haven't truly gotten past it myself. I've simply been so focused on everything happening with Rocks and the colony I've been too distracted to really deal with it. My college acceptance letters are the same.

This past year has been totally insane. When I look back at the me from this time last year, I was like a little kid. Not literally, but I acted like one. Between then and now, I've dealt with so much crap—and survived it all. Sitting here safe from Enzo's reach, I'm quite proud. I held it together with the help of Rocks and my parents. So now it's my turn to hold it together for Rocks.

The magic spell he's so keen to find out about scares me beyond words. But I'm sure he was scared for my life and Mini's when he came to my rescue. Regardless of how scared I was when I was dealing with all my crap, I held it together to get the job done. I'm going to do that for Rocks. I'm going to be the one he can lean on, while he faces the scariest moment of his life—a transformation I pray he survives.

"Rocks!" Mini announces, charging toward him.

I look up from the laptop to watch him scoop her up in his arms and raise her high over his head. She squeals with delight. He spins around and her little legs fly out, and she giggles. It's one of my most favorite sounds. He puts her back on her feet and moves to sit with me.

"Mini fly again," Mini commands. "Again."

Rocks looks to me. His eyes pleading.

"Uh-ah, don't look at me. You started her favorite game, Mister." I know how this ends—with Mini calling commands and her six-foot-four hero doing whatever she says.

Rocks stays seated but reaches down wincing slightly before sending her flying above our heads and spinning once more. "Sorry about the cedar." I ogle his biceps and triceps moving under his skin as he spins her around. He stands up for a longer flight path.

Blinking, I add, "I'm glad you found some, but how on earth did you fly with it?" I hope the fact Mini is flying around our TV room in his arms means that she won't pay attention to my reference to Rocks flying. She can be a mimic at the worst possible times.

"I'm sore everywhere. I'm not as skilled at wood carving as Moonshiner, so I wanted to have some spare wood in case I screw it up."

Mini flies down for a landing on the carpet. Soon as Rocks stands up, she wants another go. I know he can't say no to that kid and his eyes plead with me again for help. He's got dagger carving to start.

"Hey, Mini, want an ice cream cone with sprinkles?"

Bingo. What Mom doesn't know won't hurt my little sister.

We spend our afternoon on the back patio. Rocks had packed two lethally sharp-looking knives in his trunk. They shred the branch easily. Mini is covered in ice cream drippings, but she's happy riding her pony on wheels around us. I watch Rocks work away at the wood, the dagger slowly taking shape.

"Do you think it needs to be a real dagger? Like capable of cutting something? Or just symbolic?" I ask.

The knife sliding down the fresh wood stops mid stroke. "Shit! I don't know. I never asked her." Rocks frowns.

"Shit! Shit! Shit!" mimics a tiny, sweet voice.

"Oh, sugarplums!"

We watch as Mini rides around in circles cussing her little head off for the next thirty minutes. I think back to my conversation with mom about why they adopted me and telling her it was time I was allowed to cuss properly. She agreed so long as Mini doesn't learn any new words.

With all the bat craziness that's been going on, it feels good to be able to swear normally—like an adult. But we need to remember to use my swear word alternatives when Mini's within hearing range. The little brat better not rat us out later.

THE DRIVE TO Helen is uneventful. We head straight down the back streets to the river and wait for the hag to meet us.

My nerves are on high alert. I try hiding in every shrub and small clump of trees by the river. It's useless. They either aren't big enough to hide me, or I'm too far away from Rocks to hear what he whispers because of the river bubbling along beside him.

"Look, if she goes nuts when she sees me here with you, I'll wait in the car," I suggest. "I don't want to like totally annoy her when you need her help."

"You are not waiting in the car," he replies. "I'm not a colony member now, so she can talk in front of you. I'll insist."

I smile at him. I love that he wants to force her to be nice to me, but messing with Sylvana, when we need her intel, isn't high on my 'to do' list today.

"Besides, I'd rather we stick together," he adds, scanning the sky and nearby trees. "Since that bat, I don't like us being separated in Camazotz territory."

"Did you ever tell Jez?"

"No. If it was meant as a test for me, then I'm not involving him. If he says someone is missing, then I would, but it's been too long now for it to be someone from the Shadows."

Jez must know we're talking about him because he sends a text saying Sylvana has left the market and will be with us shortly.

"Jez gonna come and see you too?"

Rocks nods and continues scanning the surrounding area. He's checking no other sneaky Camazotz are in town. He's wearing his royal blue t-shirt today and it always throws me. I'm so used to seeing him in black, or dark greys, and the occasional blood red. The darkness in his full-sleeve tattoos is somewhat softened by the bright colored t-shirt.

I try hiding behind the trunk of the closest tree.

"I can hear you breathing, Connie. Just stand with me. I actually want you close. If she wants her money, she'll have to tell me what I need to know with you standing next to me."

I hate to admit that it calms me to be within touching distance of him too. Even though we don't understand the threat, I also want us to stick close together. The message was either directed at Rocks—or me. So not being alone feels safer.

The cash is in a brown, paper lunch bag. Beside his boot is a sports duffle containing his gemstones, the unfinished cedar dagger, and my filigree heart necklace. Rocks asked me if he could borrow it for the item that's close to his heart. He said I was what was closest to his heart, but he will not put me in any unnecessary danger.

The next best thing was a piece of jewelry he made with love for me. It represents me, but to an outsider who doesn't know Rocks, they could mistake it for his love of his art and trade. The necklace will keep me close to his heart but protect me at the same time.

He bends down and pulls out the rough dagger. "I'll ask her when she arrives how finished this needs to be." The wood is a perfect dagger shape, but it wouldn't cut butter. Rocks was concerned each time he thinned the blade to sharpen the edge about it breaking. Only if Sylvana wants a sharpened, wooden dagger will he risk working on it more.

Rocks puts down the cedar and stands tall. I look around and high in the branches of the tree we're standing under is a lone, black bat.

Aeronaught leave!

I jerk at the high-pitched voice inside my head.

"She stays. Flip!" Rocks answers, not looking up.

Silence.

The bat doesn't move any closer. Rocks holds up the brown paper bag near his head and waves it around.

"You want this, flip now. Otherwise, we're leaving."

The little bat's nose twitches. Rocks claims money stinks, so she must know what's in the bag. I scan left-to-right and all around, including the other side of the narrow river. It's all clear, but both of them probably already know as much. Above me, the bat lets go of the branch she was holding and plummets straight down—rocketing directly toward me.

It weaves around one branch but manages to be still above me. I stare transfixed at the small creature hurtling down. A second later, I'm yanked out of the way, and Sylvana materializes *exactly* where I was standing a moment ago.

"What the hell?" I grumble. I use my anger to hide the fact that had Rocks not pulled me clear, she would have flipped on top of my head, and I'd be sprawled over the grass right now. Just what I need— Kamikaze Camazotz!

"You okay?" he asks me, glaring at the witch.

I nod and give her my best evil eye.

"What's she doing here?"

"She is my family now, since my own kind kicked me out, so if you have a problem with that we can both leave—but the money leaves with us." I sense his anger has been forged from the threat of the dead, unknown bat.

I'm shocked he's playing hardball with Sylvana. She has the information we need, but maybe Rocks knows how desperate she is to get her hands on this kind of cash. I wonder how she earns her keep at the colony, since she doesn't have a trade that makes money. Obviously, the Sire doesn't pay her well if she's trading secrets and body parts with a banished member.

She holds out her palm, and I notice for the first time she has odd symbols tattooed across it.

"Tell me what I need to know first. I have the items, except the location of the bloodroot."

She sucks in a breath, and her eyes widen so much I can see white all around her dark iris. "You have failed! This is a bad omen." She starts muttering under her breath and looks like she crosses herself.

"I didn't say I've given up!" he rebuts.

We watch her close her eyes and continue her ancient muttering.

"Please tell me what you know." His voice has lost the demand from a moment ago.

She finally opens her eyes. "You know most do not survive," she warns.

I'm grateful when Rocks asks the questions burning across my tongue. "What do you mean most? How do you know?"

Sylvana stares at me for a long time but remains silent.

"What?" I ask, feeling defensive. I know I shouldn't piss her off, but she's stalling. By being here, she's breaking major bat laws, so I'd think she would want to hurry up about it.

"This isn't for her ears."

"Make it for her ears. Maybe those bats didn't survive because they needed an aeronaught?" Rocks suggests. She bares her yellow teeth at him.

"We will never need their help."

It takes all my willpower not to list off all the ways I have helped this so-called independent colony.

"Did you tell Celand most don't survive when she came to you? Do you even know what happened to her?" he asks.

"What you are asking of me goes against the Sire's wishes. I will only speak of the matter between us. I will not speak of what others chose to do."

Rocks groans. "By talking to me now, you're already breaking the Sire's wishes. She was my sister! If anyone has the right to know, it's me!"

Sylvana's body language closes down right in front of us. She turns to walk away.

"Wait, please," he begs. We both get another long glare before she speaks.

"I will tell you this. Casting a spell is dangerous, but reversing a spell is a whole different entity entirely. You want magic that was not performed on you but on your ancient ancestor to be reversed. Reversing a spell after five hundred years will come at a price. That's how magic works. Rockland, first-born son of Strickland, are you prepared to pay the price?"

16
Ambush

"YES," he replies.

I swallow the lump of bile in my throat. *Comes at a price...*

I hope she's talking about money and not some life for a life crap. All I can see is the mutilated body of the bat on my roof. What kind of price was paid with that? I try to remain calm. I promised myself I was going to hold it together for Rocks while he needed me, and I mean to do it now more than ever.

"Good," she replies. "A strong spirit is needed to survive. Show me your items."

She bends down to inspect what's in the bag. "That is not a dagger. Any pup could carve better. It needs to draw blood. You will be required to contribute your blood to the ceremony—drawn by this blade."

She digs into her skirt pockets and pulls out a small, wrapped piece of black velvet. She beckons for Rocks to crouch down too. "Your ancestors," she whispers, carefully unfolding the soft material to reveal three tiny bones. "Guard these. Make sure they are not broken. There is power within."

Rocks takes the wrapped bones and places them gently in the container that holds two of his gemstones. The bubble wrap to protect the stones will protect the bones too.

"You told me last time we met you would tell me the last piece today. What is it?" Rocks asks, still crouching over the bag.

"The moon. I need to throw the bones to find out what night you need to go to the sanguinaria to find the shaman."

"But I don't know where the bloodroot is."

She hisses again, standing up. She paces back and forth several times, muttering again.

She's totally insane!

When she stops, she digs around in those cavernous skirts again. "For an extra two hundred, I will throw the bones twice. Once to find out if I'm allowed to tell you what I know, and the second time, to reveal the moon you must travel on."

That extorting hag!

I never thought I'd be thanking Enzo for anything after what he put my family through, but I have to admit his cash has saved us. I keep a portion of it under the spare tire, so when Rocks gives me the head nod, I leave to get the extra bone throwing payment. I'll throw some bones in a minute for free—but they'll be hers and into the damn river.

The car is parked on a quiet backstreet a few minutes walk from our meeting place. When I get there, I'm stunned to find Jeremiah and Bailey waiting in the shade. I breathe a sigh of relief that they're both alive and well.

"Jez?"

"Hi, you done with Sylvana yet?"

"Nope. She's about to throw the bones. Hi, Bailey."

"Hi, Miss Connie. Where's my brother? Is he okay? I really need to speak with him." She stares up with her one super serious eye. Her leather eye patch is new, and I wonder if Moonshiner did the leather embossing on this one too.

"He's busy for a bit longer," I reply. "Can you wait?"

"Yes." She folds her arms as though she's not moving until she sees him. If I didn't know better, I'd swear she was preparing to chain herself to something.

Jez helps me lift the tire, and I grab the payment and an extra twenty. "Take her to the bakery and then head to the river. We should be done by then."

"Thanks," he says blushing and slipping the twenty in his back pocket.

"Hey, whatever happened to the bills you got from *that* van *that* night?" I ask without wanting to say too much in front of Bailey. The boys stole cash from the Vipers, and it was tens of thousands of dollars each.

He glances sideways at Bailey, still standing with her arms folded. "Buried it," he whispers. "Too much was going on back then, and it's never settled down. One day I hope we can use it."

"Probably a wise idea. And it's not like it's going anywhere."

Jez smiles. He looks older somehow. I wonder about life at the colony and how stressed he is without Rocks. "How's the Fold politics going?"

"I'll explain later but not good. Get back to him. I don't trust her. We'll see you soon."

When I return, Sylvana is dancing around a piece of blood red satin. She's wafting white sage smoke this way and that. Closer up, I can see she's already thrown the bones, as there's a small pile of them lying haphazardly in the center of the satin circle.

She ends her dance with a screech before collapsing onto her hands and knees. She sniffs the bones in an overly, exaggerated manner three times. I can't help but sniff the air too. She leans so close to the teeny, tiny bones, she must be going cross-eyed.

"It's decided!"

We wait. She's still peering at them, inches from her nose. She suddenly sits back on her haunches and rubs her temples, humming out loud. With her eyes closed, she reaches out into thin air, waving her fingers wildly as though sifting the air for the answer. Rocks' focus never leaves her. The crazy fingers routine has me highly dubious, but Rocks and I have failed at finding those flowers, so I guess we have to endure her theatrics.

"It is east. Go east. East. As the bat flies, it is east near the falls."

She opens her eyes, blinking. I can't stop the frown that creases my forehead. She can't possibly expect us to believe that was some kind of premonition.

"How far east? There's a lot of country to cover *east*."

"Due east!" she snaps. "Remember this is your journey."

"For two hundred bucks, I want more than 'east,'" I snap. I can't control myself. *East.* What is she on? Her evil glare bounces off my thick skin. If the bat *biatches* can't get under my skin these days, then why would I let this faker. "Tell him more about these falls."

She leans back over the bones, sniffing and making even stranger noises than before. She closes her eyes and starts garbling weird vowel sounds. Her hands shoot out in front again, and she yells, "Fall." She sways from side-to-side, sort of growling before spitting, "Creek." More weird vowels sounds, and she throws herself sideways onto the ground. "Falls!"

Rocks is transfixed by her performance. I literally have to stop myself from rolling my eyes and slapping her.

"Fall Creek Falls?" I repeat.

She gets back on her hands and knees and mumbles at the ground, "Yes."

Sylvana asks Rockland to gather the bones and spit on them. I mentally try to remember if I have hand wipes in the Honda. I can't even imagine the germs on those things if every colony member that's needed her help has had to spit on them. Fudge me, that's so disgusting.

Gently handing over the bones, she commences her whirly bird dance for a second time. I tiptoe over to the tree I was trying to hide behind earlier and take a seat. At least we have some shade while she does her witchy-whatever-this-is.

More shrieking, more chanting, more smoking sage before she proclaims, "Three cycles! You have three lunar risings to prepare! After the third, you will need to be waiting by the bloodroot when the moon is directly overhead."

Rocks confirms her cryptic announcement means three moon risings. Since it's Wednesday, he only has three nights to find the crescent moon, and then on Saturday night he needs to be ready. I want to be sick. By the weekend, he could be fixed—or dead.

My lungs constrict, but I try to stay calm. I need to be his rock this time. I need to be rock solid and reliable. I close my eyes and feel the soft grass beneath my legs, the hard trunk behind my back, and the sweet smell of a rural river. I have to believe Rocks and I have survived so much together, we'll get through this too. Maybe the others needed medical attention afterward, so that's why they died. Maybe the key is not doing this alone.

"And you're sure the shaman will be there waiting?"

The anger in her answering stare almost singes my hair. "You doubt my bones?" she shrieks.

I clamp my teeth together.

Yes, I doubt your faker bones, you fake, extortionistic, old hag!

"No," Rocks replies, handing over the paper bag and assuring her the 'golden hairs' are inside. She casts a quick glare my way, and I try to appear calm—and innocent—so she won't open the bag.

"Farewell. May the ancestors protect you. Bats allowing." And with that she turns and walks upstream.

Seconds later, a tiny Goth missile comes hurtling towards Rocks and wraps herself around his legs.

"Rockland!" Bailey exclaims. Her grin could light the darkest corner of the universe for a thousand years. It almost brings tears to my eyes. "It's you. I missed you."

He gently rubs her head, but she won't let go of her hold on his legs for him to even be able to bend down to hug her properly. It's so adorable as only Bailey can be. He pulls her wrists apart from behind his knees and finally picks her up.

"I miss you too, Bailey. It's so good to see you. But this is a surprise. I didn't know you were coming." He eyes Jez, and they do that silent communication thing where I expect to hear their voices inside my head.

"Someone's been *hanging* around listening."

I assume from his careful choice of words, Bailey isn't scared of flipping to her bat form any longer. The sneaky little bat must have overheard Jez planning to meet.

"I needed to see you. It's important," Bailey explains. Rocks places her on her feet but kneels down to be closer to her height. "I know why they banished you, and they're WRONG!" she suddenly yells.

"Shhhh… you promised to be good," Jez admonishes, looking over his shoulder.

Bailey apologizes to Jez, while looking at the ground and straightening imagined creases from her full skirt. She gives Jez a quick side-glance before focusing back on her big brother. It's the cutest fake apology I've ever witnessed.

"The Fold banished you for not having babies. Well, I told them only *girls* have babies, and they need to let you come home because they are silly and wrong. It's not your fault you can't grow a pup like Zada can."

Rocks looks at Jez. "She flew into a secret Fold meeting—down the chasm—and started yelling her theory at each member. According to Judge, Strickland nearly choked her. She had to be physically dragged from the chamber and was so worked up—"

"We don't talk about that, Jeremiah!" Bailey interrupts again, still yelling. She has also totally mastered the one-eyed, evil eye glare.

He frowns at her and continues, "—so worked up, she couldn't flip for two hours."

"It was important," she defends.

"Bailey, listen to me," Rocks soothes, "you cannot—*cannot*—interrupt a sacred Fold meeting uninvited. That's very disrespectful no matter what you had to tell them."

"But they're *wrong*," she almost sobs.

"Sweet girl, it's complicated. Thank you so much for defending me. I'm the luckiest big brother to ever live having you for a sister. But you have to listen to Zada. Zada loves me, right?"

She reluctantly nods her head.

"Trust Zada to know what's right, and what's going to get you in very big trouble with the Sire. Zada would have told you not to do what you did."

"But you were always in trouble with the Sire, and that was okay."

Rocks sighs. Her six-year-old logic makes sense. Jez shrugs his shoulders at Rocks. I'm glad I don't have to convince her of how it really is.

"Strickland doesn't like me being different from everyone. Now promise—"

Five bodies materialize in a semicircle around Rocks and Bailey. They're dressed from head-to-toe in identical black—including the hooded masks covering their faces.

"Fuck!" Jez spits, turning his back toward his brother to protect his flank as he faces the two closing in near him.

I'm on my feet as fast as they appeared. All I can see is the image of that dead bat on my roof—the murdered bat. Each of the males is armed—with deadly-sharp blades the length of my forearm. Knives, which could easily cut off wings.

"You're dead!"

I know that voice.

"Ash!" Rocks spits. "At least be man enough to show your fanged face."

"Prepare to bleed out for your sins," Ash sneers. The group takes a step closer in unison.

Jez, Rocks, and I form a tight circle around little Bailey. She's completely silent, but she's our vulnerability. We can't run. We can't fight. As a group, we take a step back toward the rushing river. It's not deep or wide, but again what will Bailey do? I don't even know if Camazotz are taught to swim.

"You have breached your banishment," another voice says. "The punishment is death. You know this."

"No!" screeches Bailey.

Rocks steps forward. "Mackie, Ash, remove those hoods, and we'll talk. Same for the rest of you cowards. Show yourselves."

Harsh laughter ripples from the group. "It's too late to talk. Judge and Zander aren't here to get in the Sire's ear. Justice is about to be served. So either kneel and take what you deserve, or we can't guarantee there won't be collateral damage," Ash commands.

I bet he'd love for me to end up as collateral damage. Even though his body doesn't move, I feel Rocks take my hand and give it one quick squeeze.

I sense he's up to something.

Too many times before I haven't listened to my gut. Rocks is so intuitive. I have to trust him. I give his fingers a quick answering squeeze. He's planning something, and I'm ready to back him. I know he would never willingly endanger me or Bailey.

One of the silent figures in front of us, flips the knife in his hands, and grips it hard with the blade facing the ground. He's ready to deliver a downward, vicious blow. I shudder when my mind wonders how deep the lethal steel would slide if it entered my neck from above—probably to the hilt. It might even pierce my heart from that angle.

Sensing the group are about to charge, Rocks steps toward them and yells, "FLIP!"

Immediately, he's a bat. I blink, totally not expecting him to change and less than a second later, Jez and Bailey have flipped too. The three bats are beating their wings to get height, but it's almost in slow motion. They're roughly at my head height.

Suddenly, eight bats appear in the cluster at eye level. Two of the male bats, from the hooded group, screeching their aerial attack as they zoom inward.

SCREAM!

The word has barely registered in my brain, and I'm filling my lungs with oxygen and unleashing the loudest, longest, highest pitched wail my body will produce. I make Horror Movie Girl proud.

Another half second, and there are eight still bat bodies littering the shady, green lawn. My ears ring from the intensity of my own scream. I fight the urge to stand dumbstruck trying to process all that's happened in less than twenty seconds. My fight or flight response is still pumping, and I try to steady my breathing.

Rocks is easy to identify as he's the biggest bat at the colony. If there was any doubt, it's cleared up by his red eyebrow ring showing on his batty alter ego. I'm thankful for the physical disfigurements the others have sustained. I gently pick up the one-eyed bat, and the bat with half an ear missing. Rocks, Jeremiah and Bailey are safely in my arms. I step over one of the attacker bats.

The bag.

I can't carry the three of them and the bag with the giant, damn, amethyst geode in it.

Crap.

Worried someone will have heard my blood-curdling scream, I don't want to linger. I take another step in the direction of my car. My stomach churns.

Listen to yourself.

You know what to do.

My gut commands me to stop and not leave these bat bullies vulnerable on the ground. If anything happened to them, their blood would literally be on my hands—or vocal cords. The last thing Rocks and I need is more trouble with the colony.

Knowing it's only Ash and his crew, I'm sure he doesn't have the stomach for actual murder. Rocks was right in calling him a coward. That's not to say he wouldn't harm Rocks, but he would probably let one of the others deliver the killing blow if Ash was serious about killing him.

I stomp my foot, but the action is futile on the soft grass. I want to have a moment of tantrum for consciously deciding to help these would-be-killer Camazotz. They wouldn't help Rocks if their lives depended on it.

But Rocks would never hurt his fellow colony members. He would never turn his back on them no matter what they do and say to him. His heart has always been with doing right by his colony. Rocks knows I won't abandon them.

"Fucking hell!" I scream up into the trees. I put the three bats who deserve my help down, careful not to hurt their wings and pull out my cell. I scroll the numbers I gave the colony after the Duskwing were bat-napped.

"Please may an aeronaught friendly person answer."

The call rings so long, I'm sure it will go to voice mail. Instead it ends. I hit the number again and pray silently. I know I only ever answer calls from numbers I recognize. I hope the colony phones haven't yet been spammed by automated voice calls. "Answer, please."

"Yes?" a deep, familiar voice crackles down the line.

"Judge, it's Connie. I really, really need your help!"

I'M SPEEDING DOWN the interstate headed for Atlanta when Rocks regains consciousness.

Pull over.

Please.

The second we stop, he flips and is sitting in the passenger seat—human again.

I wonder when the last time I will see him flip will be. I'll miss it.

"Thank you, Beans. Are they safe?" He reaches over and kisses me.

"Yep, I rang Judge. He came with Zander in the old van and took them all back to the market. I didn't want to help Ash and those murderous creeps, but I knew you wouldn't leave them knocked out on the ground."

"I love you so much. Thank you. You did the right thing."

"But how did they know you were there?" As I ask, Rocks is pulling out his phone and typing a text. "To Jez?"

"Yep. It was probably Bailey. She has a bad habit of talking to her dragon when she's about to do something wrong. She probably told dragon she was coming to see me and it got back to Ash. The colony has almost imploded on itself. Members are eavesdropping on others and reporting it to those who might want to know to gain favor. It's not how it should be."

"Will Jez be in trouble? Like will Ash report him to the Sire for seeing you?"

Rocks shrugs. "Technically, I do forfeit my life if I re-enter the colony after banishment—without an invitation. But it's got to go before the Sire. He's the only member who can issue a death sentence. But their vigilante posse is also outlawed. They were taking the Sire's power into their own hands."

"So they won't want Jeremiah telling the Sire what they were about to do either?"

He nods, studying his phone. "Jez said he's staying with Zander tonight with Bailey. Just in case anything goes bad."

"Shit. That's messed up!"

"What's messed up is we only have three nights to find the bloodroot. It's out of Shadows' territory, so I don't really know the area Sylvana is talking about. I hope the Fall Creek Falls are easy to find."

"I know you're anxious to get home, but while we're stopped, can we please eat the lunch Mom made? I don't want to lie about our picnic."

"Excellent. I'm famished. It must be being in bat form and unconscious, my metabolism goes crazy."

The idea that Rocks might have to watch his weight after the fix totally blows my mind. Maybe I should give him a Human Problems 101 course.

LYING ON MY bed, I stare at the open window. It's early evening and I know Rocks won't be flying through it any time soon. I try not to picture the vicious knives those jerks threatened us with. What if Rocks is caught alone? I sigh and push the pounding questions from my mind.

I focus on the plans that need tightening and go over them again and again until they're solid.

At two a.m., I finally give up and turn my light out. He's still out there. We used Google maps to locate the falls. It turns out there is a Fall Creek Falls in Georgia, Tennessee, Idaho, and Oregon. I now know explorers are lazy and unoriginal when it comes to naming places. I mean Fall Creek Falls is like a super obvious name—falls that fall. Wow, that's genius, and yet there are at least three other falls with the same name.

Since Alex told us it was off I-575, we know it's the falls in Georgia. We had calculated how long it would take Rocks to fly there and back. If he was successful at finding the sanguinaria, he'd be back by now. But there's nothing I can do. I'm exhausted from my hectic night.

Our next three days are going to be busy, but it all hangs on Rocks finding the bloodroot. I'm all set, packed and ready for our trip. I have a perfectly plausible lie to spin Kelly and Chad in the morning.

Lying to them again is purely out of necessity. It doesn't make me proud. It doesn't make me happy, but it is essential. Explaining Rocks is taking part in an ancient shape-shifter reversal spell so won't fly with them. Plus, who knows what the colony would do to me and Rocks if they found out we let my folks in on the colony secret.

I run my fingers through my long, wet hair. It feels the same at least, and the familiar gesture calms me. I imagine this is how a racehorse feels standing at the gates. It's excited, yet tense, and the outcome is definitely unknown. There's danger if the horse falls—it could be fatal. But success and celebration could also be moments away.

My feelings on Rocks doing this are so mixed. He originally said he was simply finding out if it were possible. Now it feels like nothing will change his mind from going through with it the way he talks. I think back to my shit with Enzo. Nothing would change my mind. I was gonna work for him until I retired if it meant keeping Mini safe and alive. I can't blame Rocks for wanting to belong and have answers too.

Tomorrow, Rocks needs to finish carving the dagger. Then we can soak it in white sage oil tomorrow night, which will give it enough time to dry before we leave.

Friday, my focus will be to get Rocks to carb load. Who knows how much energy this magic will drain from him. With his already super high, batty metabolism, I don't want to risk him being weak. He's gonna eat until he can't swallow another mouthful. When he broke his arm, he nearly died from loss of energy—not the actual bone break. We learned a great deal from that injury.

Trying to think of reasons why someone might not survive this spell is hurting my brain. I shake my head at the insanity of trying to guess the outcome of something I don't actually think exists. But my doubt always returns to the mystery and wonder of Rocks flipping and flying off. He is a magical shape-shifter. I have seen it plenty of times, so how can I still not believe?

I hope he won't need to continue his search on Friday night. I want him here and not burning up the precious carbs he will have eaten all day. I will myself to close my eyes and stop staring at the open window. All I want is for him to fly in and say he's found the meeting place. A tiny breeze shifts my lace curtains. I adjust the towel on my pillow for my wet hair and try to relax listening to the muted sounds of the night.

I TEXT ROCKS eight times throughout the morning. I'm pacing my room, willing him to wake up and come find me. With the big days he has ahead of him, I want him to get as much rest as possible. I don't want to knock on his door in case it wakes him up. Once he's awake though, I know he'll look at his phone immediately. I'm desperate to know how his search went last night. Each time I walk past the mirror, my reflection startles me. I should have gone to bed earlier, but my brain wouldn't shut down. At least, I have our plan all set.

Dad is at work, and Mom and Mini had left by the time I woke. I'm so grateful because I want to see Rocks first. Opening my backpack, I check our supplies for the third time. Unsure as to whether getting fixed will be painful or not, I have half the medicine cabinet. My brain is sifting through all the worst-case scenarios from supernatural or magical books.

What if he's stuck half-bat, half-man? Like a man with wings and fangs, but human in every other aspect. What if he gets stuck forever as a bat by mistake? I reach for my inhaler and take a puff. What if the magic wipes his memory clean—like a re-birth—and he doesn't have a freaking clue who I am? I take a second puff.

In my moments of near panic, I missed Rocks walking down the hall. The water pipes are humming, so the cheeky bat is in the shower. My phone screen illuminates with messages, but I forgot it was on silent.

I'm awake, but stink. Long flight.

Quick shower first, then we'll talk.

The shower smells of a weird chemical.

P.S. I found the bloodroot.

His fourth text makes me want to dance and vomit at the same time. In two days time, the spell is happening.

I race to the mirror and check my reflection again. I pull out my high ponytail and let my silky hair fall over my shoulders. I pull it all over one shoulder. Then I tie it back up again.

Stay calm.

The bathroom door opens and I wait for him. Rocks walks in, still drying his own wet hair, and stops dead. His eyes widen before scanning me up and down, and back up again.

"Connie, what the fuck have you done?"

17
Surprise.

"**D**O you like it?" I ask, praying the answer is yes. I'm still undecided. It's such a shock to look in the mirror.

He comes to my side. "It's... it's..." He runs his finger down the length of my midnight black hair. "This explains why the bathroom smells odd, but why?"

"My golden blonde hair is a dead giveaway I'm not a Camazotz. I figured the only way I can help you after the spell is performed is to pass for a Camazotz too."

"You aren't coming with me."

"Oh yes, I am!" I put my hands on my hips.

"It's way too dangerous. I'm not endangering you for something I want to do."

"Rocks, you have been in danger many times because of me, so that argument won't cut it. We are a team. Yes, this will be dangerous, but there is no way on earth you are going to face this alone."

"Helping you was different. I had abilities you didn't, and they were needed to rescue you and Mini. You couldn't hang upside down in the warehouse and videotape Enzo. Could you?"

"Rocks, what if something happens to you? What if you die? How guilty do you feel because Celand tried to get fixed alone? Don't you wonder everyday if things might have gone differently if she had've taken you with her?"

His silence is confirmation. "It's different," he argues.

"No, it's not. I refuse to live with that kind of heartache wondering if I could have saved you. Your wing break already proved my access to medicine can do incredible stuff. And we don't know anything about this mysterious shaman that's going to do magic on you! He or she could be dangerous."

"Exactly! That's why you aren't coming."

"Am too."

"You are not."

I glare. He sighs. "The fact is I don't want you in harm's way. You don't have any of the items we collected for me. What if they ask you where your stones are?"

"I'll tell them I'm not getting fixed, but helping you after it's done."

"No. I'm doing this alone."

"Okay, Mr. Independent Smarty Pants, how do you plan to get back here after the spell is performed and you can't *fly*? Hmmm?"

Rocks looks so shocked it's as though I slapped him. He slumps onto my bed. "You know I hadn't even thought of that."

I sit next to him and take his hand in mine. "If you haven't thought about those kinds of things, are you sure you're ready to give up all your abilities? Like you just said, you were able to help my family last year in ways only a Camazotz could. Are you ready to just be ordinary forever?"

"I don't see it as becoming ordinary, I see it as becoming who I feel I am inside. Yes, there will be an adjustment, but I know this is right for me. I've just never had to think about transportation before."

"Or paying for food I guess. Drinking blood is free."

I give him a moment to process it all. I don't mind how long this takes, because by the time this conversation ends, he will agree I'm coming with him. And that's final.

"You felt left out when I didn't talk to you about college. You said we were a team. You and I have to stop being so independent and start relying on each other. I want to be there with you. I accept the danger because I love you with all I've got."

"You don't fight fair." He smiles and kisses my lips. "It's like I'm making out with a new girlfriend."

I tickle his ribs. "Just so long as I don't remind you of anyone back at the colony."

"Not for a second. You are all you, just more mysterious now. Thank you for thinking this through—your hair, my transportation problem. Thank you. I've been so focused on the list of items and finding those stupid, little, white flowers."

I beam at him. I love helping him instead of causing trouble all the time. At the start when we became friends, I felt like I was one problem after another for Rocks. But lately, my aeronaught-ness is an advantage.

"Remember that Alex said he wished he'd gone with Celand?" I say.

"Yeah, you're right. I wouldn't want you to end up like him."

"Exactly." I smile wide and lean against his strong, hard body.

"Well, if we're doing this together, then you need to follow my lead," he says. "Please do as I say when we meet this shaman. I absolutely won't risk you, so please let me take the lead. But I'm so grateful you will be by my side. I'm starting to feel nervous."

Rocks explains about finding the bloodroot. He says it was a little too easy after he found the falls Sylvana told us about. The more he wonders about why these spellcasters chose to meet here, the more he is calmed by the fact that they aren't close to any one colony. The falls are almost in the middle of the three Camazotz colonies located in Georgia.

"Seeing where it's located makes me think of Celand out night after night a long way from the colony searching alone. I find it hard to believe she ever found it."

"Why?"

"Not that she wasn't a very capable female. I'm not saying that. She was so strong and smart. It just stirs something deep inside in my male instincts and my need to protect her. Then again maybe it's stirring up guilt. She was so far from the roost alone. I would never be happy about Zada, or Graceland flying that far alone. Poor Celand was so isolated. I mean it's no different to how you worry about me when I fly alone over a long distance. I regret not being with her."

"Maybe Sylvana told her about the falls too? Maybe like you, she only had to search a smaller area?"

"God, I hope so. And man, Sylvana could have saved me some massive flying time with that hint from the start. I was flying in circles around the Shadows and risking getting caught by the patrols night after night."

"Do you think it's odd she helped you? I mean she admitted to helping Celand. And I saw her with little Elm and Oak at the colony whispering to them before they disappeared. It kinda makes sense they went to get fixed too if Cypress loathes the fact they prefer being human. She's always been so nasty to me. I find it hard to believe she could ever be helpful." These thoughts have plagued me from the start.

"I think it's odd she hit us up for the money. If the boys did go in search of the fix, then they certainly didn't have any cash. She's up to something, but she always is," he says.

"I'm glad you found it and won't need to be out alone again."

"Absolutely. The weird part is it's still in bloom. The plant does grow in the shape of a crescent moon, but the white flowers are still blooming. Only a few of them, but they're there, and surrounded by so much rosemary, spring onions, and garlic. It burned my nose it was so strong. Like a small field of them. Had I known, I could have sniffed the spot out."

He shows me the photo. It's dark since it was after midnight, but the flash illuminates three little white flowers. The plants around it are thick and I can make out the distinctive shape of rosemary growing wild.

"Do you think those herbs have magical properties? Maybe it helps the shaman? Or do you think magic is making those few flowers bloom?" I ask.

I can't believe I'm having this conversation, but everything I learned from the Internet says those flowers should be long gone by this time in summer. Maybe I'm finally starting to believe in magic.

"I don't know, but there is definitely something about that place. I tried to pick up any scents, but there was nothing I could smell other than those pungent herbs. The place seemed deserted. I didn't linger. Didn't feel right."

I grab the laptop and ask him to find it on the map. We will need to locate the nearest road where I can leave my car for our return trip. From the amount of green on the map, it will most likely be a fire access road, so nobody will notice if I park my car there for the night.

The satellite view doesn't show the crescent moon garden, but Rocks is ninety-nine percent sure he's pointing to the correct place on the map.

When he's quiet for a moment too long, I look at him. "What?"

He reaches up and touches my hair. It matches his now. We aren't the sun and the moon, day and night. We're the same. "I don't know if I will ever get used to seeing you with black hair. I love your golden, sunny, bright hair."

I swallow. All night I was worried the darkness would make me look anemic or something. Since Rocks and I have been dating, I will admit to wanting to look pretty. Those Camazotz girls are so sensuous it drives me crazy.

"But you are the most incredible girlfriend a guy could ever have. You look sexy in a totally different way. It's hard to describe." Rocks opens his camera and holds his arm out to take a selfie. We smile at each other in our reflection.

The girl sitting next to the hottest guy in the universe so doesn't look like me, but for once the boy and girl match. The darkness, which has always surrounded Rocks, or any Camazotz, definitely isn't because they all have dark hair. I stare at the photo and hope when I get some Camazotz style clothes, I'll blend in a little more.

"What are you going to tell your parents?" he asks.

"I have it all planned out. You'll see, but more importantly, I'm going to need an undercover Camazotz name." The thought of what Rocks is about to go through makes my blood curdle, but getting to pose as Camazotz is a tiny ray of sunshine on a cloudy day. "And I'm going shopping this afternoon with Tiff to buy an outfit. She's into bodice-rippers, so she'll know exactly what I need."

"Do I want to know what a bodice-ripper is?"

"No, you don't. Let's go eat. I'm going to be feeding you up from now until we leave Saturday morning."

AFTER MY TRIP to the mall with Tiff, Rocks and I stay upstairs until Mom calls us down for dinner. The folks got home an hour ago and neither of them has seen my new look. Rocks has been busy working on his wooden dagger, and it now has a needle-tipped point on the end. I'm suddenly nervous to show my parents my home dye job. Tiff started squealing when she realized it was me. She has dyed her hair a number of times and thinks I look cool. Her suggestion was a little more eyeliner until I get used to it.

Rocks leads the way into the kitchen. Mom is slicing a loaf of bread, and I can hear Dad at the table trying to wrangle Mini into her seat. She loves the freedom of no longer being trapped in a high chair.

My jet-black locks are pulled into my signature high pony, and I will admit I selected the white t-shirt to lessen the 'Camazotz effect.'

"Ta-da! What do you think?" I announce, holding my arms out wide.

Mom's facial expression can only be described as utter shock horror, and Dad drops the glass he was holding, which smashes on the tiles, sending glass shards skittering everywhere.

"Oh, sh— I mean, whoopsy." He picks Mini up before her tiny feet become glass magnets.

"Whoop-seeeeee," she mimics loudly. "Whoop-seeeee."

I race to help him and hold my arms out to Mini. "Come here, you. Let Daddy get the broom." Mini's eyes mirror Mom's in how wide they expand, and she shies away from me, burrowing into Dad's neck. "Mini, it's me, Connie."

Her little features crinkle into the cutest Mini frown ever, as she peaks out at me from the safety of Dad's neck. The voice she's hearing sounds like Connie, but the girl trying to touch her doesn't look right. Rocks swoops in, and in her usual Mini baby-crush way, she flings herself into his arms. Little traitor.

Rocks shifts to the side talking softly about my new hair color, telling her it really is her big sister. Dad is a statue, staring at me at close range. "Did you get a tattoo as well?" he asks.

"No, Dad! I just changed my hair." A deaf man would hear the annoyance in my tone, and it snaps my Dad into action cleaning the glass.

"Sorry, I just thought..." His eyes shift to Rocks and back again.

Just thought... I want to ask. I know it appears I'm turning into my boyfriend, but it kinda hurts they assume that's what I'm doing.

I know they have absolutely no other reason for my recent cloning, but still.

"I'm simply trying a new look. It probably won't last. I thought I'd give it a go to celebrate the end of high school. Relax, both of you."

The kitchen returns to pre-dinner action, with all of us pitching in. When we take our seats around the table, Mom finally speaks.

"It does suit you, sweetheart. It was only a shock because you never said anything about doing it, but you look lovely."

Dad's eyes keep darting from Rocks to me and back again every time I look at him. I don't want to know what his gray matter is trying to process.

"I know you guys have been worried I haven't chosen a college yet, so Rocks and I are going on a little road trip this weekend to visit a few. Is that okay?"

It seems I'm batting two for two in silencing my folks tonight.

"Ah…" Dad manages, while Mom sits holding a forkful of food an inch from her open mouth.

"Are you two okay?"

They both blink and conversation resumes. The usual questions of where to, how long, and where are you staying, I have pre-practiced lies to deliver. These are what I now term 'essential lies.' They are essential to protect Rocks' secret, so I don't feel quite so bad.

Last year when I was studying my parent's facial expressions to detect if they were lying to me about my adoption, I learned a lot. Dad's face tonight shows signs he knows Rocks and I are sleeping together. I could be wrong, but there was something different about the way he was looking at us, and it has nothing to do with my new hair. Plus, the repeated 'please be *careful*,' I suspect has a second meaning.

I don't commit to an exact return date, since I'm concerned Rocks might need some recovery time. They make me promise to give them daily updates of our whereabouts, and Rocks assures them he'll keep me safe.

SATURDAY MORNING, WE'RE on the interstate by ten.

"Remind me again why we're leaving this early?" Rocks smirks from the passenger seat.

He's surprisingly relaxed considering what's happening tonight, but he knows perfectly well why we left now, because we have been over, and over, and over our plan, until I'm sure I'll remember it when I'm ninety.

What he wants is for me to say it out loud.

I grin back at him, biting my bottom lip. "Because your sexy, dark-haired girlfriend wants to spend the day with you in bed at a hotel. Preferably with no clothes on." I feel my ears burn.

Rocks had calculated the moon won't be overhead tonight until after two a.m.. To combat both of our nerves at what Rocks is about to face, I thought some alone time was in order. I want to be as physically close as possible to Rocks on the last day he's a Camazotz.

Rocks beams, winding down the window. It blows the hair back off his face, and I wish I didn't have an hour's drive north to the town of Jasper ahead of me. My need to look at him and touch him worries me. I hope my gut is simply overreacting.

"You're confident you can find it at night on foot?"

"Yep, I flew low back and forth from the falls twice, so I would be able to locate it again. I decided I wasn't going to flip or use my Camazotz senses for any part of the journey. Since I want to be an aeronaught, I figured I should only use aeronaught abilities from now on."

"I can't believe what you are about to give up. *Flying.* I imagine it's the best kind of fun. I understand why. I just don't think I would give up flying if I could. Even your eyesight makes me jealous."

He rests his hand on my knee, and we drive the rest of the way in silence.

The hotel is clean, but nothing special. We didn't have a great deal to choose from in the area at such short notice. From the hotel to the campground—where I'm planning to leave my car—it's only a twenty-five minute drive. We then have a short hike to Fall Creek Falls before searching for the crescent moon sanguinaria. That gives us until one a.m. to hang out together.

"Have you thought of your Camazotz code name?" Rocks asks, when we drive past a sign post informing us we have entered the Jasper city limits.

"I've thought of nothing else! I love the wing naming conventions. Since we don't know who these shaman, or witches, or whoever are, I thought it best to use something from the Shadows colony. They might know enough about each colony to know if it's a true Camazotz name or not. I want to be called Little Fox."

"But that's—"

"I know," I say, cutting him off. "I know I'm using the Little wing and the Fox wing. I also thought it was a bit of a test. If they know the Shadows really closely, they'll question me about it."

"Mmmm... good thinking. I like it, Little Fox."

"Plus I was able to get a fox head fake tattoo. I had to try to make my tattoos look as colony-like as possible."

The hotel has a small, outdoor swimming pool—another first for my Victorian-era boyfriend.

I 'borrowed' a pair of Dad's board shorts for Rocks—the ones from three years ago, he won't admit don't fit him. I watch Rocks' nose twitch when we sit on the reclining pool chairs. Even I can smell the chlorine, so I can't imagine what it's doing to the senses he's trying so hard not to use.

Taking the lead, I pull off my sundress. My black bikini actually suits my new, dark hair. Bending over, I spread my towel out before standing tall in front of him. I let him look at me. It's a new body bravery I have only acquired since we had sex. Rocks has never ever lied to me, so when he says he adores my body, I believe him. And besides, he picked me. He's with me, and has always risked so much to do it.

His eyes linger on my breasts, my bare belly, and finally my hips, before making a slow circuit back up again. I'm grinning by the time he meets my stare. "Your turn." I stretch out on the chaise recliner.

When Rocks pulls his shirt off and displays his hard, muscled chest and those incredible arm tattoos, it literally takes my breath away. I giggle when I realize it's the first time I've ever seen his legs bare in public. He never wears shorts. His calf muscles are sleek and toned like every other inch of him. Flying is clearly an all body, incredible workout. He slides on his dark sunglasses and rests both hands on his hips.

He's letting me enjoy his divine body. I bite my bottom lip, sighing. He's a god, and I'm a mere mortal.

"Come enjoy a little sun first," I invite, patting the lounge chair next to mine. Rocks stretches out, holding his wrists above his head. I can't look away—his triceps, biceps and shoulders are so perfect, it's as though he's been drawn. I want to reach across and trace the lines of muscle. His skin is absolutely flawless in the bright sunshine. I notice three girls across the pool ogling him. I stick my chest out a little further and revel in the feeling of being his girl.

Twenty minutes later, he can't wait to try the pool. "I love seeing the blue dots of pools from the air. They're so clean and clear. Lake or stream water doesn't look like this."

I have learned that all the Camazotz are taught to swim once they can flip into their human form. It's an emergency precaution in case they ever take a nosedive into a body of water, and the shock forces them to flip. Bats can naturally swim. Sometimes if a Camazotz is very panicked or stressed—like Bailey was recently when she accused the Fold of banishing Rocks incorrectly—it's impossible for them to flip into their bat form. So to make sure nobody drowns, it's swim lessons for every pup.

"Coming in?" He raises an eyebrow and grins.

"I wouldn't miss this for the world."

The water is cool against my warm flesh, but not so cold it's uncomfortable. The oglers have stopped mid-conversation to watch Rocks stride to the deep end and dive right in. He glides under the water and comes up near me but dives back under.

He glides around like a shark. How can he be so good at everything? Rocks surfaces behind me and tickles me under water. I squeal and try to get away, but the resistance from the water isn't helping. He stops his pursuit to float on the water. I join him, and we float together, looking up at the radiant, blue sky. No clouds will help tonight as we wait for the moon to rise fully. I reach over and pinch his butt under the water.

Caught off guard by my boldness, he sits up fast, spluttering. His eyes narrow before he sinks under the water like a silent predator, and I immediately wish I hadn't provoked him. He swims towards the deeper water. I stay safe in the shallow end, but know he'll be back. When he surfaces, he's watching me.

Rocks takes a deep breath, and I know he's coming. I make a move toward the corner stairs, but his fingers wrap around my ankles before I get there.

I squeal on instinct before he pulls me under. A second later, his arms have pulled me to his chest, and we surface together, smiling.

I wrap my legs around his waist, pulling his body flush with mine. He drags me to the deeper water, and I cling to him tightly. His eyes darken and his hands cup my butt. I flinch expecting him to pinch me in retaliation. He smiles wider and shakes his head.

"I won't do that, but I will do this." Both hands travel smoothly up and down my bare back. His touch sends a shiver through my whole body.

Next his fingers slowly slither inside my bikini bottoms to caress my bare cheek flesh. He pulls me even closer against him.

Cradling my head on his shoulder, I snuggle in underneath his chin, savoring the feel of his touch.

I listen to his steady, strong heartbeat, and the evenness of his breathing. I'm so scared about what awaits him in twelve hours. To distract myself from the rising panic, I sit up straight, grip the back of his neck and pull his mouth to mine. Rocks responds to my need and kisses me deeply.

I don't care that we're putting on a show for the other pool goers. I want him. I need him. The feel of his hard, hot body against mine in the cool water is sending my system into overload. I instinctively pull his body closer between my legs, making Rocks groan. I need some friction.

We break apart, and the look in his midnight blue eyes tells me he feels it too. He strides through the water carrying me to the stairs. Our swim time is clearly over. I expect him to let me go when we reach the stairs, but he continues holding me to him. I grip him tighter as he exits the pool still holding me cradled against his chest.

The girls on the other side of the pool are staring open-mouthed. I'm sure they're jealous I'm the one wrapped around this gorgeous man. I giggle.

"You better not drop me."

"Never. I've got you. Now and forever."

I kiss him again, as we stand dripping on the warm pavers near our lounges.

I don't remember getting back to the room, but I'll never forget him stripping me of my little black bikini. I've never felt sexier in my whole life. Rocks and I christen both queen beds and the shower. God, he's strong. He can hold me like I never knew was possible.

After round three, we drift off into a deep sleep, wrapped around each other. I wake just before my eight p.m. alarm was set to sound. Rocks is facing me but still sleeping soundly. I reach for my phone and cancel the alarm.

Taking a moment, I study him. His jet-black hair has a depth to it my dyed version doesn't. I place a lock of my hair across his and the color difference is noticeable. I pray those we meet later won't call me on being a fake.

Sliding out of bed, trying not to wake him, I take another shower. I want him to be as well-rested as possible for whatever awaits. My Camazotz outfit is harder than I expected to put on by myself. I have a low cut lace-up bodice in silver grey. It has embroidery in shiny black thread along the edges and highlighting the chest-constricting, vertical bones in the corset. I'll never get this thing tied alone.

Leaving my corset half done up, I pull on the long, black skirt. Tiff knew exactly where to find it. She had seen the Camazotz *biatches* visit the Bun Lovin' Barn enough times to know what sort of clothing I needed. I extend my leg and watch as the thigh-high split falls open revealing my whole leg. I leave my hair down and work on dark eyeliner to complete my look. A tiny hint of pale shimmering lip-gloss and I stare at myself in the mirror, pleased with the sexy Camazotz girl looking back at me.

A movement in the mirror makes me jump. Rocks is standing in the doorway watching. Sneaky bat. He closes the space between us in an instant, and has me sitting on the counter before I can even register what he's doing. He takes my face in his hands and kisses me like we're back in the pool.

Fire burns inside me as he pushes my legs apart.

"We don't have time," I gasp. He clearly approves of my Camazotz disguise.

"Yes, we do."

18
Brotherhood

WE sit in on the same side of the booth at the pizza restaurant. Rocks' fingers never leave me. He's touching me constantly, and I appreciate the closeness. I don't want to ask if he's as scared about later as I am.

I let Rocks choose what he felt like for dinner. Unsure of what will happen to him during this spell, I didn't want to select a meal which might upset his stomach.

His fingers caress the skin of my neck, pushing back my long hair. He smiles as he stares at his handiwork. A Camazotz costume wouldn't be complete without fake tattoos. Rocks insisted if I was going to pull off this madness, then I needed ink. Since I didn't want to live up to Dad's stereotype of a boy-obsessed girl, I'm adorned with the temporary artwork he applied.

My neck has a beautiful black and white fox head. It starts at my collarbone and finishes below my jawbone. If it were real, I'd be proud as hell because it's so beautiful. It looks as though someone used a fine pencil to sketch it across my skin. Rocks put it on my neck to match his cousin's fox head tattoo. It might help with my authenticity.

I lean in close to him. "Do you think you should stop at a farm for a quick sip?"

He looks down and smiles. "I don't know."

"I think it's best to be on the safe side. Blood was what saved you when you broke your arm. Maybe you should have some to be on the safe side. It's been a while, right?"

"Yes." His fingers love the thigh high split of my skirt. He pushes it aside slightly and runs his fingers over my other 'ink.' A full moon with a dozen bats flying in front of it adorns my thigh. When I look up, I catch him looking down my corset. "God, you look edible in this. I never thought you dressed as a Camazotz would turn me on the way it has. Incredible."

My ears burn, but for once I love the feeling.

"Stop changing the subject." The pizza arrives and he dives in, completely filling his mouth, so he can't talk. I give him the evil eye. "You'll have to swallow eventually, and then you can answer me. Or better yet. I've decided we *are* stopping for you to have your last drink. I'm not taking any chances."

I watch his throat bob as he swallows and then washes the pizza down with soda. "You might be right. Let's not risk it. But, no pigs. Sheep or cattle only."

WAITING ON A dark country road, while Rocks is off doing his last vampire bat meal is a little creepy. I feel as though I'm being watched, but it's probably the herd of cows in the adjoining field. My shoulders ache and won't relax, even after I roll them repeatedly.

He flies in the open passenger window, and my heart skips a beat. Screaming would be very, very bad. He lands on the seat and looks up at me—those intelligent eyes behind the bat face. I reach over and gently stroke the soft fur on his head.

I'm ready.

This will probably be the last time I see his bat alter ego. Sadness fills my chest, but I smile at him. "I'm going to miss this cute little guy," I say, stroking between his ears. Pulling my arm back, I give him all the room to flip.

"Me too," he says, grabbing his seatbelt.

"Rocks?"

"What?"

"You don't have to do this. We can make it work. I love you just the way you are—bat and all. I'm scared. Please. You don't have to do this."

"It's going to be okay, Little Fox." He pulls me against his chest, and I cling to him for dear life. "Shhh, it will be fine. I've got you on my wing. I've got all your technology, which Celand never had. I trust you."

"But—"

"Do you really mean that? That you would love me forever like this?"

I pull back, stunned he doesn't already know. "Oh my God, of course! You are incredible—every single part of you. You have to know that. God, Rocks. Do you still think I don't like the bat in you?"

"Not exactly, but I thought you were more tolerating it because you had no choice."

"No! I don't want you to do this. I don't want you to risk your life. I love you exactly how you are right this minute."

He wraps me in the tightest hug ever. The smell of him fills my nostrils, and I pray he will smell as good afterward—still reminding me of a moonlit, forest night.

He whispers against my neck, "Thank you, baby. Thank you for truly accepting me."

"So we're going home?"

"No chance. We're so close to getting some answers. I have to find out what really happened to Celand. But I promise you this. If I feel it's a really bad idea to continue after we meet the shaman, I'll call it off."

THE CAMPGROUND IS busy. I'm glad because my car should go unnoticed for the night. Sylvana gave us no indication of how long the transformation will take, so we're guessing it could be up to twenty-four hours. I check the doors are locked for the second time. Not that there's anything of value inside, I simply don't want to come back to find the car gone. We might need it to get Rocks to an emergency room fast.

The moon is low in the sky when we find the trail. Rocks takes my hand and leads the way. I tell him he's using his Camazotz gifted eyesight whether he wants to or not. He guides me around obstacles I would have tripped over for sure.

My fitness isn't really put to the test with the hike. It's short and easy. I smile when I hear the rushing water from the falls in the distance. It's sometimes nice not to depend on my sight. The cool, pine scented air is the perfect temperature for a late night forest walk.

"We don't need to go past the falls. Is that okay? Or do you want to see them?" Rocks asks.

"No, just get us to the sanguinaria."

We continue on in silence. Rocks is carrying all his items in his backpack, while mine is full of emergency supplies. Having no clue what sort of medical kit a witch would carry, I've got a little of everything.

A large owl hoots and takes flight from the tree on our right. Its silver white feathers reflect what little moonlight filters down through the trees. I nearly jumped out of my skin, but Rocks chuckles.

"You knew it was there, didn't you?" I look around at all the trees close to us, scanning for more potential heart attacks.

"Sorry. I forgot to warn you. It was a barn owl. I'll be glad to never be afraid of owls again. That's for sure."

We walk deeper into the forest. Rocks halts to listen and sniffs the air. I want to ask what's wrong but don't want to risk speaking. We stand in silence for a moment. Nothing but the sounds of a forest at midnight fills my ears.

"Thought I heard a vehicle," he says quietly, before setting off again.

We enter a thick patch of dense pine trees. I can't hold Rocks' hand and maneuver around them at the same time. My backpack catches on the low branches, and in places we have to almost crawl to escape the clinging branches. But Rocks never slows. I scramble along close behind.

As the trees lessen, I take his hand once more, and then I can smell it—the rosemary he described. A few more paces and the space opens up entirely to a small meadow and shining brightly in the moonlight is the barely blooming bloodroot.

"Will you look at that!"

We stand together—still using the cover of the tree line—staring at the crescent moon shaped growth. We made good time, as the moon isn't fully overhead.

"Can you sense anyone?" I whisper.

"No, go have a closer look."

Stepping out of the protection of the trees has me scanning all around—left, right, above, behind. Creeping toward the plants, my nose fills with each distinctive scent. I walk in a circle around the weird sanguinaria and thick herb garden encompassing it. Rocks is right about it feeling odd. The hairs on my arms stand on end. I don't waste time in the open and return to his side. We take a seat, leaning against a large trunk, both fixated on the moon slowly making it's way overhead.

Our fingers entwine, and I rest my head on his shoulder, listening for sounds on the gentle breeze.

"Someone's coming from the west," Rocks whispers into my ear.

I remain completely still listening, but my ears don't have the skills of a Camazotz. I close my eyes, willing my ears to pick up the sounds. Then I hear it—someone is coming. One, two, three, no five hooded figures walk to the sanguinaria and stand in formation.

Their cloaks are gray and must have weight to them. When the center member raises his arms to the moon, the long fabric isn't bothered by the gentle breeze. Strange, soft chanting floats over to us as multiple voices are repeating things I cannot decipher. As one, they howl at the moon—like Sylvana does—and I flinch against the unexpected sound.

The center figure speaks, "Come forward those seeking our magical assistance. Come forward. We sense your presence." His hands rest as though in prayer in the center of his chest.

Rocks and I glance at each other. It's now or never.

Rocks helps me up and together we step out from under the great tree sheltering us. We stand silent in front of the five figures.

"You are?" the males voice asks.

"I am Rockland, and this is Little Fox of the Shadows colony. We were told you could help us."

"Indeed. Greetings, Shadows' members. It is an honor. Not many from your colony ever seek our help."

The other four make their way around us. Suddenly, we are surrounded, and I don't like it.

"Who are you?" Rocks asks.

"We are the Brotherhood of the Blood Night. Most who seek us are after the fixation spell. Is that what you desire?"

"Yes. I wish to be human forever."

I flinch at his words. I don't like these dudes. I want to see their faces, instead of a dark shadow where their face should be. I want names and driver's license numbers before I even contemplate trusting them.

"You have come to the right place. Follow me." The main figure starts walking in the direction from which they all came. We don't follow.

"You won't perform it here?" Rocks asks. We hadn't planned on being taken anywhere.

"By the bat within, no! We must journey to our sacred cave. There you will take part in the rituals. As it may weaken you for days, you will need protection."

Days?

What the?

He said days! This is going to take days. Thank heavens I didn't give my folks a definite return date.

"It is preferable for travel if you flip." He holds out a canvas bag. "I will carry you to conserve your energy."

Oh, shit.

Rocks gives my hand a squeeze. "I vowed I would never take *that* form again. I would prefer to go on foot since it is my desire to never fly again," he says, giving me a good cover.

A voice behind speaks, "We would prefer it if you flip. We risk ourselves coming here and don't need any added worries of missing persons. Now flip."

"No."

"Flip!"

Modern day shaman are rude. Maybe it's all those years of persecution they can't move past. But if these dudes can really do magic, they need to cut the attitude.

"We will never take that form again!" Rocks growls back. "If you can't help us, we will leave."

"No, no, it's fine," the leader says. "It's a short walk. You will need to keep up." He sets off at a fast pace. I'm painfully aware my eyesight could let my cover be blown. Rocks takes my hand again, but we're moving at a much faster rate. I try to stay calm and I scan the forest floor for obstacles.

The leader takes us to a worn, dirt path, and the going is much easier. I wonder if it's a hiking trail and wished I'd studied the local maps better. I also wish my phone wasn't switched off and hidden in my backpack. We didn't want to risk having aeronaught technology, but at the same time, I want to be able to dial the paramedics if Rocks needs it. I don't like that we're changing location.

Rocks cut a slit in my backpack lining and we hid our phones inside. Some black electrical tape sealed them in safely. To make my new pack look worn and torn, we added a few external pieces of electrical tape as a quick patch mend.

The path starts to head downhill and over the next rise, Rocks tugs on my hand. Parked up ahead is a black van. I wouldn't have noticed it on a dark night in the forest, until Rocks drew my attention to it. Not what I was expecting at all.

A chill runs up my spine as I try to turn and look at our hooded companions. Everything about them is identical, giving no clues to their identity.

The leader stops at the van.

"Are we going in this?" Rocks asks. "Where to?"

"Our sacred cave location must never be revealed. You will travel in the back for our protection more than yours."

I notice it's the kind of delivery van with no windows. *Awesome.*

He opens up the van doors, and Rocks immediately takes a step backward. "Actually, we've changed our minds. Sorry." He pulls me with him and turns to face the four others. Their body language mirrors a solid wall of muscle.

"You aren't going anywhere, except with us. Get in!" one growls back. I don't know why Rocks is reacting this way. I can't see anything in the empty van, which might signal danger.

"No!" Rocks tucks me in behind his body. His stance changes. He straightens to his full height, and when I see his clenched fists at his side, I suddenly need more oxygen.

"We can do this the easy way, or the hard way, but you're coming with us."

Before Rocks has a chance to respond, I feel cold steel at my throat. I gasp, shocked at the kiss of hard metal on my skin.

I'm yanked back away from him and into the hard chest of the leader. "You will do as I say, or she will bleed to death right here."

"Fuck," Rocks mutters.

They push him around to the side of the van and tie his hands behind his back. None of them speak to issue orders, so this was all premeditated.

"Let me go, you bastard!" I yell, knowing nobody will hear me, but not wanting to comply without trying to free myself.

The knife blade presses harder into my flesh. I fight the instinctive urge to swallow because I'm sure the movement will draw blood.

A hooded male comes over and pulls my hands behind my back and ties them. Rocks is turned back to face me, and I want to cower in fear when I see the look of despair on his face. What on earth changed his mind about this, I wonder?

Hoods are placed over our heads, and we're shoved into the van. My chest constricts as the memory of being hooded and thrown into a van rushes through my veins. I drag air into my lungs through my mouth, praying I don't have a panic asthma attack.

"Stay calm, baby. Relax. I'm here," he whispers. I feel Rocks moving around and soon his head bumps into mine. "Sorry. Just breathe, baby. Breathe."

I focus on his voice—his calm, soothing deep voice. I am not alone. This isn't like last time. We will survive, I chant over and over.

The momentum of the van surging forward, rolls me into Rocks. "Sorry." I wonder where the others went. These vans usually only take two passengers, three at most, but there were five of them.

"Can you smell it?" Rocks whispers.

"No. Smell what?" I ask, blinking blindly behind my hood. I can't see a damn thing. I should be more used to not relying on my sight by now. But the panic bubbles up inside of me. I breathe in through my nose, analyzing the air, but smell only the dust on my hood.

"Cocaine."

"What?" I whisper yell. My heart beat thunders in my ears. My neck feels tight from the amount of blood rushing through my veins. I wheeze.

"Relax, baby. Stay calm," he coos.

"Are you sure?"

"I'll never forget that stench."

"Shit," I whisper. "Who are these people?"

The difference between now and the last time I was kidnapped is that Rocks is by my side. We're in this together. As scared as I am about who these crazy people are and where they're taking us, I'm so glad he wasn't going through this alone. I'm glad I'm here with him.

We drive for what feels like an age. We must be on an interstate because the sound of the wheels on the asphalt is steady at the same speed. Once again, I have no clue what direction we are heading.

"Do you know which direction?" I ask.

"No. Don't worry though. We'll be fine."

I know he's trying to keep me positive, and that's better than the alternative of having a panic attack and needing my inhaler. My backpack is still on my shoulders, but I'm not sure Rocks would be able to access my inhaler buried with all the other supplies.

The van slows and must pull off the highway. We slide toward the driver and then back toward the door of the van over and over again. I imagine we're in the backstreets of a city or town driving from one stop sign to the next. That's the type of rhythm to our ride now. Not the smooth continuous whirring of the highway. I start counting the seconds to gauge how long we drive around. Twenty-five minutes later, the engine is switched off, and we hear each door open and shut.

"I think we're in a city. Not near a cave," I whisper.

"Agreed. I can smell the pollution."

"Atlanta?"

"I think so," he whispers.

Then it occurs to me he's using his Camazotz hearing to try to eavesdrop on whatever those men are saying. It's completely quiet.

"Can you hear anything?"

"No. They went into a building. Let's try to unlock the door."

Rocks and I wiggle around like worms on hot concrete. We bump into each other and the sides of the van, but make little progress. Rocks tells me to keep still and he rolls over the top of me so he's closer to the doors. But before he can roll over again to try to open the door, they open.

"What are you two up too?" the same voice asks. "Move it. We need to make room."

Rocks is shoved against me. I hear the thunk of items being thrown in behind him. The van doors close and off we drive once more.

My noses twitches, and I'm transported back in time.

The stench of cash—lots and lots of cash—fills the air.

"Rocks?" my voice waivers.

"I smell it too. Don't worry."

"Who are these people?"

The smell sends me straight back to my afternoons in Enzo's warehouse. I want to scream and kick and escape.

Fuck!

What if Enzo is behind this?

How did he find us?

Why did I think I was off his radar?

It can't be him. It's impossible. Yet, he knew so much about my life. My stomach is a raging sea, rolling up and down. Maybe giving Enzo Rocks' name for the birth certificate was a really bad idea. I think I'm gonna be sick.

"Baby, listen to me," Rocks whispers. I wonder if he can hear the chaos in my guts. "Calm down. I'm here. Nothing bad will happen to you. I'm here."

"Enzo? Do you... Enzo?" I pant.

"He's in jail."

"So? He has connections, and his connections have connections," I mumble.

"But he doesn't know about my colony—"

"How do you know? He had a Camazotz working for him." My blood pressure must be off the charts.

"Joey—I mean Tronido?" Rocks says. "But that doesn't make sense."

"Oh, shit. You know what does make sense?" I ask.

"What?"

"We've been bat-napped too!"

"Oh, shit!"

19
Tunnels

I couldn't tell you how long we drove around, stopping at places. The back doors would open, and from the sounds and smell of it, either a duffle of cash was loaded into the van, or cocaine. Rocks confirmed he could smell it. However not one single word was spoken at any of the stops. After my time with Enzo, I'd say Rocks and I were passengers on a well-planned, perfectly-timed delivery run.

The van finally speeds up for more than five minutes, and I sense we're back on a highway. The metal flooring digs into my body, and no matter what position I try I can't get comfortable. My shoulders start to throb. I rest my head against Rocks and we both wait.

"GET OUT!" KIDNAPPER dude commands.

My muscles scream in protest of my small movements. Rocks' warm body suddenly disappears. Hands grab my ankles and I'm dragged toward the van doors. I'm pulled this way and that until I'm on my feet.

It must be after sunrise because there's a faint glow through my dark hood. I want to ask so many questions, but I don't want to distract Rocks from the things he can hear which I can't. The binding on my wrists is cut, and once again my shoulders protest at their sudden release. I rub my sore joints.

"This way. Come on."

We're dragged side-by-side up very uneven ground. Even Rocks trips and stumbles. The air is fresh and clean. Forest—I can smell forest. We must be out of the city. I'm having so much trouble walking on the crunchy gravel under foot that I'm half-dragged along by hands digging into my arm muscles. Grunts of annoyance surround us.

"This would've been so much easier if you had've flipped."

"No," Rocks retorts.

"Well, you're gonna be forced to soon."

I try not to panic. If I can't flip, it doesn't matter what color my hair is. I take a calming breath remembering Rocks said a Camazotz can't be forced to flip. God, I hope he's right. The path evens out, but as we continue on, the light fades. Dripping water echoes in the stillness. Cool air kisses the skin left exposed by my corset. Our footsteps have a slight echo with each step. My poor senses are working overtime.

"Stop."

The hoods are yanked off, and I blink because it's crazy dark. I turn around and see a light behind us from the entrance.

"We're in a tunnel?" Rocks asks, confirming for me where we are. "You said we were going to a sacred cave."

"We are. This is the back entrance." The three men chuckle at some unknown joke.

An underground mountain tunnel explains the change in temperature. It's wide and high and old. There are small pools of rancid water here and there. Our backpacks are removed and zipped open on the rough stone floor.

"Where's your phone, Rockland?"

"What?" Rocks replies.

The fact they know Rocks has a phone makes me shiver. The male rummages through his backpack, and they make jokes about the items he prepared. One lifts out the dagger.

"This is pathetic. It wouldn't cut snow." He tosses it back in. "Where is it? Hand it over."

"I don't have it. I gave it to my aeronaught girlfriend. I didn't think an ancient shaman would be happy if I brought modern tech with me."

The man stands and closes in on Rocks. "Body search time." Rocks is pushed against the rock wall as two of them yank and pull at his clothing and pockets.

"You're next."

"But I don't have one of those telephonic things. I want one, but I don't have one. How would I possibly get one?"

I'm shoved against the rough wall as their hands pat down my back. Camazotz girl outfits don't actually have that many hiding places. My backpack is next and when they unzip it, medical supplies spill everywhere. "What the fuck's all this shit?"

"In case we need medicine once we are aeronaughts," I lie. "His girlfriend gave us a bit of everything. She was worried about him. She said it can do magic of its own." I pray they buy my bullshit.

He pulls out handfuls of gauze bandages, aspirin, and rubbing alcohol. He eyes the protein bars, but frowns when he sniffs one.

The male stands and kicks my bag. "You have two seconds to pack that crap, or it stays behind."

Rocks kneels to help me stuff my supplies inside. I feel stupid with the items I chose now. They won't be of any help with our situation. The utility knife hidden with my phone is hardly a weapon.

"You aren't a shaman, are you?" Rocks asks.

The group all snickers but say nothing. We shoulder our backpacks, and they shove us forward toward the endless darkness. I can't risk stumbling and have them catch on that I'm an aeronaught now that the hoods have been removed. My poor heart has been given enough stress tonight, but looking into the cold, dank, stone tunnel, I feel my blood pulsing through my veins again.

Just ahead I spy a dirt hole about two feet wide, which isn't full of glistening, filthy water. I step in and dramatically launch myself onto the ground trying not to actually hurt myself.

"Agh, I'm so tired. Please let me rest."

Rocks is by my side, helping me up. I hope he understands what I'm doing. In a few feet, I won't have any light left from the tunnel entrance behind us.

"She needs food and water. Can we stop? We've been traveling for hours."

"No. You've been lying in the back of a van for hours. Get up."

"At least, let me assist her," Rocks announces.

Bingo!

God, I love how much he thinks about my needs. I can't imagine any of the boys I went to school with caring this much. They would all be shitting their little pants if they were in our shoes.

"Thank you," I gasp, allowing him to help me stand. "That will really help."

My Victorian-era gentleman offers me his elbow, which I attach myself to like Velcro. He has led me successfully through pitch-darkness so many times, I have faith he will do it now. I focus on the cave outside of Helen, and my heart rate returns to normal. He was my eyes that afternoon, and he will be now.

It doesn't take long for the light from the tunnel entrance to peter out altogether. Rocks is literally my rock. He's steady and strong and manages to subtly lead me around ground obstacles without our abductors noticing. When I do happen to stumble, I complain about how tired and weak I feel.

Since none of the men need light to see by in the utter darkness, it's a safe bet they're all Camazotz. I hope they hate aeronaughts enough to not truly comprehend how bad our eyesight is in comparison. That way they shouldn't get suspicious because I'm the only one tripping every so often.

My Camazotz outfit is a curse. The cool, dank air of the tunnel tickles my bare flesh. I wish I had a jacket and jeans. This thigh-high split isn't such a great idea either. I cling closer to Rocks to steal some of his warmth. At least, I can say it's been 'a while' since I drank blood—no lie—to explain why I'm so cold if they get suspicious.

The tunnel feels large. I try futilely to look up and see the ceiling. No chance.

Rocks leans over and says quietly, "Might have been a train tunnel back in the day."

"Shut it, Rockland. Keep walking," someone commands.

He stops. I jerk to a halt beside him, surprised he's not obeying their orders. "Will you allow me to carry her through the water?" he asks, turning behind us.

"What-the-fuck-ever. Just move it."

"My boots won't get ruined wading through ankle deep water, but your shoes..." he kindly explains. I blink at the blackness before me, willing myself to make out water. Nothing.

Stepping into stagnate water would have freaked me right out. And I bet it's super cold, and absolutely filthy! He moves his backpack to the front and bends down. I have to hitch my skirt way higher than I would like to in front of these staring freaks, but the alternative is worse. I do my best koala impression and cling to him for dear life. Resting my ear against his shoulder, I close my eyes, listening to the sloshing footfalls in the puddle, and trying to forget about the amount of leg I'm showing.

Where the hell are we being taken?

Rocks has passed through the water, but he keeps me on his back as we continue deeper into the tunnel. He walks and walks and walks.

"Stop."

I look around helplessly, cursing my reliance on my eyesight. More darkness. I squeeze his shoulders, hoping he'll describe anything he sees. He moves his arms from behind my knees, so I can slide off his back.

"Now you're really gonna want to flip. The next part is messy otherwise."

Rocks growls, "I realize you probably aren't the powerful shamans we were seeking, but what you don't understand is I'm never flipping on command again. *Never.* We can wait here another twenty-four hours for our forced flip, or we travel on foot," Rocks says. His tone is full of power.

I've never before compared Rocks and Strickland, but in the dark I hear his Sire's power. Strickland just uses way less words and glares more. But that born leader is deep within Rockland whether he can see it, or not.

"Did you hear that, boys? He's never being forced to flip again." They all laugh and it echoes down the tunnel. "You're so wrong about that, but you'll work it out. Sooner or later you might have to flip—or die."

I shiver. I can't imagine they'll be happy to know they have an aeronaught with them.

"Well, I'll make that choice when it faces me," Rocks replies, calmly. I can't believe I never saw his likeness to Strickland. Strickland wouldn't be fazed by this situation either. He would stand his ground, unflinching, showing no emotion, because that's what it requires. Be strong for those he is leading. Rockland has the same quality. One difference is he only uses it when he's forced into a corner.

"Don't get all Sire with me! On your knees and get in there. Now!" their leader yells.

I almost jump out of my skin as his harsh words reverberate right through me.

In where?

"Fuck," Rocks mutters. My heart stutters in my chest. This can't be good.

Rocks must bend down because I feel the loss of him next to me. It's confirmed when he speaks next. I look down to follow his voice, but still can't see for shit.

"That crawl space is barely over two-feet high. I think you need us to flip into badgers not bats to be any good in there!"

"Show them," the leader mutters.

Someone pushes past me and from what I can hear bends down. "Fucking hell," the strange voice mumbles. "This is gonna suck."

"Move it!"

Rocks takes my hand. "I'll go first. Stay calm and close. Since we choose not to flip, we must crawl on our hands and knees through this tunnel, just like any aeronaught would if they were here. It's good to experience aeronaught challenges."

What the hell?

Crawl where?

A tunnel within a tunnel?

I take the deepest breath my lungs will hold and blow it out through my mouth. I do it again and again. I have no other choice but to follow Rocks' instructions. Both our lives depend on it. My hands start to shake. I can't control them.

I remember all the times Rocks was there for me when I needed him the most. I push the fear down deep into my toes. I focus on my toes. Toes aren't afraid of the dark. Toes don't care if they crawl. Toes get the job done. I'm going to be like my toes—if only my toes weren't so freaking cold. My hands stay steady.

If I distract my brain with crazy thoughts, my fear won't consume me. It's logical. I just need to cling to that logic for Rocks. If I freak out now, I don't know what he'll do to protect me.

"Aeronaught challenges?" a kidnapper repeats. "Man, you're a piece of work, but I'm telling ya, you should flip," the kidnapper growls.

At this point, I don't give a shit about how much of my body these assholes perv at. My focus is on staying calm and doing what I need to keep us both alive. I pull my long skirt up and tuck it in the waistband.

Thank God Rocks is going first and can't see this attractiveness I'm oozing with my do-it-yourself mini skirt.

I get on my hands and knees and follow Rocks into the tunnel.

The ground is cold and gross, and full of what I imagine are shark's tooth rocks to split open my skin a million different ways. I bite my lip to stop from crying out in pain when the first jagged edge bites into my knee, but I keep crawling. I try not to think about how far under the surface we are, and how I'm in a tiny fucking crawl space beneath a mountain, because toes don't give a shit about that sort of thing. Toes don't get claustrophobic. Toes get the job done.

We crawl.

And crawl.

And crawl some more.

To pass the time, I picture us by the pool. I imagine each and every detail of seeing his bare chest in the sunshine. His bare, toned, calf muscles for the first time. Him diving into the pool and coming up with wet soaked hair and one hundred percent raw sex appeal. I replay every moment over, and over, and over.

When that image starts to let the reality of how far underground I might be back in, I change it to how we spent our afternoon in the hotel room. I replay every kiss, touch, and caress.

It works, because suddenly, I ram head first into Rockland's butt, not aware that he stopped. "Oof, sorry.

Rocks disappears ahead of me and there's a small glow. I make out the jagged edges of the very small tunnel I've been crawling through, and my heart does a flip. Maybe my aeronaught blindness was a gift considering the circumstances.

The second I'm free, I'm blinking my eyes because there are two tiny oil lamps flickering in the corner of what appears to be a room carved out of stone. There's a wide exit ahead—which opens to the left and right. The stone walls there have been smoothed and polished slightly.

My whole body protests as I try to stand. Rocks' hands help pull me up. "You okay? Oh, shit, your knees."

My self-consciousness returns as I tug frantically at the twisted length of material I tucked into my waist. I pray my fake tattoo hasn't been scratched to bits. I pull the split closed over my leg just in case, as the fabric falls back to my feet.

"Sit," someone commands.

"Are the dogs still out?" one asks another.

Dogs?

My patience has run out. My brain is also not computing anything from the freaking craziness of this night? Day? It was light when we entered the train tunnel, so it must still be Sunday.

"Yeah, while both lamps are lit, we gotta wait till they're put away. Unless you want to fly in?"

"He ordered me to stay with you, so that's what I'll do."

"Good. 'Cause if anything goes wrong bringing in Camazotz cargo, you know the consequences."

"No, thanks!" The thug shudders and shakes his head. Each of the hooded figures finds a section of wall and sits against it.

Rocks takes my backpack and digs around for the first aid supplies I'll need. I glance at my knees and shins, and the bloody gore explains the pain. After crawling for a while, it was almost like I couldn't feel it any longer. Now I'm impressed I kept up so well.

"I'm so sorry," Rocks says, opening the rubbing alcohol. I'm not sure if he's apologizing for getting us into this mess, or the burning pain he's about to cause me.

"Just do it."

"No, I mean—"

"I know and don't worry about it," I interrupt. Neither of us would have guessed chasing the fix would have led us to this.

The string of curses I unleash would make a sailor blush, but it's my only release. I know Rocks will be hurting as much as I am because he'll feel responsible, but I simply cannot hold my tongue. The pain is too intense. He starts to unwind some of the dozens of bandages I stupidly packed. For some reason, I had visions of all Rocks' bones shattering or something, and I thought I could splint them. There's also a packet of wooden tongue depressors in amongst the mess for exactly that purpose.

He hands me a protein bar, and I'm so hungry it tastes as good as if Mom baked it. I rub my hands on my filthy skirt and wish I hadn't. I can't see clearly, but I imagine splinters of stone embedded in them too. Before I need to ask, Rocks inspects my palms and applies more first aid and gauze.

Snuggling up close to him, I rest my head against his shoulder, waiting for whatever comes next.

HARSH WORDS JOLT me back to consciousness. I think one of those assholes kicked me.

"What's happening?" I ask Rocks.

"I think we're moving again." He nods his head to the oil lamp—one of them is extinguished.

Our captors stand in a tight circle having a hushed discussion before one approaches us.

"We're going to walk across the yard. You follow the worker bees into the hive, or else. You're gonna be given thirty seconds to flip and follow their lead before the dogs are released. And trust me when I tell you, you don't want to come face-to-face with those hounds. They haven't been fed and will shred you. So take my advice and *flip*."

The protein bar threatens to be ejected. Hungry guard dogs are going to maul me. Or worse, Rocks won't flip, and they'll maul him too. Chasing the fix has turned into a nightmare neither of us could have imagined.

"I won't leave you," he whispers, as we're shuffled out the left exit.

"That's what I'm afraid of."

I try to memorize how to get back to the 'badger tunnel' for our escape. Two lefts, one right, go straight. But my plan is annihilated before it even got going when we stop at a giant, iron cage door. This is what prison must look like. The black metal bars sink into the stone on every side. The leader punches in a ten-digit code and the lock buzzes, signaling it's open. Around the next corner must be the yard as natural light floods the corridor.

We follow and have exited what seems to be a massive cliff face. My eyes want to close for the sheer brightness of the setting sun, but I force them open to take in as many details of our location as possible. Above us to the left is the sheer rock face. On the right, an open, dirt yard stretches over to another jagged, rocky cliff face.

I notice notches in the stone high up. Further to the right is an enormous, broken-down truck. The wheels would easily be taller than me. Behind a chain-link fence at the bottom of the opposite cliff, there are people trudging one after another from a makeshift warehouse building, which almost molds against the side of the cliff. They're entering a similar entrance at the bottom of the stone face, like the one we exited. More tunnels. Fantastic.

"Welcome to the compound," the leader proclaims, before giving one of the others a high five. "Now follow them down the hole, or it's dog meat for you two."

The line of people dwindles, and when the last person in dusty denim walks past a gate, they unchain it and push us through. I turn around to look at where we came from and realize it must be an old quarry. The scars on the stone are man-made and explain the sheerness of the cliff face jutting out of the ground. The old quarry carved a passage straight through the original hillside. Up past the broken-down truck is a dirt road that winds around a bend in the mountainside. The quarry has left a man-made valley, carved into the hill.

They lock the chain fence and yell at us to run. Panic takes over and I grab Rocks' hand and we race into the cave. This entrance is different from the one across the yard. The entry starts as bare, cut stone, but about a hundred feet in, we step onto wooden flooring. The bare rock walls have been covered in plaster like my bedroom walls. Electric lights hang from the ceiling—that is also plastered—and we can hear the footsteps of the people moving ahead of us.

Turning a sharp right, there's an empty table against the wall, with crumbs of food scattered across the surface. A small boy is standing at the opposite end picking at the tiny morsels and carefully placing them on his tongue.

His eyes widen when he see the two of us. "You new?" he asks.

"Yes," replies Rocks. "Where are we?"

"Quick. The others will explain inside." He turns and vanishes around another blind corner to the left.

Racing after him, we've hit a dead-end. The hallway ends with a large, high-ceilinged room—easily twelve feet high. It's empty—except for the young boy. Where the hell did everyone go? I wonder, gaping at the dead-end.

"Up there." He points to a square hole in the plaster the same size as a manhole. "Go in there before the dogs come. Quickly." He indicates to a small, security monitor stuck on the wall below the manhole. The screen is blank. "Once you see the dogs on there, you have twenty seconds." He flips and immediately flies up and disappears into the dark hole.

I step back a ways and stand on my toes to try to look in. The manhole is higher than Rocks' head—maybe seven-feet or so. Shiny metal gleams from inside.

"Shit!" I swear. I look around the room, and there's a larger, matching manhole high on the adjacent wall, but it's covered. In the space behind us, there are high, wooden beams stretching across the open area.

White splatters are dotted here and there on the brown, wooden floorboards.

A beeping similar to a microwave starts sounding, and the security monitor comes to life. The black and white screen shows a wooden hallway identical to the one we walked down. Suddenly, two monstrous dogs flash across the screen.

"Rocks?"

"Climb!" He bends down and picks me up at the knees. Wincing as he makes contact with my wounds, I try to grip the wall to stay balanced. He pushes and shoves as I try to reach up to grip the edge of the hole. My fingers slide off the edge. He heaves me higher, and I grab hold of the edge. It takes all my strength to lift myself inside, but my arms are suddenly made of jelly causing me to slip back down.

A low growl sounds around the corner, along with the scratching of claws on polished wood. Rocks is pushing and shoving, trying to help me get higher. He grabs my foot and I straighten my knee. I'm halfway in.

"Hang on!" His support vanishes. I slip back, but spread my hands flat on the cold, slippery metal, hoping my sweaty palms will stick, and then I remember they have slippery bandages covering them. I press down as hard as I can stand to slow my backward slide. Behind me the beasts must enter the room because the growling turns to vicious barking, and the claws scratching across the wooden floorboards chill my blood.

"Rocks!" I pant.

Movement above my head lets me know Rocks is away from those teeth. He flips in the tiny space in front of me and grabs my wrists. Rocks is lying on his stomach and drags me up over the edge of the manhole into the duct with him. I bite my tongue at the pain that jettisons up my legs, as my bandages scrape over the rim.

Our ragged breathing fills the small space. I close my eyes and rest my forehead on the cool steel. "Thank you."

"This reminds me of the air conditioning ducts at Enzo's warehouse," he says, trying to look around.

When I look up, he's right. We've climbed into an AC vent. I understand why the Camazotz flip. It's going to be another crawl on red, raw knees for me, but at least it's not over jagged ground.

"Any guesses as to what we'll find at the end?" I ask.

20
Answers

MY long skirt saves my wounded knees as it slides on the metal duct. Rocks leads the way and we crawl along the shaft. I try not to focus on the fact I'm again headed deeper under some Georgian mountain.

"Not far. I can see the end," he says up front. "But I want you to wait here until I know it's safe."

"What?"

"Please, Little Fox, let me see what we're in for." I love his subtle reminder of my undercover identity.

I agreed to do what he asked when we negotiated me accompanying him. I trust Rocks, and after what we've been through so far, I agree to wait in the duct until he gives me the all clear.

I lie still, resting my chin on my folded arms and watch Rocks cautiously approach the opening.

"What on earth!" his voice sounds distant.

"Rockland?" a faint, male voice answers.

Rockland wriggles around and tells me it's safe. I crawl to his boots. "Baby, wait here. I don't know how we're gonna get you down. Give me a minute."

Flip!

He's gone.

Crawling to the edge, I can hardly believe my eyes, but my nerves get the better of me, and I slide back a few inches for safety.

Fifty-feet below is a sprawling, underground cavern. It reminds me of my visit to Blood Mountain and breaching the Shadows' sacred roost. The cavern is equally as big, if not bigger. I'm stunned so many large underground caves exist. I guess I never really thought about it and assumed the earth beneath my feet was always solid.

"Wow."

Rocks materializes into the sea of people we saw walking in a line out in the yard. For once, I have a bird's eye view. Peering down, I scan the layout. There are rough, wooden bunk beds in rows and rows along the sides and easily covering one half of the cavern floor.

The roof of the cave lowers toward the back, but I can make out a dark, gaping hole. There must be more to this underground world than I can see. The air smells cool but of hay and human bodies. I notice there's a trail of random pieces of straw leading into the maze of bunk beds.

Bodies are everywhere. Up on the bunks, standing around in a tight circle near Rocks. Bats are flying down from the ceiling to flip. When I look to my right, there are dozens of bats huddled together, clinging to the rough stone staring back at me.

Rockland.

Rockland is here?

What?

He can't be.

It's true.

There is endless chatter from those in bat form buzzing inside my head. Their words aren't harsh like some of the times when the Shadows' members were in my headspace. They're excited and shocked.

The crowd gathering slowly parts and two men step forward. I remember both of them from my visit to the Duskwing honey farm. The Duskwing Sire—with his black, spiky hair and muscular chest— steps forward to offer Rockland his forearm in greeting. Behind him is the older gent—still wearing his denim overalls—who I remember was also a Fold member.

Never in a million years did I think our journey to get Rocks fixed would uncover the secret whereabouts of the bat-napped Duskwing. This means—without a doubt—the Camazotz who brought us here are members of Vuelo de la Muerte!

Rockland turns and points to me. The whole group were so shocked by his arrival, they hadn't noticed me spying from my little perch. There's action and beds are stripped of several sheets. More discussion and then muscular males are forming a group around Rocks.

Eventually he walks over to beneath me and yells up, "We're going to bring you down in the sheets—like a swing. Just hang on." He flips and with the growing group of males takes hold of some sheet.

The large Sire, Moondust, is handing out the sheet and twisting it at the same time for the bats to grab. It turns into a thick-corded type of rope swing that glides through the air toward me. More and more bats join in and grab hold.

Come help.

It's Connie.

Everyone help.

Most of the high ceiling is now empty of bats. The organized troupe gets closer. When the swing is as close as they can get it, I pull myself out of the duct. Thankfully there's a narrow ledge to help me swing my feet around.

Step into the swing.

It's Rocks. I will not let panic get the better of me. Rocks has proven time and time again, he won't let anything hurt me. As high up as I am, I don't want to step into a flying sheet, but my alternative is to sleep in a cold, steel air duct. I step off and just when I think I'm about to plummet, the sheet goes taut and holds my weight. More and more bats are still joining the effort. I glide down—standing upright—in the middle of my sheet swing. It's almost surreal.

A sea of faces is staring at me. I take a deep breath and walk forward and extend my hand to Moondust.

"Moondust, Sir. I'm Connie Phillips. We met back in March."

He reminds me so much of beefy Pegasus at the Shadows. Corded muscles move in his arm as he extends it and grips my forearm in the traditional Camazotz greeting.

"I remember. I wish we were meeting under better circumstances. I like your new hair."

I forget about my dark, midnight locks. I feel my ears flame as I fight the urge to look at my feet.

"Thank you, Sir. I wanted to come with Rocks for... um, well, you know... Anyhow, this was the only way."

Shit. I don't know if Moondust would approve of Rockland chasing the magic fix. I remember when I visited his colony, he got upset and yelled at Strickland about many of his pups and fledglings wanting the fix.

I relax the second I feel Rocks' hand slide around my waist. His other hand rubs his nose back and forth several times. Nighthawk—the older Fold member in denim—comes forward and grips my forearm, offering his welcome. The whispers start about my hair. It's weird the whispers used to be about the fact my hair was so different, and now it's because it's just like everyone else's.

"You're a brave young lady, Connie Philips," Moondust comments. "Following Rockland into this hell hole." The Duskwing Sire raises his arms indicating to the cave around us.

The cave seems enormous from down here. I spy the lights strung across the cavern.

"You have electric lights?" I point.

Everyone looks up. "Only until they turn them off at ten," Nighthawk replies. "Every little thing is controlled by them. We—"

"MOOOOOVE!"

"MOOOOOVE!"

The crowd around us all turn to follow two little voices yelling their way through the sea of onlookers. A moment later, two identical bodies fling themselves at Rocks, hugging him around his waist.

"It is you. It is you," they chant in unison.

The twins.

"You're here too? Thank heavens you're both safe," Rocks says, hugging them back. "Cypress is so—"

"No! Oh, bats above. No. Not you too," a woman wails.

I look up in time to see a young woman, sobbing as she collapses in a heap on the ground about three-feet away.

"Celand!" Rocks yells, and pushes past the Fold members to get to his long, *dead* sibling. "Celand! You're alive?"

"Brother, you're trapped now too. I wouldn't ever wish this torture on my worst enemy. No! You can't be here!" she wails, covering her eyes with her hands as Rockland wraps her up in an embrace.

Every set of eyes in the cavern is on them. I can't hear what's being said, as they whisper to each other, but she sounds immensely sad. This moment is so private, I feel bad for the pair of them being the center of attention.

"She was here with a handful of other Camazotz when we arrived. She's been here the longest," Moondust explains to me. "I hate to tell you this, but she's right. Both of you are trapped now too. There's no escaping the compound."

A sliver of ice runs through my veins. I stare at Celand. Rocks helps her to her feet because she's skin and bone. Her clothes are faded and have been roughly mended in several places. She cups his cheeks with her long, boney fingers as she starts to cry all over again. He gently walks her this way. I don't miss the crazy twitch of his nose again, and I wonder what he smells. He rubs it with the back of his hand.

"Celand, this is my girlfriend, Connie. Connie, this is my amazing, big sister, Celand," he says, tears forming in his eyes.

"Connie?" Her sad eyes travel over me.

"I'm an aeronaught," I confirm, since my fake tatts and dye job make it harder to tell.

"But how did you get in here?" she questions, looking between the two of us. "That awful tunnel!"

I shove my leg out through the thigh-high split and people gasp at the bandages. In places, fresh blood has seeped through. I must look an absolute sight.

We're immediately ushered through the maze of bunk beds and out the opening at the back of the main cavern. As I suspected, there are a series of smaller caves connected to the larger one. In the first cavern, there is an underground water supply. A large, almost round pool with a tiny, flowing inlet at each end. Thankfully they have a natural water supply, which our captors cannot turn on and off at will.

In another cave, there are goats and large piles of hay. The smell of their waste is pungent, and I fight the urge to cover my nose.

We stop in a smaller cave filled with makeshift furniture, which resembles an office. It contains a table made from recycled timbers and several wooden crates upended for chairs. Two mismatched cups and some other random supplies sit on one end of the table. They clearly constructed it from random finds of timber. Without a saw to even up the ends of the table, different pieces of wood jut out from each other.

"Please take a seat," Moondust beckons. He apologizes for keeping us out in the main cavern so long, but says we need to understand that newcomers are the only break in their monotonous routine.

As many of the crowd that can fit have followed us into the smaller cave. "Celand, come in." Nighthawk motions. "The rest of you go prepare for bed. There'll be plenty of time to meet our new arrivals. You too, Elm and Oak. You can see Rockland tomorrow." The twins have been our shadow for the whole tour.

The shortest Camazotz adult I have ever seen rushes in. "I was helping the elderly and just heard. Rockland, are you okay? They didn't hurt you?"

She stands by his side and is actually shorter than me. Her hair is a messy, short cut—like a long pixie cut—but it's her tattoo, which I can't take my eyes off. Her right arm is a full-sleeve depicting a violent thunderstorm. Heavy, dark cloud heads loom with white lightning strikes arcing through the middle. It's so realistic it could be a black and white photograph of a powerful storm. Mom says it's rude to stare, but the art on her arm is intoxicating.

"We're fine. It's hard to say it's good to see you under the circumstances," Rocks says, gripping her forearm. He introduces her as another Fold member of the Duskwing representing the Cloud Wing. "Meet RainCloud."

Her tattoo is perfect. She has sharp, pretty eyes that I sense wouldn't miss a single thing. I love her already, even though we've only just met. She's younger than Mom and Dad, so I'd put her in her mid-thirties, but she looks like she can handle herself—a powerful, strong role model for the female pups at Duskwing.

"I finally get to meet the famous Miss Connie. I've heard so much about you." She smiles and her teeth are perfectly aligned. "I wish we weren't meeting under this mountain. But here we are."

Nighthawk and I take a seat, but Moondust, RainCloud, Celand and Rocks stay standing.

"Do you know where we are exactly?" Rocks asks.

"I was hoping you'd be able to tell us," Moondust replies. "We were at the roost sleeping. Next thing a man enters, and we're knocked out. The whole colony woke up in the bird room."

"We know—" I say.

"The what room?" Rocks asks at the same time. He looks at me. "Sorry, you go."

"No, it's okay. I want to know what the bird room is too."

"We'll get to that," older Nighthawk says. I don't know if it's the darkness of the cave, but his hair seems to be solid gray now. I don't remember him looking so old at the farm. "You say you knew?"

Rocks explains about finding poor little Moonshadow wandering around in Helen.

"She's alive?" Moondust exclaims.

"Yes, perfectly well. She's one brave, little pup. She told us what happened." Rocks puts a steadying hand on the Sire's shoulder. Moondust's face crinkles as though he's trying not to cry.

"Oh, thank the bats above. We thought she was dead. When we woke in the room, a half dozen of our number had died. We can only guess at how."

"They were probably suffocated," Rocks says. He recounts Moonshadow's tale of everything that occurred—including the leather harnesses all the bats were placed into before they flew away. "Maybe a bad position in the harness."

The three fold members are astounded we know more about what happened to them that night than they do.

Their muscular Sire dwarfs tiny RainCloud. She says quietly to him, "If only we'd known. I'm sorry, Sire."

"She died in vain," he replies.

I want to ask whom, but feel it's too personal a question from an outsider.

Moondust shakes off the grief that seemed to ooze out of him for that moment and gets right back to Sire business. "The bird room is on the other end of the air duct. At night, great horned owls occupy those perches. During the daylight hours, bat falcons replace them."

"Bat falcons aren't native to this continent," Rocks says, frowning. "They're found mostly in South America. How would they get this far north?"

"All I can tell you is they're living at this compound."

The white splatters on the wooden floorboards make sense. Their natural enemies guard these Camazotz day and night. Tronido is one sick son of a bitch.

Afraid the lights will go out any second because I have no clue what time it is, I start to unwind my bandages while the three Duskwing continue to fill us in on life at the compound. Celand takes one of the cups and returns with cool water. I rinse what's left of the gravel from my shins and grab the plastic tweezers from the first aid kit to pull out several chunks of dirt that are in deep.

RainCloud interrupts, "You have medical supplies and training?"

"Oh, no. I mean, I do have supplies but no training." She eyes what's spilling out of my backpack. "You can help yourself if you need anything, especially bandages."

"Really?"

"Go for it." I nudge the backpack toward her with my foot.

"You are too kind. These items are precious. Tronido must not have welcomed you if you were allowed to bring them in. We have almost nothing. Only what we can steal from the work room."

Rocks swears. "We feared he was running this after what Moonshadow told us."

"He's their Sire now—by force. The Vuelo de la Muerte's official Sire is still Saturno, but he's only for show."

"What do you mean by force?" Rocks asks.

"The heirs of all the Muerte Fold members are down here with us. They occupy the back far corner of the bunk beds. Tronido threatens to kill them each time their Sire or Fold member don't do what he says to keep up appearances. They were living down here with Celand and the others long before we arrived," RainCloud explains.

"Fuck! That explains why Saturno was so vague when we paid them a surprise visit. He also looked like he'd been beaten within an inch of his life. He could hardly stand."

"He probably was," Moondust replies. "When beating him didn't work, they started torturing his heir to get his compliance."

Rocks growls his frustration. "I want to kill that bastard!" Rocks notices I'm having trouble turning my leg into a Halloween mummy. "Here let me do that."

He gently takes the bandage and starts winding it up my leg. Celand hasn't taken her eyes off her little brother since we arrived. Every so often she reaches out and touches him—on the arm or hand—as though making sure he's real. I can't imagine the pain and misery she's endured all this time. When she makes eye contact with me, it's only for a fleeting second. Her eyes aren't full of sadness, but more of... nothing. Ghostly almost.

Maybe this is what one looks like after having one's spirit broken. Maybe this is the look of someone whose life doesn't belong to them now.

I explain how to use the rubbing alcohol and various other ointments and creams in the backpack. When my stomach imitates a lion's roar, all eyes are on me. "Excuse me." I can't imagine how loud that was to their ears.

The Duskwing exchange worried looks before Nighthawk says, "We're very sorry, but we don't have any aeronaught food to offer you."

"No problem. We have some."

Rocks digs out another protein bar. He offers them a bar as well, but they all agree I should keep what food supplies I have, since the goats can't nourish me."

They explain that the table in the hallway has some aeronaught food on it each day, but it's nowhere near enough to sustain all the trapped

Camazotz. Everyone is slowly starving. When they first arrived, the Duskwing killed two goats by accident because they were used to feeding more regularly. They literally drank them dry. Now food and blood is rationed strictly to ensure everyone gets some each night.

"I'm so sorry," I add. "Please have some."

"No," Moondust commands. "As the only Sire here, I command every Camazotz *not* to touch your food. I'm serious when I say you'll need it. But I do thank you for your generous offer. Let's get to the bunks."

"Um, I... ah." I look at Rocks, but I know he won't be able to help me. "Um, I need to go potty."

It takes a second for the group to realize what I'm talking about, and when they do, they all exchange nervous glances. RainCloud escorts me, apologizing repeatedly, and if I thought the goat cave smelt bad, then that was nothing compared to the bat guano cave. There is what I can best describe as a wooden camping potty resting over a deep fissure in the cave floor. It reminds me of a bathroom Dad found once when we got lost in a National Park. No water to flush, just a pit full of poo. I have a feeling I'm not going to poop ever again to avoid going back in that cave.

We return to the group, and I use half the hand sanitizer I packed. I even contemplate putting some up my nose somehow, but decide against looking like a freak. Besides, it's not their fault they have no bathroom facilities, and I don't want to make them feel bad.

A young girl waits silently at the mouth of the office cave. When RainCloud addresses her, she announces our bunk is ready.

"Come," RainCloud beckons. "You must be exhausted. All leaders are given permanent bunks in a private corner. We apologize we can only give you one."

When we walk back through the caves to the main cavern, everyone is watching. I feel exposed in my costume corset, and it hits me I'm stuck in these revealing, annoying clothes indefinitely. In all my packing, I never thought to put a change of clothes in the pack. My suitcase is in the trunk of the Honda.

Celand hugs Rocks when we're half way through the sleeping quarters. "My bunk is this way. All originals have their own space. Good night, Rockland." She stares up at him with the same dark intense eyes, only hers are full of so much sadness. "Good night, Connie. I hope you rest well."

We watch as her slender frame heads to the opposite side of the cave.

Our bed is thankfully a top bunk. We're located on the far wall with some space between us and the next set of bunks. It's a luxury compared to the tight fitting beds we walked through earlier. Rocks being Shadows royalty has allowed us into this precious corner. RainCloud bunks below us, and the next bed over are Moondust and Nighthawk. I'm grateful to be allowed in their inner circle.

Rocks sneezes and excuses himself. "You okay?" I ask as he helps me onto the wooden bunk. He nods and rubs his nose again but doesn't climb up with me.

"I'm sorry I have to ask," he says to Moondust, "Please forgive my rudeness, but why does everybody smell like cocaine?"

MOONDUST frowns. "How do you know what cocaine smells like?"

"Yes, exactly!" adds RainCloud.

Sitting with my legs dangling over the side of the bed, I place my unopened protein bar on the bare mattress. "It's my fault. Please don't think badly of Rockland. He knows because of me."

"Connie, it's unrelated. You don't have to tell them."

"No, Rocks, it really isn't. It's a tangled web, which we innocently got mixed up in, but I'd rather they hear it from me. What if he recognizes me?"

Not long after I start my tale of finding out I was adopted, the lights in the cavern flick off. I dig my fingernails into my palms to stop myself from screaming out loud. It's utterly black. Darkness. Midnight nothing. But it was the unexpected suddenness that caught me off guard.

"Fuck!" I whisper, squeezing my fists tighter.

Rocks materializes next to me and puts a comforting arm around my shoulders. "I'm here." He tries to explain to the others how bad aeronaught eyesight is in the dark.

I take a deep breath and close my eyes. I continue my story and hope they won't judge me too harshly. I wish it wasn't so dark, so I could see the looks on their faces when I explain about Enzo and Tronido working for him. I pray they believe I really didn't have anything to do with that coincidence.

"My biological father is a ruthless, ambitious, powerful business man. It was only a matter of time before Tronido gravitated toward him. I'm sorry Rockland had to enter that warehouse to—"

"Do not apologize, Connie," RainCloud says. Her voice is soothing in the pitch darkness. "Rockland is a Camazotz of honor, and I'm proud he helped save your baby sister."

Her words break whatever is keeping my emotions at bay. I burst into tears, covering my face. It's been a rough twenty-four hours. "Thank you for not judging the blood that flows through my veins. I'm so… ashamed," I sob.

"You are not your biological father, Connie." Moondust has a deep penetrating voice. "Do not waste precious time dwelling on things you cannot control. I have seen enough of you myself to know you would be a Camazotz of honor too, because you're an aeronaught of honor."

"Thank you, Sire. That means a lot to me."

It's decided I need my rest, and Rocks places the forgotten protein bar in my hands. We lay down, and I wrap myself around him. He offers to flip and sleep above on the cave wall, so I can have the whole bed, but my ironclad grip on his shirt tells him what a horrible idea I think that is.

The crinkling of my wrapper sounds so loud, but when I listen, there's the ambient noise of the colony preparing for sleep around us.

"Want some?" I hold the bar roughly where I think his face is.

"No, baby. You eat. I'll be good until tomorrow thanks to you insisting I feed."

"Holy shit!" I exclaim, actually making Rocks jump for once.

"What?"

"My phone! I totally forgot about it after we found Celand. Maybe we can call for help."

"Oh, shit!" He's suddenly gone and I hear him zip open my backpack. A second later, he places it in my hands.

Waiting for the screen to come to life seems to take an eternity. So many lives are resting on this tiny device. The subtle glow is bright down here. We wait.

No service.

"Crap."

"Can I try?" asks Rocks. "Maybe up near the vent? Closer to the surface?" I hand it over and he vanishes. Waiting in the dark makes time stretch out forever. He can't be gone more than a minute or two, but the nothingness almost chokes me.

"It's okay, Connie," Moondust's deep voice floats up from the lower bunk opposite. "We're all here with you. Trust me when I say you'll never have a moment alone here."

I bite my bottom lip because they must have all heard a change in my breathing, or heartbeat, or something, to know I'm trying my best not to freak out.

"I'm back," Rocks announces from beside the bed. "Nope, it doesn't work." From the tone in his voice I can picture his defeated look. "No service anywhere under here."

"I also smuggled in a utility knife," I say. I borrowed it from Dad. I wasn't sure if we would need a small knife, or cutters, so I hid it inside the lining with our phones.

I hear wood creaking, and suddenly Moondust's voice is closer. "You have a knife with you?"

"Yes. Rocks, it's hidden with the phones." I hear Rocks dig around in the backpack again, before he places the cold steel in my palm.

"Do you mind?" Moondust asks. I shake my head. He takes the small knife from my palm. "I will hide that to keep it safe. This is as precious as those telephones."

THE NEXT THING I'm aware of is Rocks saying my name. I blink and quickly close my eyes. The overheard lights are back on, and seem way brighter than they did last night. It cannot be morning.

"What time is it?" I ask, stretching my sore body. The trip down those tunnels has taken a toll on my arms and legs.

"It's seven," RainCloud says from below. "Off at ten. On at seven. Never any change."

"What happens now?" Rocks asks, jumping off the bunk bed, like he's twelve all over again.

"We have an hour to get to the work stations and then the falcons are released," Moondust says, climbing down from the top bunk and stretching too. "I imagine you will be summoned before Tronido goes to bed. The Muerte keep a nocturnal schedule."

Nighthawk slowly stands, rubbing his back. I know how he feels. "I suggest we get Miss Connie up and out early, so there are no problems."

"Good idea. RainCloud will show you where you can wash your face," Moondust says.

I get past two bunks in the maze of beds, and little Elm and Oak are waiting. Their identical features—except for the brutal owl scars—still amaze me. Elm takes my left hand while Oak grabs my right. "We can show her and bring her back," they say in unison to RainCloud. She nods before heading off on other business. My little helpers lead me deeper into the cave.

I really, really, really want a hot shower and a change of clothes. I guess washing my face will have to do. I stare across the sea of bunk beds and wonder about the bathroom routines of these people—that's one hell of a lot of guano.

When I return, I grab some painkillers to ease my sore muscles and the pain radiating from my legs. The twins stay close, watching my every move. Rocks ruffles their hair, making them giggle.

"Should we risk bringing my cell?" I ask, before zipping up the pack.

"No," Moondust answers. "Wait. It's too precious to risk getting confiscated without us even having a chance to use it."

We head to below the air duct and the group of sturdy males has gathered. Their Sire nods his head and the group flip. I'm airlifted to the high duct. It's not too difficult to get into again, and I crawl along and wait at the other end. There are no signs of the snapping guard dogs, but there is fresh bird poop on the floor as I peep over the edge.

Stay low.

Rocks instructs in my head. A bunch of bats fly over and out the exit. They flip and start forming a human pyramid for me to climb down the other side to the wooden floor. The drop from the duct on this side is much lower, but still too high for me to jump. It amazes me how helpful the Duskwing members are in comparison to the Shadows.

If I were stuck in here with them, I would hate to see how they would accommodate my aeronaught-ness.

"Thank you all so much," I say, looking at each of the young men and teenagers. "I guess we'll meet here again tonight."

Some of them give me shy smiles, and it transports me back in time to first meeting Rocks. He's so much more open now than back then.

Moondust and Nighthawk materialize next. "We can wait here for a bit. RainCloud comes through last when all those that can work are through. We don't get any days off and some of the elderly can't cope."

"Where are Starjewel, Ganymede, and the other Fold?" Rocks asks.

Pain spreads across Moondust's features faster than he can flip. He rubs his brow and sighs. "The three of us are all that's left of our Fold."

I gasp, recalling the other two Fold members I met on my visit to their farm. Starjewel was the first female Fold member I ever met. She had such a kind, peaceful face, and a presence I still recall, and she was little Moonshadow's mother—the brave little bat who escaped and flew to the Shadows unaccompanied.

"Shall I tell them for you?" Nighthawk asks.

"No, it's fine. When we woke here. Right here actually," he says. "We were forced down that duct. Of course, we didn't know the rules, and those beastly hounds killed the other two Fold members. They were too slow and torn apart because, to be honest, we didn't believe what they told us. Who unleashes savage dogs on other people?" Moondust looks at Rockland and me. I don't know what to say.

"Anyhow we regrouped down in the cave, stunned and… it's hard to explain. I never thought it was possible to kidnap a whole colony," Moondust continues. His eyes show confusion and sorrow. Now I understand the cause of it.

"Moonshadow was nowhere to be found. We did head counts and more checks. It must have been close to midnight by the time we were sure my young pup wasn't with us."

I recall that Moonshadow told us both her parents were Fold members, so she never had to really do what everyone else was commanded to do.

"Starjewel was beside herself. I couldn't console her. I didn't know Moonshadow's fate anymore than she did. She decided to go look for her. Celand begged her not to, I begged her as well—at least until we knew more about this place. She couldn't bare the thought of her little pup out there and scared. She flew up to the vent, and it sounded this loud alarm. All the bats in the cavern were knocked unconscious again.

"We retrieved her from the vent and waited for her to wake up. I sat with her. When she woke, she was determined. She said she couldn't live a single day without her daughter and flew up again. This time she flipped and crawled through the vent." He stops speaking and stares at the floor.

Nighthawk continues, "We heard it. Her screams and those dogs tearing her apart. The next morning when we came out, the floor was a pool of smeared blood, with large, bloody paw prints all the way down the hall."

I want to be sick. That's so cruel. Poor Starjewel was desperate to find her pup and gave her life trying, when Moonshadow was actually winging it to the Shadows colony quite safely.

"I'm so sorry. Please accept my condolences," I say to Moondust.

Rocks offers his forearm, saying, "May her final flight have been swift and smooth. I'm sorry, Sire."

"Thank you both. But it doesn't end there. That first day while we were working, Tronido came into the room and explained every member has a mate. Not a breeding mate, but a 'life mate,'" Moondust explains. "If someone tries to escape, or does not do what they're ordered, then their life mate will suffer the harsh consequences."

"What?" I ask.

"I'm sorry if this will be difficult for you to hear, but it was horrific to witness. Tronido pulled back a curtain on one wall. There was a large cage and two great horned owls perched inside. One of his goons carried in an unconscious bat. To this day, we have no idea how they caught him. He placed the bat on the floor and stood on one wing— breaking it."

I gasp and Rocks takes my hand. My memory floods with the exact scene of Tronido breaking Rocks' wing. It's painful to recall. I swallow down the bile and nod for them to continue.

Moondust speaks quietly, "Tronido looked around the room grinning at us, before he pulled out a cleaver and chopped his other unbroken wing clean off."

"Oh my God!" I gasp.

"Fuck!" Rocks swears, and his eyes dart to mine. We've seen a bat with no wings!

"Exactly," Moondust agrees. "Next he places the bloody and broken body in a drawer of the cage—down the bottom—like it pulled out for cleaning or something. The moment Ganymede awoke, screeching in pain, he slid the drawer back in, and those owls tore what was left of him to pieces in front of all of us—small pups included. He's insane. He didn't care. It was the most gruesome thing I have ever witnessed. He waited until we all knew for sure it was Ganymede by the painful voice echoing inside our heads. This is who you will be dealing with later, Rockland. Be careful what you say today. Your life and Connie's depend on it."

I cover my face with my hands. We're trapped with that maniac in charge. I drag air into my lungs. I have to stay calm. Rocks wraps his arms around me and pulls me to his chest. He's warm. He's steady. He's all that's keeping me from collapsing on the floor.

What the hell will he do to me if he finds out who I am?

"I'm sorry to upset you both, but you need to learn the rules fast here. There are no second chances. I know you will want to plan an escape, but it's not possible. Tronido has thought of everything," Moondust announces and the defeat in his voice makes the oxygen in my lungs evaporate.

We begin marching single file out through the cave and into the morning light. The fresh air is a gift from heaven and I fill my lungs over and over again. A handful of wardens are waiting on the other side of the chain-link fence watching our movements. I try not to make eye contact because I need to go unnoticed, but I'm also sketching a compound map in my head. We absolutely cannot stay here forever. In a matter of weeks, my golden hair is going to give us away.

WE'RE MARCHED INTO a giant cutting room! My nostrils want to close from the harsh smell of the cocaine. My stomach rolls as the smell transports me back in time to working at the warehouse with Enzo. This is a freaking nightmare. The Duskwing have been drug cutters, and unless we can get the hell out of here, I'm going to be one forever too.

How ironic is it that I manage to send Enzo and his crew to prison—so long as the trial does what it's supposed to and lawyers don't find some loophole—and now, I'm working for another drug lord? You wouldn't bet on it. Nighthawk tells us to stop at a table with him and Moondust.

Gone are the underwear rules Enzo enforced. We're all allowed to keep our clothes on. Or should I say rags. Some of the Camazotz, whose clothes are almost threadbare, have clearly been here the longest. Describing their attire as 'clothes' is being generous. I look at my skirt, ripped in two places, and wonder what I will look like if we don't get out of here.

Celand approaches and Moondust nods his head for her to join our workstation. There are long tables positioned with precision in a grid across the room. Each table has two sets of scales and utensils for us to weigh and cut the powder. It's not the kind of déjà vu I want to experience.

Celand whispers instructions about how it all works, and unfortunately I already know. Rocks listens intently because he never got to see the cutting room in action. Members of the Muerte enter from the opposite end of the warehouse—calling it a room feels stupid since it holds enough workstations for the entire colony. They wheel dollies in with different sized plastic wrapped bricks. The product.

Male Muerte members start distributing the uncut bricks to each table. The only sound in the room is from one cart's squeaky wheel. I can't believe Rocks and I have ended up here. Before any product is dropped at our table, in saunters Tronido. I pray all the surrounding Camazotz can't hear my sudden intake of breath. The artery in my neck starts to throb.

Stay calm.

I stare at my hand resting on the worn table.

"It really is you," Tronido trumpets to the whole room. "Rockland Shadows is working for me. What a gift!" He stops beside Rocks. "Come. We're gonna have a little chat."

They start to walk away, and I channel the ability to become invisible as I take a long, deep calming breathe.

"Wait, they said there were two of you. Who else did you convince needed fixing?" he asks Rocks.

"I didn't convince anyone."

Tronido glares. "Have it your way. Newbie, step forward now!"

His tone means business, and after what happened to Starjewel and Ganymede, I'm not going to let my nerves risk anyone's life. I faced Enzo Ascari and came out the other side. The blood that turned Enzo into the ruthless man he is pumps through my veins. I can do this. I lied so well my baby sister survived. After what my biological parents put me through this year, I know I have the strength to survive. I will play this part and convince Tronido I'm a submissive little female from the Shadows.

The stories from earlier turned my stomach, but I remember seeing the cutting room guy shot through Enzo's office window. I recall the vicious beating Enzo gave Brick—the Rambo look-alike bodyguard—with the tire iron. I remember the feeling of looking down the barrel of the gun when I was kidnapped. I have been tested over and over again, and I'm still standing.

Rocks and I can do this. Together, we will make things right.

I daren't look at any of the others. I keep my eyes on the ground and allow my hair to cascade around my face—a curtain of jet-black hair I pray will protect my identity. I curve my shoulders to hunch in on myself like I'm trembling with fear. I wouldn't say I wasn't shit scared, but evil pricks have a weakness. Rocks and I simply need to work out where Tronido's weakness is.

Tronido circles like a shark smelling blood in the water. "Who are you?" he sneers so close behind me I feel his breathe on my ear. I flinch. He laughs. Intimidation is his game. He's good at it. He one thousand percent intimidates me, but I will never give up hope of outsmarting him, because I've got Rockland on my side, along with every other Camazotz in this room.

"That's Little Fox," Rockland replies, "She's from a small wing and followed me."

"Cousins of yours, aren't they?" Tronido asks.

Fuck. The Fox wing is related to the Land wing. Tronido has been studying bloodlines.

"Yes, distant. Don't punish her for that," Rocks says.

We walk through the Muerte entrance at the far end of the warehouse. I feel as though we're back under the mountain again, but it's so hard to tell when they cover the cave corridors with plaster and paint. There aren't any AC ducts here, but the temperature is even and cool. We follow Tronido through a series of corridors with multiple guard points—like Enzo had.

What surprises me as I look around is there doesn't seem to be an alarm system, or any video surveillance.

Tronido stops at a doorway and motions for us to enter. The room is empty except for two metal chairs. There's one low hanging simple electric light. I glance at Rocks and his nose twitches. I twitch my own to fake that I can smell whatever he does, but I don't want to know what he can smell. There's a cold, nasty vibe to this space.

My gut tells me not to sit in the chair. Bad things happen to people who occupy those chairs.

"Sit."

We do. I keep my focus on my plain, unpainted nails and ignore my gut screaming at me to make a run for it.

"Welcome to my colony," Tronido gloats.

"I'm not a member of your colony." Rocks spits at Tronido's boots.

"Careful, Rockland. Today, I will tolerate your rude behavior and put it down to adjusting to your new Camazotz future but only today."

"You kidnapped them! You stole their lives! This is slavery," Rocks rants.

"Call it what you will. I choose to call it my new colony. And forget Saturno. That old man does whatever I say to keep nosy Shadows' members out of my business."

Rocks folds his arms and sits up straight. I want to be as defiant too, but I can't risk Tronido recognizing me. The Shadows don't have any female Fold members, so I channel a submissive vibe to really keep myself off his radar.

"You're jealous I dragged my colony into this century. I know that's where you want your colony to be, but Strickland and Fold members—Cypress and Macallister—will forever hold you back. Maybe you should have considered overthrowing them. Like I did here." He walks around with his arms spread—King of this mountain prison.

"Never compare us. We are nothing alike."

"Mmmm… I think we do see eye-to-eye on certain things. Technology for example. It's a modern miracle to be able to contact my legion of Camazotz when they're hundreds of miles away. And another advantage of integration is the usefulness of aeronaughts." He laughs and I force myself not to look at Rocks. All I can see in my peripheral vision is Rocks unfold his arms and grips his knees. His fingers must be hurting his knee muscles since his knuckles are turning white.

"I don't disrespect them by calling them 'naughts anymore because they aren't nothing. They are priceless, *weak* customers, who've made me wealthier than I ever dreamed I could be. Who knew there were powders capable of bringing aeronaughts to their knees? Plus, you can get them to do all the dirty work. I bet that's why you keep your aeronaught pet! Or maybe just for the physical benefits."

Rocks springs from the chair so fast I would swear he could flip into a panther. His fingers wrap around Tronido's throat, and I watch in horror as he lifts the short asshole slightly off the ground. Just as fast, the two thugs at the door slam Rockland back into his chair and hold a shoulder each.

The hatred in Tronido's eyes makes the oxygen in the room evaporate. I daren't even breathe as I study him from under my bangs. He takes two slow steps and leans over within an inch of Rocks' face. "The next time you touch me, I will remove the body part you used—but from her! Understood?"

Rocks nods his heads, and I return my stare to my lap, shaking my hair forward as much as possible.

"I promise you, Rockland, this will be the last time you are forgiven. You aren't the Sire's son here. Listen to Moondust. He's managed to stay alive all this time *and* keep *all* his body parts. You work for me now." He stands up straight and smooths out his dark shirt.

He continues, "Yes, you work for me as part of my empire. I really must send that little pet of yours a thank you gift. I don't know what she did, but I can't deny she did something to help me gain all this."

"What?" Rocks asks, reading my mind.

"Taking care of Enzo. He held a meeting with all his distributors and mentioned the long, lost daughter returning to his side. Of course, I knew from the Vipers who he meant. Next minute, the man the Feds have been trying to take down for decades—the most powerful dealer on the East coast—is arrested." He laughs. "I'll give it to you. You really know how to pick 'em."

He walks around in a small circuit with his chest puffed out. "This could have all been yours, don't you see? If you had've embraced both sides of yourself, your colony could be as powerful and wealthy as mine. You had a direct in with little Miss Enzo Jr, and you wasted the opportunity. But I'm glad you did, or you'd be dead now. Instead, I have the pleasure of killing you slowly—after I break you—from years and years of labor under my command."

Tronido runs a hand down Rockland's arm that he broke. I would kill to know what he's thinking. "I tried once, but Little Miss Fix-It healed you. I am impressed. Will have to get me one of those vet doctors under my control. But she isn't here now to save you. I will enjoy watching the spirit die in your eyes, like it has in your sister's."

I close my eyes because I don't want to witness Rocks lunging at him again. My hands make a fist, protecting the first limbs I'll part with. But Rocks shows Tronido the control that years of dealing with Strickland taught him. I can't even hear him breathing. I don't think Tronido realizes how much shit Rockland is capable of dealing with without it breaking his spirit.

Tronido chuckles again. "Oh, I was hoping to spill a little blood today, but I see you're a fast learner. Now, Little Fox."

He paces over and I stare at the scuffmarks on his boots. I pretend to start sobbing and hang my head lower. "I'm sorry. I just wanted the fix. Please. That's all. I don't understand what's going on," I sob.

"There is no fix!" He turns back to Rocks. "Did you hear that? No. Fix. It was such a laughable scheme, and never in a million years did I expect to catch you in my trap, Rockland. Never in my wildest dreams. I can't wait to think of ways to use you against your Sire."

"He's not my Sire any more."

That gets Tronido's attention. For all he knows about the Shadows, he hasn't heard about Rocks getting banished.

"Do tell. This will—" Two heavily tattooed males enter and beckon Tronido to the door. They have a hushed conversation. "It will have to wait until tomorrow. Business calls, but we will talk again, Rockland."

He walks over, grabs my chin and pulls my face up. My hair is still mostly obscuring my face. His eyes land on the fox head tattoo that covers half my neck. "If you try to escape, I'll chop his wings off and feed him to my pets. Clear?" I nod. "Rockland, she will pay the same price for your mistakes, and *then* I'll fly to Connie's house and murder her whole family. That's a promise."

I have to restrain myself from letting his words show how much they affect me. This deep primal urge inside roars to life, and I want to bite him, claw him, scratch his eyes out, anything to hurt or maim him for threatening my family. I follow Rocks' example and remain still, digging my nails into my palms.

Tronido leaves and the thugs, who are still behind Rocks, nudge him to get up. We return to the workstation with the others. All eyes are on us when we both return not bleeding, and Moondust exhales and mumbles something under his breath looking at the heavens.

Everyone works for twelve hours on his or her feet with no lunch break—all day. By two in the afternoon, my stomach is roaring, and my back is protesting loudly. I want to sit down, but will my knees to lock in place standing. I don't want to find out what they will do to Rocks if I take a seat.

I walk to the drinking fountain by the bathrooms. At least in the warehouse, there are real, aeronaught-style, flushing toilets! I nearly cried when I got to use them earlier.

A few guards patrol the room to make sure everyone is working, but we stop for water breaks or to use the bathroom without needing permission. I take a long drag of cool water. The stench from the cocaine has totally killed my sense of smell. Before I finish my drink, a young girl is beside me so closely she's totally invading my personal space.

"We met when you visited. I'm Moonlight," she whispers so quietly I only just understand her. "Tell everyone to take as much plastic as they can." She opens her fist to reveal a handful of the plastic used to wrap the cocaine bricks. She shoves it inside her waistband and takes a cup.

I return to my station and pass her message to the others. Nobody questions me, but when none of the guards are looking, everyone starts discreetly pocketing the used plastic. My flimsy skirt is no good, but I manage to shove quite a bit of plastic up under my corset. The hard bones of it hide the plastic perfectly.

Tronido clearly learned a lot from Enzo and is distributing the cocaine in lip-gloss holders too. They do make the perfect cover for a gram or two of blow. The stack of lip-gloss sitting on our worktable at the end of our grueling twelve-hour shift is mind-boggling. How on earth can he move this much cocaine? And then I remember my job in the counting room. This operation is big compared to Enzo's standards, so he must have caves full of cash around here somewhere.

Much later, RainCloud tells me to use the bathroom again, and I realize it must be almost quitting time. I'm so exhausted I understand why the Duskwing trudged back to the cave the previous night when we joined them. My legs are heavy and stiff, and my lower back is screaming with every step. The day is finally over.

One by one we make the trek back to our sleeping quarters. I want to call it our jail cell, but that indicates something connected to the law and nothing about this place is law abiding.

The table in the hallway has an assortment of sandwiches and fruit. It's nowhere near enough to feed even a quarter of the hungry Camazotz walking past. I want to snatch up as much as I can carry, but then I think of all those behind me in the long procession, and the hungry pup we met last night picking at the crumbs.

The human pyramid is waiting for me when I enter the bird room. I hand my food to Rocks and scramble up to the air duct. He steps on the back of one of the helpers to hand me my breakfast, lunch and dinner. Lying on the cool, steel duct feels so incredibly good. I'm off my aching feet. I'm tempted to have a little nap, but I need to clear out of the way so every member can get to safety before those deadly dogs come running.

Elm and Oak are waiting for me when I touch down from my aerial swing. They hold up an apple and a bag of chips. "We got this for you, Miss. Connie. We know you can't drink blood and didn't want you to be hungry."

My heart breaks a little. These super shy boys—who could hardly utter a single word to me at the market—have been forced to grow up at the compound under such harsh conditions. Yet, their kindness and compassion hasn't been broken.

Both of them were thin before they left, so now they look particularly frail. "Boys, it would make me so happy if you would eat those instead, please."

"Thank you," they echo, before leading me through the bunk bed maze to my sleeping area. They reverse up a few steps to clearly be in the permissible zone, since they are only pups and this is the Sire's quarters.

Back safely on the bunk, I want to keep something for breakfast, but decide I'll use another protein bar instead. Young Moonlight shows up, looking way too happy for a girl who spent twelve-hours cutting cocaine on her feet with no food.

"I'm collecting all the plastic. I can't wait to show you what I'm making for you, Connie. You're gonna love it."

"Can we help too?" Elm and Oak ask from behind her.

22
Face-off

"WE need a plan. I'm not living out the rest of my days like today," I announce to Rocks when he returns to the bunk.

All the Camazotz want to talk to him. They want to hear news of the outside world. The tale of little Moonshadow flying all the way to the Shadows colony alone to raise the alarm of their bat-napping is becoming legend. My heart aches each time I think of the brave little pup, and the sad news she will receive when we manage to escape regarding her mother.

"Let's go over the facts one more time with the others," Rocks suggests. "We need every little detail. I'm not living out the rest of my days with Tronido gloating the way he did. I won't be able to stand it. I want to... ugh... I want to do bad things to that bat!" His hands form fists in front of his body.

"Ugh, me too! I've never ever had the urge to physically attack someone until today in that room with him. But his ego is going to be his downfall. I pray there is something he's overlooked."

RainCloud, Moondust, and Nighthawk explain the security measures once more when they join us. There is no escape for bats because the moment they enter the duct, an alarm sounds which sends them into nap land for ninety minutes. If a human body passes down the air duct after the birds are released, the dogs are there, waiting to tear their victim apart.

The Muerte all sleep during the day, except for the workroom guards. At night, the compound is almost Muerte-less since they all take to the skies to transport and/or sell the cut drugs. We're not sure where exactly we're located address-wise, but according to the heirs of the Muerte fold members, we're very close to the Muerte headquarters.

"So that puts us somewhere in Walker County, right?" I say. The Camazotz all stare at me until Rocks explains how each state is divided into counties for the government.

"How does that help us?" Moondust asks.

"Because I have a cell phone, and as soon as we come up with a plan, I intend to use it to bring backup."

"Connie, outside help isn't going to be any use, unless we can get everyone out in one night," RainCloud says. "We cannot risk leaving anyone behind. It's too dangerous. I spent the first three weeks I was trapped here thinking about an escape plan night after night after night. It can't be done."

"But why not lock us behind iron bars?" I ask the group. "Tronido is almost daring us to escape with these crazy security measures of birds and dogs. It's a game to him."

"That's said like a true aeronaught. Birds and vicious dogs aren't your natural enemies," Nighthawk says. "They are killers, and no game to a Camazotz. This is a serious prison."

The others all agree.

"Yes, but what Tronido isn't counting on is an aeronaught on the inside willing to help you all escape. I know in my gut there is a weakness. We simply need to find it."

Celand arrives and asks Rocks to come speak with some of the others. He invites me to come along, but I want to spend the time plotting, and I need to clean the cuts on my legs before lights out.

There absolutely has to be a way to escape.

As I apply the fresh bandages, I think and think and think. There has to be a way. That a-hole planned this prison for a colony of bats—not to imprison me.

I turn my phone over and over in my hands as I stare up at the high stone walls. My charger is in the trunk of the Honda, along with all my clothes. I can't risk wasting any battery life, even though I want to check again to see if we magically have service.

The lights flick off and it catches me off-guard. I take a deep breath and remind myself that friends surround me in the darkness. Nobody here is going to hurt me.

"Connie," Rocks says from beside me. I look in his direction but can't see a thing. "I didn't want to scare you. I'm coming up. Move over."

His warm body gives me comfort as he lies down and wraps his arms around me. "I never got the chance to apologize," he says. "I'm sorry—really sorry."

"Why?" God, I wish I could see his face.

"For getting you kidnapped."

"I'm not. Now stop being ridiculous," I reply.

"I'm not! If I had been happy as me, we would never be in this mess. It's all my fault."

"This isn't your fault. You didn't know this was going to happen," I argue.

"But if I didn't want the fix, we wouldn't be trapped here."

"If you didn't want the fix, then we never would have found Celand."

He's quiet for a while.

"Rocks, this is somehow part of your journey. You learn the most when you're being tested. I learned so much about what I could endure while Mini was being held hostage. Before that letter, my life was so easy and neat. Nothing messy. Nothing complicated. It was easy to walk in my shoes. I was lucky."

"I don't see how that's relevant."

"Your life has prepared you to fight hard. Living with adversity is way harder than 'lucky' people realize. I only realize now after I felt like my luck ran out for a bit. You are so strong, and everyone in here is going to need your strength to get them out."

"I wanted the fix. How can you say I was strong? It seems so weak of me now."

"No, Rocks. You and I were meant to find this place. You had to *want* to be fixed in order for this to happen. It was fate. Sometimes the worst moments in your life make you the strongest, but it's not until later you see it. That letter showing up on my doorstep was fate. It brought me to you. It made me see what I can endure to protect my family. Did I want to crawl into a ball and give up? Yes, so many times.

"Did I want my life to return to easy and neat? Hell, yes. But all of it led me here. It led you here. Now we've found the Duskwing and Celand, you and I are going to fight to free everyone. My parents never looked at me the way Strickland looked at you when you were growing up. You never let him break you. Can't you see how incredible you are?"

"I'm not incredible."

"Oh my god, you are. You've had to justify who you are to your wing your whole life. They've judged you. But you stood up to them."

"No, I didn't."

"Yes, you did. You would sneak off with Judge to buy donuts. You read aeronaught comics. You slept in your wagon instead of as a bat at the roost. You were brave enough to trust me and to take a chance on a human to discover your human side. You fought for who you are, but it's an ongoing battle. Many people hide their differences or diversity for their entire life. But you did what was comfortable to you, despite their sneers.

"Rocks, you've stood your ground. Don't ever think otherwise. Just because you haven't convinced them to be open-minded doesn't mean you failed. That's on Strickland for not seeing the beauty and courage his son possesses. That's his fault—not yours. Hasn't it ever struck you as odd every time I've dealt with Strickland, he's been human? You taught me how to listen for your telepathic messages, and I hear them whether I want to or not. Strickland—who claims being in bat form is so superior—is never a bat when I'm around. I'm not a threat to him when he's a bat. He knows that, but why is he always in the form he persecutes you so badly for preferring?"

"Shit. I never thought of it like that."

"Exactly. So don't feel bad for wanting to get fixed. You didn't fail. Your Sire failed you and made you believe that was the only way. But it was actually meant to be. In the bigger picture, you and I were meant to end up here, because we're going to find a way out. You are going to prove to Strickland what an incredible Camazotz you are and always have been. I believe it in my heart. And I want you to as well."

He sighs. I reach up to cup his cheek and he guides my hand to his face. "Believe in what you are capable of, Rocks."

"You're the most incredible woman. I love you more and more everyday." He leans over and kisses me. "It's funny because I've often thought of how fate did bring us together, so you're right. I am meant to be here. Thank you."

MY BODY GROANS waking up on day two at the compound. I pray Mom and Dad haven't been texting me, as they'll be really worried since I haven't replied. Our plan for today is to see if my phone has service outside. I dig it out of the backpack, while Rocks gets his wooden dagger.

"You can use the utility knife if you need," I suggest.

"No, this will work," Rocks replies.

The Muerte confiscated all items that can be used as weapons from the Duskwing. The idiots who allowed Rocks to bring his dagger, and me the utility knife might be wingless if Tronido finds out. RainCloud suspects it's to make blooding items for transportation as a bat harder. The Camazotz need a tiny amount of their blood on any personal items for them to vanish with them when they transform. Rocks pricks his skin and we both watch the blood pool on his fingertip.

"You sure you don't mind?" he asks again.

I sigh. "I'm not answering that again. When are you going to accept I have fully accepted every part of you? Plus, it's the safest way."

He grins before smearing a little blood on my phone and the case, then tucking it in his back pocket next to his phone.

"We're ready," he announces to the Duskwing fold members.

A murmur of excitement suddenly starts to ripple through the bunk beds. Moondust pulls himself up, so he's standing on the bottom bunk and looking out over the sleeping area.

"This sometimes happens, but I don't know what could possibly be good news this morning," he explains. He looks all around, even toward the sheer rock face. "Oh my goodness."

Rocks asks him what he can see, and when he steps down, he directs his answer at me. "You're going to love this."

We follow him through the beds toward the exit—the only exit in the series of caves we now call home. Pushing through the crowd towards us is young Moonlight. "Miss Connie, I did it. I worked all night and did it. Look," she says, pointing up at the vent.

Hanging from the air duct is a ladder.

A ladder!

"What? How? You made that?" I ask her.

She positively beams with pride. "Yes! With all the plastic and some of the goats' straw. Do you like it? I've tested it. It's very strong. Plastic makes good rope if you have enough of it."

The ladder is a flexible rope ladder construction. I approach the end of it and pick up one of the rungs. Just as she said, it's made from woven straw and plastic strips. There are ends poking out every so often along the length of it.

"I'm sorry it's not very pretty, because I don't have a knife to cut off all these bits. But now you can climb up and down yourself."

I'm stunned. These Camazotz are so kind and welcoming. I wish Rockland had grown up amongst them.

"I love it. Thank you so much. You're so clever. This is really incredible."

Moondust comes and inspects the weave. "Very well done, Moonlight. You can have my food this evening as well as your own share. Excellent work."

The young girl—with the pretty smile—grins from ear-to-ear. "Thank you, Sire. Thank you."

Moonlight explains to the group how she secured it to the air duct rim. Rocks gives it a hard yank and it doesn't fall. "Do you mind if I test it too?"

I indicate for him to have a go. He takes hold and starts the climb. It reminds me of those ladders trapeze artists use to climb to their death-defying heights above the circus. I study his technique, so I'll be able to make it to the top while the whole freaking colony watch. Don't want to embarrass myself now.

Rocks waves down from above. He's sitting on the small ledge of stone by the duct. I take a deep breath and start my ascent. The rope is surprisingly solid and with the help of those below, it doesn't sway too much. I don't look down and keep putting one foot after the other, until I see Rocks' hands waiting to help.

Once I'm in the vent, I give a shout of triumph, and the spectators below cheer. It was something nice to break the monotony of their daily life.

Outside in the morning light as planned, the group forms around Rocks and I. When we're certain no guard is looking, he slips out the phones. The wait for each device to activate is agonizing. More Camazotz flip and join the group, pretending to enjoy a moment in the fresh air.

I'm so delighted when fourteen texts messages appear on my screen. Only three are from the folks. Tiff wants updates on my college choice and my road trip with Rocks—she can wait. I quickly send a message to Mom telling her we're still in Georgia on a slight detour. I hate lying, but couldn't bring myself to type the words 'we're fine' or 'safe.' That would be a huge lie.

Rocks sends Jez a text saying he's found the Duskwing and the fix was a trap. Celand requested he not tell any of the Shadows she's alive. He tried to argue with her, but she was so upset about it, he eventually agreed.

We wait as long as we can risk for any replies, but Mom must be busy with Mini. Moondust says it's too unusual to loiter any longer and requests we turn them off. He's probably right. Our goal was to check if they work, and they do in the middle of the quarry. I take a quick screen shot and hand it over to Rocks. A moment later, he flips and flies the phones back down to the safety of the cavern.

He doesn't join me at our table until RainCloud appears. I frown at him because I was starting to panic. "She needed help with several of the elderly. They're too old to be working these hours," he whispers. "I have to do something."

RainCloud stands on my other side. She leans in close to me. "What you said to Rockland last night about his inner strength and what he's capable of?"

I look at her and nod to show I know which conversation she's referring to. There isn't any privacy in the cavern.

"It almost made me cry and not much makes me cry. You are a special young lady, Little Fox. And from this day forward can consider yourself a member of the Duskwing."

I gasp and look at her, then Moondust standing opposite us. He gives me a slight head nod in agreement with her. I feel Rocks lean over and bow back at the Sire and Fold members at our table.

"Thank you," we both say in unison, aware the day is about to commence, and we need to keep quiet.

The entrance at the end of the long warehouse opens and carts deliver the bricks to each table. I want to scream at the thought of weighing and bagging for the next twelve-hours straight with nothing but a few bathroom breaks to break the monotony.

"Tell Tronido I need to speak with him," Rocks commands one of the thugs.

This kind of thing clearly never happens because several of them huddle around discussing whether to listen to him or not. Last night, we all agreed the only way out was to have every single detail of the operation. A huge unanswered question is how the Muerte got involved selling drugs to begin with. They've been capturing workers for a long time since Celand is here, so Rocks and I want to make sure we know everything possible. It feels like we're missing something.

"Start working," the thug orders when he returns.

"I will after I've spoken with Tronido."

Rocks folds his arms over his chest the same way I've seen Strickland do almost every time I've seen the man. The thug hesitates and then delivers some product to the next table, deciding not to challenge him.

Tronido walks in with a blank expression. I know every set of eyes in this room is on him, and he probably knows it too.

"This is very dangerous, Rockland. Commanding to speak with me? It better be good." He stops opposite Rockland and mirrors his stance, but it doesn't look as powerful on the much shorter male.

"I want to discuss the labor conditions."

Tronido's eyes widen before he gets control of his features. He stares at Rocks and then starts to slowly shake his head. "You've finally found your balls. I have to admit it's ballsy to be here five seconds and now you're representing *my* workforce. Maybe you stole Moondust's balls, yet he's never had the stupidity to do this. I won't punish you—or your life mate—because this is exactly what I would do if I were in your shoes. I'm impressed. Tell me what you want."

"You're working your captives to death. Plain and simple. Connie told me every single detail about Enzo's operation. Enzo said he was successful because of the people he had working for him. He looked after them, he even paid them money, because without them he had nothing. You need us strong, healthy, and standing at these tables everyday for a long time to come, correct?"

Tronido's nose flares. Rocks has hit his mark. Telling Tronido he knows about the business from Enzo was Rocks' idea, and I think it's about to work. It evens up the playing field between the two males and actually gives Rockland the upper hand because Enzo had been doing this for decades.

"Yes."

"At this rate, you're going to kill half of us. Look at my sister. She's underfed, dressed in rags, and is completely exhausted. You broke her, and soon she won't be productive. Can you afford to lose the workers you have?"

Tronido frowns, but Rocks doesn't wait for him to answer.

"Of course, you can't. Have you worked out the return you get on your investment in each of us?"

Now he waits. Tronido doesn't answer, and his eyes hold a tiny moment of fear before he closes down. Rocks was counting on him not having an answer to that question.

"Smart businessmen always study returns," Rocks continues, spouting what I learned in accounting class this year. "Then they can work out how much to reinvest in their workers. You admitted to making more money than you ever dreamed possible yesterday, so it's time to invest some more of it back into a very essential part of your operation. Us.

"We need twenty-four hour access to a hot shower and flushing toilets. You need us happy in human form for twelve-hour shifts, so indulge our human needs. We need more aeronaught food—at least six times what you're currently leaving out. I have a list of bargain, bulk items Connie brought to the Shadows after you kidnapped the Duskwing. These will feed us and won't break your budget. Next, we need one day off a week to rest. Lastly, new clothing."

Tronido doesn't say a word and a slow smile creases his face. "I never knew you had a mind for business. You really did waste such an opportunity with Enzo. And now I think you know it."

Rocks agrees, "As much as I hate to admit you're right, you are. I did miss an opportunity, but what I can't work out is how you managed to get an in with Enzo. He is a shrewd man, who is very difficult to fool, or deceive, and yet you managed to do both. Now, that's what I call ballsy."

My thought is Tronido is riding his ego way too much. He thinks he's untouchable and is therefore bound to make a mistake, or at least, underestimate us. Rocks is trying to flatter him just enough to trick him into telling us his whole story.

Tornido's eyes narrow slightly, but then he breaks into a wide smile. "Thank you. I think it was ballsy myself. What I will share is that a Camazotz true power lies in embracing both sides—human *and* bat."

We've got him.

"You already know the old Vuelo de la Muerte way of thinking matched Strickland's—bat form is everything. I discovered otherwise! As Camazotz, our bat form gives us power in the aeronaught world. We have advantages, and the upper hand if we play our cards right."

He starts pacing in a wide circle around Rockland. Not another soul dares to speak as every member listens to him spill his secret of creating this compound and enslaving his fellow Camazotz. Even his worker thugs are standing still and listening to every word.

"I don't understand," encourages Rocks.

"My goal was money but easy money. I saw all these aeronaughts with so much wealth, but getting a job was not an option. I sent my crew out night after night to lurk in the shadows and see what business opportunities I could take advantage of. Sex and drugs happen in the dark corners of every city. The thought of having to run aeronaught women was too hard—too many problems. But trafficking drugs? Easy for a creature who can fly over a border under the radar. Literally, under air traffic radars. We were born for it, Rockland." He laughs to himself.

If I didn't know any better, I would swear he was slightly manic, but I think he's getting off on his own genius. I'm not sure which is more disturbing.

"But that doesn't explain how you got in?" Rocks pushes. "I can't believe you did it so quickly."

"Humans are so ignorant. Nobody cares about a little bat clinging to an alley wall. My crew and I listened and watched and followed. We found the users, then the buyers, then the suppliers. And eventually, we found where they were bringing in the cocaine from South America."

"They?" Rocks asks.

"The Vipers. Such a sloppy operation. It was easy to infiltrate for anyone with bat ears and half a brain. When I made my first contact as a human, they thought I'd been in the business for years, because being able to eavesdrop in the dark, gave me prices and how deals went down, who was dirty and who was solid. It was easy to start distributing for them. They lacked leadership, so I climbed their ranks quickly."

He explains how the Vipers were obsessed with stealing some of Enzo's territory, since they were archrivals from way back.

"So that became my pet project, and I was good at it because of my other side—my bat within. When I took my first block of Enzo's soil, I was promoted, and they soon learned I had a stomach for blood. But when the Vipers' boss got arrested for those trumped up murder charges, the shit hit the fan."

He walks back to stand directly in front of Rocks and spits on the floor. His eyes are hard and angry when he continues. "Those fools, ugh, so weak and useless. Mitchell Jones was the brains and balls of the Vipers. When his brother was forced to take control while he was on trial, it fell apart. His brother wasn't cut out for the hard side of things. Connie for example!"

He stares at Rocks. My blood has frozen in my veins as I recall that horrible, decaying house those two thugs locked me in, and the moment

'Joey' showed up and everything that followed. I'm glad I didn't eat breakfast earlier.

"What about Connie?"

"Oh, Rockland, Connie's kidnapping. His brother has his biggest enemy's daughter tied to a chair, and he didn't pull the trigger himself? Weak! That's what it was. So weak it made me sick."

"He *really* wanted Connie dead?" Rocks' voice is barely above a whisper.

23
Played

TRONIDO'S face displays an expression of 'hells yeah, fool' spread across it.

"Of course, he wanted her dead. But your brothers interfered. She was lucky, because Mitchell's brother could never stay around to witness if his orders were carried out. He also hired half-brained buffoons to save money, but they always screwed up. I mean, they were supposed to kidnap *Sophia* Ascari, and they got your little angel instead—such amateurs. But, I started to take care of things properly. Camazotz have the stomach for blood letting." He sneers, licking his lips.

Tronido walks around again and is looking at the Fold members standing on either side of me. He wants an audience with power.

"Slowly, but surely, I gained authority until their boss was calling me directly. I had his trust and was basically running their operation, and any of the old boys who didn't like it didn't last long. And my bats had my back. But the Vipers business was nickel and dime stuff compared to Enzo Ascari. He was a hard nut to crack. He doesn't trust easily, but he understands the importance of blood. Blood—how perfect. It's what Camazotz know best.

"With patience, I was able to make a buy. I moved the product quickly in the Vipers' territory, so I could increase my next buy. I paid cash in advance because I had heard Enzo respected that. Enzo likes to know his product can be moved without raising alarms, and he's hesitant to increase supply if it will jeopardize his whole operation. He's smart."

"Yes, he is," Rocks agrees.

"But I'm smarter. I spied on his other suppliers and began reporting any who were breaking Enzo's rules. Enzo wasn't very forgiving of anyone who broke his rules. When four of his key players were out of the way, it left it open for me to offer to take up their turf. Enzo tested me, and I passed every time. Camazotz hearing means I always had the right answer. But I wanted to *be* Enzo."

Tronido describes in detail how he became obsessed with finding a weakness in the Ascari organization. He listened and spied and followed, but it only got him so far. Enzo was safe and strong and not going anywhere.

"You could have killed him?" Rocks suggests.

"No. Enzo had an empire, and it was organized. If Enzo went down, Sophia would take command. After her, he had a chain of lieutenants waiting for their chance at promotion. Even with all the ground I had gained with Enzo, I was still a mere foot soldier—maybe a sergeant at best. The death toll would have been too great for a bloody takeover, and the cops would have gotten involved. No, I was trying to work out how to take Enzo down the smart way."

He strides around looking at all the shocked workers, holding his arms out wide. He's a showman taking center stage. Listening to him tell his tale, as though it's full of glory, when it's deadly and illegal is making it hard to stand still and focus on the scales before me. I want to slap his smug face more than ever.

"And who should wander in one day?" His eyes are wide and crazed as he stares up at Rocks.

"Little Miss Blondie! Wasn't I surprised to see the father-daughter reunion? I knew if I just waited long enough, things would fall into place. And seeing what Connie would do for her sister, gave me ideas to deal with my annoying Fold and Sire. I'll give you one thing, Rockland. Your taste in women is impeccable. Blondie is smart and patient. I trusted my intuition and it paid off. Little Blondie took care of everything I needed. I already had information on where Enzo got his product, and the channels of how to bring it in under Border Control's noses.

"We don't need to worry about shipping. My Camazotz fly it in using the harnesses on a moonless night. Sometimes we fly as a colony of bats and each bring two or three bricks—depends on what's happening with the cops. I was bringing in as much as I could cut, but I needed more worker bees.

"When aeronaughts go missing, those pesky police officers hunt around like bloodhounds on a scent. I decided it was too hard to use humans for workers. I couldn't risk them seeing what we are, so I had to keep it in the 'family' so to speak. I needed Camazotz who didn't mind being human for twelve-hours a day.

"My trusted comrades were busy with importation, so I needed factory workers to command. My crew drives off the property in vans because of the owls we feed regularly to encourage living here—"

"You encourage those fowl creatures to live around here?" Rocks clarifies.

"Yes, that way I know no nosy Shadows' member will discover my compound. The owls are smarter than you might think. They can be trained too."

"But don't they risk your own members?"

"We know they're there. But the owls tend to stay within a certain boundary near their food source, so like I said, we drive out of that zone safely. Once we are out of hunting range, my soldiers take to the skies to deliver the cut product, or collect the pure coke, or our cash. It also protects my operation here because nobody could locate it following my soldiers by air. But can you see my problem?"

He waits for an answer and looks around the room.

"The cutting needed to be done, and more and more of it needed to be done as I expanded. None of my colony would volunteer for that shit when they could be winging it at night at altitude, so I naturally thought of the one group of Camazotz who don't mind a little human time."

I want to look at Rocks, but I won't risk a single move that might distract Tronido from spilling his guts. Now we know the night sky around the compound is full of owls—a detail we didn't have before, and a crucial one for a successful escape plan. Nobody is going to be flying out of here.

"I set my plan in motion to acquire a free labor force. What I discovered with my owl releases at both your colonies," he says, gesturing to Rockland and Moondust, "was that when a Camazotz goes missing, or is killed, nobody notices except his wing. So a colony of missing Camazotz wasn't going to cause a problem."

One of the thugs delivers more bricks of product to each table, but Tronido doesn't seem to care. He must crave an audience to listen to how great he thinks he is.

"But why attack aeronaughts? Couldn't you just kidnap the Duskwing in secret? You risked our exposure," Rocks asks.

"Of course, I could have." He laughs like the devil. It's cold and makes my skin turn to gooseflesh. "But what would be the fun in that?"

"Fun?" Rocks asks. The set of his shoulders tells me he's a heartbeat away from grabbing Tronido and having some 'fun' of his own. I know Rocks won't lay a finger on him because he's too concerned with what will happen to me. But I sense he wants to more than ever.

"I wouldn't have been able to terrorize the Shadows. Make your Sire worry he's not as solid and capable as he once was. Destabilization is the key to my success. I've done it repeatedly—with the aeronaught dealers, and then to prevent your nosy, bossy Sire getting wind of my business."

Tronido goes on to describe Strickland as being similar to Enzo— nothing much gets past him. Tronido was concerned Strickland would notice the amount of money they were making and start asking how and why.

"I needed to distract him, so I thought I'd fill in his free time with worry over his own colony—and it worked. Strickland didn't know which direction the attack was coming from. His dislike of technology put him in a dangerous position. He had isolated himself beyond saving. He couldn't text or call his troops to warn them of danger. No, his pups and fledgers were easy pickings for some blooded owls."

A ripple passes down Rocks' arm. My brain is trying hard to block the bloody images of young pups attacked, of Decker ripped to pieces in their defense, of little Bailey's missing eye, the dead Shadows' members, and it was all a game to Tronido. I side-eye RainCloud and her lips are pulled back over her teeth in a silent snarl. She must be remembering all the injured and dead from the Duskwing, and wants to tear Tronido limb from limb.

"When we started the aeronaught attacks, I knew your little 'naught would come running to tell you—and in turn Strickland would hear about it. It weakened his position by having to rely on an aeronaught for information about the Camazotz. Without little blondie in the mix, my plan was all for nothing. She was the connection, but just the bare minimal connection to the modern world. Enough to spook them into chaos." Tronido rubs his hands together, looking like a mad man.

That fucking bastard.

He played our weakness to his strength, and if Strickland isn't careful, the colony won't survive. I feel sick I was part of his plan and never realized it. I did exactly as he predicted, reporting the terror and causing more uncertainty. He manipulated us all.

Not only did I help destabilize Strickland, but I handed Tronido the Ascari drug trade by taking Enzo out. He needs all the Camazotz trapped in this room, because I freed my baby sister, giving him more territory and a bigger need for workers.

Fucking hell!

We were all played and for such a long time. I thought I was helping the colony by reporting the news. I swallow the disgust bubbling up in my throat.

Tronido is watching Rocks, and I'm guessing Rocks is trying to process this tangled web too.

"But you? Ah, catching you in my web was the last thing I expected," he says to Rocks. "I never thought you'd dare try for the fix after Celand. Getting you into my labor camp is a real feather in my cap. In the early days, Sylvana did all she could to recruit sad, little, lost Camazotz who wanted the fix—"

"Sylvana?" Rocks growls.

"You hadn't worked that out? Yes, she's my third cousin," he states, like it's old news.

That ugly, fake hag is a double agent. I will strangle her with her sage sticks when I get my hands on her. But then I think of what Strickland will do when he finds out she betrayed him. She'll make Rockland look like the golden child. I focus back on Tronido's words. My visions of revenge can wait for another day.

"She spread those ludicrous rumors around each colony, until it felt like part of our myth—a real part of our creation history. And one by one, little bats joined my humble beginnings. There's no fix, Rockland."

"Are you sure about that?"

He laughs. "Were you not listening? I am the one who started the 'tale of old.' It's bullshit. A lie. We are what we are, and there's no changing that. The Camazotz curse can never be broken."

"But how did your Fold allow you to recruit workers back when Celand went missing? How did they not punish your crimes?" Rocks asks, frowning.

He's got a point. If Rocks had gotten involved with the aeronaught drug trade, Strickland would have locked him in a small, iron cage and thrown away the key.

Tronido laughs again. "You have to be one step ahead, dear Rockland. I never rush in. I'm patient, and patience pays big dividends. When my business was still in the pup stage, I kidnapped the three eldest children of each Fold member and each Clip. That gave me my first hit of workforce to really start things moving. Where are my originals anyway?"

He looks around the room, leaning around workers to try to find the heirs of the Vuelo de la Muerte. He waves at the table in the far corner and laughs. The workers standing there are deathly thin and almost dressed in rags. Half of them aren't even looking Tronido's way, but just going through the motions of preparing the cocaine. My heart aches for them. I remember being Enzo's puppet—forced to do what he wanted to save Mini. They were the puppets that forced their whole colony to conform. I thank up above Mini is too small to ever remember how Enzo used her.

"Then with the help of my wing—who agreed my way was the only way into the future for the Camazotz—we took over. The Fold was to act and appear as though all was happy and well. Nothing was amiss. If Strickland came sticking his annoying nose into our affairs, and the Fold didn't set him straight and tell him nothing was wrong, then one child from each wing would lose a wing—literally. I would chop off their wing, cauterize the bleeding, and let them suffer a slow painful death. No father or mother would risk an ugly death for his or her child—

especially after I chopped off my first wing. Only had the pleasure of doing it three times. Once to show my Sire I meant business, then again when the Duskwing arrived."

He's referring to Ganymede. He's a sick, twisted bat. If it's the last thing I do, I'm going to ruin him—exactly like I did to Enzo. Somehow I will find a way to end him.

"And lastly when I needed to keep the tension level at maximum velocity at the Shadows. I want every detail of how Strickland reacted when Connie came running to you with the body I left on her roof. Do tell." He bows down with his arm out wide as though he's giving Rocks the spotlight.

"Strickland doesn't know," Rocks says, quietly.

Tronido's nose flares wide. "What do you mean he doesn't know?"

"Connie and I decided not to tell him. The murdered bat wasn't a member of the Shadows."

RainCloud flinches at my side. I risk a quick glance at her. She's staring at Tronido with such loathing, I'm surprised she isn't burning up from the inside out—her rage a lethal inferno.

"Ah, what a shame. I was hoping he would panic and move the whole colony. If you're curious, it was some old female who didn't have the energy to perform the work I need. She was the last one out each morning, so chop-chop, and she was the perfect scare tactic. But I'm betting Connie hasn't slept well in her room since." He chuckles to himself.

I realize now why RainCloud is the last member out each morning. She's protecting the other elderly members of her colony. The Duskwing are so caring and honorable. I wish they were my introduction to the Camazotz world.

A muscle in Rocks' cheek flinches. He looks as though he's made of solid steel. "You're a sick bastard," Rocks growls.

"I'm itching to chop off another wing, Rockland, so don't go giving me any reason to. Any more questions? You take after your nosy father I see."

"No more questions for today. Perhaps I'll have one for tomorrow when you give me an answer about my labor requests." Rockland stands tall again and folds his arms.

"I'm glad to see you've embraced the idea of staying."

"I've analyzed your security measures, and regretfully, you've given me no choice but to stay. A little over the top for my taste but definitely effective."

"If any nosy aeronaughts came wandering in, I didn't want it to look too much like a prison. You know those crazy aeronaughts will climb any mountain, hill, or rock they can find. If they come to the quarry for an adventure, then hunting birds and dogs aren't illegal." Tronido smiles.

For the life of me, I couldn't work out why he went to such lengths with securing us. He could have just put up a big iron fence, but now I understand. It does have the appearance of an abandoned quarry and seeing a savage guard dog isn't unusual on private property.

"You really have thought of everything, Tronido," Rockland says. His Adam's apple bobs in his throat as he spits out the compliment.

"Glad I have your approval," he sneers, sarcastically. "I'm off to bed if we're done. Work hard for me now, won't you all?"

The whole room is buzzing—with anger. I glance around and everyone is looking at each other—not game to say a word—but the message in their eyes is all the same. I pray none of them resent me for the part I played in his grand plan.

When Rocks comes to join me, we look at each other. It's so frustrating knowing we have over eleven-hours before we can discuss everything we learned.

I take the gram of powder off the scales and carefully pour it into the lip balm tube. I will spend every single minute between now and then planning our escape.

My gut is telling me there's a way out, and for the first time in my life, I'm going to believe it.

24
Dogs

"WE can't fly out because of the owls or falcons. We can't crawl out because of the dogs," Celand says again. "Rockland, you need to accept it can't be done. And even if we were to get past those two attacks, then we'll be picked off in the skies trying to leave the compound. It can't be done."

"Celand's right," Moondust echoes. "There are too many of us. And with the life mate threat, we can't risk a few escaping because those left behind will be slaughtered. You heard how Tronido wants to have a reason to torture us. He wants to chop off wings."

I watch from the top bunk while the lights are still on as the group discuss our options—or lack thereof—yet again. Rocks and I gave our condolences to the Duskwing as soon as we were out of the warehouse and allowed to talk. The elderly bat was RainCloud's grandmother—SilverCloud. The Duskwing were grateful we buried her, and Rocks performed the rituals as best he could with what he had. RainCloud had hugged each of us for several minutes, clearly relieved to know her beloved gran's body is resting at peace.

"If we can get everyone out of here, then I can help with getting us away safely," I add. All eyes are on me. "Judge can bring the Shadows' van and my parents will bring theirs. All Rocks and I need to do is call."

"But we don't know our location, Connie," Rocks rebuts.

"I took a screen shot of our location on my GPS app. I'll email that and get Mom to locate my phone. Lots of parents can track where their kid's phones are. Mom's never done it, but I know she has the feature turned on."

Rocks and I discuss how we could send Judge with Jeremiah to my folk's house, and then we would have two vans to fill up with bats. The Camazotz would only fit if they were in bat form. But it's a safe way to get us past the hunting owls surrounding the compound.

The others don't seem convinced of this part, since they don't believe Rocks and I can truly get word out. I guess they'll need to see it to believe it.

"Let's say we manage to get past the dogs and owls somehow, how long do you think it would take us to get everyone out of the cave and up the road out of sight?" Rocks asks.

"It takes us an hour to get out of here and to the workstations each morning," RainCloud replies. "But that's with us all flying out. There is no way past the alarm, so I have no idea how long it would take for everyone to crawl out. Several hours at least."

"Mmmm... that's too long," Rocks says. "Too long to not be noticed."

"What if some of us brought dozens of bats through unconscious?" I ask, thinking out loud. "That would speed the process up, but we need something to put everyone in."

"Ropes!" Rocks announces, smiling. "Where's Moonlight?"

The young weaver is brought to the group, and RainCloud speaks with her.

Watching young Moonlight stride off into the sleeping area with her task makes me smile. I could tell she was super proud to be summoned for a job critical to our escape plan. She promised to make as much rope as she could, so long as everyone brings her plastic tomorrow.

RainCloud leaves the group to calculate how much hay they can spare for the rope construction, while still keeping the goats healthy.

"Celand, do you think some of the Muerte would talk with us about what they know?" Nighthawk asks.

"I think so. Let me find out." She promises to bring anyone who will talk tonight, even if it's after lights out.

Nighthawk explains the original Muerte members—who were imprisoned at the start—have chosen to seclude themselves from the Duskwing. They feel too ashamed about Tronido rising to power in the way he did, they barely speak to anyone. Celand has been with them since the beginning, they trust her, and she feels more comfortable bunking amongst them. Solidarity through the hardships they've all endured over time.

"Do all the Muerte members happily follow him?" Rocks asks.

"No, before we arrived, Tronido imprisoned any from his colony who fought against his plans. Some of them tried to escape, but he had the life mate system in place for them too."

"Apparently, one night some of the Camazotz didn't return from a flight, and the next day their life mates were dragged down here. But they'd been brutally beaten first. Eleven of them died from broken bones which made flipping impossible," Moondust says. "Celand said it was hideous to watch helplessly."

"I wonder if Tronido told the remaining members he had imprisoned them, or whether he let them think they all were dead?" I ask. Tronido has some sick psychological warfare he uses. I bet he told the trapped Fold and Muerte he killed the life mates of all those who flew away to prevent anyone else doing it.

"Good question, and you're probably right," Nighthawk agrees. "He's evil enough to do that since he's so sure we can't escape. He loves the fact the door is wide open—so to speak—but we still can't leave. He's proud of his mental torment, so if there was an opportunity to torment those who aren't fully loyal to him, I'm sure he jumped at it."

The lights flick out before Celand returns. I lie down and close my eyes. Keeping them open—when it makes me feel blind—pushes my blood pressure up. I like to trick my brain into thinking it's so dark because my eyes are closed instead. Rocks had this genius idea last night, and it does help me stay calm.

"You wish to speak with us?" A voice I don't recognize says.

I sit up looking around, and then try to hide my growl of frustration. A second later, Rocks flips next to me and whispers in my ear that two of the Muerte heirs are here and one other male. He says Asteroide is the eldest born of their Sire, Saturno. And with him is Mantarraya, who is the second child of Océano—the female Fold member he saw when Strickland sent the envoy to gather information. But it's the third of their group I really wish I could see. Rocks says Willow is the son of

Cypress and Venus. Venus is as beautiful as her name suggests, and she mated with Cypress twenty years ago.

"Rockland wishes to know the percentage of Vuelo de la Muerte members who joined forces with Tronido agreeing with his plan," Moondust states. "Will you help him?"

Rocks disappears from my side, so I lay back down and close my eyes again. I want to hear every word spoken, so I must focus on my sense of hearing.

"I'm trying to get a feel for what I witnessed when I visited your headquarters. How many are truly followers?" Rocks asks.

A new voice speaks, "I don't see how this will help you plan an escape, but less than a third really have Tronido's back. The rest are all keeping their heads down to stay alive." I assume this must be Mantarraya talking.

"Why didn't the majority overpower him?" Rocks is almost reading my mind. "Surely there was time if you had the numbers in your favor?"

"Because Tronido took all of the heirs before he made a move. One night, he brought us all together and made an elaborate show of matching us to life mates. I was imprisoned down here when that happened, but some of the others who joined us later for rebelling told me. They had no clue what he was planning. The owls were attacking us and there was chaos.

"Tronido announced his plan for the members up there, and Saturno called for everyone to stand against him—to help him put an end to this madness," Mantarraya continues. His voice is even and calm, but I realize he's only relaying the events. He wasn't a witness himself. "After Saturno made his request for Tronido to be arrested, they chopped off the wing of Ciruela. It was the first time he had mutilated a bat that way. He saw how effective it was. I think you know our Fold member Sandia? Ciruela was his heir."

"Oh, God," Rocks gasps. "Yes, he greeted us when we came. It explains the vacant look in his eyes."

"Only one of the members living down here would talk of it. None of the others will because it was so traumatic. Every member witnessed the bloody, violent, slow death. The group was too shocked to listen to Saturno's plea to fight. It crippled his power instantly."

"But if we could get up there, do you think those members would help us take back the power?" Rocks asks.

"It's hard to say. I couldn't say for sure because none of us know what they have been through. After Ciruela finally died, Tronido's gang grabbed Saturno from the crowd and beat him viciously. The whole colony stood and watched too stunned to step forward. I do not know if any would step forward now either."

"Thank you for your honesty. I know it's difficult to speak of this," Rocks says.

The third new voice speaks, "I know my father and yours have not always seen eye-to-eye, but please don't hold that against me. I too would like to help any way I can." I guess this must be Willow and am surprised he knows of the bad blood between Strickland and Cypress.

"It won't. I don't hold grudges," Rockland assures him. "I will gladly accept any help we can get to free us all."

"Whatever you plan, it will fail," Asteroide states. "But I will help you. I know assisting you will risk my Sire's life, but his life is over already. The humiliation he must feel as each night passes, I can't even imagine. If I am dead, then Saturno won't be forced to bow to them. Sires are a proud breed, as you well know, Rockland. So if we fail, and Saturno is sacrificed along with us, then at least I know I will have aided in ending his suffering and dishonor."

"Thank you, I will call on you when we have a solid plan. Is there anything else you think might aid us?"

"The forest around here is teaming with owls. Before Tronido let the owls go near the Shadows and Duskwing, he experimented here. At the time, none of us realized he was behind the sudden appearance of the winged beasts. Lots of pups went missing. I suspect he used them to blood the birds. Even his right-hand man got attacked and almost lost an eye. Did you ever have the misfortune of meeting Temblor?"

Asteroide describes the large male as obsessed with having his bones tattooed on his skin above the corresponding real skeletal system. "He was seriously attacked by the owls, but miraculously survived. Everyone thought he would lose the sight in his eye, but he showed up weeks later with a rough scar across his left eye. Now having heard the stories of your recovery from a broken wing, I know Tronido must have sought medical aid from the aeronaughts."

"Yes," Rocks says. "He was guarding Sandia and Océano. I asked him about his luck with the scar crossing his eye. There was no way he kept it without modern medicine, but he wouldn't admit it to me."

ON DAY FOUR of our captivity, there are three tables laden with fruit, fresh muffins, and granola bars. My mouth waters as the scent of baked treats hits it. There's enough food laid out for every member to have two items for breakfast. I'm so grateful because I ate my last protein bar yesterday and had no clue how I was going to last twelve grueling hours on my feet without breakfast.

"Mmm-uph, vese ah dericious," a young pup mumbles, around a huge mouthful of blueberry muffin. Everyone has a spring in their step this morning heading to the warehouse.

The whole group is on a mission to get as much plastic as possible for Moonlight. I send up a silent prayer today will be uneventful.

When Rocks and I walk into the huge room, Tronido is standing by our table.

"Nice to see you set an example of coming in first, Rockland. That's good for morale. Did you get my gift?"

"Yes, and the members are all in good spirits this morning because of the breakfast buffet you left. Thank you. You will see the benefits once everyone gets a little stronger. When can we start taking days off?"

The confident smile vanishes and is replaced by a scowl. "No time off. I need every set of hands at the workstations everyday."

"But some of—"

"I SAID NO!" he screams.

I feel as though I jump a foot off the ground. Moondust rests an assuring hand on my back, but removes it quickly. It's never good to make someone stand out in the presence of Tronido.

The cruel Camazotz tries to rein in his emotions, but it's too late. He breathes out through his nose. "Tell me why Connie isn't with you?" He takes another deep breath. "I can't believe she would let you do this craziness."

Rocks takes a moment to respond. "Firstly, she doesn't *let* me do things. We have a relationship based on mutual respect. Secondly, Connie is not your concern."

Tronido glares at Rocks and comes up very close to him. "Tell me now!" He pulls out a long, gleaming knife from inside his boot. "We don't want blood spilt this early, do we?"

Rocks doesn't look Tronido in the eye. He stares straight ahead before answering, "She's gone on a road trip to see colleges. She will be gone a few weeks. Are you worried about her springing *me* out this time?"

Tronido smiles. "No, I'm not. But thank you for telling me the truth." His voice is level and calm. "You passed my test and will be rewarded with clothing and two extra goats when you return tonight. If you behave Rockland, the whole group benefits."

My heart is beating so fast. This crazy motherfucker was pretending to be angry, and for a split second, I thought he must have seen through my disguise.

"How do you know I'm telling the truth?"

"Because I paid her family a little visit last night. Mommy and Daddy were talking about Connie's road trip. They aren't sure when she will return and that suits me perfectly."

My fists clench and I have to look away. That bastard was at my house, near my family last night. I'm so grateful the folks didn't mention my text while he was listening. I think of little Mini alone and unguarded upstairs in her bed without me there. The folks are usually downstairs for a few hours each night after they put her to bed.

If he touches her, I will kill him.

"I have no reason to lie. I only want to protect her. If I do whatever you ask, will you stay away from them all?"

"Maybe. Now get to work!"

As promised at the end of our shift, there is three times the amount of food, stacks of clothing, and two goats waiting in the bird room. After I climb the human pyramid, the goats are shoved into the duct. They bleat and complain as their hooves slide on the slippery surface.

While I climb down my ladder, I watch the bats swoop low with clothing clutched in their feet. Some of them dump the items from a great height and head back down the duct to make a second trip. I help the others collecting the scattered garments and sort them into stacks for distribution. I eye a pair of black jeans and wonder if I will be lucky enough. My skirt is a mess, but it's in better condition than many others.

The goats get airlifted to the cavern floor.

In the privacy of the bunk beds, I pull the roast beef sandwich out from down my corset. It's squashed, but edible. I lift the pink, shaved meat to my nose and breath in long and slow.

"Oh, that smells good. Meat."

The idea hits me like a wrecking ball.

"Holy shitballs, that's it!" I say out loud, dumping my prized sandwich on the top mattress and running through the maze of bunks towards the office.

All the supplies Rocks and I brought in with us are being kept in the makeshift office—except our phones. The first aid supplies, like rubbing alcohol and bandages, are neatly stacked on the small table for use. I unzip the backpack under it and start grabbing at bottles.

Since Rocks was reluctant for any of the Camazotz here to take any aeronaught pain medication, we left them zipped away. I brought a whole pharmacy worth in case he was in incredible pain after his fix.

"Where are they?" I try two more bottles. "Oh, thank God!" I clasp the bottle of pills to my chest and walk slowly back to our bed.

Rocks is waiting, holding a precious pair of black cords. "For you. I know that skirt is driving you crazy."

I throw my arms around his shoulders and kiss him repeatedly. He laughs but steps back out of my embrace. Moondust and RainCloud have joined us. This day could only get better if we're rescued right this minute.

I stand before the three of them. "I've got it. I know how we're gonna get past those dogs."

The small bottle gets passed from one person to the next. Moondust doesn't seem convinced. "So what will this *valium* do exactly?" He sniffs the bottle and wrinkles his nose.

"It will put them to sleep, and that's when we sneak out!"

When Mini was with Enzo and Mom lost it, her Doctor gave her two bottles of Valium to help her sleep. She only ended up taking a few tablets, and I borrowed her unopened bottle as a just-in-case for Rocks.

"And now that we've got beef sandwiches and probably cheese too, I can hide the tablets in that, and those dogs will gulp them down."

Moondust calls a meeting. Celand, Asteroide, Mantarraya, RainCloud, Nighthawk, Moondust, Rockland and I sit in a tight huddle working out the steps of the jailbreak. It's good to be able to see Asteroide and Mantarraya at last. Both are around the same age as Rocks. Asteroide's arms are covered so I don't know what tattoos he might have, but Mantarraya has a dozen stingrays swimming down one arm. He winks at me when he notices I'm checking out his ink.

"We'll need lots of rope. Celand, go check on Moonlight and explain to her how we're going to use it please," RainCloud asks. "I'll make sure everyone has handed in their plastic and get more members to help her weave."

I turn on my phone and start typing out a detailed email to the folks. I have to ask them to rescue us, without them calling the cops, or even discussing what they are about to do out loud with each other. If Tronido is sending nightly eavesdroppers to listen to what's going on, then we certainly can't risk my folks speaking about their part in our plan. I delete and edit and ask Rocks to read it over and over. When we're both happy, I attach the screen shot of the map showing our exact location, and save it for sending when we're ready.

Rocks and I snuggle together when the lights go out. I'm so excited, but amped up on nervous energy, I don't know how I'll sleep.

Only two more days until freedom.

"Do you think it's gonna work?" I whisper into Rocks' neck.

He kisses my forehead. "God, I hope so, or we're all dead."

25
Secrets

THURSDAY morning, I send my email to Mom with a request she replies by seven a.m. Friday. Before we risk everyone's neck, we need confirmation there'll be a vehicle waiting to drive us all to safety.

Rocks is more nervous than I've ever seen. Jez, Judge, and Zander aren't answering any of his text messages. He frantically types out another three texts to Jeremiah asking him to convince Judge to drive to my house Friday afternoon. Rocks sends a list of items we need them to bring for our plan to really be a success.

Work is exhausting. I don't know if it's the nervous energy, or the fact we are all stealing as much plastic as we dare, but everyone is on edge. I pray the dumb guards don't sense a change in the group. Tronido doesn't grace us with his presence today, and that is definitely a blessing.

All day my brain goes over the email I sent Mom and Dad and whether they will do as I ask. I told them this was as serious as Enzo having Mini, and it was equally as important they don't say a word to anyone about it.

After dinner, the whole colony gets to work on the ropes. All the beds are stripped of sheets as we construct our own harnesses for carrying unconscious bats.

Just before lights out, I climb the ladder with my pockets stuffed full of sandwich meat. If these guard dogs are properly trained, they won't eat a thing I drop down for them. I'm hoping Tronido isn't a guard dog expert and only had them trained to maim and kill.

The alarm is almost deafening as I crawl down the air duct. I'm sure all the Muerte know what I'm up to, and I'll be facing an angry mob of them when I stick my head out the other end. The crawl seems to take forever. About three-feet from the end of the duct, the alarm thankfully silences.

When I do make it to the end of the air duct, the guard dogs are snarling up at me from below. When I lean out, they start to jump up and down as though they could pull me from my hole. The great owls sit not even flinching as the dogs circle and snap.

I drop my fist-sized lump of meat, and the three dogs swarm on it, snapping at each other.

Success!

By the time I empty all I have for them, the three dogs are sitting looking up at me, hoping for more. Their coats aren't shiny and thick, so I'm guessing they too are underfed. The owls haven't moved and I hope they won't when we all dare to step out tomorrow night.

The alarm sounds when I return through the air duct. We all wait to see if anyone comes to check, but nobody does. According to the routine, all the bats—including Tronido—are out making deliveries. Only a skeleton crew is left here and all of them are sleeping to rest up for their next day shift.

I fall asleep without Rocks against me. Once the lights went out, I was of no use to the team.

Friday morning dawns and the team is out the duct the moment the birds are put away. Mom has replied with a very long, very upset email. She promises to do what I have asked, but her tone is extremely cross, at best. It finishes with "you have a lot of explaining to do, young lady!" and I try not to laugh. I know I do, and I'm not looking forward to it.

Rocks swears and all eyes are on him. "Nothing! No replies. I doubt Jez has gotten my messages. I don't know what to do."

"Text him again. We can only hope," I say, sending an amendment to my instructions to my folks before switching off my phone. We're gonna need every second of battery life possible. "It will work. Don't worry."

The shift on Friday is agonizing. Every second takes forever. With only an hour to go, every member tries to use the bathroom to be as prepared as possible. The meat filled sandwiches are waiting on the table like a gift from heaven. The whole colony is down the air duct in record time.

The groups start organizing themselves, while I crush the Valium to lace the meat and cheese for the dogs. I have no clue what amount to give and I don't want to kill them, but at the same time, I don't want to be torn to pieces either.

I force a few bites of the unused bread, but I'm too nervous to eat much. I notice there is almost complete silence in the large cavern. Everyone is nervous about how tonight will end. All the groups are waiting in position. I watch RainCloud walk amongst the teams and can only imagine the words of encouragement she's whispering. People smile and take deep breaths as she leaves them.

Rocks stands beside me and slides his hand into my back pocket. It settles my heart rate, and I'm so grateful he'll be by my side the entire time. "Oak and Elm, I want you to wait with me. You're going with Connie, okay?"

The boys look up at their hero and nod their heads.

"You ready?" he asks me.

I nod too. He wraps me up in the tightest bear hug. We cling to each other, oblivious of our audience. "You have my utility knife and phone?"

"Yep. I'm all set. I love you so much," he says.

"I love you too."

"It's time," Moondust announces.

Again, I climb the rope ladder to visit the dogs. For some reason, I'm equally as nervous as last night about the dogs refusing my offerings. If they smell the Valium and decide not to eat it, I don't know what I'll do.

But my worries are for nothing. They gulp it down greedily, and I settle in for my vigil of watching when they pass out. Ten minutes after the last one collapses, I throw a rock at one of the sleeping mutts.

Nothing.

The owls twitch a little and seem to give me an evil glare, but I yell the okay and lower the second rope ladder.

"Connie, wait—" I hear Rocks saying down the duct before the blaring alarm cuts him off.

The sleeping dogs below don't move a muscle. I step down and tie their back legs together, just in case. The alarm keeps blaring and blaring and blaring. Rocks is soon with me and runs off down the corridor. He has to plant my phone up the road for my folks to be able to track the signal to meet us.

Soon all the strong males are climbing down the ladder. My job is to keep an eye on the owls. They haven't left their perches and I hope they stay that way.

Maneuvering the bed sheets full of unconscious bats out of the duct without dropping them takes a little longer than we anticipated. Our hope is if the owls can't see the unconscious bats, they won't try to attack.

"It's all clear," Rocks announces to the team when he returns. "The moon hasn't risen yet."

When every single Camazotz is down from the duct, the teams grab hold of the ropes and bat-filled sheet hammocks, and we start our trek to the cave entrance. Rocks has one end while I have the other. I don't know how many bats exactly we're carrying, but it's almost too much for me to lift. Moondust and RainCloud follow closely behind with their hammock.

Rocks stops at the cave entrance. We've made good time but need the lights to go out. Just outside the cave are two large floodlights—probably from when it was a working quarry. In preparation, I close my eyes and wait, appreciating the rest from lifting my cargo.

Right on time, every single light flicks out and floods the open space we need to cross in complete darkness. When I open my eyes, I can see a little more than in the blackout cavern.

"Let's go!"

We shuffle across the compound. I trust Rocks will lead me on a smooth path. We stop at the chain-link fence, and I watch Rocks bend down and crawl through the opening he cut with the wire cutters on Dad's utility knife earlier. We carefully guide the hammock through the hole ensuring no snags rip the threadbare sheets.

Next, Rocks and I are moving as fast as we can along the bottom of the cliff face which borders part of the road. I try to focus on breathing in and out through my mouth to distract from the pain of the ropes digging into my shoulders, and the precious cargo swinging between us. We're almost there.

Hoo-hoohoohoo Hoooo Hooo.

We have owl company. High across the quarry another great horned owl replies with an equally haunting call. The birds hoot back and forth, and we continue up the road. When we round the corner, blocking us from view of the compound, I do relax. Out here, we should be safe.

But I can't see my parents. "Can you see a van?" I whisper, out of breath.

"Not yet." He stops, signaling for me to lay our bat hammock on the ground. He steps under the tree and brings out my phone.

I text Mom, and we watch the other teams carrying their Camazotz passengers making their way up the dirt road.

I quickly cover my glowing screen when she replies.

Almost there. ETA six minutes.
Are you okay?

"They're coming!"

"Let's go further up the road," Rocks suggests, shouldering his load.

Sweat is pouring off my forehead when Rocks tells me the best news ever. "I can see them. Not much further."

Up ahead two vans are waiting on the road, their headlights out. When we get closer, I spy Mom and Dad getting out of one van. I can't imagine their confusion at seeing Rocks and I dragging what probably looks like a dead body wrapped in a sheet. The hammock is of a similar shape I now realize.

"Connie, what on earth?" Mom says when we get closer, eyes wide.

"Shhhh! Please!" I whisper yell back.

At the van, we gently lay down our hammock. Mom pulls me into a hug before declaring I absolutely stink!

"Did Jeremiah show up?" Rocks asks Dad.

"No, that's why we were a little late. We waited as long as we could for him. What's going on?"

"Mom, Dad." I look from one to the other. "You just have to trust us. Please! We don't have time to explain, but I swear to you we will before sunrise. We need you to load these hammocks into both vans carefully and then drive to Helen. Dad, I'll go with Mom and you follow us. Okay?"

"Connie—"

"Please, Daddy. Please."

"Sir, this really is life or death," Rocks states, backing me up. "I know it doesn't look it, but it is."

Moondust and RainCloud arrive and gently place their load of unconscious bats next to ours. Moondust greets my folks, and his authority sets them into action.

"I will forever be indebted to your family for saving mine. We should load up and get moving right away," he says.

Dad opens one van, while Mom does the other. Both are work vans from his company. Dad drives one as his company vehicle, even though he works in their office. This morning my amended email asked if they could bring two vans, since Jez hadn't replied to Rocks.

Each team brings their load and helps place them in the back. I see Dad frown and mumble under his breath. Rocks walks over and says something to him. Dad's eyes almost fall out of his head he opens them so wide, and then he stares at the hammocks laid out in his van.

Rocks takes the items Mom and Dad brought with them and assures me he'll see me at the market. I want to change our plans and stay, but I know under these extremely suspicious circumstances my parents won't let me out of their sight.

"Don't worry, Beans. I'll be there by eleven. I promise." He kisses me quickly, and I don't miss Dad's second look of shock.

Rocks, Moondust, and six of the young males that form my human pyramid each day, jog back down the dirt road to set the trap for Tronido.

Asteroide, Mantarraya, Willow, Nighthawk, and four other males leave us and disappear into the trees. They are headed for the Muerte headquarters to free the Fold.

I'm told Willow takes after his mother in looks. I believe it because he doesn't remind me of cruel Cypress one bit. He's very good-looking but not my type. All the female Camazotz would clear a path for him when he walked through the bunk beds. On the inside of both forearms, he has the Plant wing crest. It's a bold move to tattoo a crest from another colony so openly, but he's clearly proud of his bloodline. On his right arm, the tattoo is visible in his human form, while his left arm has a swirl of ink in the same position to show off his heritage in bat form.

RainCloud pats my shoulder. "Connie, this will work. Trust them. In my opinion, we've gotten over the biggest hurdle. We're out and your parents are here."

"You're right. I know," I say, watching Rocks disappear around the quarry wall. "Go easy on my dad please. He doesn't know yet."

She smiles. "I will."

I walk over to my father who is by the open driver's door. "Please trust me. Nothing bad will happen, but take it from me you will want to keep your eyes on the road. Ignore whatever goes on back there." I kiss him before running around to the passenger side of Mom's van.

"Let's get out of here!"

I instruct Mom to turn on the headlights so we can drive faster down the dirt track. Calling it a road is really a bit of an exaggeration. As I watch the scenery go past, it's a miracle they actually found us.

"Connie?"

"Mom, please. Just drive. I need some distance before I explain."

"Are those sacks full of bats?" she asks, looking at me and not the track.

"Yes."

She swallows, and I remember the fear I felt when Rocks was a bat unconscious on my bed the first night we met.

"They won't hurt you. I swear."

"Did you join some animal liberation movement, and you and those hippies have stolen these bats? Is this a humane rescue team? Is this legal? Were you trespassing?"

I laugh. The Duskwing in their out-of-date, home-sewn denim could be mistaken for hippies in the dark, I guess. "No, Mom, I didn't join anything, but what you're doing is a rescue. Now drive as fast as you can. Please."

I plug in my phone and navigate the windy, back roads. When we reach the highway, I almost cry. Nothing will stop us now. If the Muerte have noticed our escape, they won't be able to track us with all the other traffic on the interstate. I worry about Rocks though if we have been discovered, but my gut is telling me everything is still going to plan.

We drive down the interstate in silence. I try calling and texting all the Shadows' phone numbers, but nobody answers. I can't understand why the phones aren't being used. It's starting to worry me because they're about to get a rude shock if they aren't expecting us.

I warn Mom of the upcoming exit. We're going to be on smaller country roads for a bit, but we're making great time—only another hour to Helen.

The van swerves from our lane into the oncoming traffic lane before Mom takes control.

"Mom!"

"What the hell is going on back there?"

Oh, crap.

I glance back, but can only see the lumpy sheets on the floor.

"Connie! What the—" She turns her head, glancing in the back and swears—something my mother *rarely* does.

"Yes?"

"I know something is going on. I know when we left that place, there were only the sacks you put in the back, but I swear I just saw…" She looks across at me for longer than is safe.

"Mom, eyes on the road, please." The last thing we need is a head-on accident.

I know the feeling of not believing what is before your very own eyes. I look over my shoulder and see a young girl sitting on the floor blinking and looking around. Before I turn back, Celand flips too.

I stare at Mom. "Don't be afraid and whatever you do, please do NOT scream."

Her eyes dart from the mirror to me. "There are people back there. People who remind me a lot of Rocks." Her eyes scan the rear view mirror.

"Mo-om, eyes on the road. Or should I drive?"

"No. Oh, God save us." She plants her foot on the accelerator, and we speed down the county road. I glance in the side mirror to see if Dad is able to keep up.

There's a thud and a male has flipped. I can't lie to her, because by the time we get to the market, the van is going to be packed to capacity. Several of the bats start to screech. Celand and the young girl flip back into bat form because there isn't enough room for everyone to be human.

"Mom…" I honestly don't know what to tell her. "Some secrets are not mine for the telling. This one belongs to Rocks and his family. You trust Rocks, don't you?"

She glances at me again. "I trust you," she whispers. Her knuckles are turning white she's gripping the steering wheel so hard.

"I should've trusted you years ago with your own identity, but it was too difficult to tell you, so I didn't. Look where that got us. I'm not going to make the same mistake twice, just because I'm freaking out. I love you, and I do trust you."

"And Rocks?" I ask.

"Of course, I trust Rocks. He saved Jasmine. Without him, God only knows what could have happened. If you tell me to keep driving and forget what's going on back there, I will."

I've never been more proud to be her daughter than right this minute. Despite the supernatural freaky thing that's happening in the back of our van, my mom is trusting me. She's fighting for me, not against me. She's treating me as an adult which, given the circumstances, is a miracle.

"I love you, Mom, so much. Now drive."

We both let out short half laughs. I can tell she's as nervous as I am, but for entirely different reasons.

"I hope your father is coping back there. I knew there was something about Rocks. Right from the start, I always knew it."

26
M.I.A.

"WHY'S the market closed?" Mom shrieks, pulling up at the gate.

"I don't know. Don't panic." I jump out and drag the heavy, wooden gate open as far as I can manage. Mom eases the van through, and I wait for Dad to enter too. They park next to each other and I jog to Mom's door and open it.

It's two a.m. and the place seems deserted. Rocks texted me on the way and assured me there will be someone here. He used to do the nightly market patrols, since he slept in the wagon behind his shop. With him gone, the duties will probably fall to the regular patrols, so they will fly over at some point.

RainCloud opens the back of the van and lets the Camazotz flip as they exit. Since they're at a location they don't really trust—and after what they've all been though—dozens and dozens of people start exiting the van. Mom and Dad are standing together watching the spectacle with surprising restraint. This would make the world's best magic trick—ever.

"We're home!" Elm and Oak cheer.

My parents stand together between the two parked vans. I join them in case they start to freak out, but stand a little further away so I can have a clear view of the path, which leads up through the pine trees to the market. Celand walks over and extends her hand to my mother.

"I'm so grateful to you. You saved us all. Thank you. It doesn't seem like enough to say it, but I will be forever indebted to you."

I explain Celand is Rocks' oldest sister and hasn't been home for a very long time because she was trapped at the old quarry.

Many of the Camazotz follow Celand's lead and walk up to thank my parents. I see it calms both of them a little. Maybe for my parents having the Camazotz show them gratitude, shows they aren't evil shape-shifters, but more like them.

"Connie, I'll go let them know we're here," Celand says.

"Be careful. I don't know if there are still owls around. I'm a bit out of touch with what's going on."

Without walking out of sight of my folks, she tells the others to wait quietly, then flips. I try to see it through my parents' eyes, as they aren't used to witnessing the magical transformation. It really is a miracle, and I'm glad Rocks can't alter this incredible part of himself. She flaps her wings hard to gain immediate height.

RainCloud comes to stand with me, now all the Duskwing are awake and out of the van. She was concerned about members getting suffocated, like when they were transported to hell.

"Everyone's alive and well," she reports. "Your father is an aeronaught of worth. He handled the first flip with surprising dignity," she says quietly to me and smiles.

When I look over at my parents, they're looking straight up with their mouths hanging open, following Celand's flight path. I join RainCloud, grinning. "He's not so dignified now," I comment.

"It's a lot to take in."

Dad's eyes are still wide, but when he sees the two of us looking at him, he grins back. I walk over to stand next to him, so proud he held it together when he witnessed the Camazotz secret. "Those bats in the cave up on Blood Mountain were these, um… type, right?"

I bite my bottom lip. "Yeah, they were, Dad. I'm sorry I couldn't tell you."

"It was Rocks we returned, wasn't it?"

"Yes. You helped me save his life. It's partly why he risked his own for Mini. He would've done it even if he didn't feel indebted to you because he loves Mini like his own little sister, but yes, you helped save him."

"I had no clue. All I knew was those bats were watching me funny," he says, shaking his head. "And I swear I heard voices when I was in the cave. I never told you that because I thought you'd think your old man was losing his mind."

I lean over and wrap my arms around as much of both of them as I can manage. "Thank you for trusting me and for following my crazy instructions. You'll find out everything soon. But I can't tell you what it means to me—and to Rocks—that you did this."

"I knew it," Mom says, smiling at Dad. "I just couldn't believe it was possible. I also thought I was losing my mind for even thinking it." She laughs.

"Connie? Is that you? What's going on?" a deep male voice says from up the path. "RainCloud?"

I turn, peering into the darkness. Zander comes striding down with Pegasus, Foxfire and several young males I don't recognize. His frown indicates he never found Celand.

"We sent you text messages. We rescued the Duskwing. Rocks might need your help. Why isn't anyone answering their phones?" I realize I've dumped way too much information when all their expressions show a mix of surprise and confusion. "Sorry, but did you happen to see, um, Celand?"

"Celand? Connie, you know she's de—" Zander says, but before he can finish his sentence, Celand materializes beside me.

"Hello Uncle," she says.

"By the bats above! Celand?" He rushes forward and grabs her by the elbows, looking her over from head-to-toe. "You're alive! What happened? How?" He pulls her into his chest, and I watch her face break into a massive smile when she hugs him back. His hand runs over her hair and he keeps talking, but it's not making much sense.

When he pulls back, he suddenly notices my parents, and his eyes widen to the size of dinner plates. "Celand, you just... in front of... oh, shit!"

"Zander, these are my parents, Kelly and Chad Phillips. This is Rocks' uncle, Zander." Zander is the perfect gentleman and shakes both of their hands, but the crease on his brow shows his concern. "My parents have seen quite a bit tonight. Without their help, none of us would be here. They saved us. But you really need to help Rocks. He's setting a trap to catch Tronido right now."

"What? Where?" Zander looks from me to Celand and back again.

"Uncle, we need to give shelter to the Duskwing. They've had a long day, and we're all exhausted. Can I take them to the shops?"

Zander takes a few steps past me and sees the Duskwing colony all standing around the vans and spreading into the trees that line the parking lot. "My goodness, you really did rescue them. I have so many questions, but first we need to get organized."

His shock dissipates as he starts giving orders to each of the young males. Foxfire and two others are to return to the roost and alert Strickland of what has happened.

I want to text Rocks to tell him, but I know he'll be in the cavern and won't have cell service. I wish I could ask him if he does need back up, or whether he's okay. I explain as much to Celand and Zander.

Zander is worried and explains Strickland was forced to take away all the phones because there was an uprising. In order to maintain his position, he gave in to their demand. It happened after Ash and Mackie told the Fold about Jeremiah meeting with Rockland in Helen. They blamed the technology for allowing them to still communicate. It was all very political, and in the end, the phones were confiscated. Jeremiah and Bailey were punished harshly.

He swears colorfully when we explain how we had sent text messages asking for assistance tonight, and because nobody replied, I had to get my parents to rescue us. He walks over and thanks my parents, adding he's sure they have lots of questions—as he does—and if they give him time, he will do his best to answer them.

Sweet, gentle giant Pegasus comes over and introduces himself to my folks. I must give them credit for not freaking out at his name, or any of the other Camazotz names they have heard tonight.

"Miss Connie is an incredible young lady," Pegasus says. "You must be very proud. She's accepting and ever so generous. She must get that from both of you."

"Aww, thanks, Pegasus," I say. "Wait until you taste Mom's cooking. You won't believe food can taste that good."

"The tatt suits you, but I think a winged creature would look better," he jokes, looking at the fox head on my neck. I pull my hair over my shoulder to hide it, knowing it's political significance like everything here.

"It's fake, Mom. Don't worry," I add.

My parents are smiling, but I know they're having trouble taking everything in. Mom finally finds her voice, "We are so proud of her. She's a very special daughter, and we're so lucky to have her."

I hug my folks again, as Pegasus starts ushering everyone up the path and down toward the dairy. RainCloud goes to assist the older Camazotz from her colony, since they're in unfamiliar surroundings.

"Do you guys want to stay? It's okay if you want to head home."

"I'm not leaving here until I know Rocks is safe!" Mom exclaims.

"And I'd like some more answers," Dad adds.

"Okay, but if all goes to plan, Rocks won't get back until eleven a.m. or so. Come with me, and I'll find a seat for you. I might have to do some explaining with Celand to Rocks' father."

"Well, so long as we get to hear it too," Dad says. "We still need to apologize for sending the police."

"Dad, I wouldn't bother mentioning that tonight please."

I don't know how Strickland is going to feel about more aeronaughts being involved, even though Rocks and I couldn't have arranged the escape without them. I can just imagine how Cypress will react to my folks being present. He better not be rude to them.

"Zander!" I yell, suddenly remembering a vital piece of information I should have told him first. "Zander! Oh, God!"

Celand comes to my side and Zander isn't far behind. "What's wrong?" he asks, frowning.

Holding Celand's hand, I lean in to Zander's ear and whisper one name, knowing she will hear me.

Leaning back, I continue in a hushed tone, "We need to find that hag immediately!"

"Yes!" cries Celand. "How could I forget too? Get a cage."

ZANDER OPENED THE dairy and is giving out chunks of cheese and milk to anyone who's hungry. He tried to force Celand to take some, but she refused, offering it to others. His eyes roamed her thin frame, and I'm sure he wants answers for her condition. I'm thankful she at least had new clothes to wear for her homecoming.

My parents, Celand, RainCloud, Moonlight, and I are sitting at the picnic table in front of the dairy. The Duskwing are all in human form, sitting or standing around the open space. Almost an hour later, Celand nudges my elbow and points straight ahead into the dark sky. The moon has risen and is high overhead so it helps my poor eyesight greatly.

Dozens of bats, flying in formation, are headed this way. A silence settles over the large group.

Strickland flips and stares at the crowd of Duskwing. He turns around and around. "Where is she? Is it really true?"

His voice is so different. It's soft and—even though it's hard to believe—loving. He continues to turn around, scanning the faces. "Celand?"

The rest of the Fold and their heirs flip around their Sire.

Celand stands up from the picnic table. "I'm here." She leaves us, stepping around the fledgers sitting on the ground to get to him.

He strides toward her, but his face is hard. It doesn't match the tone of his voice a moment ago. She stands still as he charges her way. My stomach tightens with fear he may reject her for leaving the Shadows to get fixed. RainCloud stands and moves closer to Celand. She must be feeling the same as me about this reunion.

"Celand."

Her name is all he says before he embraces her. He pulls her tight to his chest, lifting her off the ground, and I have a clear view of his face over her shoulder. His eyes close as he rests his head on top of hers when her feet touch the ground once more.

And then he starts to cry. I hear his first sob, before I make out his scrunched up features. He starts to rock both of their bodies from side to side. I don't know if it's to calm her, or himself. He says her name over and over like a prayer. The moment is so intimate, but part of me is relieved to see this man actually has a heart. He eventually pulls back and cups her face in both his hands.

Judge, Levi, and Carnelian all flank him. "Look," Strickland says to his fellow leaders, "she's alive and has come home."

Judge opens his arms and Celand rushes to him. She hugs him like the stepfather he's always been to all of Zada's young.

Cypress notices RainCloud and asks her. "Where's Moondust?" he asks.

I doubt my dislike of that man will ever ease. Of course, he wants to talk with the *male* in charge!

"Moondust is assisting Rockland to capture Tronido. I am the only Duskwing Fold member present and can answer all of your questions, *Cypress*." She spits his name with such contempt everyone present now knows she isn't a fan either.

He looks away from her, and I glare as his eyes pass over me. "Who are they? Aeronaughts? Explain!" He stares hard down at tiny RainCloud.

I launch myself off the bench and join her. "Those aeronaughts saved your sons!" I spit.

All eyes are on me and then murmurs start as they recognize me with my new hair and fake tattoo.

"Strickland! Come see to this madness!" Cypress commands, like he's calling a dog. But he's ignored my comment.

"Oak? Elm? Willow?" I remind him.

"What?" he gasps, "Where are they?" Like Strickland, he turns around scanning the crowd for his boys.

A soft cry is heard up past the dairy, and when we all look, two women are hugging the twins. Each woman picks up one of the thin boys and runs toward Cypress.

"Elm and Oak are fine, as you can see," I add.

"Willow?" he asks. Strickland is now standing with Cypress.

"He's doing his duty and taking control back from the Muerte," RainCloud states. "Strickland, on my blood oath, I swear to you we only involved Connie's wonderful parents because your colony couldn't assist. We tried your phones, but nobody answered our distress call. It was a life or death choice."

So there! Suck on that, Sire!

I have to calm down, but being in the presence of hateful Cypress gets my temper primed for a fight. Particularly after how welcoming the Duskwing have been to me and my parents.

"Strickland, without Connie we wouldn't be here. Her bravery, magic Valium, and her parent's willingness to answer her distress call and bring their vehicles, without question saved us," RainCloud continues.

"I didn't do this alone," I remind her.

She gives me the fastest wink, and I know she's highlighting the fact that having an aeronaught on your team, or using technology, won't make one any less of a Camazotz.

"Foxfire, bring those devices."

I wonder if Foxfire survived the political wars and has been chosen by Strickland to replace Rocks. Strickland listens as RainCloud explains the part Chad and Kelly played in freeing the Duskwing, Celand, Elm and Oak, and Rockland too.

Cypress leaves the group when the two women arrive, placing Elm and Oak on their feet. The boys stare at their dirty boots when their sire kneels down. He too pulls the young pups into an embrace. "I was so worried about you, boys. I'm so glad your safe. Hannah, PurpleSky, see that they're fed. They're too thin," he commands.

Hannah is the mother of Ash and Cedar, and I wonder why she's helping. I remember her from the night the angry mob came to lynch me for the boys going missing in the first place. She has a huge Cypress tree covering her bicep from shoulder to elbow. On the other shoulder is the Hebrew wing tattoo.

"We have cheese," Elm replies.

"We don't need blood," Oak adds. I bite my lip, hoping my folks are still coping with the crash course in Camazotz 101 they are experiencing.

A moment later, I'm engulfed in a bear hug from Judge. He lifts me clean off my feet. "You are our little miracle worker. We're so fortunate you entered our lives," he says, placing me on the ground. "Now, please introduce me to your parents."

JUST AFTER DAWN, Zander returns with Pegasus and has an unconscious bat in a small, rusted, iron cage. The cage looks like it was made at the turn of the century. The metal bars have artistic swirls on the ends where they join the base of the cage.

I explain to my folks quietly the Camazotz cannot flip back into human form when they are surrounded by iron or steel. Or if the space is too small for their human counterpart to fit and would injure them, then they can't initiate the change. It was part of the perfection of the original magic spell to ensure their safety.

"Magic?" Mom whispers. I put a finger to my lips and she zips hers.

"Sire, we have the traitor in custody," Zander announces, holding the cage high for all to see.

"Hand her to me. I will guard the witch day and night," RainCloud requests.

"We all will," Zander assures her. Celand begins explaining to the group how evil and fake Sylvana really is. She's not a medicine woman or shaman, but Tronido's third cousin. Anger emanates from every muscle on Strickland, and I pray I'll be present when he unleashes his wrath upon her. One day that man's gonna blow a valve if he doesn't rein his temper in, but I hope it's after he deals with the lying little witch.

When Foxfire returns with the stack of phones, Jeremiah and Ezra are with him.

"What did you do to your hair?" Jez asks, loudly.

"I had to go undercover. Couldn't let our boy out of my sight for one second," I joke.

"And we're grateful she did," Celand adds.

Jeremiah and Ezra look as though they've seen a ghost, and Celand is hugged so hard, I'm sure she'll have bruises. She answers the same set of questions of how is she alive, and what happened as best she can in under a minute before Strickland asks about the messages.

"Connie, show me Rockland's distress call."

The phones are dead. "They need to be charged, Sire. I'll take them to the dairy," I offer.

"I'll help," Jez offers.

As we walk across to the dairy, I tell him everything that happened. The emotions that flit across his face show me he's stunned but relieved. "Thank you for having his back."

"No, Jez, don't thank me. Rocks has always had my back. He's saved my skin more times than I care to count."

"Yeah, but you risked a lot pretending to be one of us."

I shrug my shoulders 'cause it was my only option. We plug in the phones, but don't turn them on. I want each phone to buzz and vibrate like it's coming to life with each and every message Rocks sent asking for help. A little extra theatrics to help prove the Shadows turned their backs on fellow Camazotz won't go astray.

Rocks' phone goes straight to voicemail when I try him again. I send yet another text. "Rocks should be replying by now."

"What?" Jez stares at my screen.

"Rocks, Moondust, and the others stayed behind to trap Tronido and rescue the rest of the Muerte. He should have done that by now and be in phone range."

Jez pulls his pocket watch from his jeans. "It's eight-thirty."

"I know. If everything went to plan, he should have called me half an hour ago. I think he's in trouble and needs our help."

27
Justice

SILENT tears run down Celand's face. "I knew I shouldn't have left him there. I knew it!" she shrieks.

"I should have stayed too," RainCloud admits to Judge. "I'm sorry I didn't."

"It's not your fault," Judge answers.

"Should we drive back there?" Dad asks.

Judge has welcomed my parents as though they are long lost relatives. He has such a genuine, beautiful soul, and it still hurts my heart when I think of Decker not being here. Decker was so much like his sire in every way, and I will miss him always.

"He's an hour late, correct?" Zander asks.

I nod and gnaw on my fingernails—something I never do. "I don't understand why he's not answering!" I check my phone again.

The sun beats down from directly overhead. At this time of day in full sunlight it's far too dangerous for a colony of bats to fly across state.

"I would appreciate it, Chad, if you would take assistance to him," Strickland says. I wonder what it cost him to ask an aeronaught male for help with a very Camazotz problem. "Do I have any volunteers?"

A discussion breaks out about how many to send and where to send them—the quarry compound, or the Muerte headquarters.

I pace back and forth, willing Rocks to call. My brain can't even begin to imagine what went wrong.

"Sweetheart, are you coming?" Dad asks.

"Of course, I am! Let's go." We head toward the parking lot, and I realize dozens and dozens of Camazotz have volunteered. Strickland is sending a small army. For once, he's doing the right thing by his son. "Thank you, Strickland."

He nods his head. "Bring him home please."

Home.

I pray I'll be able to tell Rocks the amazing news of him being welcome once more. I swallow my fear and march down the path with the others.

Dad opens the vehicle and stands witnessing all the Camazotz flipping and entering the back of the van. I warn him this trip won't be so quiet if he was able to hear the bats inside his head the day we visited the cave.

Mom looks so out of place as the only aeronaught. I realize I stand out that much normally when my hair is golden instead of ebony. She hugs us both before we get in the van. Dad puts the van into reverse, and Carnelian opens the main gate. Poor Dad checks his mirror twenty-five times before moving to ensure he doesn't annihilate Camazotz-Aeronaught relations on day one by running over someone.

"Stop!" yells Carnelian. Dad hits the brakes, and I brace myself on the dash. "Go back in. Move forward."

Looking out the window behind us, I see one headlight of a vehicle blocking our exit. Jumping out of the van, I race to join Carnelian at the gate.

Rocks is sitting behind the steering wheel of a strange van grinning like a lunatic. He winds down the window and leans out. "Sorry we're late. Driving on the interstate is very different from a parking lot!"

"What the—" I mutter, taking a deep breath.

We clear a space so Rocks can park. "Mr. Phillips, stay behind the wheel. We need you," he says, as Dad starts to get out of his van. "Connie, one of those dogs attacked Moondust. I think his arm is broken—or worse. We need to get him to the vet!"

All chaos breaks lose, but eventually Mom and Dad agree to take Moondust to Dr. Gandy with RainCloud, Moonlight, and Celand for support. I hope his wing hasn't been ripped to pieces because young Moonshadow cannot lose her only surviving parent today—not on my watch.

Most of the Shadows' females, fledgers, and pups were ordered to stay at the roost when news of the Duskwing showing up reached them. I'm stunned Zada is still there, and not even sure if she knows Celand is alive and well.

The blood on Rocks thankfully isn't his. Once my folks leave, he opens the back of the Muerte van to reveal one very, very full Chinchilla cage. When I see the stack of bats—literally stacked on top of one another—completely filling the tiny cage, I laugh so hard I can't stand up straight. Some of the bars are pushing against their little faces and distorting them, because there are so many bats crammed in tight. Nighthawk and Asteroide laugh too, and in the end, everyone who sees the tiny, cramped prison can't keep a straight face.

Tronido and his goons are done! Those bats deserve exactly what they're about to get.

I lean down next to the cage, trying to straighten my face. "Hey, Tronido, guess who?" I run my fingers through my black hair. "Tricked ya, sucker! Can you believe you let an aeronaught past your super Camazotz defenses?"

Silence.

"What was that?" I taunt, cupping my hand to my ear, waiting for him to speak in all of our heads. "You're done, asshole. I can't wait to witness what the Sires and Fold members of all three colonies decide to do with you."

Strickland brings the cage holding Sylvana and drops it in the van next to the others. He closes the doors, and we all listen as Sylvana and Tronido begin to argue about who's to blame.

A cacophony of voices rings in our heads.

> *You idiot!*
> *Get off me.*
> *Move your claw.*
> *You're to blame for this!*
> *Can someone itch my nose?*
> *How is this is my fault?*

I have to bite my lip to prevent myself from laughing again.

Rockland faces his father and goes to speak, but before he can, Strickland embraces his heir. "Welcome home, son."

A cheer goes up from the surrounding crowd. Finally these Camazotz are treating Rockland the way he has always deserved. Judge hugs me and Jeremiah howls—he's the happiest and most animated I've ever seen.

"Am I truly welcome here again?" Rocks asks.

"Yes. There will need to be a meeting to make it official, but you are under my protection until that happens."

"Thank you, Father. Thank you." They grip forearms, and I breathe a sigh of relief that Strickland is being human for once.

Rocks walks over to Judge and after they embrace hard, he says, "I avenged him. I finally did it. Tronido is behind bars and will pay for taking Decker's life. Now I know my brother may find peace on his final flight."

Judge puts a hand to Rocks' neck and brings his head forward so their foreheads touch. Both of them close their eyes.

"Thank you," Judge says quietly. "Peace on your final flight, Decker. Be at peace, my boy."

A whisper of the loving words Judge spoke echoes through everyone present. People bow their heads and close their eyes. The words get repeated and repeated as a soft blessing for a beloved and greatly missed member of the Shadows.

Back at the dairy, when everyone is seated and quiet, Rocks begins his story. Nighthawk, Asteroide, and Willow are standing in the center ring with him.

"We snuck back down the air duct and laid our ambush," Rocks says. My parents gave him Feathers' old metal carry case from the shed. It was exactly the right size to fit down the duct. "Moondust and I flipped into bat form when the lights came on at seven."

"I waited, crouched on the ledge by the opening," Nighthawk adds. "We were set."

At eight a.m. when not one single member was at their workstation, Tronido and his crew came looking. Rocks and Moondust heard them in the bird room and told them telepathically the workers were going on strike until they received better conditions.

"I've never heard cuss words strung together like that before," older Nighthawk jokes, making the whole crowd laugh. "It hurt my ears."

"I kept communicating with him. Trying to make him so mad, he'd flip and fly down to punish us," Rocks says. "It worked. The next second, Tronido issued the command to his gang to come get us, and he flipped too. I could hear him in my head screaming that I would pay in blood for this rebellion."

"But timing was everything," Nighthawk adds. "Rockland and Moondust flipped just as the first bat flew out of the duct. And once we had a dozen of them circling, I let it rip!" Nighthawk holds up the air horn my parents gave him.

Rocks describes watching Tronido and his gang fall from the heavens unconscious and getting them in the cage—the captor was now the captive. The team hauled the cage back down the duct—collecting those that were unconscious in there too—and went to check if all the goons had followed Tronido.

"We snuck back through the warehouse and headed into their area. Sure enough, four of them were unloading the van with the drugs they had brought in overnight," Rocks says.

I feel my heart rate rise as I worry those goons had guns like all of Enzo's men. He explains they armed themselves with the heaviest things they could find and were able to knock two of the goons out cold. The last two flipped and tried to fly away.

"But I got 'em," Nighthawk announces, holding up the air horn again. Many in the crowd cheer.

After the warehouse was clear, Moondust started up their drug van and drove over to the headquarters main gate.

"That's where we already were," Asteroide takes over. "Willow and our team had arrived before dawn. We took out two guards, who were snoozing on the job, and freed the Fold. I'm pleased to let you all know Saturno is recovering well. All the Fold are safe."

"There was a fight with the more alert guards. But we managed to get them out of the way as the bats out on delivery duty began returning. We knew who was on Tronido's side, and who we could trust. But as the vans returned with dozens of bats hanging in the back, we knocked them all out cold. Our friends we let wake up, but the enemies are stuck in that tiny cage," Willow reports.

"Moondust got injured when we were doing a final check of their facility. Tronido had built a large structure at headquarters and only his closest creeps knew their way around," Asteroide explains.

"Moondust opened a door and there was another guard dog. It latched onto his arm before we could blink," Rocks explains. "By the time we subdued it, he was badly injured. Let us hope he will fly again soon."

I'm pleased to hear Rocks talking of flying. I know we need to discuss how he feels about staying as a Camazotz forever, but there's so much else to do first.

"My phone got smashed when we all tackled the dog to save Moondust. We found a cell phone on one of the warehouse guys we had tied up, but I couldn't remember Connie's number," Rocks admits, looking at me and shrugging his shoulders. He mouths the word sorry and everyone—except Jeremiah and me—laugh.

To think I was so worried, and the dingbat couldn't remember my phone number! I'll tattoo it on him next time he storms a drug lord's headquarters.

"Thanks to Connie teaching me how to drive, I was able to get us all back here safely since Moondust was injured. The Duskwing are free. The Vuelo de la Muerte's rightful Sire is back in power. And three lost Shadows members have returned home at long last," Rocks says.

"No," Strickland interrupts. "Four Shadows' members have returned home."

THERE ARE SO many questions to be answered. Rockland, Nighthawk, Asteroide, and Willow try to answer as many as possible. I sense this will go on for days to come, but I'm exhausted. Now that the adrenaline has finally stopped pumping, I need to lie down.

I glance at my phone and can't believe I've stayed awake for almost thirty hours straight. I yawn, pressing send on the reply to my folks.

Rocks bends down in front of me. "Come on, let's go. I'm beat too." He helps me up and I show him the text from Mom at the vet.

"Good, I'll tell Strickland."

I'm too tired to even bother listening as he speaks briefly with his father. Strickland announces something about sleep and a meeting. I'm trudging towards Rocks' shop when his warm arm wraps around my waist.

"I'm so tired all of a sudden," I explain.

"Me too. We've got six hours before your folks will be back and then a tri-colony meeting." Rocks bends down in front of me and tells me to get on his back. I gladly accept the ride and scramble on, resting my head between his shoulder blades like I did in the train tunnel. His strides are much longer than mine, and we make it to his wagon in no time.

His gypsy wagon feels strange because it's locked up tight, and none of his belongings are scattered around, but his bed looks like heaven.

For the first time ever, he closes the little door behind us. Once he pulls the thick, velvet curtains closed, it's super dark. Perfect.

Stripping off my filthy clothes feels amazing. Rocks hands me a dark, long-sleeved shirt that comes down to my knees. We snuggle up in his bed with Rocks curled around my back, his arms holding me tight. It's like we're in the bunk bed, but with more space. His bed is like sleeping on a cloud.

Rocks speaks softly, "Thank you for helping me see my true place in this world. Without you, I don't know that I would ever have discovered it."

I roll over to face him. "What place is that?"

"Here at the colony. And with you in your world. As a modern Camazotz—not one form, or the other, but both."

I smile, kissing him repeatedly until he laughs.

"Both parts of me were crucial in our escape. You were right. I was exactly where I was supposed to be. And we needed both your modern world, and my magical one to succeed. With you, I'm the luckiest Camazotz on the planet, because I have the freedom to embrace both parts of me, because you have told me again and again that you love me just the way I am."

"I do! I really do!" I half shout. "Oh, Rocks, it makes me so happy hearing this. So no more crazy talk of getting fixed?"

"Never again. I don't see the Camazotz curse as a curse any longer. It was a magical, mystical gift that has given me incredible powers. From now on, I'm living my life, and I don't care what people say or think. I'm going to be me—your one and only bat boy."

I feel so happy I could fly. Rocks has finally found his place in this world. We snuggle up once more and drift into the most peaceful sleep I've ever had.

JUDGE AND ZANDER enter the parking lot in the Shadows' old, beat-up van, returning from their important task. Rocks and I are waiting for my folks to return from the vet with Moondust. I feel upside down and twisted inside out because the six hours sleep was not enough. I don't know which way is up. All I know is that I want to be back in the wagon curled up around Rocks' warm body.

Asteroide flips at the van door, opening it immediately. He's checking his Sire is safe. Saturno is still in bat form and the young male takes him from the rows of hanging bats and lets the wounded bat cling to his shoulder.

Greetings.

The Vuelo de la Muerte's Sire's voice echoes inside all our heads. Rocks bows his head slightly as Asteroide walks past with his Sire. "He's saving his energy for the meeting," the young male explains.

"Very wise. If he needs my goats, please let me know," Rocks replies.

I watch as the stream of Muerte members exit the van in human form. It really is the best trick ever. When my parents pull in next, Rocks breathes a sigh of relief when he spies the Duskwing Sire clinging with one wing to RainCloud's shoulder. The other wing is bound up in bandages with a small splint sticking out—exactly like the one Rocks had.

"Dr. Gandy said he'll be fine," Mom coos. "And he was so pleased to hear that his last bat patient can fly perfectly well." Mom raises a hand to cup Rocks' cheek. "I'm so glad he saved you."

"I'm so glad you both have accepted me," Rocks replies.

"You're still the same young man you were last week to me, Rocks," Mom replies, opening her arms to hug Rocks.

"We need to go," Judge interrupts. "Strickland is waiting."

The wing-shaped clearing in the forest is packed to capacity. As many members that were able from each colony are present. Zada escorts my parents to the Land wing platform. She can't stop thanking them for bringing Celand home to her at long last. Mom and Dad finally apologize for sending the cops up here, and she waves their apology off as though it doesn't matter in comparison to what they did for the Shadows last night.

Instead of moving to the Z wing platform, Zada sits next to Celand, holding her hand, never taking her eyes off her first-born daughter.

Strickland calls the meeting open, welcoming the other colonies. Saturno has flipped and is standing, leaning on a cane with Strickland. Tiny RainCloud is on his other side with Moondust still draped over her shoulder.

He speaks of colony relations, blood, power, and where the colonies should go now after such a breach of trust. I zone out as I glance around the clearing. I never thought aeronaughts would be given such honor as being guests to the Sire's wing. My parents have no clue how monumental their welcome really is.

Duskwing members are still thanking them, and now that the Muerte members are here, they are filing past my folks to give thanks as well.

I look over to see how Elm and Oak are being treated at the Plant wing. The young boys are on the laps of the two females. Cypress is standing, arms crossed at the edge of his platform, closest to Macallister. Ash and Mackie are standing there too. My eyes narrow because I sense they're not celebrating with everyone else.

"The trials of those who have committed unspeakable crimes across the three colonies will be held a week from tonight," Strickland announces. "During that time, we will gather evidence, so if you witnessed their treachery, please see your Clip or Fold member in the coming days. Any questions?" His powerful voice echoes over the crowd.

"I have one," Cypress answers.

Strickland turns to face his Fold member. "Yes."

"Why is a banished member present? Will Rockland be on trail for breaching his banishment along with Tronido?"

A gasp sounds around the clearing, including from my mom. Her eyes are wide as she stares at me. I indicate for her to keep her questions silent for now. She frowns at me, but keeps quiet as Dad takes her hand in his.

"I have granted Rockland blood clemency," Strickland replies.

Cypress, Macallister, Ash, and Mackie jump down from their wing's platform and stride through the crowd, before stepping up on the main platform meant for Sires.

"I challenge your clemency," Cypress spits, inches from Strickland's face.

A second later, Judge, Zander, Levi and Carnelian materialize behind Strickland. I take a breath of relief counting the four-to-two numbers of Fold members supporting Rocks. Judge pushes Cypress back and stands protecting his Sire.

"You are not permitted to question the Sire's clemency, and you know it," Judge snarls. "Our law stands, and you will follow it. If the Sire grants clemency, then no Fold, Clip or colony member can question his decree."

"He's unfit to be Sire," Cypress continues. The hundreds of Camazotz present are deathly silent. "I challenge you!"

Strickland doesn't even flinch. He steps past Judge and stands his ground before Cypress. For once his angry energy is focused on a member who actually deserves it for a change.

"Part of the sacred oath each and every Fold member takes—whether it was today, or dating back to our first ancient ancestors—they swear on the blood in their veins to protect their colony. To strengthen and secure it, even in death. The Fold swears to protect their Sire. You swore on your blood to protect me." Strickland states. "You broke your sacred oath."

"I have fought harder than any to strengthen the Shadows!" Cypress yells back. "I have fought to uphold our values to keep us strong. To keep our blood pure!"

Strickland starts calling out names from several wings. Female names. When he calls on Rebekkah and Phoenix, my stomach twists. He's summoning the blood-bonded females to the platform.

The girls slowly gather. He commands them to swear on the blood in their veins and the veins of all their ancestors watching from the night skies to tell their story. One by one, they all accuse Ash, Mackie and Malachite of forcing their bonds, forcing them to corner Rockland, so the Sire would have no other choice but to banish him. Phoenix and Madison then retell overhearing Cypress and Ash in the forest and their plan to force Strickland into banishing Rockland.

Cypress glares at Ash, then at Macallister. It's clear he didn't see this coming.

"But—" Cypress starts. "These females lie! They should have given evidence at Rockland's trial."

"They were unconscious," Judge informs the listening crowd. "They were so worried about saving Rockland, they flipped and were discovered in bat form. We caged them for punishment during the trial without hearing why they broke the law."

"Law-breakers can't accuse me!" Cypress defends. "They are unworthy members."

"Quiet!" Strickland roars. He nods his head to Judge.

Judge holds up a paper and begins to read. "Cypress, son of Dogwood, and Macallister, son of Macadam, you are stripped of your positions on the Shadows' Fold. You have committed treason by conspiring to weaken the colony for personal gain and power in a coupe to overthrow your Sire. By Camazotz law, Sire's can only be challenged when they themselves pose a threat to the survival of the colony. Strickland, son of Richland, has never endangered us. He has fought to protect us, even at great personal cost. From this moment on, you and your heirs, and their heirs, are forbidden to hold positions of power."

"No," Cypress cries. "Levi. Carnelian, you can't agree to this! This can't be."

"You didn't think I knew what you were doing behind my back?" Strickland asks, his voice as calm as the ocean on a still day. The deadly power hidden beneath the still surface.

"But?" Cypress looks around. For the first time ever, he's floundering. I'm break dancing on the inside at the sight of that cruel, hateful Fold member being put in his place at long last.

"We have more than enough witnesses to your attempts at encouraging the chaos Tronido unleashed on us. Instead of fighting for the colony, you fought to weaken it for your own gain, and for that, your wings will pay with servitude. And there is the matter of attacking the aeronaught, Alex Greene. Don't even bother trying to lie about it, or your punishment will be far worse." Strickland says. He points to the Plant and Mac platforms. "Return to your wing's platform for the last time in a very long time. Or face us." Strickland indicates to himself and the four strong males on his flanks.

"And us," RainCloud steps up beside Strickland, joining support.

"And us," Saturno adds, doing the same.

Cypress and Macallister, and Ash and Mackie have no support left. They're done. Finished.

The four males step off the platform and slink into the darkness.

Judge reads another decree stating that young Malachite from the Gem wing is also banned from ever holding a position of power in the colony and his heirs after him as well. Carnelian hangs his head in shame and takes a knee before the Sire. He swears he was not aware of what his son was doing to weaken the colony. He offers to resign from the Fold, but Strickland states that all evidence proves Carnelian is innocent and refuses his resignation.

"Rockland," Strickland calls.

He leaves my side to stand before his father. "You owed the colony twelve lives for the life giving blood you received. Today, you gave hundreds and hundreds of Camazotz their lives back—their freedom. The Duskwing and Vuelo de la Muerte are free because of your actions and bravery. You repaid your blood debts, and then some. Thank you, my son, for fighting for our survival, even when it cost you everything."

Strickland takes a knee before his son, and an instant later the entire gathering follow and all kneel to pay respect.

Rocks is the only member standing.

And I couldn't be prouder.

28
Family

A MONTH later, summer is in full swing, and the Appalachian Trail is busier than ever this hiking season. Business at the Sanguine Mountain Market is at an all time high. Zada has recruited many of the Duskwing to keep Cappella's beautiful scented candles in stock. They're a customer favorite and sell out most weekends.

Pegasus huffs and puffs as he assists the truck driver to load the last box of cheese. Zola is shipping her artisan cheese to farm-to-table restaurants now across four states. At the moment, she's taking phone orders, but I'm working with Dad to get a website up and running shortly.

"Tiff, help those ladies with their order, will you?" Mom says, from behind the coffee machine. She adds over the noise of the milk she's steaming, "Celand, we're going to need more milk. Will you run and fetch me some from Zola's?"

Rocks and I are clearing the tables of the outdoor coffee shop Kelly opened at the market. When she discovered there wasn't any food or drinks offered to customers at the market, she almost fainted. Strickland can say no to many people—including his first-born son—but he hasn't worked out how to navigate his way around Kelly Phillips on a mission.

That's not to say he hasn't yelled and screamed at Rocks and I when she's not around. He has. Several times. But when he gets the update on the daily takings at the market—now that the world's most delicious baked goods can be sampled while sitting in the shade of two-hundred-year-old, ancient pine trees—he soon shuts his mouth.

Cypress and Macallister fought tooth and claw to prevent their demotion, but when three Sires agreed—for the protection of all—they didn't have a wing to save them. Literally.

The Sires also agreed to merge into one joint colony. If each Sire is true to his word about protection and strength, then moving forward together was the only way. Together, they are still working out the details of the new mega colony, but so far the majority of members are happy.

Mostly it's the Duskwing and Shadows members who work closely together between their farm and the market to produce even more goods for sale at the Sanguine Mountain Market. Construction on the new general store, to promote the wild honey and fresh local cheese, is still underway.

The Camazotz who prefer to be bats have mostly moved to the Vuelo de la Muerte headquarters. They're still governed by their Sires. The colonies ruled against having a single leader. The merged colony decided to keep Strickland, Moondust, and Saturno in power, until an election can be held in six months. Everyone felt it was time for a change of leadership, and Zada is particularly pleased about the chance to finally vote for females.

Sylvana's isolated little shack has been turned into a wooden prison. It houses Tronido, Sylvana and every sentenced member of their deadly gang. The room is filled with tiny steel cages, so small a bat can hardly spread it wings, hanging in rows at four different heights around the space. It reminds me of the wall of cages at any cat shelter, but those animals deserve a second chance. The bats are given access to fresh goat's blood once a day and then locked away in the dark. A rotating guard—made from members of all three colonies—sits outside twenty-four hours a day, ensuring those inside will never be released.

Under the old Camazotz laws, their crimes justified a blood sentence, but the option of banishment—allowing them to be free in society—was unacceptable. A unanimous vote was cast that blood sentences from now on will consist of life imprisonment. Camazotz that betray their colony will never be given the freedom to do it again.

"Here's your vanilla latte," Tiff says with a smile to the young girl holding three Sanguine Mountain Market shopping bags.

"What's the WiFi password?" The young teenage aeronaught asks, holding up her phone.

I pause with an armful of cups and shake my head. Never in a million years did I think Rocks would succeed in getting the market fully wired for WiFi. That was one argument where I thought Strickland would have a stroke, he was so red in the face.

But Rocks stood his ground, insisting if the colonies didn't enter this century, they would slowly fade out of existence. Moondust had thankfully backed him up, and Strickland couldn't argue with the Duskwing Sire. Dr. Gandy skillfully saved Moondust's wing and he's recovering well. Now that all three Sires run all three compounds, they all have to agree on everything. After what Moondust and Saturno experienced under Tronido's reign, they never want to be 'offline' and out of touch ever again.

I glance over and check on Mini. Bailey adopted her the second she laid her eye on the kid, and I know nothing bad will ever happen to Mini when Bailey's on duty. That little mother hen is still a force to be reckoned with. Bailey is also Mom's chief cupcake frosting designer, and she has a natural flare for ingredients and combinations that work to rival any professional pastry chef. It's a common sight to come home and find Bailey and Mom testing out new recipes in our kitchen. The kid will write her own cookbook one day.

Judge and Dad run the hot dog stand on weekends only. Tiff was instrumental in setting it up with her years of experience at the Bun Lovin' Barn, and the two men rarely let anyone else behind the counter when it's open. I swear those two knew each other in a past life.

Moonshiner asks Mom for a free cupcake when there's a lull in coffee addicts. "I haven't had one today, Mrs. Kelly," he says, smiling up at her. Clinging to his shoulder is Moondust, with his wing still in the splint Dr. Gandy put on it. We're all hoping he'll be able to fly good as new in the coming weeks.

Understanding how important it is to know where you come from, I was delighted to watch the Moon wing of the Duskwing adopt Moonshiner. His Sire spends most of his waking hours on Moonshiner's shoulder, and it melts my heart listening to the pup telling his dad about his life here.

"Jez!" Rocks yells, waving to his friend. "It's break time."

Rocks helps me place the dirty plates and cups on the cart to be washed in the new kitchen in the dairy. Tiff brings a tray with two milkshakes, two coffees, and four gleaming cupcakes. Celand gives instructions to Jez, Phoenix, and Pegasus about what needs to be done to fill the couple of orders waiting while we're on our break.

We take a seat in the shade by the small stream away from the tables the customers use. I'm going to miss these weekends working together when I head off to college. I finally decided that vet science is for me, and I know exactly what mammal I'm going to specialize in. Even though it will be years before I'm fully qualified, Rocks is so excited the colony will have medical access at long last.

Rocks grabs his vanilla milkshake and tucks the fingers of his free hand in my back pocket.

"I know we've talked about this before, but do you really think shape-shifters exist, Tiff?" I ask.

Vanilla milkshake sprays everywhere. Rocks coughs and chokes, thumping his chest. He glares at me from the side, still coughing and wiping his nose and mouth.

"Are you okay?" Tiff asks, handing over a tissue.

"It came out my nose," he complains. "That's not pleasant."

I try not to laugh. "No, it's not. Are you okay?"

"Yes," he says, still glaring at me.

"So, Tiff?" I ask again, rubbing the filigree heart necklace that rests above my throat. I can feel those dark blue eyes of his burning into the side of my head, but I ignore him.

"Oh, God, I hope so. Wouldn't that be ah-mazing?" She sighs.

"Would it bother you dating a shifter?" I continue. "Like the fact they can be an animal too?" I raise one eyebrow back at Rocks, and he can't contain his grin.

"You need to read this new series my mom just started." She wiggles her eyebrows and whispers. "So H.O.T." She fans herself, grinning. "But seriously, I'm so over being single. Hey, Rocks?"

Rocks looks like a deer caught in headlights. He's wide-eyed and looking from me to her, with his cupcake hovering near his open mouth. I don't know why he gets nervous when Tiff asks him questions directly, but it's another thing I adore about him.

"Yes, Tiff." He places the cupcake on the tray, preparing for the Spanish inquisition. Celand joins us, grabbing her treat and coffee.

"Is Jeremiah single?"

His brow crinkles in the cutest way I've ever seen. Knowing Rocks, he won't want to lie to her, but he now understands what 'single' in the aeronaught sense of the words means. Celand giggles and watches her brother.

"Ah, I guess. Why?" Rocks asks.

"Oh, Rocks," Celand reprimands, taking control of the conversation. "Guys are hopeless. The question is, Tiff, do you like him?" I smile at Celand and she winks back.

"Well, he is, um, well, he's Jez. I guess," Tiff stutters. "I don't know him that well, really." Her face turns the hottest shade of pink I've ever seen on the girl.

Tiff never gets flustered. Ever. "But I'd like to get to know him."

Celand leans over closer. "His missing ear doesn't bother you?"

It's my turn to choke on my cupcake. Frosting on the lungs is about equal to vanilla milkshake out your nose on a discomfort scale.

"No, I don't mind. It sort of adds to his mystery. He's very dark and silent and mysterious," Tiff says, watching Jeremiah across the way delivering hot coffees to exhausted shoppers.

Celand rolls her eyes while Tiff is perving. Jez and I have definitely bonded in the time I've known him. For the longest while, I thought he hated my guts, but now I know he was only looking out for his friend. Jez knew the trouble I would add to Rockland's already complicated life. It wasn't anything personal. He's loyal to the very end, and Tiff would be lucky to have him as her boyfriend.

Rocks gives her a massive grin. "Maybe the four of us can go on a double date."

"Great idea," I add, putting my arm around his waist and kissing his cheek.

"Hey, brother, make that a triple date! Alex Greene replied to my text."

"What?" I half squeal.

Celand blushes and gives me the same shy smile her younger brother has. They are so similar some days it scares me. She shares her contact with her old aeronaught boyfriend, leaving out enough details in Tiff's presence.

Alex was over the moon she was safe and well, but he's apprehensive about seeing her again. I don't blame the poor guy, but that's not fair on sweet Celand. By the time our coffee break is over, we have a plan.

Tiff and Celand hurry back to Mom's side as a huge group walk down the path holding shopping bags, heading straight for the coffee stand.

Rocks doesn't follow the girls, but instead pulls me closer to him as I stand up. "You sure about this?" He points to Tiff, where she's taking the tray from Jez and grinning up at him. Jez smiles back, shoving both his hands in his back pockets. He stands there in front of her not moving and they do a 'I go left, you go left, I go right, you go right' dance around each other. It's adorable to witness.

"I think they'd be good together. They both deserve someone amazing."

"Yeah, they do." He leans over and kisses me, pushing me up against the trunk of the tree our table is under. I grab his neck and kiss him back. His touch still ignites every bone in my body and I know it always will. We break apart before either of our folks spy us.

Rocks walks to Jez and I follow. "Thanks for covering our break."

His friend nods, not wasting any words, but before he leaves, Rocks adds, "You got plans this Thursday, Jez? Cause Connie's got an idea I think you're gonna love."

Rockland's Fudged Up Family Tree

ScarletFall 32 — F ✦

Strickland 42 ☽ ✦

Zada, 40 F ✦

Judge, 36 ★ ☽ ✦

Moondust 34 ★ ☽

Starjewel 42 ★ F

Ireland, 8 F

Celand, 23 • F

Decker, 17 • ☽

Moonshiner 9 ☽

Shadowmoon, 12 F

Rockland, 19 •

Baxter, 12 • ☽

Graceland, 15 • F

Bailey, 5 • F

★ Fold ☽ Sire • Raised by Zada

DUSKWING

Shadows

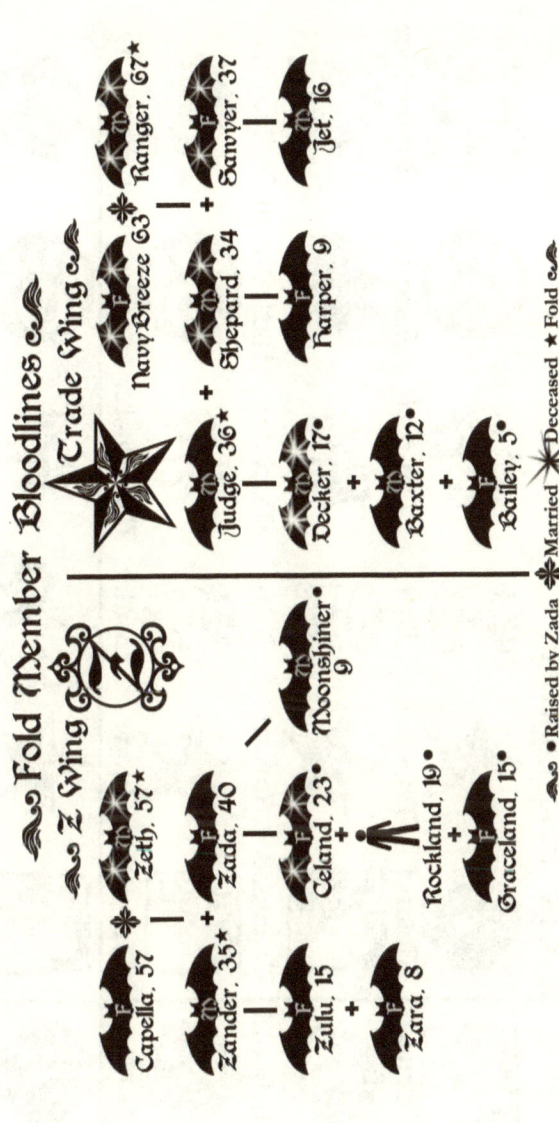

Fold Member Bloodlines

Trade Wing

Ranger, 67★
Sawyer, 37
Jet, 16

NavyBreeze 63
Shepard, 34
Harper, 9

Judge, 36★
Decker, 17•
Baxter, 12•
Bailey, 5•

Z Wing

Zeth, 57★
Zada, 40
Moonshiner• 9

Capella, 57
Zander, 35★
Zulu, 15
Zara, 8

Celand, 23•
Rockland, 19•
Graceland, 15•

🦇 Married   ★ Deceased   ★ Fold

• Raised by Zada

The Fold History

Sire

Spruce · Roland · Marshall · Zan · Panther · Joaquim · RustyMoor

Richland · Dogwood · Ranger · Zeth · Macadam · LittleStorm IndigoRiver

Strickland · Cypress · Judge · Zander · Macallister · Levi · Carnelian

Rockland · Ash · Decker · Pegasus · Mackie · Mazal · Malachite

Character List

Ash (Plant Wing) — m. Son of Cypress and Hannah. Older brother of Cedar and half-brother of Elm and Oak. Aeronaught hater like his father. Tattooed fangs on his lips and chin. Potential heir of the Plant Wing.

Asteroide (Vuelo de la Muerte - Planetary Wing) — m. Son of Saturno and future heir. His name means asteroid. Very confident young male who takes pride in being the Sire's heir. Tattoos: his back is a full planetary system with the Planetary wing crest in the center position instead of the sun.

AuburnSky (ColorNature Wing) — f. A young female chosen by the Sire to bond with Rockland. Appearance: short bob length hair. Tattoos: both hands are tattooed with a design that can only be seen when she's a bat.

Bailey (Trade Wing) — f. Daughter of Zada & Judge along with Decker & Baxter. Half-sister of Celand, Rockland, Graceland, and Moonshiner. Acts like she's forty-five-years-old instead of five-years-old. Only has one eye after surviving an owl attack.

Baxter (Trade Wing) — m. Son of Judge & Zada along with Decker & Bailey. Half-brother of Celand, Rockland, Graceland & Moonshiner. Very quiet and shy boy.

Carnelian (Gem Wing) — m. Fold member. Father of Jet and Malachite. Uncle of little Sapphire. Appearance: thick dark hair. Only one visible tattoo high on his shoulder of the Gem Wing symbol. Wears leather cuffs on his wrists. No visible scars.

Cappella (Star Wing) — f. Rockland's only live Grandparent. Mother of Zada. Appearance: thin, short, slightly gray hair. Tattoos: the ink on her arms can't be distinguished since they have blurred. But she has stars and bats tattooed on her neck. Needs glasses because her eyesight is so bad.

Cedar (Plant Wing) — m. Second son of Cypress and Hannah. Brother of Ash and half-brother of Elm and Oak.

Celand (Land Wing) — f. Daughter of Strickland & Zada. Rockland's mysterious older sister. Half sister of Decker, Baxter, Bailey & Moonshiner. Dated aeronaught Alex Greene.

Concha (Vuelo de la Muerte - Ocean Wing) — f. Daughter of Fold member Océano. Her name means seashell. Sister of Mantarraya. Tattoos: Both forearms have crashing waves from elbow to wrist.

Cypress (Plant Wing) — m. Fold member. Father of Ash, Cedar, Elm and Oak. Also fathered Willow from the Vuelo de la Muerte colony. His Grandfather Spruce was the Sire in his day. Aeronaught hater. Tattoos: humans and animals all over his body gushing blood from neck wounds.

Decker (Trade Wing) — m. Son of Judge & Zada along with Baxter & Bailey. Half-brother and best friend of Rockland. Cousin of Jet & Harper. Potential heir of the Trade Wing. Super nice guy who everyone likes.

Elm (Plant Wing) — m. Human born twin of Oak. Son of Cypress and PurpleSky. Half-brother of Ash and Cedar. Appearance: shoulder length, dark hair. Almost delicate facial features. Has three puckered,

red scars down his neck from an owl attack.

Ezra (Hebrew Wing) — m Second son of Levi and Sunshine. Younger brother of Mazal. Half-brother of Jeremiah and Odeliah. Tattoos: the Hebrew Wing symbol on his left forearm. Very deep voice and looks similar to Jeremiah.

Foxfire (Fox Wing) — m. Son of Foxhunt. Third cousin of Rockland through Rockland's Great Grandmother Foxtail. Is waiting for his chance to be groomed for leadership. Appearance: shaggy hair. Tattoos: fox head on the side of his neck, and a tiny bat with three stars trailing in it's wake high on his left cheekbone.

Foxhunt (Fox Wing) — m. Father of Foxfire. Clip of the Fox Wing. Trying to position his son Foxfire for a future Fold position. Has a loud, booming voice.

Foxpaw (Fox Wing) — f. Sister of Foxfire. She is mate of Mazal — who is trying to play political games with the Trade wing to replace Decker. She is ambitious and clever as a fox.

Ganymede (Duskwing — Planetary Moon Wing) — m. Is named after the largest moon of Jupiter. Fold member for his wing. Tattoos: a blazing sun inside his forearm.

Graceland (Land Wing) — f. Daughter of Strickland & Zada. Sister of Celand and Rockland. Half-sister of Decker, Baxter, Bailey, Moonshiner and Ireland. Not a fan of aeronaught interaction.

Harland (Land Wing) — m. Rockland's hard-edged cousin. Son of Kirkland & Snowflake. Appearance: shoulder length jet-black hair, viper bites on his lower lip. Likes grape soda a lot.

Harper (Trade Wing) — f. Daughter of Shepard and Lotus. First cousin of Decker, Baxter, Bailey, Sapphire, and Jet. Was rescued by Decker in the owl attack, but bled to death.

Ireland (Land Wing) — f. Only daughter of Strickland & ScarletFall. Half-sister of Celand, Rockland, Graceland, Decker, Baxter, Bailey & Moonshiner.

Jackson (Son Wing) — m. The Shadows' resident tattoo master. Appearance: In his early sixties with slightly gray hair. The skin on his hands is rough and stained from years of rubbing ink into his work.

Jenson (Son Wing) — m. Grandson of Jackson and apprenticing to become a tattoo master. Appearance: He's in his early twenties and covered in tattoos. His right side is all bat tattoos while his left can all be seen in his human form.

Jeremiah (Hebrew Wing) — m. Son of Levi and Neon. Older brother of Odelia. Half-brother of Mazal and Ezra. First cousin of Ash and Cedar. Appearance: missing half his ear. Tattoos: the Hebrew wing symbol on his right bicep and the Elemental wing symbol on his left bicep. Mr. McChatty.

Jet (Gem Wing) — m. Son of Carnelian and Sawyer. Half-brother of Malachite. First cousin of Decker, Baxter, Bailey, Harper and Sapphire. Appearance: thin and wiry build.

Judge (Trade Wing) — m. Fold member. Father of Decker, Baxter, & Bailey. Brother of Shepard & Sawyer. Uncle of Jet. Step-father of Rockland. Appearance: has a massive, puckered scar that runs down his face from temple to chin. Very muscled with a thickset chest. Likes sweet potato fries.

Kyanite (Gem Wing) — m. Father of Sapphire. Brother of Carnelian. Uncle of Jet and Malachite. Was killed in the first owl attack on the colony.

Lavender (Plant Wing) — f. A young girl who was chosen by the Sire to feed Rockland and form a blood bond. Tattoos: sprigs of lavender all over both arms.

Levi (Hebrew Wing) — m. Fold member. Father of Mazal and Ezra with Sunshine, and father of Jeremiah and Odelia with Neon. Brother-in-law of Cyprus through his sister Hannah, and second cousin once removed of Carnelian. At age 50, he is the oldest living fold member. Isn't team aeronaught but accepts Connie's offer to try a burger.

LittleSong (Little Wing) — f. Mate of Zander and mother of Zulu and Zara. Her father, LittleStorm, was a fold member, but the Hebrew wing took over from the Little wing since LittleStorm only had female offspring. Her sister LittleBee is mated to Carnelian. Aunt of Malachite and Jet.

LittleStar (Little Wing) — f. Potential mate for Decker. The Little wing is trying to position themselves to return to power in the fold with future offspring and the support of powerful wings. Tattoos: single star on her chin.

Macallister (Mac Wing) — m. Fold member. Father of Mackie with MagentaSpring. First cousin of Cyprus. Hates aeronaughts with a passion. Appearance: hard, solid man with dozens of faint, thin scars down his left arm.

Macantia (Mac Wing) — f. A young female chosen by the Sire to feed Rockland and form a blood bond. Has a bit of an attitude. Appearance: short and overweight. Tattoos: has the Mac symbol tattooed on both shoulders.

Macaulay (Mac Wing) — m. Macallister's half-brother. Works at the tannery. Appearance: has three fingers missing on his right hand.

Mackie (Mac Wing) — m. Only son of Macallister and MagentaSpring. First cousin of Elm and Oak. Second cousin of Rockland, Decker and Jet. Frowns a lot. Tattoos: a large Mac wing crest in the center of his chest. Potential heir of the Mac Wing.

Madison (Son Wing) — f. A young female chosen by the Sire to feed Rockland and form a blood bond. Appearance: high undercut half way up her head. The remaining hair is long and hangs forward almost covering her eyes. She's very sweet when not being manipulated by the *biatches*. Tattoos: lace collar that covers her neck from collarbone to chin.

Malachite (Gem Wing) — m. Son of Carnelian and LittleBee. Half-brother of Jet. First cousin of Sapphire, and third cousin of Jeremiah, Ash and Rebekkah. Appearance: large, predominant nose. Was the Camazotz that tried to scare Connie away and is Graceland's boyfriend. Potential heir of the Gem Wing.

Mantarraya (Vuelo de la Muerte - Ocean wing) — m. His mother is the Fold member Océano. Younger brother of Concha. His name means stingray. He's very confident with girls being the heir to his Fold. Tattoos: has a dozen stingrays swimming up his right arm.

Mazal (Hebrew Wing) — m. Son of Levi and Sunshine. Brother of Ezra. Half-brother of Jeremiah and Odelia. Mazal has one pup called Joaquim II with mate Foxpaw. Appearance: deep age lines from a hard life. Looks older than his 28 year. Has a buzz cut to show off his head tattoo. Tattoos: a gothic bat that wraps around the back of his skull and the wing tips end on his temple almost touching his eyes. Potential heir of the Hebrew Wing.

Moondust (Duskwing - Moon Wing) — m. Sire of the Duskwing colony. Father of little Moonshiner from the Shadows colony with Zada. Father of Moonshadow with Fold member Starjewel. Appearance: spiky, black hair and very muscular chest and arms. Tattoos: full arm sleeve depicting the planets and solar system.

Moonlight (Duskwing - Moon Wing) — f. A young female at the Duskwing colony. She is Moonshiner's first cousin. Appearance: slender with fine hair and a pretty smile.

Moonshadow (Duskwing - Moon Wing) — f. Daughter of Moondust and Starjewel. Half sister of Moonshiner. Appearance: wears her hair in two braids. Has stunning blue eyes that she inherited from her mother.

Moonshiner (Shadows - Moon Wing) — m. Son of Zada and Moondust—from the Duskwing colony. Is the sole member of the Moon Wing at the Shadows. Half brother of Celand, Rockland, Graceland, Decker, Baxter, & Bailey. Has a half-sister called Moonshadow at the Duskwing colony that he has never met.

Nighthawk (Duskwing - Night Wing) — m. Oldest Fold member at the Duskwing. Appearance: could be mistaken for an aeronaught farmer.

Oak (Plant Wing) — m. Human born twin of Elm. Son of Cypress and PurpleSky. Half-brother of Ash and Cedar. Appearance: shoulder length, dark hair. Almost delicate facial features. Has three puckered, red scars from his elbow to his wrist from an owl attack.

Océano (Vuelo de la Muerte – Ocean Wing) — f. Fold member of the Ocean Wing. She has two children—Concha and Mantarraya. Her name means ocean. Appearance: Looks sad with deep age lines around her eyes. Dresses from head-to-toe in black at all times.

Odelia (Hebrew Wing) — f. Daughter of Levi and Neon. Little sister of Jeremiah. Half-sister of Mazal and Ezra. Bailey's best friend who didn't have a beanie baby to love.

Pegasus (Mythical Creatures Wing) — m. Eldest son of Peryton. Older brother of Phoenix. Appearance: looks like a body builder. Has shark bite piercings on his lower lip. Tattoos: three crescent moons with a set of huge wings high on his shoulder. Is being groomed as the potential heir of the Z Wing.

Peryton (Mythical Creatures Wing) — m. Clip for the Mythical Creatures Wing. Father of Pegasus and Phoenix. Has worked his whole life supporting the Z wing in the hopes that his only son may be voted in as a Fold member with the Z wing's support.

Phoenix (Mythical Creatures Wing) — f. A young female chosen by the Sire to feed Rockland and form a blood bond. She is a good friend of Rebekkah and Zabreena. Is madly in love with Rockland. Appearance: slim, pretty, young Camazotz. Tattoos: stars around her eyes.

Rebekkah (Hebrew Wing) — f. Daughter of Gavriel and Helium. Older sister of Isaiah, who was killed in one of the first bat attacks. Second cousin of Jeremiah, Odelia, Mazal, Ezra, Ash and Cedar. Has been groomed to be Rockland's future mate by her wing, and was chosen to create a blood bond with him while he was recovering. Appearance: elf-like features and fine waist-length hair braided with black satin ribbons.

Rockland (Land Wing) — m. Son of Strickland & Zada. First born male in Strickland's bloodline & potential heir. Has seven siblings. Appearance: over 6'4", lean, muscled and toned, ridiculously good-looking. Has long raven-black hair at the front that hangs over his eyes when he wants to hide from the world. Tattoos: full black and grey sleeves on both arms. The design is the Shadows bat but can only be seen when he's a Camazotz.

RedFaith (Red Wing) — f. A young female chosen by the Sire to feed Rockland and form a blood bond. Appearance: extremely tall with one brown eye and one blue. Camazotz Supermodel. Has butterfly kiss piercings under each eye and studs implanted along her collarbones. Tattoos: vivid colored butterflies covering both arms and the tops of her thighs.

RedWish (Red Wing) — m. A young male trying to gain popularity to win a position as a potential future Fold member. He is also Malachite's second cousin. Appearance: totally clean-shaven head. Tattoos on his ears that can only be deciphered in his bat form.

Sandía (Vuelo de la Muerte – Fruit Wing) — m. Fold member of the Fruit Wing at the Vuelo de la Muerte colony. His name means watermelon. Appearance: Dresses in black from head-to-toe. Has a scar across his left temple and small beady eyes. Tattoos: vines wrapped around his wrists that twist up his forearms.

Sapphire (Gem Wing) — f. Daughter of Kyanite and Snowflake. Niece of Carnelian and first cousin of Malachite, Jet, Decker, Baxter, Bailey, and Harper. Decker rescued her in the owl attack.

Saturno (Vuelo de la Muerte) — m. Sire of the Vuelo de la Muerte colony. Walks with a cane and is hunched over from deep internal wounds in a recent owl attack. Father of Asteroide.

Sawyer (Trader Wing) — f. Mother of Jet with Carnelian. Sister of Judge and Sheppard. She was killed in the first owl attack protecting a group of pups.

ScarletFall (Color+Nature Wing) — f. Mother of Ireland with Strickland. Her father, IndigoRiver, was a previous Fold member, but was only blessed with female heirs, and their wing lost power. Half-sister of MagentaSpring and PurpleSky. Aunt of Mackie, Elm and Oak.

Shepard (Trade Wing) — m. Deceased brother of Judge and Sawyer. Father of Harper with Lotus.

Snowcap (Snow Wing) — m. The colony treasurer who works for Strickland. Appearance: small, wiry, elder male in his 60s. Has a limp like he's got a bad knee.

Snowflake (Snow Wing) — f. Mother of little Sapphire with Kyanite. Aunt of Malachite and Jet. Appearance: short, bob hair with black satin ribbons braided through it.

Starjewel (Duskwing – Star Wing) — f. Fold member for the Star Wing at the Duskwing colony. Mother of Moonshadow with Moondust. Appearance: bright, blue eyes. A kind, peaceful face. Tattoos: has stars tattooed on the palms of her hands.

Strickland (Land Wing) — m. The Sire. Has children with Zada and ScarletFall. Is responsible for the entire Shadows colony. Appearance: shorter than his son Rockland. Hard, muscled, and strong. Highly judgmental. Usually scowling and/or frowning. Tattoos: three thick bands of black ink circle his forearms.

Sylvana (No Wing) — f. The medicine woman & shaman of the Shadows colony. Traditionally the medicine man or woman should not belong to a wing so that they don't favor any one wing. They need to be concerned and focused on the colony as one. Appearance: long, wild, grey hair. Full skirts and flowing clothing that smells of incense and healing herbs. Tattoos: pagan signs and symbols inside her wrists.

Temblor (Vuelo de la Muerte – Mother Nature Wing) — m. Guard at the Muerte compound. Appearance: has a barely healed, ragged scar that runs from the middle of his forehead across his left eye to his ear. Scruffy, dirty hair. Tattoos: anatomically correct bones tattooed on the back of his fingers and hands. His name means earthquake tremor.

Tromba (Vuelo de la Muerte – Mother Nature Wing) — f. Guard at the Muerte compound. Appearance: extremely thin with dead straight should length hair. Wears gold hoop earrings and dozens of gold bangles and chains on both wrists. Black leather pants and vest. Her name means whirlwind.

Tronido (Vuelo de la Muerte – Mother Nature Wing) — m. Troublemaker extraordinaire who is highly ambitious and ruthless. Appearance: medium height and weight with dark, short hair. Likes wearing mirrored aviator sunglasses. His name means thunderclap.

Venus (Vuelo de la Muerte – Planetary Wing) — **f.** Sister of the Vuelo de la Muerte's Sire. Mother of Willow with Cypress from the Shadow's colony. Appearance: middle aged, yet super model gorgeous with thick, long hair worn in two braids over her chest. Her name means Venus.

Violet (Plant Wing) — **f.** A young female chosen by the Sire to feed Rockland and form a blood bond. She is a good friend of Rebekkah and Zabreena. Has had a huge crush on Rockland since she was a pup. Appearance: tiny, petite girl with scars from the early bat attacks across her forehead and down her arms.

Willow (Vuelo de la Muerte – Plant Wing) — **m.** Son of Cypress. He lives at the Vuelo de la Muerte colony, and at twenty, is the oldest member of the newly formed Plant wing. Appearance: is a very handsome young guy that takes after his gorgeous mother. Tattoos: the Plant wing crest on the inside of his right forearm. A matching swirl on the inside of his left forearm that shows the Plant wing crest when he's a bat.

Zabreena (Z Wing) — **f.** Daughter of Zambia. Second cousin of Celand, Rockland, and Graceland, and Decker, Baxter, and Bailey. Best friends with Rebekkah. Appearance: angular, hard facial features. Wavy, wild hair. She wears very low cut and revealing clothing that shows off her assets. A large scar runs from the corner of her lip down under her chin. Tattoos: half-inch wide bands across her eyes creating the look of heavy eyeliner.

Zada (Z Wing) — **f.** Mother of Celand, Rockland, Decker, Graceland, Baxter, Moonshiner, & Bailey. Sister of Zander. Appearance: long, dark brown messy hair. Tattoos: colored flowers on her neck, chest, and back.

Zander (Z Wing) — **m.** Fold member for the Z Wing. Father of Zulu and Zara with LitteSong. Young brother of Zada. His father, Zeth, was a fold member, and his Grandfather, Zan, was a fold member. Uncle of

Celand, Rockland, Graceland, Decker, Baxter, and Bailey. Uncle by marriage of Malachite. Appearance: shoulder length, straight black hair. He has the same high cheekbones as Rockland and is very good-looking for a thirty-five-year-old. Has a nice, kind smile. Tattoos: like Rockland has swirls and patterns covering his arms which only create a tattoo when he's a bat.

Zola (Z Wing) — **f.** Zada's cousin and Rockland's first cousin once removed. She runs the dairy and makes cheese to sell at the market. Rocks swapped her some goat's milk if she would charge his phone since she has an industrial refrigerator in the dairy.

Glossary

Aeronaught: an ordinary human that cannot fly.

Blood bond: when a member needs blood to keep them alive, another member can regurgitate blood they have drunk recently. Camazotz can't share their own blood. It must be the blood of another animal. Members might need feeding if they are too sick or injured to go out to feed. Since the member sharing their last meal will need to feed again quickly, they are owed a blood bond in return. A blood bond can be called in as a free meal in hard times, or as a new life given by a successful mating.

Blood Clemency: when the Sire dissolves a colony member of any and all crimes. This is generally only used for crimes that carry a blood sentence. The Sire has the right to reverse any punishment, but it must be based on reasonable grounds and evidence.

Blood Sentence: the ultimate punishment for breaking serious Camazotz laws. For many laws the Sire and Fold members vote on the punishment. A blood sentence, however, cannot be negotiated. The guilty member is either put to death instantly, can choose a death flight to fight for their life, or is banished from the colony for the rest of their natural days. A blood sentence brings humiliation and dishonor on the guilty and their wing.

Camazotz: a human with the ability to shape-shift into a vampire bat. Any offspring born of a Camazotz will also have the ability to shape-shift—even if one parent is an aeronaught.

Clip: the leaders of the other smaller wings not represented in the Fold. Each wing votes for a leader. From these leaders the seven Fold are chosen. When the colony faces grave danger, the Clip are invited to help the Fold and Sire make a decision.

Death flight: when a Camazotz is sentenced with a blood sentence, the guilty member can choose to fight for their right to life. They face three opponents, in bat form, separately. The fights take place one after another with no time for the guilty to rest. Most often by the third fight, the guilty member is mortally wounded and left alone to bleed out while the colony turn their backs on them.

Fledgers: name given to Camazotz aged fourteen to eighteen years of age.

Flip: the involuntary shape-shift from human to vampire bat that occurs thirty-six hours after their last shift. This prevents the Camazotz from choosing to stay in their human form forever. However, Camazotz can choose to flip at any point in time as well.

Naught: a derogatory term for a human.

Pups: name given to young Camazotz from birth until thirteen years of age.

Roost: the top-secret location where the Camazotz live as bats.

Shaman: someone who can cast spells or curses of great power. They can summon good or evil spirits and were labeled witches throughout history. The Camazotz rely on the shaman for healing.

The Fold: the members of the ruling council that create the laws and decide the fate of the whole colony. There are seven members in the Fold. They are usually the heads of the most powerful wings, but are voted onto the ruling council by all adult and fledger colony members.

The Sire: the leader of the colony voted into power by the Fold members. The Sire will rule indefinitely until he decides to step down or is challenged by another Fold member. This usually consists of a fight to the death.

Wings: family bloodlines within the colony. Each member sees themselves as part of a wing rather than part of this family or that. Members born into each wing are named for that wing to identify their father's bloodline.

About The Author

Sanguine Mountain—Book One in the Camazotz Trilogy—was the debut novel of Jennifer Foxcroft. The story of Connie and Rocks continues in Sanguine Moon and comes to an end in Camazotz Curse.

Jennifer was born and raised in Australia. She spent her youth dreaming of far away lands and the crazy critters that inhabit them. When she wasn't swimming in the backyard pool or training the family pet to ride a bicycle, she would visit those magical lands and accompany her characters on their exciting adventures. Even as an adult, her daydreaming of fanciful lands never ceased. To this day, she regards herself as a teenager trapped in an adult body. This series is a glimpse of the characters and places she often visits.

For more information about the author and her series, please go to

www.jenniferfoxcroft.com

Twitter: @MsJenFoxcroft

Instagram: @foxcroftfiction

Facebook: facebook.com/jenniferfoxcroft.author

Help An Indie…

Indie authors need you!

Yes, we need your amazing book reviewing skills. If you enjoyed reading Camazotz Curse, Jennifer would greatly appreciate a review. And you know how obsessed with technology Rocks is. Imagine his smile when he checks the review count on his phone and sees one written by you. You'll make his day.

Reviews are welcome on Amazon, GoodReads, iTunes, and Barnes & Noble.

Thank you so much. You helped an indie author today.